The Talus Slope

A Cortlandt Scott Thriller

Lee Mossel

ISBN: 0-6157-6965-9
ISBN-13: 9780615769653
Library of Congress Control Number: 2013933890
The Crude Detective, Parker, CO

Dedication

The Talus Slope is dedicated to Jan who lived through the long slog of getting my first book, *The Murder Prospect*, written, edited, proofed, and published. She's been there for it all.

Thanks, Special!

TALUS: (*TAY*-lus), noun, geology: the sloping mass of rocky fragments at the base of a cliff; a high angle rock or boulder pile; a rock slide

chapter

ONE

I hadn't seen Hank Francis in over ten years. When I heard the outer door to my office suite open and close, he was probably the last guy I expected to see as I strolled out to the reception area. We'd gone to graduate school together and received Masters Degrees in geology in the same year. Then, we'd both worked for Shell Oil Company with me in Denver and Hank in Farmington, New Mexico. Later on, Hank had been transferred to Denver and we worked on a couple of projects together until I left to become an independent geologist. A couple years later, Hank left Shell for the United States Geological Survey and what became a distinguished career at the USGS. He'd advanced to regional director in a group charged with evaluating future domestic oil and gas reserves. Along the way, we'd been good, if not close, friends. I didn't know why we hadn't been in contact in so long…I guess even friends drift apart.

"*Check the head on that one*! Hank, you sorry bugger, *how the hell are you?* I haven't seen you in forever."

"Hi, Cort, it *has* been a long time, hasn't it? It's good to see you. You're looking well."

"I try to stay in shape, not that it's easy anymore." I regretted saying it as soon as the words were out of my mouth. Hank had battled a weight problem his entire life and looked like he might've been losing the fight for a few years.

He laughed. "Well, as you can probably tell, I've pretty much quit trying. I'm fat as the town dog!"

I laughed. That'd been one of my old friend Hedges' favorite sayings and Hedges had a saying for everything. Some didn't make much sense but they always seemed appropriate. "God, I haven't heard that one in a while."

Hank chuckled. "You know what? I'd been trying to think of one of Hedges' sayings all the way down here. I didn't come up with anything until right now. Funny how things like that work, isn't it?"

"That's a fact. Hey, come in and sit down. You want a cup of coffee or a drink?"

"A little early for a drink and I've got to be back in the office this afternoon… I'd go for a cup of coffee if it's made."

"You know I always have coffee, buddy. You take it with cream and a couple sugars, don't you?"

"You've still got a hell of a memory, I see. Yeah, I take it with everything you've got."

I showed Hank into my private office and pointed at one of the leather guest chairs. "Sit down—I'll get us the coffees." I got a couple mugs with *Crude Investigations* printed on the side, poured coffee, added cream and two sugars to Hank's, and carried them back. I took the other guest chair instead of going behind the desk.

"What brings you downtown, Hank? It's not Friday so I know you're not going to a RMAG meeting." The Rocky Mountain Association of Geologists had a luncheon every Friday followed by a professional paper. The USGS guys usually attended. I had attended regularly for years although as I got deeper into the private investigation business and did less geology, I'd quit going.

Hank blew across his coffee. "I don't know if you read the newspaper like you used to, but you probably heard about the USGS geologist who was killed over in the Piceance Basin in western Colorado last spring."

"I still read the paper cover to cover almost every day—and I do remember reading something about that—a woman, right?"

"Yes, Martie Remington. She'd worked for me about five years. She was heading the field mapping group for our Green River oil shale project. It's the first year of two or three mapping seasons we'll need to get ready for the resource evaluation. There are several billion barrels of oil in the shale and some industry companies are getting close to figuring out how to get it out."

I said, "I thought Exxon bent their pick on that stuff back in the eighties?"

"They did. They were looking at it strictly as a mining and retorting process and couldn't make the economics work. Now there are two or three companies developing new techniques that won't be nearly as expensive or as destructive to the environment."

"That would be a good thing. What kind of oil price do they need to make money?"

"Hard to say although Shell thinks they can make a go of it at forty or fifty dollars a barrel."

"Hell, West Texas Intermediate was seventy-five bucks yesterday. What's holding them back?"

"Leases—most are federal with some state and a few private ones mixed in.

We—I mean the feds—don't know what to do about royalties, or term, or anything else. And no decisions will be made until we get an estimate of how much oil we're talking about."

"So what brings you to me?"

"I don't think Martie's death was an accident, Cort. The county sheriff looked at it and the medical examiner said it was an accident, but I've got some questions."

"So, what's wrong about it? Why don't you think it was an accident?"

"It's hard to put my finger on. I've just got a nagging feeling from knowing Martie and how she worked. They said she fell down a talus slope, hit her head on a rock, and slid all the way to the toe of the slope. I spent two field mapping seasons with Martie and I don't think she would've put herself in a position like that. I mean, she was ultra-cautious. She wouldn't have been at the top of a pile of loose rocks in the first place. Christ, she grew up in Boise, went to school at Montana State, and did her thesis work in Nevada. She's been around talus slopes and rock piles and cliffs her whole life. The other thing is—she was working in a four-person team and it wouldn't have been like Martie to go off on her own. She conducted a daily safety meeting and not going on your own was lesson one every goddamn day!"

"Did you or the sheriff question the other team members about why she was by herself?"

"Sure, nothing came of it though. Martie split the team so they could cover more ground. Her field assistant, a girl by the name of Judy Benoit, was a summer hire. She's a grad student from Berkeley in her second summer with the Survey. She said they'd taken a lunch break and were resting under some big junipers on the side of a ridge. Martie had to answer a nature call and was going to walk across the ridge top. When she didn't come back in ten minutes or so, Judy called for her but she didn't answer. Judy started looking along the crest of the ridge where she could see down both sides and didn't spot anything. She got worried, called the other team on the walkie-talkie, told them where she was, and they started her way. It took them about twenty minutes and Judy kept trying to raise Martie on the walkie-talkie. She never answered." Hank took a drink of coffee, wiped his palms across his knees, and stood.

"When the guys got there, they talked it over, decided to split up along the ridge, and walk ten minutes in each direction. That was as far as Martie could have gone before Judy went after her. There was no sign of her. They met up back where they started and made the decision to call it in. Believe it or not, there's good cell phone coverage up there and they were able to call the sheriff's office."

I sipped my coffee which was cool, pointed at Hank's cup, and raised my eyebrows. He shook his head. I asked, "So what'd the sheriff do?"

"He had a helicopter there in under an hour and it only took a few minutes to spot Martie's body. She'd gone maybe a hundred feet farther along the trail from where Judy said they ate lunch but was all the way at the bottom of a rock slide on the other side of the ridge.

"The pilots patched into the team's cell phones and led them to where they'd spotted the body. Unfortunately, the closest place to set the chopper down was over a mile away and they didn't have enough daylight left to land and walk back. So the three members of the mapping team went down the brushy part of the slope, away from the talus, and walked to where she was laying. Randy Joyce, one of the guys on the team, checked her vitals and said she was dead. They tried to call the sheriff but couldn't make a connection from down in the canyon. They decided Randy should stay while the others climbed to where their phones would work. When they got back to the ridge top, they phoned the sheriff and told him what they'd found. He told them not to disturb anything, leave the body like they found it, and hike out to their field vehicles. They called Randy on the walkie-talkie and told him what the sheriff said. He said he'd rather cold camp and stay with Martie until morning. So that's what he did." Hank was pacing now as he told the story.

I asked, "Who's the other guy on the team?

"Rick Russell."

"Not the Rick Russell who worked for Pan American? He must be seventy-five years old!"

"No. This is Rick Russell, *Jr.* He's been working with us for going on fourteen years."

"How come he's still doing field work? He should be a desk jockey by now."

"Doesn't want to—he's asked for field mapping for as long as he's been there. He doesn't want to be a crew chief either. He just wants to be on a mapping team."

"So why are you having trouble with all this?"

Hank returned to the chair. "Like I said, Martie had worked around rock slides for a long time, plus the ME concluded Martie slipped and fell *during* a slide. Rick said there were no signs of a slide. When I looked at it, I agreed. Nothing was turned over or disturbed. The sheriff's investigator found a single rock several feet from Martie's body with blood and hair on it that turned out to be hers. They'd picked it up by the time I got there so I don't know if it was in place or not." Another thing—the site wasn't far from where the girls had lunch. If there'd been a rock slide, Judy would have heard it. Plus, she didn't hear Martie yell or scream."

"Are you saying somebody killed Martie?"

"I don't know what I'm saying. I just don't think the evidence fits a fall-down-by-yourself-and-hit-your-head story. That's all."

"Who'd have a motive for killing her?"

"Now, I'm really lost. I don't have the slightest idea of who'd want her dead."

"How did she get along at work?"

"Good as far as I know. Everybody seemed to like her okay. We've had good funding for several years so there've been lots of promotions. I don't think anyone was jealous of her or anything. The mapping team, draftsmen, and computer people she supervised all seemed to get along with her fine."

"Was she married?"

"No."

"Anything in that fact?"

"What the hell do you mean by that? Are you asking if I think she's a lez or something?" Hank's face got red and his eyes took on a hurt look.

"I don't mean anything, but since you raised the issue, *was* she a lesbian?"

Hank settled deep in the chair, took a deep breath to regain control of his thoughts. "I honestly don't know. She didn't seem like it. She was pretty feminine if you know what I mean. She usually wore slacks or jeans but so do the rest of the women in the office. I guess I never thought about it. I don't even know if she had a boyfriend or dated. She used to come out with us on TGIF days and I never saw anything strange there."

"Is there anything in her work or her projects that would provide a motive?"

"Not that I'm aware of. She worked for the federal government in the oil and gas division of the USGS, as do several hundred other people. I don't know why that would get her killed."

I got up and walked to the window. "I don't either, Hank, but if she was murdered, there's got to be a reason. Is the oil shale project sensitive to anybody?"

"*All* our projects have become sensitive. There're lots of people who don't want oil or gas exploration anywhere—look at Alaska. We've had people claim the USGS is just a tool of the oil industry and we're all on the take. There are militant, green organizations who don't even want us walking around on the ground. Last summer, one of our pickups burned under mysterious circumstances. The official investigation said some brush got caught up underneath and caught fire after touching the muffler. The trouble was ... the fire didn't start until two hours after the crew had parked the truck. Then we got a fax saying the fire was no accident. It was a warning."

"Who sent the fax?"

"Don't know—it was generated from a computer at an internet café and there was no way of knowing who'd sent it."

"Did anybody sign it or claim responsibility?"

"Nope, it was totally anonymous."

"Where'd the truck burn?"

"That's the other interesting thing. It was about five miles from where Martie was killed. In fact, the truck was being used by the mapping team working for Martie."

"That sounds like more than a coincidence."

"I know."

"What do you know about the girl working with Martie?"

"Well, like I said earlier, her name's Judy Benoit, she's a PhD candidate from Cal Berkeley, and it's her second summer working for us. She already has our permission to incorporate the project findings into her thesis but that won't come out for a couple years. I think she may have some family money because she flew home almost every weekend they weren't in the field."

"Did *she* have a boyfriend here?"

"Not that I know of; maybe that's why she went back to California so often."

"Did she get along with Martie?"

"As far as I know—like I said, Martie split the crew into two person teams. The guys were one team and she and Judy were the other."

"This has lots of moving parts, Hank."

"I know. That's why I'd like you to take a look at it. Will you?"

"It's pretty intriguing. It's not every day the USGS gets involved in murder and arson. Sure, I'll take a little time and sniff around. If something turns up, we can get the law people involved."

Hank squirmed around in the chair. "I don't know what you make in this line of work, Cort, and I'm not sure I can put you on a retainer as a PI. Since you're a petroleum geologist, I can probably list you as a consultant and slide it by that way."

"I make about the same as a well-site geologist—seven hundred a day plus expenses. Let's do this—I'll check it out with the sheriff in Garfield County on my own dime. If it looks strange, I'll take the case and we'll work out the cost stuff."

"That's generous of you and I appreciate it."

"No problem. Can I talk to the other people on the mapping team?"

"Sure—we haven't restarted the field work so everybody's in the office for now. Judy Benoit spent a month here and has gone back to Berkeley. She was too shook up to keep her mind on her work and wanted to go back to school. She'll finish her course work next June and said she'd like to come back next summer and then spend a year writing her thesis."

"Okay. I'll be in touch."

We shook hands and I showed him out. Back in my office, I poured fresh coffee, and sipped as I looked down Seventeenth Street. I spotted Hank crossing Stout Street and hurrying toward the parking garage. I hoped I could give him some answers.

chapter

TWO

I was anxious to get started on Hank's "case" since I hadn't worked in a while. It had taken me two years to partially recover from the devastation of my girlfriend Gerri German's murder. We hadn't been a "couple" in the traditional sense because we'd lived separately and never made marriage plans. But, we'd been much more than friends with a close, intimate relationship that had lasted nearly twenty years.

I'd suffered mind numbing, bone crushing guilt over Gerri's murder because, in part, it had resulted from my investigation of another killing. I'd been working my first case as a private investigator by advising some friends about an oil deal that turned out to be a scam. I'd told my friends to run away as fast as they could. When a scheme to launder drug money through a bogus drilling program blew up, the bastards promoting the deal murdered one of my client friends. When I began investigating, they murdered Gerri to send a message and teach me a lesson. It was a heavy burden—so heavy I'd spent month's self-medicating with alcohol and talking only to my closest friends.

My best friend, Tom Montgomery, is a homicide detective in the Denver Police Department. He's seen violent death from every angle and its effects on far too many people. He'd spent uncounted hours on my back deck or in front of the fireplace sharing a bottle and talking. Tom's talks probably saved me from falling into complete depression. He convinced me that although Gerri's death may have been directed at me, there was nothing I could've done to prevent it. That was a hard pill to swallow. It'd been my decision to change careers from petroleum geology to investigating oilfield crime. Maybe if I'd continued pursuing drilling prospects instead of crooks, Gerri would still be alive.

Adding to my guilt was my relationship with Lindsey Collins. Lindsey's a crime scene investigator whom I'd met at the murder site of my client. We'd started up before Gerri was killed and what began as a dalliance had rapidly evolved into something more. I hadn't considered telling Gerri; I didn't think there'd be cause to tell her. That doubled my guilt load when she was killed.

After the murders and during the months of trials that followed, Lindsey and I intentionally stayed apart. She worked for George Albins, the lead homicide investigator for the Arapahoe County Sheriff. George had become deeply involved in solving the murder of my client and not only because it was his job. He and the victim, Mary Linfield, had been an "item" many years before. Lindsey's job provided her a good living and an independent lifestyle. She had a nice condo in an upscale neighborhood.

Being apart was tough on both of us. It had taken several months and lots of intervention from both Tom Montgomery and George Albins to finally affect a rekindling of the flame.

Now, we spent most of our time together at my house in Parker. However, occasionally, Lindsey would disappear for a day or two and stay at her condo. We always seemed to sense when each of us needed to be alone for a while.

***

I walked the two blocks from my office to the parking garage and headed home. As I turned in the driveway, I hit the garage door opener and saw Lindsey's Ford Edge parked in her normal spot. She'd been gone for a couple nights and it would be good to see her. I'd enjoyed the time off, but didn't like cooking for one. Being alone also meant I had to finish a bottle of wine by myself each night. Hedges would've said, "You gotta take the good with the bad."

I saw Lindsey standing on the back deck looking out through the trees toward the big park on the hill. I called, "Hey, welcome back. How the heck are you?"

She turned, smiled, and pointed back to the bar. I saw an open bottle of 2004 Domaine Drouhin Pinot Noir. I poured a glass and raised the bottle at Lindsey. She shook her head and held up her glass to show me it was full. I liked using sign language to communicate. I stepped onto the deck and Lindsey slipped into my arms. We held the embrace for a moment and stepped back without kissing.

"It's good to see you." I said.

She smiled. "It's nice to be seen. I hope you don't mind me raiding the wine cellar for top-shelf stuff. I was hoping you'd be in the mood for a good one."

"It's not a raid when you do it."

"That's a nice thing to say. And see, I've been learning a lot about wine. This one tastes really good."

"It'd better. It's about seventy-five bucks a bottle. I bought a couple of cases three years ago. So, what's for dinner?"

"*Dinner*—surely you don't think I'm going to cook too! I was hoping we could go out. You know, there could be special rewards for treatment like that." When she wanted to, Lindsey could display an absolutely lascivious smile. She wanted to now.

I opened my eyes as wide as I could in shock. "What is this—an extortion plot?"

"Damn! The super sleuth private detective has winkled out my devious plan once again." We sat in the Adirondack deck chairs. "Glad to see me?" She asked.

"Yep, I miss you when you're gone."

"That's funny—funny odd, I mean—I miss you too, and yet I need time alone."

I sat silently for a moment. "I know what you mean, Linds. I'm the same way. I can't explain it because it feels so good when you're here. Yet I like the down time, too."

We sipped the wine for a few minutes without talking. It was comfortable.

I broke the spell. "So you want to go out to dinner, do you? What variety of food do you have in mind?"

"I don't know—something light. What about fish or southern Italian?

"Sounds good to me—let's go to Antoinette's in Castle Pines. It's got light stuff on the menu."

"Perfect."

We finished the glasses and put the bottle in the wine fridge. Lindsey was wearing salmon colored linen slacks and a beige silk top, a lot more casual than my sports coat and button-down dress shirt. I said, "Give me a minute to put on some golf slacks and shirt. These duds are pretty formal for Antoinette's."

"Okay. I'll meet you in the car."

It was a twenty minute drive to the Village at Castle Pines. Antoinette's has a west side patio with a great view of the Front Range. We took a corner table, ordered a glass of prosecco each, and asked for the wine list. Our server, an earnest young man a bit light in the loafers, brought the dinner menus and wine list with our spritzers.

Lindsey waited for him to get out of earshot and said, "Ooh, I think he likes you, stud muffin."

I glanced over the wine list. "Better that he likes me than dislikes both of us, I guess."

She laughed. "What kind of booze are you going to ply me with this time?"

"I don't know what you're going to stuff yourself with so I'm keeping my options open."

"Good answer. I'm having the antipasto plate and bread. What're you having?"

"I didn't have lunch today. I think I'll have a salad, prosciutto and melon, and the Tuscan chicken—how about a bottle of Pinot Grigio?"

"That sounds good. What kept you downtown so long? Usually, you're home before me."

"I had a visit from an old friend. He's regional director of the USGS and wants me to look into the death of one of his employees— a girl. He doesn't think some things about her death add up."

"What's the *U-S-G-S*?"

"USGS is the United States Geological Survey. I thought you knew that. Weren't your folks at Colorado School of Mines?"

"Yes, but that doesn't mean I know anything about geology. They were both math instructors. You act like you're disappointed in me."

I was but said, "No, I just thought you'd have heard of it before—no matter."

"What's bothering your friend?"

"His name is Hank Francis. He said the dead girl was always super careful in the field, even conducted safety meetings, and didn't seem like someone who'd fall to her death. He said the rocks where she supposedly fell weren't disturbed like they should've been in a slide"

"Did a forensic investigator look at the scene?"

"I don't know. I'm going to check it out. It's a remote location. After they found the body, they had to leave it overnight before bringing her out."

"Well, if I can help, let me know. That's what I do, you know."

"Thanks, Linds. No telling what I'll find so there's always a chance I'll need help."

The waiter brought the wine, an ice bucket, and two new glasses. He opened it with a good sounding pop, poured about a teaspoon full, and backed off for me to taste. I motioned to the glass, "Pour about an ounce for proper tasting. I could inhale this by just sniffing it." The waiter did a sniff of his own, then poured enough to taste. I swirled it vigorously, checked the nose, and sipped a little. I held the wine on the back of my tongue and swallowed. Pinot Grigio is best when kept cold and allowed to warm slightly before serving and they'd done a good job with the temperature. "It'll be fine. Go ahead and pour, please." I'd added the "please" for Lindsey's sake. She had a "you're-a-wine-snob" look. She'd relaxed when I said "please."

The waiter said, "Very good, sir." He poured, picked up our empties, and said, "Your dinner will be out in ten minutes. Would you like the antipasto plate now?"

Lindsey shook her head. "No, I'd like it with his entrée, although you could bring the bread."

"Yes, madam, right away. Thank you."

After he left, I looked at Lindsey, grinned, and said, "Want to bet he sticks his thumb in my melon and prosciutto?"

She grimaced. "Or worse—you're acting like a damn wine snob. You thought you'd get away with it by saying 'please' but I'm onto you. Straighten up your act, or the surprise tonight might not be what you expect."

"Yes, madam, I'll do just that, madam."

"Wise ass—you'll get yours."

"I'm planning on it, madam." Our dinners arrived and we dined as the sun set behind Sleeping Ute Mountain.

"What are you going to do about your friend's case?"

"I don't know if there *is* a case. I'll drive over to Glenwood Springs, talk to the sheriff, and see what he thinks."

"Like I said—if you want help, I could go along."

"If Hank's right and it doesn't add up, we'll go back another time. How's your wine?"

"It's okay, nothing special. What do you think?"

"I agree. How's the antipasto plate?"

"It's really good and goes with the sunset."

I looked toward Sleeping Ute. It was like one of the film editing tricks directors used in biblical epics and happy endings. The main orb of sun was behind the peak of the mountain with shafts of golden light splayed out from behind. It was too bad there were no clouds; it would've been a spectacular sunset.

We finished our meals and had another glass of the "okay" wine. I paid cash and left a ten percent tip. Lindsey looked at me, didn't say anything until we were back at the car, and then said, "Short on cash, are you?" Luckily, she said it in a nice way and with that smile.

"I didn't like his attitude. He was condescending and way too smug for me. I should have stiffed him."

"If you'd done that, there would be no nooky for you."

"If I'd left five percent, could I've gotten a kiss on the cheek?"

Lindsey slugged me in the shoulder.

chapter

THREE

I picked up *The Denver Post* from the driveway, poured two cups of coffee, and went into the master bath. Lindsey sat at the vanity putting on her makeup. "Are you off to Glenwood Springs today?"

"Yep, I'm taking off soon as you leave. That'll put me there about 9:30 or so. After I talk to the sheriff and maybe the ME, I'll give you a call. Unless something weird pops up, I should be home by mid-evening."

"Okay, sounds good to me."

I sat in a deck lounger, sipped my coffee, and read the business section of the paper. The *Oil & Gas Activity* column was down to just a couple inches. Lindsey came out dressed for work and with a comment. "Be careful driving. You always drive too fast in Glenwood Canyon."

"Yes, mommy dear, I'll be careful." I gave her a kiss and swatted her bum as she turned to leave.

She grinned over her shoulder, "Hold that thought."

***

I opened the gun safe and took out my 9 millimeter Beretta. I wouldn't need it, but since Gerri's murder I never went anyplace without a piece. I put it in a pistol case, grabbed a light jacket, and headed for the garage. Today would be a top down, fun drive so I took the 'Vette.

I went west on the 470 loop to I-70 and started up Mt. Vernon Canyon where the scenery started to unfold. Near the buffalo overlook for the City of Denver's herd, the highway department had constructed a bridge overpass that framed a panoramic view of the high mountain peaks. I never tired of seeing it.

In Glenwood Canyon, the rock exposures were spectacular. I was glad I could still get excited about geology even when observing it doing the speed limit.

I exited the canyon and dropped into Glenwood Springs. The old mining and railroad town boasts one of the great natural hot springs hotel resorts in the Rockies. I'd found one of the real pleasures of life was soaking away an afternoon in the pool, having dinner in the historic dining room, and slipping between cool, starched sheets in one of the hotel's suites.

I got off I-70 and crossed the river toward downtown. The sheriff's office was west a couple blocks. I checked the dashboard clock as I pulled in: 9:35 a.m. I'd made good time. I popped the trunk, put the gun case inside, and walked to the cavernous lobby atrium where a uniformed guard motioned me through the metal detector gate. No bells or chimes erupted and the guard said, "The sheriff's office is straight down the hall at the back of the building."

Inside double glass doors, a matronly receptionist in civvies looked up as I entered. "Good morning, sir. How may I help you?"

I tried a TV detective voice. "Good morning to you. My name is Cort Scott and I'd like to see the Sheriff."

"Sheriff Colby is in a meeting at the moment. May I inquire what you want to see him about?" She didn't sound like she watched much TV.

"I'm looking into the death of the geologist killed last spring and I'd like to ask the sheriff some questions."

"Oh, yes...the young lady who was with the USGS?"

"Yes, she's the one."

"Well, Mr. Scott, the sheriff will be in his meeting for another half hour or so, but his schedule is fairly open this morning. Would you like to make an appointment for, say, ten-thirty and come back?"

I glanced at the wall clock behind her desk and saw it was nearly ten. "If it's all the same to you, I'll wait here."

"That's fine. You can have a seat over there." She pointed to a couple of uncomfortable looking chairs near the entry doors.

First impressions proved correct—the chair was uncomfortable. I picked up an out of date edition of an outdoor magazine and thumbed it until a woman and two men came out of an office at the end of the short hall behind the receptionist's desk. All three wore uniforms and baseball hats with "Sheriff" on the crown. I looked expectantly at the receptionist who spoke into her headphone mouthpiece. "Sheriff Colby? There's a Mr. Cort Scott here to see you concerning the girl who died in the rock slide." She looked at me. "You may go in now. The sheriff's office is the last door on the right."

"Thanks." The last door on the right was solid wood with *Sheriff Robert Colby* lettered in gold. I knocked, opened the door, and walked in. The sheriff was seated at a small, dark walnut desk inside the modest-sized office.

"Howdy, I'm Bob Colby. What can I do for you, Mr. uh...Mr. Scott is it?"

The sheriff rose and extended his hand. We shook and I said, "Yep, that's me. Cort Scott." He was a muscular man with a firm grip. I judged him to be about forty-five. He was wearing Wranglers and a polo shirt with a decal star. Another sheriff's baseball hat was on the credenza behind the desk.

"Have a seat." He motioned to a leather side chair against the wall. Three straight-backed visitor's chairs were aligned in front of his desk. The uniforms must have been lined up for a lecture.

"Sheriff, first of all, thanks for seeing me without an appointment. I appreciate it."

"No problem, Mr. Scott. We haven't been too busy around here lately. In fact, the gal falling off the ridge is the last bit of excitement we've had."

I decided to get straight to business. "Her boss, Hank Francis, asked me to look into her death. Some things don't seem to be adding up and he wondered if fresh eyes could answer some questions for him."

Colby sat back in his chair and raised his eyebrows slightly. "I remember him. We met the day after she was killed. I didn't know he had more questions though. Doesn't he think we investigated it properly?"

"He just thinks there are a few loose ends."

"Like what?"

"Like the fact Martie Remington grew up around cliffs and rock slides, she'd studied them for years, and was known to be super careful. Hank doesn't think she was the kind to fall off someplace. He's bothered she was found only a few hundred yards from where her field partner was having lunch but who *didn't* hear her scream or yell or the sound of a rock slide. If she fell, she would've had time to yell before she got to the bottom."

The sheriff steepled his fingers in front of his chin and let his gaze climb up to the ceiling. He took in a long breath and let it out slowly. "Francis didn't mention her background when he was here. We questioned Judy Benoit three or four different times over a couple of days and she was pretty adamant about not hearing anything. Of course, there's almost always wind up there and they were on opposite sides of the ridge."

I asked, "Was there anything unusual about the autopsy?"

The sheriff thought for a few seconds. "Maybe one thing—the body wasn't as bruised up as I would've expected from falling the whole length of the slide. There was a big bruise where she'd hit her head and fractured her skull and a few smaller bruises on her back, right side, and elbows. Her field pants were ripped at the buttocks although not real torn up. To tell you the truth, I didn't think too much about it at the time. It looked pretty cut and dried—she tripped, fell on the rocks, slid down until she hit her head, and then on to the bottom."

I considered that for a moment. "Did your ME or coroner raise any issues?"

"We use the medical examiner from Grand Junction over in Mesa County. We don't have enough county funding to have our own. He didn't go out to the scene. One of my deputies hauled in the rock with the blood on it and the ME said cause of death was blunt force trauma to the head resulting in a fractured skull and a blood clot on the brain. He matched the hair and tissue on the rock to the girl's and wrote a report saying she hit her head on the rock. He didn't make any comments on how it might have happened."

"You got any theories?"

"No. I listened to what the ME said and read his report. It looked straight forward at the time."

"Did you go to the scene?"

"Not until the next morning. After the chopper pilots radioed they'd found her, I drove out. There were only a few minutes of daylight left so I waited for the others to walk out and made the decision we couldn't get her out. I gave the USGS guy permission to stay with the body. I didn't like it much, but figured we were better off looking at the scene in daylight. One of my deputies, Jonas Welker, and I returned first thing the next morning with an ambulance. Jonas and I crawled down, looked at the body, and talked to the guy who'd stayed the night. He was pretty spooked by then—it couldn't have been much of a night for him."

"Any of the stuff Hank mentioned to me seem strange to you?"

"I don't know—looking back I guess it was unusual she didn't touch off a rock slide if she fell up near the top. I mean, if you throw a big rock onto the pile, the whole damn thing will slide."

"Would you have any objection to me taking a look at the scene and then talking to your deputies?"

"No. Anything you find that sheds light on it is fine by me. Let me ask you something, though, do you think we missed something?"

"It's not like that, Sheriff. I'm not looking for anything you might've missed. I'm just trying to help out my friend, Hank. I'll have to come back another time to look at the scene though. I didn't drive a rig I can take up there."

"I'll tell you what—if you want to look now, I'll get Jonas Welker and we can go."

"That would be great. I'd really appreciate it."

Colby picked up his phone, pushed a number, and said, "Marge? Hey, would you call Jonas and ask him to bring his truck around? I want him to take Mr. Scott and me out to the accident site. Yeah, yeah, I know he's off today. This is important. Unless he's got a problem, have him meet us in the lot in fifteen minutes." The sheriff hung up and said, "Jonas lives about five minutes from here. It's his day off, but he won't have a problem with taking a run out there."

We stood, the sheriff put on his hat, and motioned toward the door. We went down the short hall to the reception area where Marge was finishing her conversation with Jonas Welker. "Jonas will be right in, Sheriff. He said he was glad to have something to do. He was bored sitting at home."

Colby winked at me. "I told you he wouldn't have a problem. Are you ready to do some crime scene investigation?'

chapter

FOUR

Colby watched as I got my jacket, put the ragtop up, and got my pistol case out of the trunk. "Aren't you going to lock it up?"

I shook my head. "When I put the top up, I leave it unlocked. I'd rather somebody open the door and look inside than slash the top to do the same thing. The trunk stays locked and I've got a key activated disabler on the ignition so it can't be hotwired."

"Hmm, first time I've heard about leaving it unlocked. I guess it makes sense. It'll be fine here anyway...no one's going to bother it in the justice center parking lot. At least, I hope not. That would be embarrassing." He grinned and continued to watch as I strapped on my shoulder rig, put a clip in the Beretta, and slipped it into the holster. "I assume you've got a carry permit for that?"

I nodded. "Your receptionist said you only had a few minutes for me. Am I taking you away from something?"

Colby kicked the ground a couple of times. "That's just my standard line. It gets people out of my office if I don't want to spend time with 'em. This is important. I need to know if there was anything wrong with our investigation or the ME's report on that death."

We looked up as a Ford F-250 pick-up pulled in and drove toward us. The truck had a police light bar on the top and was painted like the other sheriff's cars in the lot. A young guy dressed in Levis and a golf shirt like the sheriff's climbed down and approached. Colby said, "Jonas, this is Mr. Cort Scott from Denver. He's a private investigator the USGS has asked to look into Martie Remington's death. We need to take a run out to the scene. Cort, this is Jonas Welker."

We shook hands and the deputy said, "Nice to meet you—you ready to go?"

"You bet. Good to meet you too, Jonas. I didn't expect to be able to view the scene today so this is a bonus. I appreciate your taking the time on your day off."

"No problem, I was just laying around the house with nothing to do anyway. Is this your car? *Nice*."

Welker drove, the Sheriff was shotgun, and I got in the second seat. It was about thirty miles west to Rifle where we turned off the interstate and headed north into the hills. It took another twenty minutes on a one track dirt and gravel road to a trailhead where Welker pulled up and shut off the Ford. "OK, we've got to hoof it from here."

Jonas led the way up a well-marked trail through the sagebrush and junipers. The climb was moderate although steady. It felt good to be out in the fresh air even at seven thousand feet elevation. We walked about fifteen minutes eventually topping a north trending ridge that fell off steeply on both sides. To the west, most of the slope was covered with talus from the rock outcrop forming the ridge. Several slide chutes were visible, interrupted by areas of sagebrush, junipers, and buck brush. Another hundred yards up the ridge Jonas stopped and pointed over the side to the west.

Colby said, "She was down at the bottom next to where that clump of sagebrush is sticking up."

I looked down the slope, although I was more interested in the trail where we were standing. It was narrow but not knife edged— probably four or five feet wide. The slope was steep but not precipitous. It looked like an unlikely place to fall and roll all the way to the bottom. I studied it for a moment. "Sheriff, do you mind if I kick a couple rocks off and see what happens?"

He looked at me and nodded, "Nah, go ahead. I'd be interested myself."

I walked a few feet and selected a rock just below the top. It was about the size of a beach ball and blocky. I scraped off the soil around it, sat down and put both feet against it, and gave a shove. The rock tumbled over a few feet until it hit another rock, slightly smaller, which also dislodged. Both rocks rolled another twenty or thirty feet until they reached the head of the slide. When they bounced into the rock field, they each set several others tumbling down. The slide gained a little volume but died out before it reached the bottom. From a geologic perspective, the slide was more aptly described as soil creep than a rock slide or an avalanche. The rocks were too blocky to pick up enough speed and cause a true rock slide.

I walked back to Welker and Colby who were standing near a vegetated area between slide chutes. It took some searching before I found another rock partially buried in the dirt and sand directly above the brushy slope. I dug it out and gave it a good kick. It bounced a couple of times and slid to a stop fifty feet down the hill.

We all looked down the slope without saying anything until Jonas finally broke the silence. "It looks to me like it would've been tough for someone to fall off the trail and then roll all the way down. I mean, it *could* have happened that way but, unless they got turned sideways, it would've been tough."

The sheriff didn't say anything for several seconds and then spoke softly. "Jonas, would you climb down about halfway to the bottom and when you get there yell '*help*' as loud as you can. Scott and I'll go down to where Benoit said they had lunch. We'll be there before you get down so yell as soon as you're set. I wanta find out if we hear anything."

Welker nodded and started side stepping down the slope. The sheriff and I walked back to the grove of junipers they'd pointed out as the lunch stop. The wind was blowing from the west and the sheriff said it was about the same velocity as the day Remington was killed. After three or four minutes, we heard a distinct "*help!*" from the other side of the ridge. It wasn't loud, but we heard it. Colby looked at me, shook his head, and said, "I don't like the way this is looking. I mean, if that gal *fell* off the trail, she would've screamed like hell and probably a lot louder than Jonas did. She'd have been closer to the top too. From the way those rocks stopped, I don't think she could have rolled all the way to the bottom either."

We returned to where Jonas was climbing up. I turned to Colby and said, "I need to check into this some more. I don't know what'll turn up, but a lot of this package is developing loose ends." Bob Colby just nodded.

Jonas regained the trail; we hiked back to the truck and returned to Glenwood Springs. Colby asked what I planned to do next. "I'll go to the USGS office and talk to the guys who were in the mapping party. I'd like to look at their GPS units and see if we can detail their movements—I'm hoping Benoit left hers in Denver. Depending on what I find, I'll probably go to California and talk to her."

Bob Colby kept nodding and finally said, "I don't know what I can do to help; I'd appreciate it if you keep me in the loop. If there's any proof a crime happened out there, I'd like to know about it. I'm getting a sinking feeling we may have screwed this up royally. I sure hope not, although I'm damned concerned."

Jonas pulled the truck behind my car, we got out, shook hands, and I said, "Thanks. I'll be in touch." I hit I-70 eastbound and roared out ahead of an eighteen wheeler who was definitely exceeding the speed limit. I glanced at the clock: 3:59 p.m. I'd be home by seven. I thought about what to do next and decided the plan I'd outlined to Colby was as good as any. Hank had been right—things didn't add up.

chapter

FIVE

The next morning I drove to the Federal Center in Lakewood on the west side of Denver. It's a two hundred acre complex surrounded by an eight foot wire mesh fence with razor wire slanted out at the top. The rent-a-cop on the gate checked my name and ID against his list. "OK, Mr. Scott, you're on the list. Go straight ahead, take the first left, go about two blocks, and look for the USGS building on your right."

The buildings were sixties vintage red brick, mostly two or three stories. The complex looked more like a minimum security federal pen than a research center. The lobby of the USGS building was small and cramped with molded plastic chairs and a gray metal receptionist's desk that looked like it might have come from navy surplus. The receptionist, Jamie Pearson according to her desk nameplate, was not a small person. I hate to stereotype, but Jamie could've been the poster child for a government employee lifer. There were few papers on her desk, no one sitting in the chairs, she wasn't talking into the telephone headset, and yet she looked harried, behind schedule, and in need of a break.

I gave her a happy face. "Good morning, uh, Jamie...my name is Scott and I have an appointment with Mr. Francis."

Jamie picked up a clipboard similar to the gate guard's and scanned it from top to bottom. I could see the top sheet with only three names. She took several seconds, tapped the clip board, and sighed, "Oh, yes, here it is, Mr. Scott...10:00 a.m. right? Would you please sign in on the visitor's board?" She pulled out a drawer and extracted still another clipboard with the kind of sign-in sheet found in a doctor's office. She handed it to me with an official USGS pen. I signed my name and put in the time: 9:59 a.m. She looked at my signature, punched in a three digit number on her desk set, waited for the connection, and said, "Mr. Francis? Mr. Scott is here to see you." She nodded, broke the connection, and looked up at me. "Mr. Francis will be right out, Mr. Scott. Would you like to sit?"

I smiled at her...it never hurts to be friendly to government employees. "No thanks. If he's on his way, I think I'll just stand." I didn't have the words out when Hank appeared at the door to the stairs. "See? That didn't take long. I'm not even tired standing yet."

Jamie didn't smile. She went back to being overworked.

Hank and I shook hands. "Thanks for coming, Cort. You mind taking the stairs? It's only two flights and faster than the elevator."

I didn't say anything, just started walking toward the door. Hank followed and we went up the two flights. "To the right—end of the hall and right again." The hall was carpeted with a good grade industrial although it felt like they'd scrimped on the pad. Hank used a key on his office door and led me inside. His office was surprisingly spacious and well furnished. It was in the northeast corner of the building with enough elevation to see downtown Denver twelve miles away. Since the brown cloud of the seventies and eighties had abated, the buildings were visible instead of just their tops. Hank motioned me to a comfortable looking chair and went behind his desk. "You want coffee or water? I can't offer you a drink like you did me." He laughed.

"I'm good, Hank. Thanks."

"You said you needed to talk to me and the guys. Did you find something in Glenwood?"

"Nothing earth shattering, although I agree something strange is going on. You want me to tell you everything and you'll repeat it or do you want to bring your guys in and I'll just tell it once?"

"Good thinking. Let me get 'em in here."

He picked up the phone and punched in a number. "Hey, Rick...Cort Scott is here. He's the geologist PI I've asked to look into Martie's death. Would you grab Randy and come to my office?" He hung up and said, "They'll be right in."

I stood, walked over to his east window, and looked downtown. "Better than it used to be."

A knock sounded and Hank pushed an electronic lock release next to his telephone. The door buzzed and two guys came in. I looked at Hank, raised my eyebrows, and nodded towards the door. He smiled and said, "Ever since nine-one-one."

Hank stood and said, "Rick, Randy...this is Cort Scott. He's a geologist gone wrong. He's doing investigations these days and I've asked him to look into Martie's death. He came by to fill me in and you guys might as well hear what he has to say. He'd like to talk to you, too."

I didn't have any trouble figuring out who was who. Rick Russell, Jr. looked exactly like his old man: medium height, stout but not heavy, and bald as an egg. Randy Joyce was about my size, younger than Rick, and looked athletic.

"I knew your dad, Rick. He was still working for Pan American when I came to Denver."

"Yeah? That's great. He was a neat guy even if he was my Dad." Russell laughed. "Did you work at Pan American too?"

"Nope, I was a Shell guy back then."

"Ah, the dreaded Shell—big competitors in those days I hear."

"They were for a fact. I had lots of good friends on both sides, though."

I filled them in on my trip to Glenwood Springs and Rifle and the hike up to where Martie Remington was killed. When I finished, I asked them what they thought.

Randy Joyce got out of his chair and walked to the window. "I think we're all on the same page. Rick and I mentioned most of that stuff to Hank before he went to see you. The part bothering me was the lack of footprints around Martie or up on the trail. We weren't worried about tracks when we first got there because we were looking for Martie. After we found her body and started paying attention, we only saw our own tracks...no others. That seemed really weird."

Rick Russell agreed. "You know, I spent parts of four different summers working with Martie and she was as careful as anyone I've ever been around. She didn't just *fall* off that trail and even if she did, she didn't get to the bottom of that slide without help. It couldn't happen that way."

I asked, "Do you guys have the GPS units you had that day?"

They both nodded and Rick said, "We damn sure do. We've downloaded all the data to our mainframe and plotted out a trail map of where we were. It's on a topo sheet so everything is in context. You can even run it chronologically and watch our day progress."

"You guys are way ahead of me. I wanted to know if there's a way to do that. Do you have Judy Benoit's GPS?"

Randy kicked the floor and shook his head. "No, we don't and it's a pain in the ass. I asked her to leave it when she took off, but she didn't. I even called her in California and asked if she'd send it back. She said she wasn't unpacked yet and it must be in her moving boxes someplace. She said she'd ship it back overnight when she found it."

"When did you talk to her, Randy?"

"Two weeks ago tomorrow and I haven't heard a peep from her since."

I looked at both of them and asked, "How did you guys get along with Martie?"

After a quick glance at Joyce, Rick spoke first. "I'd say both of us got along with Martie just great. I broke her out on field mapping and Randy was her first field assistant. I'm sure Hank has told you I don't like routine office stuff. I don't want to be an administrator so I keep going back to the field. Martie actually became *my* supervisor and was one of the best bosses I've ever had. No reflection on you, Hank, but I really liked Martie."

Randy picked up the conversation. "I feel the same way. She was great to work for, very fair in her evaluations, always gave credit where it was due, and we never had any friction."

I tried another tack. "How'd you guys do with Judy Benoit?"

Again, they exchanged glances before Randy answered. "We got along fine with her too. She's a lot different from Martie, though."

"How was she different?"

"That's kinda hard to explain. She always wanted to know the *big picture,* you know, how whatever we were doing that day or week fit into an overall scheme. She was always asking 'where are we going with this' or 'what's the Survey's *real* objective' for mapping something. Sometimes she was hard to keep on track with a mapping project."

Rick added, "She always wanted to review the regional work we were doing. It didn't seem like she was interested in the day-to-day stuff. She wanted to look at our mission statements and directives."

I asked, "What the hell's a mission statement?"

Hank laughed at that. "Man, you've been out of the corporate and government business for too long, buddy. You absolutely *have* to have a mission statement these days. It's usually some kind of inane platitude about how each project or each employee's efforts contribute to the greater good. It's the kind of stuff you used to see in needle point hanging on the wall in your grandmother's house."

"Sorry I asked. How come Judy was so into the big picture?"

They all shrugged and were silent until Rick said, "I think she's kind of an idealist. I think she's trying to figure out where she fits."

I thought about that for a bit. "Aren't we all?"

We talked more about their work in the field until I finally asked the sixty-four dollar question. "How come Martie worked with Judy and had you two together?"

Randy answered. "I think Martie felt she could do more teaching if she worked with Judy. She didn't think Judy would get along with either one of us on an everyday basis."

"Okay," I said. "Hank, do you have an address and phone number for Judy Benoit? I'll make a trip to California and have a talk with her."

"Sure, I'll pull 'em up and print it out. When do you think you'll go?"

"I'd say in the next couple of days."

Hank handed me a sheet with Judy Benoit's address and telephone number. I shook hands with Randy and Rick and thanked them for their help. I told Hank I'd give him a call when I got back. Hopefully, it would be a quick trip.

chapter

SIX

Back in Parker, I pulled up a travel website, booked a flight to Oakland, reserved a Toyota Camry, and clicked through hotels in Berkeley.

I googled Judy Benoit and was surprised to find several hundred hits. Most of them weren't relevant. The ones worth something were extremely interesting, however. The most recent entries were about Martie Remington's death and some newspaper quotes from Bob Colby's investigation.

Earlier articles were about Judy Benoit being an outstanding student from Yreka, California. As a high school senior, she'd been involved in demonstrations protesting the logging of old growth forests in northern California. She hadn't been arrested but was pictured carrying signs and offering quotes about the unconscionable destruction of our natural environment for profit. That struck me as odd for a person who was now following a career in a resource industry.

Maybe it was just youthful exuberance. She'd probably matured after college, even if it was Cal Berkeley.

Next, I googled oil shale and got over six million hits. I read several papers and came to the conclusion that Colorado's deposits alone could amount to over a trillion barrels of oil. Everybody who'd ever published an opinion, good or bad, believed there was more oil than in Saudi Arabia. The problem was getting it out at a cost that would provide a profit. Since the US doesn't have a national oil company like mid-east countries, oil shale extraction would have to be a profitable enterprise conducted by a company. The scale of any such undertaking dictated only *major* oil companies need apply. It was going to cost billions and the extraction process hadn't been invented yet.

It was easy to understand why the federal government and the oil companies were pushing the USGS to get an accurate estimate of recoverable oil. The resource presented problems for the feds. They were being asked to subsidize companies trying to figure out the extraction process. Hank had said there were a couple of competing processes being developed on small test plots. One would involve the historical method of strip mining the shale, crushing, heating, and extracting oil. The newer thinking involved heating the oil shale package underground to the point where oil would flow to a conventional oil well bore and could be pumped to the surface.

The first method caused surface disruptions and disposal problems with the waste after the oil was extracted. The new technology meant using huge amounts of electrical power to heat up the ground. Both required lots of water, too. In western Colorado, Mark Twain's words rang true. "Whiskey is for drinking and water is for fighting."

Water was going to be hard to obtain for developing oil shale. Of course, if it *was* developed, the reserves would make the country energy independent. The whole thing was complicated.

Interspersed with the professional papers and reports were off-the-wall articles by environmental and conservation groups opposed to developing oil shale by any method. Some were concerned with water, some with surface disruption, some with wildlife, and still more were just anti-government. The usual suspects were represented. The Sierra Club, World Wildlife Federation, Wilderness Society, Audubon Society, and the Nature Conservancy all had position papers. I altered my search and looked for oil shale protests. There hadn't been any group rallies, just lots of fringy sounding outfits publishing some vitriolic papers.

***

Done with my computer research, I set the deck table and moved a wine bucket outside with a chilled bottle of Mud House New Zealand Sauvignon Blanc. I mixed a batch of margaritas, got out two giant glasses, and salted the rims. I was ready.

I heard the garage door open, grabbed the blender, and was pouring the second margarita as Lindsey came in the door. I didn't even say hi, just handed her a glass and stood back.

She smiled that wonderful smile, sipped the drink, and stepped close for a greeting kiss. It wasn't a peck-on-the-cheek kind, either. It was the real thing.

"Hi, baby." She murmured. "This is a *really* nice way to come home. I could get used to this."

"I hope you do, Linds. It seems like a long time since this morning."

"More like forever. Would you take my drink to the deck while I get out of these work clothes? I'll be out in a few."

I kissed her again, took the drinks, and strolled out. A magpie and a large squirrel were having a loud conversation in the scrub oak thicket behind my house. The screen slid open and Lindsey came out. She'd slipped into a pair of loose shorts and a thin camisole top. She wasn't wearing any underwear that I could discern.

She picked up her margarita and slipped into the lounge chair next to mine. "So, how was your day sleuthing around, sweetie?"

"Just the normal private detective stuff, I guess. I talked over Martie Remington's death, came back here, and did some internet research. I need to go to California and talk with the woman who was working with Remington when she was killed. She took off right after it happened."

"Is there something wrong with her story?"

"I don't know what her story is—I just need to talk to her. She took a GPS unit with her and hasn't sent it back and I'd like to take a look at it too."

"So...you've decided to take this case on for sure?"

"Yes. I haven't done much for a while. I could use the income."

"Oh *crap*, Cort. You don't need money. You just want to help your friend." Lindsey took a bigger drink this time and looked directly at me.

I grinned at her. "Whatever. You're right of course, but having *some* income doesn't hurt. I'm determined to make a go of the detective business and unless I can keep getting clients, that's going to be hard."

She set her drink down. "You know we've never talked much about finances. I mean, I can see how you live and it takes some pretty substantial resources to support this house—and your cars—and your wines. I know you and Gerri traveled quite a bit and that takes money too. I'm not trying to pry into your business or anything; however, you know I could be helping out around here some if you want."

I sipped my drink and smiled. "I know we've never talked about stuff like that, Linds. Frankly, it's still hard to talk about Gerri—at least about her money and such. However, I owe you that much. I'll tell you what...let me light the BBQ, pour us another drink, get dinner started, and we'll talk." I walked to the other side of the deck, lit the grill, and went inside to get the drinks.

"What are you fixing, Chef?"

"Bacon wrapped scallops, steamed veggies, and a spinach salad. How's that grab you?"

"Wow, sounds great! You start cooking—I'll pour the drinks."

After we'd eaten a little of everything, I looked at Lindsey and said, "It's a fairly long story. I'll shorten it as much as I can."

I took a couple more bites, a drink of wine, and told her what had led to forming Crude Investigations. "I came to Denver as a new-hire geologist for Shell Oil Company after a stint as an army ranger. Shell was good about hiring veterans and especially officers.

"I had some early success with Shell and parlayed it into a job for one of the most successful independent oilmen in Denver. My good luck continued and I found a couple nice oil fields in the Denver Basin northeast of Denver. My income grew rapidly and I got the itch to do my own thing. I kicked it around with my boss and he hooked me up with an account executive at Merrill Lynch who became my business partner. We found a handful of backers, including my boss, and some other oilmen around Denver. We did a private placement to raise some seed money and got an underwriter for a stock float as a public company. Our timing put us in the first wave of companies about to flood the market with stock offerings. Our shares were gobbled up in the first two hours of trading and we were on our way. We named our new venture The Crude Company. It got a lot of laughs, but it was a name that stuck in people's minds. The stock ticker symbol was CRDE.

"My hot streak continued and we made a number of small discoveries. They weren't company makers although they kept our name in the news and our stock, which had come out at a dollar a share, was steady at three-fifty after a year. Then we found a good one—we drilled the Linfield Ranch discovery in Arapahoe County, Colorado. We had fourteen producing wells and the stock soared to eight bucks, plus I had a nice override from the production. By most any measure, I was a millionaire. It was more money than I ever thought I'd have."

Lindsey air toasted and asked, "What's an override?"

"It's a percentage of oil that's produced. In this case, I had two percent."

"What's that mean in money?"

"Well, at the time, oil was about twenty-five bucks a barrel and the wells were averaging seventy-five barrels a day each, so my share turned out to be over fifteen thousand dollars a month."

"Holy Crap! Are you still getting that?"

"Almost ... the production has declined over the years, although oil's worth a lot more now. I probably still get twelve or thirteen thousand a month. It's what I call mailbox money." I poured the last of the wine and continued the story.

"Frankly, after a year or so, I got bored—I wanted to do something new and different. The business was changing and I couldn't see doing the same old things another twenty-five or thirty years. As soon as the holding period for my stock shares expired, I cashed out my part of the company. My timing was good as far as stock price but poor when it came to paying my fair share to Uncle Sam. When the dust settled, I cleared a little over four million dollars. I immediately invested half of it in Gerri's new gas exploration company because I believed in Gerri and what they were doing. Then I bought this place for cash and that used up half of what was left."

Lindsey stood, walked to the edge of the deck and looked back at me. "How'd you hit on being a PI?"

I thought for a moment before answering. "It took several months before I settled on it. And then the unthinkable happened—the first case I took, for the Linfields incidentally, led directly to Gerri's murder. When her will named me as the beneficiary of her shares in Mountain West Gas Exploration, I almost went crazy with guilt.

"With my shares plus Gerri's, I became the majority shareholder of a company with the biggest gas field discovery in the US in over twenty-five years. I didn't want the emotional burden of benefiting from Gerri's death and I sure as hell didn't want to run her company. After consulting with several attorneys, a tax guy, and Gerri's partner, Marty Gear, we hit on a solution. I agreed to place all of my shares and half of those I received from Gerri in a second offering designed to raise enough money for Mountain West to develop the field. After the sale, I formed a charitable trust with the money plus the remainder of Gerri's shares. The trust was dedicated to Alzheimer's research—my mother and Gerri's father both died from it—and we'd talked about doing something. The total endowment was fifty million dollars. The gift was irrevocable. It left me with money in the bank, this place, and a huge tax deduction. The problem with a deduction is having income to use your deduction against. Other than the override, I haven't managed much income for the last year."

Lindsey had listened intently to my story. She sat for several moments before she said anything. When she did speak, her voice broke. "I had no idea. I mean, I knew you had been in the oil and gas business and made a lot of money. I had absolutely no clue you'd done all that. You're quite a guy, Cort. There's a lot more to you than I thought."

"You think so? Hold that thought and I'll keep trying to fool you as long as I can."

Lindsey's voice was serious when she said, "You aren't fooling anyone."

chapter

SEVEN

I spent two more days researching oil shale potential and the probable economic and environmental impacts if it could be developed. Everything was a trade-off. There was enough potential to end the US dependence on foreign imports and just the promise of development would probably cause world oil prices to fall. It was possible the US could even leverage that promise against the big oil exporting countries to force short-term reductions in oil price.

The trade-off came in the environmental impact. If mining and retorting the rock became the preferred method, the surface disruption was incalculable. All of northwestern Colorado would be turned into a virtual moonscape of gray, powdery rock piles. If the underground heating method won out, massive power plants would be built to provide the electricity needed. They'd be fueled by nuclear reactors or natural gas. Could the state and nation live with those costs and that kind of infrastructure? The battle lines were being drawn although they certainly weren't firm. The feds couldn't weigh in on either side of the equation until they had a legitimate assessment of the potential.

Monday morning I caught a 9:30 a.m. Southwest flight to Oakland. Lindsey drove me to Denver International Airport at 7:30 a.m. She dropped me off with a long kiss. "You take care of yourself, sleuth. I'll pick you up when you get back. Call and tell me how things are going."

"I'll do it. Don't drink all my good wines."

She slugged my arm and laughed. "Just for that, I'm going to drink a top shelf bottle every night you're gone...that'll encourage you to get your butt back here."

"You're not kidding—I might try and catch a return tonight." I went through the automatic doors into DIA's circus tent main terminal.

At Southwest's counter, I presented my ticket, ID, carry permit, and PI license. I told the agent I had an empty 9mm Beretta and two clips in a locked gun case inside my bag which I intended to check. He took me behind the counter to a small office where he had me take out the gun case. He told me to jack the receiver, show him the clips, then put everything back in the case, lock it, and repack it in my bag. He filled out an orange tag, slipped it through the handles of the bag, and put a piece of orange tape over the lock. I would have to claim my bag at the special baggage office in Oakland. The agent carried the bag back to the counter and put it on a special handling cart. I had time to kill before the flight so I got a *Denver Post* and a cup of mocha coffee with a shot of vanilla. The Rockies were now in an official losing streak, five games, and falling out of contact with the Dodgers in the National League West.

I used the pedestrian bridge from the main terminal to the A concourse and cleared security with nothing except the newspaper. I'd forgotten to wear slip-on shoes though and had to retie my Nike's before heading to the departure gate. The damn shoe bomber had made flying a pain for everybody—I was glad he was serving life without parole at Super Max in Canon City.

The flight boarded on time and I took my row nine window seat on the port side. I was in front of the wing and would have a good view of everything to the south. For most of the boarding process, I thought I was going to have the row to myself. However, five minutes before we were due to shove off, a passenger hurried in and took the aisle. Rats.

My seatmate fell asleep within ten minutes of takeoff. From the look on his face and his slight snore, I knew I wouldn't have to come up with any conversation for the two hours to Oakland. I watched the geology of the Colorado Plateau and the Four Corners areas play out below me. I still got a kick out of identifying the famous geologic features. The blue of Lake Powell appeared and I could spot the marinas from Hatch's to Glen Canyon dam at the southern end. It was a great day for flying.

As we started the descent into Oakland, my flying companion awakened and looked around. He blinked a few times and said, "I must have really been tired. Sorry about sleeping all that time...it probably made for a pretty boring trip."

"No problem, I get a kick out of watching the geology and the scenery."

"Oh, yeah?" He leaned over to look out the window and catch a glimpse of the Sierra Nevada Mountains. "You a geologist?"

"I used to be." I answered.

"How do you *used to be* anything?" He asked.

"Good question—I guess you quit what you were doing and do something else."

"I see. What do you do now? You don't look old enough to be retired."

"I'm a private investigator."

"Really? That sounds like a big change. What do you investigate?"

"Whatever people ask me to. Mostly, I look at stuff related to the oil and gas business...drilling deal scams and stuff like that."

"That must be interesting. Are you working right now?"

"Yes."

"Can you tell me what you're working on?"

"I'd rather not. I don't know if anything will come of it and I wouldn't want to give you, or anybody else, the wrong impression."

"You sound like a lawyer." The guy smiled and brought his seatback up when the announcement sounded.

I brought my seat up. "Don't accuse me of that, it's a dirty word."

He laughed out loud. "Do you know the difference between a dead coyote and a dead lawyer in the road?"

I hunched my shoulders and shook my head. "No. Tell me."

"There are skid marks in front of the coyote."

I laughed and filed it away to tell my attorney. "What do you do?"

"I'm a lawyer." That gave both of us a good laugh.

We dropped into clouds and fog at ten thousand feet and flew blind for several minutes. The lawyer looked at the fog. "Welcome to the Bay area." I nodded and gripped the armrests. I hated flying when I couldn't see the ground.

I found the office for special-handling baggage on the wall opposite the carousels. The glass door was locked but I spotted two agents standing inside behind a counter. I knocked on the window and one of them looked up, nodded, and reached beneath the counter. I heard an electronic buzz and the door lock clicked open. "Morning fellas, my name's Cortlandt Scott. I've got a firearm in a bag that just arrived on the Southwest flight from Denver."

"You got some ID, Mr. uh—Scott?"

I pulled my driver's license, PI card, and the receipt from Denver. The bigger of the two guys took it all and looked it over carefully.

"Looks like you're who you say you are. Hang on a minute while I take a look at the stuff that's in." He turned to the baggage slide on the back wall. I could see my bag with four others. Mine was the only one with orange tags and tape over the locks.

"Would you mind opening the bag, taking out the firearm, inspecting it, and then signing the bottom of the receipt, sir?"

I did as he asked. Everything was fine so I signed the receipt and gave it back to him. The other guy said, "Nice piece, man...we get a lot of guns through here—not many Berettas like yours." The whole thing made me nervous as hell. It was Oakland for chrissakes!

chapter

EIGHT

I took a shuttle to the car rental, got my Camry, exited the airport, and headed for Berkeley. I wanted to check out the campus before I looked up Judy Benoit. I hadn't been here in twenty years so I wasn't surprised to see changes in the peripheral areas around campus. Most of the sixties-vintage coffee shops had been replaced by Starbucks and Peabodys, which was a shame. Some of those places had been the heart of the Berkeley spirit. I didn't see how today's free thinkers would be as inspired over a seven dollar cup of triple espresso skinny latte as the potheads back in the day.

I parked in a visitor's lot, put the gun case in the trunk behind the spare tire, and locked everything up. On campus, I strolled around checking out the thirty-five thousand full-time students who filled the sidewalks and plazas. They looked a lot younger than I remembered. Of course, to me, even the players on the Rockies and Avalanche didn't look like they were old enough to shave.

I located the Geosciences Building and scanned the directory. Judy Benoit's office was #314B. The building map indicated it was on a crossover bridge connecting the geology department to geophysics.

I climbed the stairs to the third floor crossover and found the office suite. The name plate indicated four students occupied the office. I glanced through a vertical slit window. I couldn't spot anyone on the one side of the office I could see. I tried the door, which wasn't locked, and stuck my head in. The suite was one large room with two credenza type desk slots on each side wall. A wild haired guy was sitting to my left behind the door. He looked up and said, "Can I help you?"

"Maybe—I'm looking for Judy Benoit. Is this her office?"

"Yeah, that's her desk over there." He pointed to the desk closest to the window on the right.

"Expect her back anytime soon?"

"I don't know, man. She comes and goes a lot. You wanta leave her a note or something?"

"No, I'll try her at home."

"You wanta leave your name? I can give it to her in case you don't connect."

"Sure—tell her Cort Scott from the USGS office in Denver stopped by."

The kid looked around, found a piece of note paper, and wrote on it. "Okay, I'll tell her if I see her."

"Thanks, pardner."

I returned to the Camry and plugged Benoit's address into the GPS. She lived west of campus near Ohlone Park on McGee. I drove to the neighborhood and located the address. It was a Victorian house converted to apartments. I parked a half block away, near the park, and walked back. Several old fashioned mail boxes were on the front wall next to the single door. A wide, covered porch with five steps rose from the sidewalk. I checked the mail boxes, found her name, glanced around and didn't see anyone so I lifted the lid to look inside. The box was empty so I looked in a couple of others and found mail.

She was either home or had picked up her mail recently. Through the oval window in the door I could see a small entry foyer with an inside security door. An old-fashioned buzzer intercom was mounted next to the security door so I entered the foyer and took a look at it. There were six name plates, the same number as mail boxes on the porch. So far, Hank's information had been accurate. Judy Benoit was at the address she'd given the USGS.

I pushed Benoit's call button and after a few seconds, she answered, "Yes?"

"Hi, Judy, my name is Cort Scott. I'm here from Denver following up on Martie Remington's death. Could I have a few words with you?"

She paused a few beats before saying, "Sure, come on up. I'm in number five. Turn right at the top of the stairs." The lock on the security door buzzed, I pulled it open, and entered. I climbed the stairs, turned right, and found number five. Judy Benoit answered my knock immediately.

"Hi, Judy, like I said, my name's Cort Scott." I put out my hand, she took it in a firm grip, and we shook. She was not a beautiful woman, although she wasn't ugly either. Plain would have been a good description. She was a little taller than average with a nice figure. Her hair was pulled back and reached her shoulders.

"Come in, Mr. Scott. Have a seat. Would you like something to drink...a glass of iced tea or lemonade?"

"Sure. How about mixing the two and making an Arnold Palmer?" She gave me a quizzical look, nodded, and went into the little kitchen. The place was spacious taking up one whole side of the upstairs level of the house. There were four rooms with a living/dining room, a bedroom, bathroom, and the kitchen. I sat on the couch near a window looking south and over the top of a single-story house next door. I could see the trees in the park, but not the street or the Camry. "Nice place, have you lived here long?"

She carried two iced tea glasses from the kitchen and handed me one with an odd color. She'd made an Arnold Palmer with pink lemonade. "Well, yes and no. I've had the apartment for three years, although I've spent the last couple of summers in Denver. So, what about Martie?"

"Hank Francis is bothered by the circumstances of her death and thinks there're unanswered questions. He asked me to look into them."

"What do you mean *asked* you? Don't you work for the USGS or the FBI or the Justice Department?"

"No. I'm a private investigator. I've known Hank for a long time and he asked me to follow up."

Judy Benoit's demeanor changed. I watched as a blush spread up her neck and face and her expression hardened. "I don't think I have to talk to you then. If this isn't an official, sanctioned inquiry I don't see why I should. I've given statements to everybody who's asked. I gave statements to the Sheriff, the Garfield County DA, Hank, and a couple of other people from the Interior Department. Why should I go over all of it again with you?"

"Hank thought I might be able to clear up some things the others didn't have time to look at. That's all—we're just trying to finalize everything."

She took a drink of tea, set the glass on the coffee table, and said, "Okay— however, I don't have a lot of time. A friend is coming by and we're going to San Francisco for dinner. What do you want to know?"

"First, do you have your GPS unit handy? Rick and Randy would like to have it so they can download the information and plot it with theirs."

She blushed again, clasped and unclasped her hands before saying, "Uh, no, it's not here. It's, uh, it's down at my office on campus. I've been meaning to send it back to Denver. I'll do that first thing tomorrow."

I knew she was lying—and she wasn't very good at it. The needles on a lie detector would've gone off the chart. "I can haul it back and save you the postage. I'll be going back in a couple of days, anyway."

"Oh, uh, yeah, sure, why not...do you want to come by my campus office and get it, then?"

"Yes, I'll do that. So, may I ask you a couple of other questions?"

"Go ahead."

"You told Sheriff Colby and Hank you waited about ten minutes after Martie left before you started calling for her. Is that right? Is that how you remember it?"

"If that's what I said, it's what happened."

"You also said you never heard Martie answer, you never heard any rock slide, or heard her scream. Is that right too?"

"That's what I said." She was sitting stiffly and her voice was becoming shrill.

"You know, Judy—may I call you Judy? That doesn't square with the physical evidence and the distances involved. I went to the scene and the Sheriff and I tried hollering from where the body was found to where you were. We could hear each other clearly even with the wind blowing. How do you explain that?"

She sat her glass down with enough force to splash out some tea. *"I don't have to explain it. I've said what I had to say and that's what happened. I think you need to leave."* She stood up and motioned towards the door.

I put my glass down, stood, and started toward the door. "I'm sorry if I've upset you, Judy. I'm just trying to get everything worked out. Do you still want me to pick up the GPS?"

"No! I'll send the goddamn thing like I said. Now, please leave."

I left and heard the door slam behind me. I returned to the Camry, got in, rolled the windows down, and pushed the seat back to settle in and watch her apartment for a while. Judy Benoit was lying about what she knew and I needed to find out why.

chapter

NINE

An hour passed and I was getting antsy. I had to take a leak, I was thirsty, and it was getting hot. I'd about decided to sprint into the park and use the public restroom when a platinum colored late model Lexus ES350 came down the street, made a U turn at the park entrance, and pulled up in front of the house. I got a look at the driver, a tall Asian male, and wrote down the tag number. Benoit sprinted down the sidewalk and hopped in. Damn, no time to go to the can now. I waited until the Lexus started away and was almost to Francisco Street before I pulled out. Luckily, there were no other cars on the street and I made up some time before they turned south on Sacramento and back west on University. There was more traffic on the main streets so I closed to a couple of cars as they took southbound 580. It looked like Benoit was telling the truth about going to San Francisco for the evening.

So much for that assumption…the Lexus didn't take the Bay Bridge exit and continued south. I closed the gap to one car and stayed in the lane to their right. I could see Judy carrying on an animated conversation with the driver who only occasionally turned his head toward her. I followed them to a subdivision near a marina east of Washington Park. I hung back while they parked and went into a house on the east side of a cul-de-sac. I pulled away from the curb and drove past the house to get the address: 22 Waterfall Isle. I made a U-turn, returned to the main street, parked four or five car lengths from the cul-de-sac, and prepared to wait again. This time I took a chance and sprinted across the street to a port-a-potty in the beach park. I hoped Benoit and the Asian weren't making a quick stop. I gulped a drink from a fountain and walked back to the Camry. Other than feeling hungry, I thought I was set for a while.

By 8:00 p.m., I figured dinner in San Francisco was out for sure. They'd been in the house for almost three hours. I was starving but would have to wait it out. I had to pee again, though, and thought I would risk another trip into the park. Just as I opened the door, the Lexus emerged from the cul-de-sac and accelerated up the street. I closed my door, started the car, and followed.

There were three people in their car now. Another woman was in the back seat on the passenger side. They went back the way they'd come with me keeping a loose tail. Back in Berkeley, they drove almost to the campus before stopping at an Indian takeout restaurant. The Asian guy got out and went in while Benoit and the other woman remained. They must have called ahead because I saw the clerk setting bags out on the counter; the driver taking out his wallet, and then packing everything back to the car. There were a lot of bags for three people; they must not have had dinner at the house. My stomach was growling and I had to pee like a racehorse. I decided to tough it out long enough to make sure they were going back to Benoit's apartment.

This time I was in luck. They headed directly to her place. I didn't pull onto McGee, deciding instead to drive around the block and head back to University Avenue. I'd spotted a Subway shop near their food stop, so I dashed in, ordered a toasted Italian sub and a large diet soda. While they assembled the sub, I used the restroom... for about five minutes. The clerk had the sandwich at the register when I returned. I paid and hurried back to the car. Back at McGee, I parked in the same place as before. The Lexus was still in front of Judy Benoit's house.

One thing I *don't* like about being a PI is conducting stakeouts. I'm kind of a gregarious guy. I like to talk to people, have a drink, tell a few stories, and enjoy myself. On a stakeout, even if you've got a partner, you sit in one spot until your ass goes numb. Usually, long before my ass goes numb, my brain leads the way.

I checked my watch and was horrified to find only forty-five minutes had passed. It'd seemed like several hours. Two cars turned in and parked across the street from Benoit's place. Two people got out of each car and went into the house. Assuming they were going to Benoit's, they would make seven. That was more than a casual dinner; that was a meeting. I hoped their curry was still hot.

I stayed put for another couple hours until six people came out all at once. I couldn't tell gender anymore. Two people got in each vehicle and pulled away. The last two cars to arrive drove toward me, made a U-turn at the park, and left. I decided not to try to follow any of them tonight. I needed sleep and a fresh start tomorrow.

One of the hotels I'd checked was near campus. I drove back and pulled into the entrance of the Bancroft. According to their website, the place only had twenty-two rooms so I was hoping for a vacancy. I was in luck. I took a junior suite, got the key, returned to the car, and parked in an assigned spot. From the lovely Victorian lobby, I took an antique lift to the second floor and found my room. If this was a suite, I would have hated to see a single. Like my long dead friend Hedges used to say, "There wasn't room to swing a cat." It was nice though, and besides, I didn't have a cat to swing anyway.

I unpacked, hung up clothes, and put my gun case on the telephone desk. I checked out the bathroom and decided on a shave and a shower. The water was hot and the amenities basket filled with good stuff so I emerged a new super sleuth. The place was high enough in the hills I could make out the bay, the bridges, and some scattered ships. I sank into an overstuffed chair and gave Lindsey a call. "Hi, greetings from the Bay area—how are you?"

"Hey, baby, it's good to hear your voice. I'm fine—how about you?"

"Okay, I guess. I'm tired though all I've done is sit on my butt and watch people."

"Found somebody to watch, did you?"

"Yeah, I found Judy Benoit with no problem. She's not very forthcoming though, and I'm pretty sure she's lying about Martie Remington's death. I don't know why she would be lying but she is. After I talked to her this afternoon, she's been running around all over the area, plus she had a meeting at her place tonight. It just broke up so I grabbed a hotel and I'll pick it up first thing tomorrow."

"What are you going to do then?"

"That's a good question. I think I'll just tail her for a day or so and see what pops up."

"You don't need to be talking to me about things *popping up* when you're on your own and *tailing* another woman." Lindsey laughed and I heard her set a glass down.

"Hey, are you drinking the good wine? Are you sitting on the deck?"

"Damn right, I am. I'm having a 2005 Yalumba Barossa Valley Shiraz."

"Oh, man, that's one of my favorites. Don't drink the whole thing at one sitting, though. You'll never make it to work in the morning."

She laughed again. "Don't worry—I'm just having one glass on the deck and then going in the hot tub for a while. Besides, I looked and you have four more bottles."

We made more small talk until I felt myself slipping away. We said our goodbyes and I told her I would be back as soon as possible. After we hung up, I thought it was nice to have someone to talk to who cared about me—and who I cared about. I wondered who had cared about Martie Remington—who had cared enough to kill her.

chapter

TEN

I got up at 5:30 a.m., dressed, went downstairs, and looked in the dining nook although it didn't open until 6:00 a.m. I could hear people in the kitchen, though, so I stuck my head in and saw four kitchen staff furiously chopping, stirring, and pouring the breakfast makings. I asked if any coffee was available and a pretty girl, who looked about twelve years old, said it was on the sideboard in the dining nook. I nodded and retreated. If I'd looked more carefully, I would have seen the three big urns. There were pretty china cups and saucers and a tea basket with about fifty different packets inside. I looked in the cupboard under the sideboard and found plastic go-cups and lids. I grabbed the biggest one I could find, filled it, added a little cream, and snapped on a top. Outside, the car was covered with heavy dew, although the sky was clear and bright. The sun was rising over the east hills and it was a beautiful morning.

I ran the swipes to clear the window and drove to Judy Benoit's. When I got there, I parked five car lengths from her front sidewalk and behind two other cars. I didn't know if she had a car or where it was parked if she did. I took the lid off the coffee which immediately steamed the windows so I lowered the side window an inch. It was the best coffee I'd had since being in France three years ago. I regretted missing breakfast.

At 7:30a.m., Benoit came out and walked up the sidewalk away from me. She was carrying a briefcase in one hand and a cup in the other. She walked past two more cars and stopped beside a beat up Volvo XC70. She must've been trusting because it wasn't locked. She started the car and pulled away from the curb. I waited until she was at the end of the street before I followed. She surprised me by turning left at the corner, away from campus. I followed as closely as I dared with few other cars around. She seemed to be driving aimlessly as she made several turns and doubled back on her route a couple times. I wondered if she suspected she was being followed so I stayed as far back as I could and still keep her in sight. After ten minutes, she pulled to the curb in front of another Victorian two miles from her place. I got behind a Dodge 4X4 a block away, crawled across the console, and got out on the passenger side leaving the door open. I turned sideways and leaned on the roof as if I was talking to someone inside the car. She looked up and down the sidewalk before opening the Volvo's passenger door, grabbing the briefcase, and walking into the house. Whoever was inside must have been expecting her because the door was unlocked.

I didn't know what to do next. I wasn't keen on another long stakeout, plus there was a lot of foot traffic. After I got back in the car, several people looked at me as they passed. Finally I gave up, started the car, pulled up to the house, and memorized the street number. I'd written down the Volvo's tag number earlier and noticed a small green sign with yellow lettering in the back passenger side window. It had the initials E-C-F separated with little *love* hearts.

I drove back to the Bancroft hoping breakfast was still being served but they were picking everything up as I walked in. I did manage a cup of the coffee and used one of the china cups this time. The aroma made my stomach growl. The same girl who'd directed me to the coffee earlier looked at me and said, "We've got some pastries left over if you want some?" I nodded and she went into the kitchen reappearing with a loaded tray. I took a lemon Danish and an apple fritter.

"Thanks," I said. "You're saving a life with these."

She giggled and took the tray back.

I went back to my room and put the Do Not Disturb sign on the door. I got out my notes, sat in the club chair, and decided to call Tom Montgomery. It was only 7:45 a.m. in Denver so I had time to eat the pastries and drink the coffee. Both were wonderful.

***

"Tom? It's Cort. I'm in Oakland. Do you have any contacts in law enforcement out here in the land of fruits and nuts?"

"Of course I do, I know somebody nearly everyplace. What the hell do you need now...and what're you doing in California?" It sounded like Tom could have used some of my coffee and sugary carbs.

"Short answer is I'm working on a case for Hank Francis. I'm tailing a woman who knows something about the USGS geologist who was killed out in Rifle last spring. Longer answer is she seems to have an awful lot of friends or associates and I need to find out who some of them are. I've got some tag numbers and addresses and I wondered if you could find out who goes with them."

"Christ, I don't hear from you for weeks at a time and then you call at 8:01 a.m. with a bunch of requests. What the hell do you think—I've got nothin' better to do than run stuff down for you?"

"I guess that about sums it up. What else *do* you have to do?"

Tom laughed, which was a good sign. "Okay, let me have 'em and I'll see what I can do." I read him the tag numbers for the Lexus and the Volvo and the addresses where I'd tailed Benoit.

"Oh, yeah, one more thing—"

"One more thing my ass—there's always one more thing with you. What now?"

"The woman I'm tailing, the one driving the Volvo, has a window sticker with the letters E-C-F separated by little hearts. Have you ever seen the logo or know anything about it?"

"No, that's a new one on me. I'll put it in the computer and ask if anyone knows anything about it. Where can I get ahold of you?"

"Right now I'm at the Bancroft Hotel in Oakland, room two-twenty-five. I'll probably be moving around quite a bit. Call me on my cell if you find out anything, Okay?"

"Yeah, I'll call you."

I hung up and finished the coffee...it was better hot...and decided to make a list. I didn't know exactly what I was going to list, but it sounded good. It made me sound organized. I needed to know who Benoit was meeting and how to get my hands on her GPS. I needed to talk to her some more too, although that was probably out for now.

I decided to stay on Benoit so I drove back to where she'd parked. For once, my timing was good. She was just coming out of the house and getting in her car. I made a turn at the next corner, sped around the block, and was approaching from behind as she pulled away. I followed her to campus and watched as she parked in a student lot near the Geosciences Building. She took the backpack and entered a side door that must have taken her to her office. The parking lot was not visible from her office so I waited five minutes, drove up, and took the spot next to her Volvo.

A few students walked through the parking lot. I stepped out and tried the Volvo's passenger side door. It was unlocked. I looked around again, opened the door, and slipped inside.

Her car was a traveling rubbish bin. If I'd had time, I would've tried to get a time line from the layers of trash piled on the floor. In geologic terms, it was a layered conglomerate of fast food bags, newspapers, take-out cups, and even clothes. It was hard to reconcile this with the neatness of her apartment. I opened the glove box and found several maps of the western US. A small plastic folder looked promising. I opened it and found a car registration for the Volvo. It was registered to Victor Benoit of Yreka. I wouldn't need that one from Tom. There wasn't much else of interest so I put everything back in the glove box and got out.

I drove straight to her apartment, went into the foyer, and pressed a callbox button for an apartment on the third floor. When a woman's voice answered, I said in my best Spanish accented voice, "'Allo, Mees Smeeth? Jew Pee S delibery. Jew push door, I put jour package inside, hokay?" The door lock buzzed and I rushed in, ran down the hall to the first corner, and ducked around. I had to wait five minutes until finally hearing footsteps descending the stairs. They headed toward the entry, milled around some, and started back up the stairs. "Mees Smeeth" was muttering under her breath although I couldn't make out what she was saying. I don't think it was complimentary about Mexican immigrants, though.

I waited until I heard a door close, walked silently to the stairs, and up to the second floor. At Benoit's door, I listened for a few seconds and tried the knob. No luck this time, it was locked. I remembered there was a knob lock and an inside dead-bolt but no exterior key slot for the bolt. She couldn't have locked the bolt from outside so if I could get the knob lock open, I was in. It took a few seconds of wiggling and prying with a credit card until it worked. I ducked in and quickly closed the door behind me.

The place looked the same as the day before, very neat and carefully arranged. That seemed odd compared to her car. I started pulling out desk drawers and checking their contents. There were lots of computer disks, files with thesis research papers, and some day runner calendars. I took a quick look at them but couldn't find the current year. That would have been too much luck for one day. I left the desk and went into the bedroom.

This was more like her car—it was a mess. I guessed that Judy was a slob who put up a good front for visitors or guests. She had clothes scattered everywhere and the bed wasn't made. I checked the closet and found a two-drawer file cabinet inside. This one wasn't locked. I pulled the top drawer out and found several files with labels: National Forest Service Actions; USGS Actions; Department of Interior Actions. I opened the USGS file and found a series of newspaper articles and internet downloads describing resource evaluation projects. All had one thing in common: if the Survey determined sufficient resources existed for commercial development, the projects would have major effects on the environment as well as the economies of the areas involved. I replaced the USGS material and pulled the National Forest Service file. It was more of the same and described several proposals for leasing timber rights in national forest tracts throughout the Pacific Northwest. The other files were similar.

I put the top drawer files back in order and pulled the lower one. There was only one file labeled: E-C-F. It contained newspaper articles about environmental monkey wrenching like tree spiking and equipment sabotage at construction sites. No single group had ever claimed responsibility for any of them. In total, there had been a few hundred thousand dollars damage. None of the incidents involved deaths or personal injuries, although the property damage was extensive. In some cases development had ceased and never restarted. I couldn't find anything that identified what the initials stood for.

I closed the file and did a quick check of the rest of the bedroom and the apartment without finding anything else interesting. I didn't find the GPS unit so she must have told the truth about that. I tried to make sure I hadn't disturbed anything although it would have been hard to tell in the bedroom. I cracked the door and listened, twisted the knob lock, and left. When I got to the entry foyer, a UPS guy was entering with two packages. I asked, "Hey, do you have something for Miss Smith?"

He looked at me and said, "Who are you?"

I said, "I'm just a visitor. I was talking to her a few minutes ago and she said UPS rang her apartment and she buzzed the door to get a package but there wasn't anything here when she came down to check. She was pissed."

"Well, she's not pissed at me, man. I haven't been here today. And I don't have anything for anybody named Smith either."

"It's a mystery, I guess. Have a good day." I left and walked away thinking I had better check delivery timings before using that dodge again.

Back at the Bancroft, I had just sat down when my cell buzzed. I glanced at the screen and saw it was Tom Montgomery. That was quick work.

"Hey, buddy, doesn't take you long. What've you got for me?"

"A shitload for a shithead would be a good way of putting it. You got a pen and paper handy?"

"You bet, go ahead, I'm ready."

"First, the Volvo is registered to a Victor Benoit in Yreka, California." I didn't want to tell Tom I'd got that by breaking into Benoit's car. "I've got an address on him in Yreka. Does the name do anything for you?"

"He's Judy Benoit's father. I checked her out a little before I came out. She grew up in Yreka."

"That makes sense then. Next, the Lexus is registered to Jon Feng with a Pacifica address." I wrote down the address. "The addresses you gave me took some digging. Luckily, California has a quick search feature on their tax records and you can find out all sorts of shit. The place in Berkeley has changed hands several times in the last five years. The current owner is a corporation: ECF. I tried to get my contact to dig deeper and get some names but he didn't have the time. Interesting, huh? Those are the initials you gave me...*now*, get this—the previous owner was Jon Feng."

All at once, I had several people and places tied together. "What about the house in Alameda?"

"Owner is Gail Porter and she's owned it for years."

I thought about it for a moment and said, "I don't know what ties them all together unless they're friends or relatives. I know Benoit lied to me about going to San Francisco last night. She and some Asian guy, probably Feng, went to the Alameda house. I found out a little more about Benoit this morning. She's been following several different governmental agency studies, both federal and state. They're all making resource evaluations like oil and gas or timber and if they ever get developed, they'll have a big impact on the environment. She also has a file on monkey wrenching incidents. The label on that one is E-C-F."

Tom was quiet for a few seconds. "How the hell did you get that information?"

I hated to tell him. "I did a quiet B&E of her apartment and read the files."

"You stupid bastard! You can't run around breaking into people's houses and reading their mail. Jesus Christ, Cort, you're going to get busted for that shit and then what happens?"

"I know. It probably wasn't the smartest thing. Still, I needed to find out about her and she isn't talking anymore. I was careful. I didn't leave anything and I didn't disturb anything. I doubt she'll even know about it."

"That's what every second story guy I ever arrested said—'I didn't leave any evidence.' You always leave something, you jerk."

"Whatever. It looks like Judy Benoit is tied in with E-C-F, whatever the hell that is, and E-C-F is probably tied into screwing up governmental agency studies and construction projects. It makes Remington's death even more suspicious."

"I'll give you that. What are you going to do now?"

"I'm going to get on a computer and try tracking down some of these names. If I'm lucky, I might figure out who's in E-C-F."

"Let me give you some advice, *don't break into any more houses*. I can't take the time to come out and bail your dumb ass out of jail if you get caught."

"I hear you. You've convinced me it was a dumb thing to do." Tom made my ears ring when he slammed down the phone. I checked the time and decided I could do some research before I went back to campus and broke into Judy Benoit's office.

chapter

ELEVEN

I found the hotel's business center and was pleased no one was there. The two computer terminals, fax machine, printers, and scanner all looked and smelled new.

I booted up a computer, went to Google, typed Victor Benoit on the search line and sat back. It took 0.337 seconds for seventy-two hundred hits to come up. I clicked on the first one under the main heading because I didn't feel like surfing the pop-up ads to buy Victor Benoit Discount Merchandise displayed in the right column.

Victor Benoit owned three lumber mills in northern California all under the name of NoCal Lumber. There were several articles about NoCal Lumber having trouble finding enough logs to feed their mills and the moratorium on federal timber sales was driving out everyone except the big national lumber companies. On Google page fifteen, I found an article describing how Victor Benoit and his oldest daughter, Judy, had a very public falling out over the issue of harvesting old growth timber. Judy had been a senior in high school at the time. I tried several links but couldn't find whether they'd ever reconciled. I knew she was driving one of his cars although I didn't know what that meant.

I spent an hour studying Victor Benoit and he seemed like a good guy who was trapped in a no win situation with the lumber supply. He'd served on local school boards, donated lots of goods and services to relief organizations, paid his taxes, and hadn't made headlines for any criminal offenses.

Next, I typed in Jon Feng and a different story unfolded. Jon Feng was the middle child of three kids of one Feng Li of San Francisco. Feng Li had come to the US in the early 1950s soon after Chaing Kai-Shek had bugged out from mainland China to Taiwan. Although there wasn't much documentation, he must have arrived loaded with travel bags full of gold bars. He'd been a lieutenant general in Chaing's army and, from the looks of things, had done very well for himself. He must have been an equal opportunity thief because both Chaing and the mainland Red Chinese government wanted him back. There was no mention of a wife or the mother of the three kids. Simple math indicated the kids' mother must have been a late-in-life acquisition. At a minimum, Feng Li would've been in his fifties when the kids were born. He'd been murdered in an unsolved car bombing outside his import-export business in South San Francisco in 1988. Apparently, Chinese of any persuasion had long memories.

The oldest kid, a girl, was reported to be in Vancouver and married to a banker. Jon and his younger brother, Robert, were listed as president and chief financial officer, respectively, of Feng World-wide Products, Inc. The company had been investigated by the state when the old man ran it although nothing recently. John and Robert had both gone to Cal-Berkeley, but there wasn't much information about them except they both lived in San Francisco.

Next, I tried Gail Porter. This time, Google took the better part of a second to turn up over thirty-thousand hits. Her name had been splashed across the news for twenty-five years and not always in a good way. Gail was an activist. She was "active" in everything from tax and war protests to environmental demonstrations. She'd joined the Sierra Club, the Audubon Society, The Wilderness Society, and several other mainstream environmental causes and had dropped out of most of them. She was suspected of being involved with the Earth Liberation Front, E-L-F, and had been questioned about some of their actions. She'd sworn she didn't know anything and would never have been associated with any kind of violence or property destruction. The acronyms E-L-F and E-C-F *had* to be related. I just hadn't figured it out yet.

Porter was in her early sixties and had first appeared on the Berkeley scene during the Free Speech protests. She was getting a little long in the tooth for some of her old- time escapades like sitting in trees and blocking logging roads by laying in front of the Caterpillars.

It took money to be a successful activist so I dug as deeply as I could into her background and that's when things really got interesting. After one arrest on the Cal-Berkeley campus, the local paper ran an article about how she wasn't a student at Cal at all. They'd found she was the only daughter of a San Francisco couple, Jim and Maxine Porter, whose liberal causes and protest roots went all the way back to before World War II. They were both acknowledged members of the Communist Party of the United States as well as every other left wing organization of the times. Although both had come from well-to-do families, they were children of the depression and had spent a lifetime working to force change on the upper classes.

Even farther back, Jim Porter's parents had lived in China around the turn of the twentieth century. They amassed a sizeable fortune in the opium trade, returned to the States in the 30s and, like Feng Li twenty years later, had a lot of money mostly in gold. They established an import/export company in San Francisco and managed to prosper during the Great Depression. I wondered what the connection was with import/export companies in these families.

There were several lengthy time gaps in the information about the Porter family. Whatever changed them from wealthy entrepreneurs to protestors and activists a hundred years later was hard to decipher. This much was clear though: Gail had never suffered from a lack of finances for her activist agenda. It was too much of a coincidence that the Fengs and the Porters were both in the import/export business in San Francisco. How Judy Benoit fit in wasn't clear, but there had to be a connection.

I returned to the campus; Benoit's Volvo hadn't moved. I found a space several rows back, parked, and took the path to the Geosciences Building. I climbed the stairs to the bridge office and walked swiftly past, glancing in as I did. I saw Benoit sitting at her desk staring out the window. I continued into the Geophysics department, down the stairs, and out under the bridge walkway. I spotted a bench under a low-crowned tree about thirty yards away. If I sat there, Benoit would have to turn directly away from the parking lot to spot me. I'd picked up a brochure for the graduate program in Geophysics which would afford cover at that distance.

This time I didn't have long to wait. I read the brochure once, glanced up, and spotted Benoit coming out of the stairway. She didn't look my way. I let her get to the lot before I went to the door she had exited. I waited several minutes to give her time to leave or return if she'd forgotten anything, sprinted up the stairs to her office, and tried the door. It was unlocked and no one inside. Good old trusting Judy had left another door unlocked.

I didn't know how long before one of her office mates would return so I crossed quickly to her desk slot. Like the living room of her apartment, her desk was neat and carefully arranged. She obviously had different public and private personas based on her bedroom and car versus her apartment and office. I perused the bookshelves above her desk, didn't see anything of interest, so started with the lower left drawer of her desk. Bingo—the GPS unit was at the rear of the drawer. It wasn't concealed or covered—just laying at the back of the drawer. I didn't trust my luck much further so I grabbed the

GPS, closed the drawer, wrapped the grad school brochure around my prize, and left the office. I hurried to the car and drove back to the Bancroft.

chapter

TWELVE

Back at the hotel, I packed my bag and put the GPS in the gun case. As I checked out, I asked the desk clerk if she'd look at Southwest's schedule for Denver. She made a few keystrokes and told me there were four flights to Denver. The first was at 3:50 p.m. arriving at 8:45 p.m. with ninety minutes in Salt Lake City but no plane change. I glanced at the wall clock behind her: 12:07 p.m. I should be able to make the 3:50 even with a rental car return.

I drove to the airport, dropped off the rental, and fidgeted waiting for the shuttle. It got me to Southwest's gates at 1:57 p.m. This was going to be tight. I sprinted to ticketing, bought the ticket, and told the agent about needing to transport my gun. She looked at me for a moment then repeated the same drill I had gone through in Denver. She made out the same forms as before, I signed, and she put everything on the cart for special handling.

Near the departure gate I grabbed a coffee and a newspaper and settled in. I had sixteen minutes until boarding. For some reason, I turned to the second section of the paper and was surprised to see a photo and article titled: *Sixties Protest Redux*. The caption read: *Gail Porter, a staple of 60s activism, accompanied by several unidentified persons, protest at the USGS Menlo Park research facility*. The article described how Porter and the others were protesting the USGS involvement in oil shale research. She was quoted as saying, "Anything they do is going to be destructive to the environment. Every place they work is going to be destroyed. These are public lands and we don't want Big Oil and Big Government on them. We've got to stop this in its tracks and any means of doing so is justified." The reporter had done background and described how Porter had been involved in protests dating back to Berkeley in the sixties. She'd been linked to several violent demonstrations but had never been charged with anything other than trespassing and interference with a law enforcement officer. She was suspected of providing money for several groups who were involved with monkey wrenching activities. I thought the article was both ironic and timely.

I got Lindsey's voice mail and left a message I would be arriving at 8:45 p.m. I asked her to pick me up on the west side drive up at a quarter past nine.

***

The sun was setting as we touched down in Denver ten minutes early. I claimed my bag, wandered out to the sidewalk, and was surprised to see Lindsey's Edge—she wasn't noted for being on time. She hopped out, popped the rear lid, and greeted me with a hug. I loaded my bag and climbed in the passenger side as she got behind the wheel. She leaned over and kissed me hard on the mouth.

"Mmm, that was nice," I said.

"It's good to have you back. Three days isn't very long, but I missed you. What would you say to a fast ride home, a hot tub, and a couple glasses of wine before I take you to bed and give you a proper welcome?"

"You've become a mind reader in only three days—how wonderful!"

"I thought you'd like the change. You know me—always into self-improvement."

"I thought as much. Why are we still sitting here? You need to move before I institute a citizen's arrest and clap you in irons."

"Oh, promises, promises...are you going to severely discipline me, too?"

"Could happen. One can't take chances with a desperate felon like you."

Lindsey laughed, fastened her seat belt, and pulled out into the airport traffic. She pushed the speed limit all the way home and we made the usual forty minute run in thirty.

I went straight to the bedroom, unpacked my gun case, and took out the GPS. Lindsey gave me a surprised look. "How'd you get that? Did the girl just give it to you?"

"Nope, I stole it out of her desk."

"You did *what?*"

"I said, 'I stole it out of her desk'. I did it right after I broke into her house."

"Oh, god—too much information, too much information." Lindsey put her hands over her ears and stepped back in mock shock. I hoped it was mock.

"Somehow, I managed to piss her off when we were talking and she wasn't going to give it to me."

"Gee, I can't imagine you ever pissing anybody off. I mean, aren't you the cool, super smooth interrogator? What'd you ask her, anyway?"

"Why did you kill Martie Remington?"

"She must be totally narrow-minded to get pissed off at something as silly as that. Go figure."

"That's what I thought. Hey, how about the hot tub and wine?"

"Listen, bub, if you're waitin' on me, you're backing up."

Lindsey was out of her clothes and into a short robe by the time I had my shirt off. She stood with her arms crossed and tapped her foot as I got undressed. I was pleased to see an open bottle of red wine on the countertop: Silver Oak Cabernet, 1994. It was another top-shelf selection...just what I wanted.

I poured, Linds slipped out of her robe as I turned on the music, and we stepped into the tub. "This is perfect. It's everything I imagined, or maybe I should say fantasized, on the flight home. When did you open the wine?"

"It was the last thing I did before I left. About 8:00, I guess. Is that too long?"

"Obviously not...although I suggest we drink up. We wouldn't want something as good as this to go over the edge."

Lindsey drank off nearly half a glass, looked at me, and grinned, "Doctor's orders, I presume."

"*Holy Cow, girl.* If this was by-the-glass, that was a seven dollar swig you just took. Don't get *too* relaxed before bedtime, if you know what I mean."

"Don't worry about me, sleuth. You're the one who needs to avoid being too *relaxed,* if *you* know what *I* mean." The lascivious grin flashed and I felt a stirring of the rudder below the waterline. I hit the jets and we both sank down a little. The music channel was playing *Ebb Tide.*

Reuniting after long absences makes for great sex. Reuniting after short absences makes for great sex. We had great sex. I think long absences are overrated.

chapter

THIRTEEN

The next morning, I made coffee while Lindsey showered and got ready for work. I'd just finished the sports section—the Rocks had finally broken the losing streak—when she came out. "What's up for you today, sweetheart?"

"I'm taking the GPS to Hank's office. Then, I need more research on the people I saw with Benoit. I'm going to be busy."

"That's probably just as well. We've got a huge backlog of evidence to process from a big drug bust and shootout in Greenwood Village. I'll probably work late tonight."

"Greenwood Village? That's a pretty upscale area to be having drug busts and shootouts isn't it?"

"Yeah, it's unusual, although lots of retired athletes live there now. Some of those guys seem to have a penchant for being involved in drugs. Hey, I gotta go. I'll see you when I see you. If it's going to be real late, I'll call."

"OK, babe, have a good day."

I poured more coffee; it was only 7:15a.m. Hank wouldn't be in for another hour. I got online and Googled Earth Liberation Front. Lots of stuff came up, including an article I was looking for about the Two Elks ski lodge fire near Vail a few years ago. ELF had taken responsibility for burning down the lodge which had been built on federal land on top of a mountain. That was the first time I'd ever heard of them and I vaguely remembered reading about some of their other "interventions." The stuff I was looking for referred to bombings of electrical transmission towers in the Northwest and in Arizona. In each case, ELF claimed the facilities were on federal lands belonging to the people and private companies shouldn't be allowed to profit from them. There were lots of other position statements about exploitation and environmental damage. Near the end of a piece about who was in ELF, I found what I was looking for: Gail Porter, of Alameda, California, was suspected of being a member of ELF and providing monetary support for their actions. In addition to Porter, several other Bay Area residents and businesses were listed. I still couldn't find a connection between ELF and the initials, E-C-F.

I began processing and organizing the information: Martie Remington worked for the USGS, a federal agency, and was evaluating oil shale deposits, most of which were on federal land. If they were commercially developed, it would be by private industry. Judy Benoit had been involved in environmental causes since she was a teenager. She went to school at Cal-Berkeley which had been a hotbed of activism since the sixties. Gail Porter was also connected to Berkeley and environmental causes since the sixties. Her parents had inherited wealth but were left wing radicals from before WW II. Their wealth had come from her grandparents' import/export business. Feng Li immigrated from China or Taiwan in 1950 and arrived with lots of money. He was in the import/export business and now his company was run by his sons. I had seen Jon Feng with Judy Benoit and they had both visited Gail Porter's house.

There were way too many associations here to be coincidental. Still, it was a hell of a leap from staging environmental protests to murder.

***

I called Hank to say I'd collected the GPS unit and would bring it to the Federal Center. He asked, "How'd you get it? Did Judy just hand it over?"

"She said she'd give it to me, got mad about some of the questions I asked, and threw me out of her house...so I broke in and stole it."

I waited for the explosion that didn't come. "Well, at least you got it. Bring it out. I'll phone the gate to let you in."

Inside the USGS building, Jamie Pearson glanced at me, nodded, and punched in Hank's extension. "Mr. Francis? Mr. Scott is here. Yes, sir, I'll send him right up." She closed the call and said, "I believe you know the way."

At the top of the stairs, Rick Russell and Randy Joyce came out of an office, nodded, and we all shook hands. Randy said, "Hank says you got the GPS from Judy. That's good. We should be able to retrace all of her steps."

I handed it to Randy as we entered Hank's office. "She told me she downloaded the information to her computer. Doesn't that remove it from the device? How are you going to get it?"

Randy said, "It doesn't remove it entirely. I have to hook into our reader program and access the memory directly. I can't display to the GPS screen without a little manipulation, however the information is still there. I'll get it."

Hank walked around his desk and shook hands. "You guys get started on it. I want to visit with Cort." The geologists left; Hank said, "Sit down a minute. What the hell did you mean when you said you stole it?"

"Just what I said—Benoit got defensive when I told her I didn't work for the USGS or the Justice Department. At first, she said I could come by her campus office and pick up the GPS—later she said to forget about that. When I started questioning her, she said, 'I don't have to talk to you' and threw me out. She said she'd mail it here. Since I thought she was lying, I decided to grab it before she dumped it off the pier or something."

"What did you think she was lying about?"

"Everything. She was nervous as a whore in church the whole time I was talking to her. What's even more interesting though, is the company she's keeping."

"How's that?"

"For starters, she's running around with a guy named Jon Feng. He runs an import-export business, founded by his father with money, actually gold, smuggled out of mainland China when the commies took over. Second, Benoit and Feng met with a woman named Gail Porter who's an old time rabble rouser from the Bay Area. She's been tied into every environmental protest for forty years. I think it's more than a coincidence her money comes from a San Francisco import/export company started by her grandparents who were also in China. Porter's been tied to the Earth Liberation Front, the same bunch who burnt down the Two Elks ski lodge. Benoit has some activist roots too. She was protesting her own father's logging operations in northern California."

Hank's shoulders drooped. "Jesus Christ, I had no idea. You don't think she actually killed Martie, do you?"

"I don't know. Like I said, she won't talk about it."

Hank sighed. "God, I hope not. I don't want to believe something like that. But, what motive would she have? Surely, it can't just be about the environment?"

"I don't know that either. Some of these groups get some really crazy ideas."

He walked back behind his desk and sat heavily in his chair. "I'm getting way too old for this kind of crap."

"I hear you—me too. How long will it take to process the GPS?"

"It could take a while. I'll give you a call when we get something. What're you going to do now?"

"I'm stopping by my office to see what's happening downtown."

chapter

FOURTEEN

I was feeling the six floors by the time I got to my office. I definitely needed to get more exercise. I set up a pot of coffee and read a week-old copy of the *Rocky Mountain Oil Journal* while I waited for the coffee. I was saddened to see an obit for Sid Bonner. This had been his office. Sid had been in a care facility for Alzheimer's patients for several years. He'd given me some leads in Gerri's murder case. The coffee maker beeped, I poured a cup, and toasted Sid. Too many of the old timers who'd been the heart and soul of the Denver oil and gas business were dying.

I started searching the web for anything I could find on Feng Li or the Porters. There was a lot of information but most was buried pretty deep.

The most interesting things were newspaper articles printed after Feng Li was murdered in 1988. Both the Nationalist Chinese on Taiwan and the People's Republic on the mainland were listed as prime suspects in his car bombing death. One enterprising reporter traveled to both places to research his story on the mysterious Feng Li. The reporter hadn't reached a definitive conclusion as to which side Feng Li had been on. In the early going, he'd been allied with Mao's bunch and had risen as high as a colonel in the Red Army. Sometime right before Chaing Kai Shek was forced to abandon the mainland and move his forces to Taiwan, Feng had switched sides. The reporter concluded Feng was being paid by the communists to spy on the Nationalists. However, he became a double agent and was playing both sides against each other. He kept getting enough good information that each thought he was working exclusively for them. He was simultaneously looting Nationalist sympathizers who remained on the mainland. His scam was to promise them an escape to Taiwan; all they had to do was "trust" him with their money, preferably in gold, until he could arrange for their escape. Unfortunately, as soon as he got his hands on the gold, the families would suddenly be apprehended by Mao's boys and charged with trying to escape or with espionage. Most were never heard from again.

On the other side, Feng was approaching rich families in Taiwan who had managed to escape. He would convince them he could get other family members or friends out of China although they would have to fund some enormous bribes to get the Red Army to look the other way. As soon as he got the money, he would again alert the mainland Chinese who would, in this case, actually catch people trying to flee. Eventually word would get back to Taiwan, but Feng would just tell the survivors something had gone wrong; that he had done all he could and had paid off the right people. It was just tragic luck. Since everybody had been sworn to secrecy, he was able to run the scam for several years. When too many people began comparing stories, he bagged up his gold and cash, bribed a few Taiwanese officials and defected to the US. He told the FBI and CIA he was escaping from the Reds by way of Taiwan and they bought it. They gave him political asylum and even recruited him to give them information on the People's Republic. Feng was happy to do so…at a price.

Part of the price was allowing him to set up a business in South San Francisco. It was unclear what kinds of merchandise Feng Worldwide Products imported. The company was privately owned and not subject to public audits. It listed its business as import/export and maintained an office and small warehouse in the dock area of South San Francisco. After the airport relocated to the area, business boomed according to the tax returns which had been faithfully filed.

When the car bomb blew Feng Li's Lincoln to smithereens, the local police started an intensive investigation that was soon preempted by FBI teams. While it had been front page headlines for a couple of days, it disappeared from the papers entirely after a week. At the time, the local cops said the Feds were conducting the investigation and they were not at liberty to discuss the case. No arrests or charges were ever reported. In the early days, the papers mentioned Feng's history and speculated either the Reds or the Nationalists were paying off old debts or, more likely, one side or the other had discovered he was a double agent.

I printed several of the articles for a reading file and switched gears to look at the Porters. Gail's grandfather had even written a book about his adventures in turn of the century China. For a guy who started as a student of ancient Chinese medicine, Grandpa seemed to have settled quickly into a practitioner who prescribed only one drug...opium. Somehow, he'd managed to get in the middle of the opium trade between Indo-China and China proper. I found an outline of his book which mentioned rugged horse and mule trips to present-day Laos to organize poppy growers, transportation, and prices, as well as storage and distribution back in China. He had headquartered in Nanking.

He, his wife and son, Jim, returned to the US in the early thirties, a few years before the Japanese invaded China and destroyed Nanking in 1937. They settled in San Francisco and built a palatial home not far from the Presidio area. I found it interesting they were able to do this during the depths of the Great Depression. It was equally interesting they started a Chinese import/export company at the same time. Although I didn't know much about 1930s and '40s Chinese history or economics, I didn't think they had much to trade during those times...legal things anyway.

I kept looking for a connection between the Porters and Feng Li. So far, I wasn't coming up with anything. As I tried to look deeper into Feng Li's murder, I found the internet search engines didn't have much information. I knew it would cost me another ass chewing, but I decided to try Tom Montgomery.

***

Tom picked up on the third ring, "Montgomery."

"Hey, Tom, it's Cort. How're you doing?"

"I'm just ducky. Whadda ya want?"

"Who said I want something? Can't I just call an old friend to chat?"

"You never just want to *chat* and I'm not old." Tom sounded like he was in a good mood or at least his normal one.

"Yeah? Well, that sounds like bad information to me. You're a hell of a lot older than me. Fifteen days to be specific."

"Well, give me some respect then and answer the question. What the hell do you want?"

"Okay, you've got me. You remember that guy, Jon Feng, you ran the plate for out in California?"

"Yeah."

"I dug around in his background and found out his father immigrated to the US in the fifties, set up an import/export business with help from the feds, and then got blown up in 1988. Nobody's ever been pinched for his murder. It was probably either the Red Chinese or the Nationalists on Taiwan. The old man was working for either or both outfits during the Chinese civil war. Would you contact the cop shops in the Bay Area and see what they've got on the murder?"

"Christ, you don't want much do you? Twenty year old, cold case homicides aren't going to be at the top of anybody's wish list. Most of the cops who would've worked it are probably gone. What're you trying to find out?"

"Anything I can...mostly if there's a link between the Porter family and Feng Li. It would help to know which Chinese side blew him up, too."

"Well, it's your lucky day. We haven't had a murder in almost two weeks and I'm sitting here twiddling my thumbs. One problem though, I don't have many contacts in that area...at least in the local police departments. I do know a guy in the California Bureau of Investigation. He was a state cop for years and went into the Bureau about three years ago. I haven't talked to him in a while—I'll see what he can find out. This might take a while though."

"That's okay. Anything you find out could help."

"I'll give him a call. Hey, where are you? Are you home?"

"No. I'm at my office. Why?"

"I thought maybe you'd want to get a beer after work if you're downtown."

"Works for me, you wanta go to the Sounds?" I suggested. Our mutual friend, Andy Thibodeaux, owned a Cajun restaurant called Sounds of the South on Glenarm Street just off the 16th Street Mall.

"That's what I was thinking. How's Denver's most famous coon-ass doing anyway?"

"Same as ever I guess. Every time he has more than a couple of beers, he gets harder to understand. He starts speaking French and not very good French either."

Tom laughed. "It'll be good to see the goofy bastard. I'll meet you there about 5:30 p.m."

I went back to searching for anything I could find about the Benoits, the Porters, or the Fengs and kept seeing the same articles over and over. I gave up, logged off, and started reading back issues of the *Oil and Gas Journal*. One article caught my eye. It was a lengthy story about several places in the world where oil shale deposits were being produced.

Projects were underway in Morocco, Jordan, and western China. Interestingly, the Chinese were involved in Morocco and Jordan as well as in their own backyard. Each country had a national oil company which gave them an advantage over the US. Shell Oil Company was working with the Jordanians though, and they were trying new technology that might have application in Colorado. I called Hank but he was in a meeting. I left a message on his voice mail, "Hank, call me when you get a chance. I need your take on the oil shale projects going on overseas. I'll be in my office until about five and home tonight. Thanks."

***

It didn't look like Colorado's anti-smoking law had hurt Andy's business too much. People were standing three deep at the bar. Andy was behind the bar; he glanced up, spotted me, and waved. I waved back, signaled for two beers, and pointed at one of the narrow booths along the back wall. Andy nodded, said a couple words to the girl working the floor, and motioned in my direction. She delivered the beers and said, "Hi, Andy said the first one's on the house."

"Well, tell Andy thanks and that Mr. Tom Montgomery will be along in a few minutes. My name's Cort Scott, by the way, what's yours?"

"I'm Lisa. It's nice to meet you, Mr. Scott."

"Call me Cort, please. When did you start working here?"

"Oh, about three weeks ago, I was at Pappadeaux's down in the Tech Center before here."

"Can't get enough Cajun cooking, huh?" I asked.

She chuckled, "Yeah, I guess that's it. Actually, business is slowing down there and I had people tell me the tips are better downtown so I thought I'd give it a try."

"Good reason, Lisa. I hope you like it."

Tom came in, looked around, and saw me in the booth. He was carrying a thick file folder. "Whadda ya say, sport?" Tom sat down across from me and slapped the folder on the table. "Couldn't wait, I see." He motioned towards my beer.

I replied, "If you're waiting on me, pards, you're backing up. When the austere Tom Montgomery suggests a beer after work, I want to be first in line."

"*Austere*—man, you've started using some real four-bit words in your old age."

Lisa arrived with two more bottles and set one down in front of each of us. She raised an eyebrow and bent down to check the fluid level in my first bottle. It was only half gone; I picked it up and drained it in two gulps. "Andy said you'd be ready by the time I got here."

"Doesn't it look like I'm ready? Lisa, this is Tom Montgomery, another of Andy's many friends and a member of Denver's finest."

Tom said, "Hi, Lisa, nice to meet you. I hope this guy hasn't been giving you a bad time. He can be a pain."

Lisa smiled. "Why, he's been a perfect gentleman, at least so far, Mr. Montgomery." She smiled and turned back to the bar.

Tom took a long draw from his bottle and exhaled. "That tastes pretty damn good. Wow, it's cold, too. Man, we haven't been in here in forever!"

"We haven't been anywhere in forever, buddy. We've got to do better."

Tom drained his first beer. "There, I've caught up. Like I said, it's your lucky day. Take a look at this folder. Those are all faxes and emails from my bud in California *and* from his buddies in the FBI. I don't know what the hell you've stepped in...I hope you've got some high boots because this is deep shit, bucko."

chapter

FIFTEEN

Tom flipped the folder open and started paging through the papers. I noticed several were stamped *Private and Confidential* or *Privileged Communication, Recipient Only*. "You're not supposed to see most of this; of course, I'm not either."

I hefted the folder. "It looks like you hit the jackpot."

"This ain't all of it, either. The feds are sending more tomorrow. Your timing is just right. They lose interest after twenty years or so and are willing to start sharing info even if it's still considered sensitive. My contact in California, his name is Harry Thornton incidentally, said the locals and the California Bureau were hot and heavy on this case when it happened. Two days later, the feds came in, took it over, shut the Sunshine Boys out, and said not to worry about it. It's still a cold case file in California although nobody's turned a tap since the feds took it over.

"Harry put me onto an agent in Quantico who remembered the case because he was in San Francisco when it happened. I talked to him, name's John Nelson, and he's still pissed that nothing ever happened. He told me, totally off the record of course, the word came down from the Attorney General to shut down the Californians, let it die, get it out of the papers and off the news, and then do nothing. He said it still gnaws at him."

I thought for a moment as Lisa brought Tom's second beer. "Why would they do something like that?"

"Because something or somebody *real* important was involved, that's why. No other explanation makes any sense."

I thought about that, too. "Did you get a chance to read much of this stuff?"

"Yeah, I read it all as it came in."

"What's the gist of it?"

"Another good word, '*gist*'...well, if I may summarize—." He looked at me with a sarcastic grin. "Feng Li was, in fact, a double-dipping agent. He started out working for the Communists, he was the old foreign minister, Chou En Lai's special boy, and it looks like Chou got him into deep cover and into the Nationalist's army intelligence group. What gets murky, though, is who he was working for from about the end of WW II until he bugged out with the Nationalists for Taiwan. There's lots of suspicion he was feeding the Commies a shitload of intelligence about Chang Kai Shek's whole operation while, at the same time, he was giving Chang's bunch info about Mao and the cadres. When the Nationalists were forced onto Taiwan, he went with them. It's pretty clear he was, literally, the last guy to arrive."

We both had a drink and Tom continued. "When he approached the Americans about coming here, he told them he'd gone to Beijing to get orders from Mao himself before he went to Taiwan. He told the FBI he was a double agent and it was getting too hot for him in both places. He said he wanted to come here and work for us. I guess that would make him a 'triple' agent, if there is such a thing.

He told our side he had good contacts in Beijing *plus* he could keep an eye on the Nationalists at the same time. The US was supporting the Nationalists and we were scared they were just lining their own pockets. And then, to make matters worse, Korea erupted.

"The Office of Strategic Services, the OSS, was in the process of becoming the CIA and was desperate for eyes and ears in both places. They thought Feng was the greatest thing since sliced bread. The CIA brought him in although they're not supposed to be involved domestically, so they got the FBI to set him up in business in San Francisco. Here's where the story gets muddied up. Feng was playing all sides against the middle. He was definitely on our payroll and it looks like he was still working for *both* the Nationalists and the Commies. I found one report, written a couple of years before he got blown up, that the CIA was getting suspicious and decided to tail him for a while. Turns out, Feng flew to Taiwan supposedly to arrange for some cheap-ass toys to be imported and while he was there, he 'disappeared' for three days." Tom made the two fingered quotation sign when he said disappeared. "Our spooks had a couple guys in Beijing who saw Feng go into the building where the Red Army kept their spies. Nobody saw him entering or leaving Beijing and he came back to San Fran from Taiwan."

"Jesus Christ! Was this guy that good or were we that dumb?" I had listened with my jaw hanging down.

"Probably both—this guy was good, no doubt, but he had so many handlers by that point it's a wonder they didn't all meet in a noodle shop to compare notes."

"So who killed him? It sounds like Taiwan, Beijing, and Washington all had reasons to want him dead."

"I don't know the answer. If I were a betting man, my money would be on the Nationalists. They had the most to lose with him working for Beijing and Washington versus what he could tell them about us or the Reds. I don't know how or when they figured it out because back then guys were defecting back and forth so it had to come out sometime. I hate to think *we* snuffed the son-of-a-bitch. I can't say for sure we didn't though."

"Did you ask this agent Nelson about that?"

"Sort of—he didn't say much. He figured the Taiwanese did it and our side shut down the investigation to keep any mention of the CIA or FBI out of the news."

"You buy that?"

"Maybe...I don't know. There's lots of scary shit goes on I don't know about and, quite frankly, I don't *want* to know about. Hell, three or four years ago, the goddamn FBI tried to infiltrate Denver PD to see if we were doing everything we should about illegal immigrants and Mexican drug dealers. They didn't ask us any questions; just tried to get a guy transferred in, at a sergeant's level, from Baltimore. We figured it out when there was some screw-up on getting his stuff from Baltimore PD. The Chief called him in, grilled his ass, and the guy told him what was really going on. Man, the Chief was *pissed*. He went all the way to Washington, got an interview with the Assistant Director of the FBI, and ate his ass out. Anyway, it just shows you that everything the feds do isn't always what it seems."

I signaled Lisa for two more beers. "This may be too much information. I have no idea of how all this ties into some girl falling down a talus slope in western Colorado. There are too many moving pieces."

"That's why you make the big bucks and I don't. I'm just a messenger here, you know. I sit around all day waiting to do your bidding."

"What you *really* are is a professional wise ass. Is there anything else of interest in the rest of the file?"

"Yeah, the feds haven't kept close track of the Feng family since the old man got whacked...hang on, let's see if I can find it in here—." Tom shuffled through the papers and pulled out a couple of pages. "Yeah, here it is. It seems your buddy, Jon Feng, has made several trips to Hong Kong, supposedly to arrange for imports, although nothing seems to get imported as far as the feds can tell. On at least two occasions, he's also disappeared for a couple of days." Tom made the quotes again. "There aren't any reports of him showing up in Beijing, but it seems damn suspicious to me."

"Christ, you don't think he's working for the Chinese, do you?"

"That's above my pay grade, pards. It's just strange. After I read it, I called Harry Thornton and asked him to check out Feng's company. He hasn't gotten back to me yet—" Tom checked his watch "—they're still working on the west coast. I'm guessing it'll be tomorrow, though."

We talked more about the info he'd gotten on Feng and how it might be connected to Martie Remington. Neither of us could come up with anything that sounded plausible. We had one more beer, paid the tab, and left. Tom said he'd let me know when he got the rest of the stuff the feds had promised. He gave me the file; we shook hands, and went in opposite directions.

chapter

SIXTEEN

I stepped into the house and saw Lindsey sitting in a glider on the deck. She stood and put her arms around my neck. "Hey, babe ... I'm glad to see you remembered your way home." She kissed me, pulled back a little, ran her tongue over her lips and said, "Whew, you smell like a brewery. You're not driving under the influence, are you?"

"I'm probably border-line. You playing cop again?"

"I probably should. You know better than that. You could have called me—I would've picked you up."

"I know. I only had four beers over a couple of hours and, besides, I was with Tom."

"*Oh*, well, *hell*, that makes all the difference. Surely, Tom wouldn't let you do anything illegal, would he?" I knew where this was going. I also knew she was right.

It didn't keep me from being defensive, though.

"Okay, Linds, I'm sorry. I'll try not to do it again, okay?"

She knew when to back off and did it now…with perfect timing. She moved in close, kissed me again, and said, "I'm just glad you made it safely. What would you like for dinner?"

"I don't know. Why don't you just call for a pizza delivery?"

"Suits me, I'll do it. So, what did you find out today—anything interesting?"

"Tom used some contacts and found out a whole bunch. I hope I'm not getting into something way over my head on this case. I've got the CIA, FBI, Red Chinese, Nationalist Chinese, and the California state cops involved and it was from one phone call to Tom."

"Yikes. Sounds scary." Lindsey spoke over her shoulder as she strode to the phone.

I followed her inside. "It's definitely got my attention."

"What's next for you?"

"I need to hear back from Hank about the GPS and I need to talk to him about the Chinese interest in oil shale, too."

"*Damn it*, I'm sorry—he called and left a message. The light was blinking; I picked it up, saw it was from Hank, and left it for you. Sorry, babe, I spaced it."

"Hey, no big deal—I'll pick it up." Hank's message said he'd been meeting with Randy and Rick about the GPS and something really weird was going on with the memory chip in the unit. They couldn't retrieve any data to map. He said some kind of wiping program had been run and the memory was virtually blank. He said they'd keep trying although it didn't look good.

He also confirmed the Chinese were involved in oil shale plays worldwide. He knew they were doing research on their own deposits and experimenting on different types of deposits in other countries. He'd met with a delegation from their national oil company about the possibility of working in Colorado. Our position was that nobody was going to work domestically until we knew what we had. There wasn't a snowball's chance in hell our government would let the Chinese work in the US. So what the hell was going on? The Chinese seemed to be everywhere. That's all I had heard today. What was the connection?

The pizza delivery pulled up, I answered the door and paid the kid.

"So, was the message important?" Lindsey inquired.

"Hard to say, I don't know much more than I did before. It doesn't look like we'll learn anything from the GPS and that's a bummer. I was hoping we'd find out Benoit was with Martie the whole time and was guilty as sin *or* she was right where she said and was innocent. Hank said it was tampered with though. If that's true, I've got more investigating to do."

"What's that mean for you?"

"Another trip to California for one thing; I need to talk to some of the people I saw hanging out with Benoit. I think she's mixed up in this. I just can't put my finger on exactly how."

"When are you going?"

"Monday—I want to spend the weekend with you."

"You're a good man, Charlie Brown, and you bake a helluva pizza!"

I began to wonder how appreciative she could really be.

chapter

SEVENTEEEN

It turned out to be a great weekend. Lindsey allowed me to have wine with dinner plus margaritas on the deck Sunday afternoon. I was suitably rewarded for my sobriety and decorum.

On Monday, we got up at 5:00 a.m. and she drove me to the airport to catch my flight. As she dropped me off, she said, "Be careful, babe. Those outfits you mentioned, ours and theirs, sound dangerous. If you *do* feel like you're in over your head, get some help. Promise me, okay?"

Lindsey had never asked me to get help. I looked in her eyes and said, "I promise, sweetheart. If it gets too deep, I'll call somebody. I don't know how long this'll take. I'll try to give you a call every night."

"You better—I'll miss you, you know." Her eyes misted so I made her close them by kissing her and scrambled out of her Edge before either of us could say anything else. I opened the back hatch, grabbed my carry-on, waved at the rear view mirror, and turned for the door. *"You call me!"* She yelled. I looked back and blew her a kiss.

I went through the gun drill, got a croissant and coffee, and took the moving sidewalk to my gate. I was surprised to find twenty or more passengers waiting at the gate. They must have spent the weekend in the Colorado mountains and were returning to work. A couple hours on the plane, a car and driver, and the time change would put them at their desk at normal time. Not a bad way to spend a weekend.

We pushed off on time and I slept most of the way, awakening as we started the descent into San Francisco International. SFO is one of my least favorite airports because of the approach over the bay so close to the water you feel like you could touch it. The instant land appears under the wing, the wheels touch and the plane decelerates so quickly the seatbelts put bruises across your hip bones. It was a normal landing.

I picked up a rental car, made the quick drive to South San Francisco, and cruised past Feng Worldwide Products, Inc. I didn't know what they imported or exported because they didn't have much room to do it. The one-story, stand-alone, metal and fake stone building was close to the docks, but not on them. It stood by itself on a dead end street. There were small, fenced parking lots on both sides with a loading dock on one side. Both lots had double wide, chain link gates wrapped with heavy chains and padlocked. The entrance door looked like a heavy duty security model, with a small, barred window at eye level. Security cameras were mounted in the eaves of the roof and on poles in each parking lot. There were no cars in the lots or signs of life around the building. I saw a printed sign on the door and pulled up in front to read it. The sign said By Appointment Only and a telephone number. I wrote down the number and tried to look in. The glass was either a one way mirror or opaque; I couldn't see inside.

I drove most of the way back to the airport to an Embassy Suites hotel. The southwest Asian girl at reception, a Pakistani or

Afghani, spoke beautiful English with a lovely lilting accent. She apologized that check-in wasn't until 3:00 p.m. and currently it was not yet noon. I put on my best smile and asked if there were *any* rooms available now. She tapped a few keys on the computer, smiled back, and said some upgrade suites were available. I said fine...even at $249...and gave her my credit card.

My room was on the second floor with a nice view of the bay from the little balcony. The day was clear and sunny and I could see the Oakland hills across the water. I hung up the few things in my carry-on, checked out the mini-bar, selected a five dollar Snickers bar, and sat at the desk.

I dialed Feng Worldwide Products and, surprisingly, got a live answering service who told me a company representative would be happy to return my call if I cared to leave my name, number, and a brief explanation of my business. I checked the telephone for the number and extension and was glad to see it was a blind switchboard which didn't match room numbers to telephone extensions. I told the answering service girl my name was Tom Montgomery and I was interested in talking to the company about importing some products from China. I didn't tell her what kind of products and she didn't ask. I asked if she knew how soon someone would call me and she said she didn't know, however someone from Feng Worldwide checked messages every day around 4:00 p.m. I thanked her and hung up.

I used my cell to call Gail Porter's number and, again, was moderately surprised to have her pick up immediately. She had a Julia Childs voice, high and slightly wavering, but friendly nonetheless. I said, "Hello, Ms. Porter? My name is Bob Colby and I'm a feature writer for an online magazine based in Denver. I'm interested in interviewing you about your long career in environmental activism." I hoped she belonged to the school of "any PR is good PR as long as they spell your name right." I was right.

"I'm *always* interested in talking about the environment and the multitude of challenges it faces. Mr. Colby, did you say? Where are you staying and when did you wish to see me?"

"Actually, I haven't checked in anyplace yet. I've just arrived and I'm calling from the airport. To tell you the truth, I was hoping you might be available this afternoon. Is that possible?"

"Yes, I suppose so. I'm not busy until this evening. If you could come right away, I can give you a couple hours if you think that's sufficient."

"I'm sure it would be, Ms. Porter. If you'll give me your address, I can leave right away."

She gave me the address and directions. It was where I'd tailed Benoit and Feng: 22 Waterfall Isle.

I hoped Gail Porter didn't ask for ID or copies of any articles. I'd have to play it by ear...lie if I had to...and hope for the best. I put my gun in my briefcase although I assumed I wouldn't need it to talk to a sixty-something woman about hugging trees or protecting field mice. Traffic was light and I made good time to Porter's house. I cruised through her cul-de-sac looking for Feng's Lexus or Benoit's Volvo but didn't spot them. I pulled up in front, grabbed my briefcase, and walked to the entry. Gail Porter answered her bell quickly, looked me over for a second, and invited me in. Her looks matched her telephone voice...like Julia Childs.

As we stood in the entryway, Gail appraised me again and said, "Well, Mr. Colby, you certainly made good time getting here from the airport. I assume since you landed in San Francisco, you must have people to see over there. You could have landed in Oakland, you know. It's a perfectly good airport although I consider it to be a waste of space and energy to have it right across the bay from SFO."

"Yes, ma'am, it does seem like duplication doesn't it?" I thought I'd try to be as accommodating as possible, at least for a while.

She motioned toward the living room and said, "Why don't we go in here... or maybe you'd prefer the deck? I have a nice view of the harbor and docking areas if you'd rather. I don't think it's too breezy today."

"That would be nice, let's try the deck."

She led the way through a nicely appointed room and through glass sliders to the deck, which did have a nice view of the boats. She indicated a couple of rattan chairs, one in the sun and one under an umbrella. "Take your choice, Mr. Colby. I'll sit in the lounger." She sat in a cushioned lounger in the shade. I took the chair under the umbrella.

"Tell me again who you write for?" She asked.

"Well, ma'am, I—"

She interrupted to say, "Please call me Gail, everybody does."

"Okay, uh, Gail, you can call me Bob then. Anyway, we're just getting started with this web magazine. It's called *The Examiner's Eye* and will publish only online. There won't be any hard copy unless someone chooses to print an article. We haven't got it up and running yet so I can't give you any examples of my work. I don't even have business cards printed. In fact, you're the first person I've talked to so I'm playing it by ear." At least that last part was true. It bothered me that the lies came so easily.

"I see, well, what possibly led you to me, Mr. ah—I mean, 'Bob.'"

"I've been researching environmental protest groups and some of the more notable events—let's call them actions—of the past few years. In Colorado, the biggest thing, probably ever, was the burning of the Two Elks ski lodge and restaurant near Vail a few years back. The Earth Liberation Front took responsibility. I started looking into them and ran across your name so I followed up. You've been involved in the movement for a long time, Gail. I decided I should talk to you and get your perspective."

"My goodness, Bob, I had no idea I was so famous. Do you believe everything you've read?"

"I have no idea of what's true and what's speculation. I wanted to talk to you, if you were willing, and go from there. Do you mind if I take notes?" I took an old-fashioned stenographer's pad out of my briefcase being careful not to let her see the Beretta. I slipped a pen out of the spiral and gave her my best cub reporter look.

She nodded appreciatively. "I admire your spirit, Bob. Go ahead—what would you like to know?"

I hadn't thought my cover through as well as I should have so hesitated a moment before coming up with a legitimate question. I wrote the date and her name at the top of a page to stall. Finally, I asked, "How did you get started in environmental activism?"

She didn't have to think about the softball lob question. "Oh, that's easy. My parents were active in all sorts of political and social protest going clear back to before WW II. I just carried on the family tradition, I guess. I started with demonstrations at Berkeley in the sixties and it's evolved from there."

So far, so good. "Doesn't it take a lot of money to actually be a physical presence at demonstrations and protests?"

"I suppose so, although maybe not as much as you'd think. Most gatherings are sort of communal I'd guess you'd say. But for me it was easy, my folks were well off and I inherited a substantial amount of money from them."

"Have you used your money to fund other activists?"

"Sure, why shouldn't I put my money where I think it does some good?" Her voice took on a sharper tone.

"No reason, no offense intended—I'm just trying to get a handle on your life as an activist. Where do you stand on acts of civil disobedience or even violence in pursuit of social goals?"

"That's a loaded question. How do I answer in a way that won't get me arrested? Let's see, I'd say I don't mind partaking in non-violent demonstrations and even some things that might cause a little property damage. I don't support violent acts. This, I suppose, brings us to the Earth Liberation Front. Early on, I supported many of their actions in defense of the environment—like opposing uncontrolled growth and urban sprawl and gas-guzzling cars and so forth. I can assure you, I've had nothing to do with any of their damaging, hurtful, and dangerous stunts. I was particularly mad about being connected to that fire in Colorado. I'm not saying I don't support their point of view…I just draw the line at arson and dangerous things like that. I haven't had any contact with those people in years and I don't intend to renew any."

I smiled and underlined her last statement. "I'm glad to hear you say that, Gail. Let's move on if you don't mind. Are you familiar with the initials E-C-F and how they might be associated with ELF?"

She said, "I'm not familiar with anything called ECF." She said it too quickly, I thought.

"What are you involved in now that you feel passionate about?"

"For starters, I'm passionate about everything I do. Right now, I'm working to preserve old growth forests in northern California and Oregon. I'm trying to get dams off the rivers in those same areas, and in preventing new ones from being built virtually anywhere. Those are my biggest projects currently."

"Where do you stand on renewable energy, oil and gas drilling, coal mining, and things like that?"

"Where would you expect me to stand? We need to use *all* green energy and we need to stop those damn polluting and profiteering oil companies from drilling in all the beautiful places, including offshore. Coal mines should be shut down and the owners made to pay for reclaiming every square inch of ground they've ruined."

"I see. You sound pretty adamant about that. Have you heard of oil shale and how it might solve the US's need to import foreign oil?"

"That's an outright lie propagated by the oil companies. They don't even know how to develop it, nobody knows how much there is, and besides, it would ruin most of Colorado and Wyoming and Utah if they try. I'm against developing even one square foot of oil shale."

"That seems pretty harsh, but at the same time it sounds like you know quite a bit about it. Have you been studying the subject or talking to anyone about it?"

"I research lots of things."

"Gail, do you know Jon Feng?"

She hesitated a moment and sat forward in the lounger. "Sure, Jon is a friend and we share a lot of interests."

"How did you meet him?"

"I met him a year or so ago when he attended a rally about offshore drilling here in California. He's very well informed and impressed everybody with his commitment. Why are you so interested in Jon?"

"His name has also come up in my research about people associated with environmental activism and who support causes with money. Do you know where Jon gets his money?"

"I don't think that's any of your business. It's certainly not any of mine."

"Would you be surprised if I told you Feng's money came from his father who emigrated from Taiwan and set up an import/export business?"

"I didn't know that, but it's interesting if true, because my grandparents returned to the US from China in the nineteen-thirties and they had an import and export business."

"Have you, or maybe your parents, ever had any business with Jon Feng's company?"

"How would I know? I was never involved in the business. My parents sold their company about the time I was born. They put the money in investments and trusts."

She sat even straighter and stared at me. "Mr. Colby, your questions seem very pointed. I'm starting to think there may be more to what you're asking than you indicated. What business of yours is it who my friends are or where my money comes from? That goes a lot farther than just *background* for some article. I think there's something going on here I don't like and it's time for me to end this interview. I would appreciate you sending me everything you intend to write about me before you publish it and I think you'd better leave now." She stood and pointed toward the door to the house.

I put my pen back in the spiral, put the pad in my briefcase, and followed her into the house. She marched directly to the front door, opened it, and pointed outside. As I stepped onto the porch, I turned and said, "Gail, I'm sorry if I've made you mad. I'm new at this and just wanted to get as much information as possible."

She looked at me very pointedly. "I don't believe you, Mr. Colby. I'm wondering if you represent a publication at all. Please don't bother me again."

I turned without saying anything else, walked to the car, and put my briefcase in the back before looking back at the house. The door was closed and there was no sign of Gail Porter. I didn't know if she'd lied to me like Judy Benoit but she absolutely knew a lot more than she was telling. It would be interesting to see how her story matched with Jon Feng's.

chapter

EIGHTEEN

I returned to South San Francisco through a rapidly developing fog bank that reduced visibility on the Bay Bridge to a few hundred feet. Amazingly, the South Bay was still clear, although by the time I got to the Embassy Suites it was fogging over. From my balcony, I watched Oakland quickly disappear. The message light on the telephone was blinking.

I listened to a completely unaccented male voice identify himself as Jon Feng. "Mr. Montgomery? Jon Feng returning your call—your message indicated you're looking for opportunities to import products from China. I'm afraid we can't be of any help to you. Our business is limited to investing in China's manufacturing infrastructure. We no longer operate as an import/export company. Thank you for your interest in our company and we wish you good luck in your venture." There was so little inflection in his voice and the message was so scripted it could have easily been a recording. The message had been left at 3:59 p.m. I checked the time: 4:10, I'd only missed his call by eleven minutes. I decided to take the drive to Feng's warehouse office.

It took fifteen minutes to get to the warehouse. The fog was so thick I was within fifty feet of the place before I saw the silver Lexus and a black Suburban parked in front. I stopped behind the Lexus, got out my gun, jacked a round into the chamber, and clipped the holster to my belt. My windbreaker hid the gun and holster.

I pushed the buzzer at the security door and for several seconds there were no signs of life. Finally, I heard footsteps approaching and two bolt locks being thrown. The door opened slightly and I saw a very tall Chinese guy standing behind it. It wasn't Feng. The guy said, "We're not open." He didn't have an accent either. These guys were either the best linguists in the world or they'd all been born here.

I said, "*You're* here, the door's open, and I'm here so why don't you just let me inside so I can talk to Jon Feng?"

The tall guy thought about it for a couple of seconds. "What's your name?"

"I'm Cort Scott—you can call me Tom Montgomery."

The guy looked confused and said, "Wait here." He closed the door and I heard one of the bolts slide back into place.

I stood in the fog for a couple of minutes before I heard the bolt again and the door opened. The tall guy said, "Jon Feng is in the office. Follow me." I liked following him better than having him behind me. We walked across the floor toward a set of wall-mounted steps to a mezzanine level with a couple of glassed-in offices. One was lighted and I saw the outline of a man standing at the windows watching us. Most of the main floor was empty except for some shipping containers near the back wall.

My guide led the way to the office, opened the door, and stepped aside to follow me in. Feng had moved from the window and was seated behind a small, metal desk. There wasn't much in the office: a couple of two drawer files in opposite corners behind the desk and a couple of molded plastic chairs in front of the desk. It wasn't much of an office for an international investment company or, for that matter, an import/export company.

Feng was also tall for a Chinese, although it was harder to tell as he was sitting down. He was wearing a burgundy sweater over an open neck, light blue, button-down collar shirt. He had a stylish American haircut. He was the guy I'd seen driving the Lexus with Judy Benoit.

Feng said, "So, Mr. uh, Scott, are you the Mr. *Montgomery* who called earlier?"

"Yep, one and the same."

"Why the alias—what do you want?"

"I wanted a chance to talk to you. By now Judy Benoit has told you who I am. You wouldn't have talked to me so I made up a name and a business. It looks like it worked."

Feng obviously didn't like the way this was going. He shifted positions, glanced at the tall guy who was now standing to my left, and said, "You're right on a couple of points. I know who you are, or at least who Cort Scott is supposed to be, and I wouldn't have talked to you. I assume your call was to see if I was here?"

"When you returned my call, I took a chance you were calling from here."

"Now that you're here, albeit under false pretenses, what do you want?"

"I want to know about your involvement with Judy Benoit, Gail Porter, and the ECF."

"What makes you think I know any of those people or how it could possibly be any of your business?"

"Let's not start off with a load of bullshit, Feng. I've seen you at Gail Porter's house and driving around with Judy Benoit. Benoit is the only person who knows who I am. I also know you've been giving money to ECF." I actually didn't know for sure but Feng's reaction proved my point. He blinked his eyes a couple times, glanced at Mr. Tall, and shifted his gaze from side to side.

"So you've been spying on me. Okay, let's say I do know them and I give money to causes I support. It's not illegal, it's my right."

"Unless the money you give leads to murder."

"*Murder! What the hell do you mean by that?*" Feng stood up quickly. He *was* tall.

"I think the ECF has been mixed up in a lot of shit and has burned up a lot of property, including Two Elks Lodge in Colorado. I think Martie Remington was murdered. I think you're involved in all of it and I plan on proving it."

Mr. Tall made his move. He wasn't quick enough. He stepped back to get behind me. I pivoted and hit him with a hard right hook. It was one of the better punches I'd thrown in a long time. His eyebrow split and he sagged but didn't go down. As he started to come up, I hit him right on the beak. I felt his nose go and this time he went to the floor in a heap. He was done.

Feng started around the desk. He stopped when he saw his man collapse. "You fucked up, Scott. You don't know what you've got yourself into. You're in way over your head and don't even know it. I advise you to get the hell out of here and stay away from me and everybody I know."

"Advice is worth exactly what you pay for it and I'm not giving you a dime, Feng. You're the one who's screwed. Your man is going to be in the hospital a few days, Porter and Benoit know I'm after your ass, you're going to have more three initial agencies sniffing around than you can count, and somebody is going to be on your tail twenty-four-seven from now on."

I stepped back and looked at the guy on the floor. His jacket was open and I could see the butt of a pistol in a shoulder rig. I reached down and pulled it out. It looked like a 9 millimeter although I hadn't seen one like it. The numbering and lettering along the barrel read QSZ-92 and contained some Chinese characters. I dropped the magazine, jacked the slide, and a round popped out on the floor. I looked at Feng. "Heavy artillery for an honest businessman. Too bad your boy didn't know when or how to use it. Keep looking over your shoulder, Jon Boy, you're going to see your new shadows...even in the fog." I threw the pistol on the desk. "If it turns out you're as conflicted as your old man, there's no telling which one of those shadows is going to take you out. You better help your buddy. He's going to need some assistance getting down those stairs." I backed out, turned, and went down the stairs. As I was crossing the floor of the warehouse, I heard a groan from the office and looked back in time to see Feng, supporting my sparring partner, start down the stairs. That had been a good punch; I hoped later rounds would go as easily.

chapter

NINETEEN

I drove back to the Embassy Suites through the pea soup fog. I thought the airport might be shut down because I couldn't hear any planes.

I opened the mini-bar and took out a bottle of Anchor Steam beer. It was $5.50 according to the price list. As Hedges used to say, "It would be a good deal at half the price." I opened the beer, took a long pull, kicked off my shoes, stretched out on the bed, and called Tom Montgomery. It was almost 6:00 p.m. Denver time. I was hoping Tom would still be around. He was.

"Hey, Tom, Cort—what've you got to say for yourself?"

"I say we drank too many beers last Friday, that's what. Jesus, did you drive home? I staggered back here, grabbed my stuff, went to the gym for a half hour, and then took a steam. I finally felt sober enough to drive home."

"I hear you. Lindsey ate my ass out about it. I made it okay by promising not to do it again. I blamed it on you."

"Thanks for nothing. You turn up anything in San Fran?"

"I think so, though I'm not sure exactly what. I talked to Gail Porter for quite a while before she figured out I wasn't a magazine writer by the name of Bob Colby. She's an old line liberal environmentalist although I didn't get the feeling she'd have anything to do with murder. She didn't have a problem telling me she knew Feng. She drew the line at the ECF. She says she doesn't hold with violence."

Tom took it in before saying, "That would match with some more info I got from the FBI guy, John Nelson. He went back through everything they had on Porter and her parents to when Grandpa and Grandma returned from China. He says all of them were on every watch list the feds had. They didn't have a single bit of evidence the Porters ever did more than peaceful protests and sit-ins. The old folks *definitely* made their money in the opium business, but it doesn't look like they were involved in drugs once they came back. You know, that shit was legal in China at the time."

Tom's words made me feel better about Gail. I'd liked her and didn't want to think she was a conspirator in a murder plot. If she was mixed up in it, it was probably unwittingly. "You know, that actually makes me glad. What else ya got?"

"Hey, you tell me. You're the guy on the ground. I'm just a paper shuffler."

"I ran down Feng and we had a little talk. I checked out his warehouse and office and guarantee you it's a front. Other than a few shipping containers, there isn't anything in the warehouse. There are two filing cabinets in the whole office."

"So what did you talk about?"

"Not much. I basically accused him of being involved in Remington's murder and of bankrolling the ECF."

Tom laughed. "Subtle technique, dip shit. What'd he say?"

"He overreacted and sicced his body guard on me so we had a little tussle."

"Well, since you're talking and I don't hear any emergency sirens, you must have handled it."

"I got in a couple and dropped him. He's going to have a real black eye and an even flatter nose...of course, he *is* Chinese. He was carrying a 9 millimeter in a shoulder rig. It's Chinese too."

"What happened to Feng?"

"We *talked* and I told him I was going to haul his ass back to Colorado."

"What'd he do?"

"Warned me off and said I was in over my head."

"He's right about that. Where are you now, incidentally?"

"The Embassy Suites by SFO, why?"

"When I talked to Nelson, he said he'd accessed more files, some above *his* pay grade, and now he's *really* interested. He thinks Feng Li was a Red Chinese agent all along and the sons have picked up the baton. The old man was probably a double or triple agent, just like Nelson originally thought. The kids are working strictly for Beijing. Anyway, he's flying into SFO, even as we speak, and wants to see you there tomorrow. Can you make that?"

"Absolutely. This is getting interesting wouldn't you say?"

"Interesting is probably a good word although dangerous may be more like it. You better watch your ass, buddy."

"Yeah, I'm getting that same feeling. Where's the FBI office?"

"Downtown San Fran: 450 Golden Gate Avenue, 13th floor. Nelson said he won't be in until about ten o'clock tonight so he'd like you to come by at 9:00 a.m. tomorrow. He seems like a good guy, at least over the phone, so I think he can help you. Besides, it always helps to have the feds on your side. You probably don't want to take on the Chinese intelligence service all by yourself."

"You got that right. I'll be there. Thanks, Tom."

"No problem, but keep me up to speed, will you?"

"Sure." I hung up and thought I had come a long way from looking at drill cuttings on an oil rig to meeting with an FBI agent about Chinese spies. I wondered where this was headed.

chapter

TWENTY

I pulled into a parking garage across the street from the federal building at 8:45 a.m. the next morning. I parked on the second floor and noticed the ramp entrance to the third floor was closed off with heavy duty security gates. Outside, yesterday's fog had been replaced by bright sunshine and a clear sky. There aren't many places as beautiful as San Francisco on a clear, sunny day.

I caught a pedestrian walk signal and crossed Golden Gate. Everybody with federal business to conduct must've had a 9:00 o'clock appointment. Seeing thousands of people on a sunny day in San Francisco is an eye-opening experience. Some of these cats had just stepped out of the Summer of Love, 1968, and hadn't shaved or bathed since then. Others were dressed at the height of fashion. Couples, whether straight, bi, or homosexual, made up at least half the crowd. Even at this hour, the smell of pot was heavy. I presumed it was all *medicinal* which the State had legalized, although the feds hadn't legalized anything.

Security was tight. Everyone passed through metal detectors and a sniffer booth that blew a jet of air up your ass to see if you were concealing explosives. I'd left my gun locked in the trunk of the car and passed without a problem. Inside, a guard asked which department or agency I wanted and directed me to a queue where another guard checked my appointment. The line for the FBI was the shortest. The guard entered the information, leaned forward to scan the screen, and logged me in.

The elevator only had two buttons marked up and down. I punched up and watched the floor numbers light in the display. It stopped on thirteen which I found ironic since lots of buildings don't have a thirteenth floor. The doors opened and I stepped off into an elevator lobby with security doors bracketing the elevator. The door to my right opened and a medium height, solidly built guy with well-trimmed, graying hair came out.

"Cort Scott?"

"That's me." I answered. He came forward, stuck out his hand, and we shook. "You must be John Nelson." I said.

"Right—it's good to meet you. Montgomery's told me quite a bit about you over the last couple, three days. I'm looking forward to discussing this case. You've stirred up a bunch of ghosts for me and I hope we can tie up a lot of loose ends."

"I hope we can help each other. I don't know what I've gotten myself into and I'm hoping you can shed some light on it."

"We'll see, I guess. Where'd you park? It can be a real bitch to find space around here for a civilian. The Bureau keeps a fleet of cars on the third floor of the garage across Golden Gate. It's secured so we don't have to check the cars for bombs." He laughed at his own joke. "I just put my name on a register when I check in and show my ID if I want to go somewhere."

"Nice," I said. "I didn't have any problem and I parked in the same garage. It was tougher getting across Golden Gate without cracking my neck checking out all the citizens."

"Isn't that the truth? They've got some real beauts here. I'd forgotten how many weirdoes there are. I was in this station for eight years in the eighties, but I don't think the streets have changed since the sixties. Come on in, we'll go back to a conference room and talk."

Nelson keyed in a code on a lock pad and we entered the sacred inner sanctum of the FBI. It was a standard government design with narrow halls between cubicles, some bullpen areas with four or five desks, and closed offices around the outside. People sat at about half the desks, but papers were piled on nearly every one so there must've been more people around. We entered Nelson's "conference room" which was obviously an interrogation room during normal working hours. I said, "Whoa, which way do I stare to give you the best picture?"

He laughed and said, "Yeah, conference room was a little optimistic, wasn't it? You'd think they'd have some real offices for visiting firemen. I'll tell them to turn down the heat and shut off the cameras right away." He laughed again. I hoped he wasn't serious. "Do you want some coffee or tea?" He asked.

"Coffee—as long as it doesn't have the truth serum in it."

Nelson laughed again. He was a jolly guy. "Believe it or not, the coffee here is surprisingly good...not like the battery acid we have in Quantico. It's one of the things I remember from when I was assigned here. Hang on for a minute and I'll have one of our admins get us some. What do you want in it?"

"If it's as good as you say, I'll take it black."

"Good choice." He opened the door, looked both ways, and waved his hand at someone. A cute, severe looking Asian girl appeared and Nelson said, "Jen, would you please get us two black coffees?" The girl nodded and Nelson closed the door leaving it ajar. "It's not like the old days when you could just say 'Get us coffee' and they would all jump. In the *new* FBI, everything is please and thanks—that's not all bad, I guess."

The door pushed open and Jen brought in two coffee mugs emblazoned with the FBI's logo and seal. She set them down, nodded to me, and started out. Nelson said, "Thanks, Jen, I appreciate it."

"No problem, Mr. Nelson, my pleasure." I thought this team would be really tough if they conducted a water boarding interrogation. They'd drown the suspect in kindness.

I sipped the coffee and it was as good as advertised. Nelson motioned to a chair and took the other one...at least we were both on one side of the table.

"Okay, Cort, let's get to it. Here's what I know or suspect: Feng Li started out working for Mao, himself. His direct contact was Chou En Lai until Chou got too high and Feng was switched to military intelligence...their spies. We don't know who ran him. He infiltrated the Nationalists early on in the civil war and was accepted by them as a defector from the Reds. He was able to give Chaing's guys enough intelligence they thought he was for real. In the meantime, he was feeding the Reds the real secret shit from the Nationalists. It looks like it was planned for him to bug out with Chaing when the Nationalists left for Taiwan." John paused and sipped some coffee.

"When he got there, he kept up the same gig until 1950 when Chaing's intelligence operation started getting some bad vibes. Feng probably started feeling some heat so he approached our guys and said he wanted to come to the US. He said he would work for us against both groups of Chinese. We didn't have many eyes and ears over there and jumped at the chance. We got some dope about both sides and since it was more than we had before, it seemed good at the time. Looking back, we think he was working *all* sides. He was taking money from the Nationalists and telling them about us. He was taking money from the Reds and telling them about us and the Nationalists...and, he was taking our money and telling us about both sides." John picked up his coffee and strode to the window. I swiveled around in my chair and watched him stare outside.

"Once we let him come here, the information flow got better and better. We think the Taiwanese were the first to figure out he was a double agent. We think they blew him up. For us, that was where the story ended. We knew he hadn't done much business through the import/export company, although he did enough to pass it on to his kids. Obviously, we didn't check the kids out enough. We thought they were running the company as a legit operation. We didn't keep on top of it because the kids weren't working for us. We let it fall through the cracks." He returned to his chair and sat heavily.

"When Tom started sniffing around, I started digging deeper and was surprised to find we picked up on the Fengs again about five years ago. Most of what we know about them comes from the CIA. Since nine-eleven, we actually cooperate a little bit and the CIA watches foreign comings and goings. The Feng brothers started going to Hong Kong regularly about then. They went together at first, although lately they've been going separately. Almost every time, they drop out of sight for a day or two. Our spooks think they're going to Beijing. As soon as I found out about that, I pulled their tax and business records. They continue to list their business as import/export but haven't had any licenses for years. Their returns show hundreds of thousands of income for which they've paid the correct taxes every year." Nelson paused and drained his coffee.

I said, "Why would the People's Republic want one of their agents involved in domestic environmental protest activities?"

"That's the sixty-four dollar question, isn't it? Okay, this is just my speculation...I don't have a shred of evidence...but I think this is part of a much bigger operation. I think the Chinese have their eyes on oil and gas deposits everywhere in the world and I don't think they're just looking at the next few years. I think they've got a long range plan that might reach out fifty years or more."

I took that in, thought for a moment and said, "So what? I don't see how that leads to a Colorado murder. What's the connection?"

He tapped the empty cup on the table before replying. "Cort, you're a geologist so you probably know a hell of lot more about this stuff than me, however I'm a quick study and I've been doing a ton of research. Again this is pure speculation on my part—but here goes... I think the Chinese have developed a methodology for developing oil shales and tar sands. I don't know how they've done it— maybe they've stolen or adapted Shell's technique for heating up the rocks underground and pumping out the oil by conventional means. Shell has taken some special project leases in western Colorado and installed a couple of pilot projects. They're required to share their technology with our Energy and Interior departments and they're having some success. They don't tell us anymore than they have to so we don't know everything they're doing. I've called people in both departments, but all they care about is having the reports filed on time. I don't think they even read them. Here's the deal, Shell is applying the same thing in a couple of other places, like Jordan and Azerbaijan, and those projects are bigger and further along than in the US. I'm betting the security is a lot looser there too. Azerbaijan is in China's back yard for chrissakes." He hopped up and began pacing back and forth.

"Now, without telling you too much, let me just say we have a few of our own *assets* in China. Word is their intelligence service, the MSS, have more agents assigned to industrial espionage, in particular energy projects, than all other groups combined. I'm guessing there are more people looking at energy than looking for nuclear secrets and that's a scary thought. The CIA has lots of eyes and ears in Jordan and they're telling Langley the Chinese are all over Shell and the Jordanian energy ministry. I mean, it's like there's a Chinese agent assigned to virtually every petroleum engineer in the country. We don't have as much evidence although we're getting similar reports about Azerbaijan. And, here's the jackpot, the only computer hacker attack we can document at our Interior Department was directed at the files where Shell's reports are stored. The IT guys think they successfully fought it off and the reports are secure—frankly, though, they're not a hundred percent sure.

"I think the Chinese are running around the world making production sharing contracts with the countries that have major oil shale deposits. They've done it in Jordan, Libya, and in the Baltic States…we got that from our good friends, the Russians, who are plenty pissed." John chuckled at the thought of working with the Russians.

"Apparently, the Chinese tell these countries they'll use their technology to develop and produce the oil shale *but*, in return, they get the lion's share of the reserves and the countries can't share the technology for at least twenty-five years."

Nelson sat down again and swiveled his chair toward mine. "Now, here's where things really get interesting and I believe relate to your case. The Chinese know the biggest oil shale reserves in the world are in the US. Because of our business structure and the fact we don't have a national oil company, we aren't about to do a deal with them. Therefore, what's the next best thing? It would be to keep us from developing our reserves while they gain control of the rest of the worlds'. If they can do it, they'll control world oil price. They'll fulfill their energy needs while keeping the price so low we can't afford to develop our reserves. From what I'm reading and getting from the Energy Department, it takes anywhere from $75 to $100 a barrel to stimulate oil shale development. If the Chinese satisfy their demands and can keep the price below that, maybe *way* below, we won't develop ours."

The light bulb went on. *Jesus*, if John Nelson is right, Martie Remington's death evolved from a deep cover plan, hatched in Beijing, to slow leasing and research on the US oil shale deposits. If the Chinese already had a viable production process, they were five to ten years ahead of us. Keeping the USGS from completing a resource evaluation for another couple or three years would make the gap even larger. That kind of head start would allow them to dominate world oil markets. Time was on their side. How the hell did this guy, an

FBI lifer, figure this out? Why couldn't I have seen it, or, better yet, Hank?

I was choking back coffee and bile. "I don't know if you're right about everything, John, but it makes a lot of sense to me. Feng supports these radical environmental actions wherever he can and establishes his bona fides as an activist. He gets people like Gail Porter involved as cover and increases his street creds while he backs outfits like ELF or ECF who monkey-wrench all sorts of deals. The Chinese play the waiting game with his deep cover until they find something important enough to warrant deploying him openly. What I don't know yet is if somebody like Judy Benoit is an unwitting accomplice or if she's in on the ground floor. What do you think?"

John shook his head. "I'm hoping that's where you can help. I don't know the answer. I'd like to believe Benoit isn't directly involved although there's a lot of circumstantial evidence stacking up against her. It would help me if you keep on her and see what she's doing with Feng. That'll free me up to stay on the Fengs and the Chinese. Will that work for you?"

"Yeah, I can do that. How much of this should I be sharing with the locals in Colorado or with the USGS guys?"

"For right now, not much—except for Tom Montgomery—if it wasn't for him, I wouldn't be on this. Harry Thornton called me and said Montgomery was doing a favor for you on a Colorado case when the Fengs' names came up. He knew I'd been involved when the old man got blown to hell and wasn't happy about being told to shut it down."

John did an over-the-shoulder double take. "To tell you the truth, I haven't told Quantico or the special agent here what I'm doing. I don't know how sensitive it might be. About the only advantage of getting old is they pretty much leave me alone and let me do my own thing. I'm nearing the end of my career and the one big scab I've kept picking is Feng Li's killing. We pulled SFPD off it as quickly as we could and then I got shut down too. I never knew why other than he was an *asset* and neither the FBI nor the CIA wanted any publicity about how the good old U. S. of A. might employ a *spy*. Remember, we always want to be the good guys and don't want our own people thinking we engage in nasty things like spying. This is probably my last chance to clear it off my desk—and my conscience. I'd like to get everything wrapped up before I hit the bricks."

"I hear you, John. I'll keep everything under my hat except for Tom." I hated to tell him about my visit to Feng, but he needed to know. "John, you're not going to like this...I braced Feng and his body guard yesterday. I told them I thought they're involved in a Colorado murder and I was going to be on their ass. I wish I'd known yesterday what you've told me today. I wouldn't have confronted him."

"*Shit!* I sure wish you hadn't done that. It's going to make this harder. They're going to be a lot more careful."

"I'm sorry, John. I didn't know the big picture. I was trying to get under his skin and push him into a mistake."

"I'm betting that son-of-a-bitch doesn't make mistakes. I think he's pretty well trained."

I wouldn't have taken the bet. "When was the last time you or the CIA had direct contact with the Fengs?"

"Good question—I checked it out. We've never had direct contact with the kids. We pretty much closed the file when the old man got scragged. The CIA just happened to see them in Hong Kong and opened a file on them."

"That might work to our advantage. Feng is going to think I'm acting on my own or for the USGS. He probably isn't going to figure he's under a spotlight by the feds particularly if you really haven't let anybody know what you're doing."

"I hope you're right, although I wouldn't bet my life on it. How are you going to follow up? Do you have a plan for checking out Benoit and Porter?"

It was my turn to stand and look out the window. "I'll go right at Benoit. She's going to be a hell of a lot easier to spook than Feng. If I can scare her enough, I might get something out of her we can use. I'm going to watch her for a while first though. I'd like to know if there's anyone else tied to this."

"Okay, sounds good to me. Would you give me a call every day and let me know what's going on? If I get something on this end, I'll let you know."

"Where should I call?"

He took out a business card and wrote a number on the back. "This is my personal cell number. You'll be the only one with it."

We shook hands and John took me back to the security lobby. I nodded at Jen as we passed her desk. "Good coffee. Thanks." She smiled but didn't say anything.

chapter

TWENTY-ONE

I hoofed it back to my car, got my pistol out of the trunk, and clipped the holster on my belt. I changed my mind about watching Benoit and decided to confront her and shake her into action. At 10:30 a.m. the traffic was light and I made good time to Berkeley.

I searched the Geosciences Building parking lot for Benoit's car. Her Volvo was parked in the second row, but I had to go up and down five rows before I found a cramped spot. I squeezed out, walked quickly to the crossover stairway entrance, and took the stairs two at a time to Benoit's office.

I glanced in the window, saw her sitting at her desk, and walked in. She was alone which was good for me. She jumped up and yelled, *"What the hell are you doing here? You stole my GPS. You've* got a hell of a lot of nerve to show up here."

I pulled a chair from the desk next to hers, sat, and said, *"Shut up, Judy.* You're in big-time trouble and I'd like to help you get out of it. Sit down and listen, don't interrupt and I'll try to figure out where you stand." She looked stunned, flushed deeply, and sat down.

"Judy, I've been working with Hank Francis, Rick and Randy, Sheriff Colby in Glenwood Springs, San Francisco PD, *and* the FBI. Here's what we know: One, you have a history of involvement with environmental activism; two, you know Gail Porter and Jon Feng; three, you either know more about what happened to Martie Remington than you're saying or *you* killed her; four, Jon Feng is a goddamn Chinese spy.

"Now, here's what we suspect. Gail Porter is an unsuspecting do-gooder Feng is using to give himself some credibility with environmental activist groups. The Chinese have a long range plan to control oil prices by bringing worldwide oil shale deposits to production—*not* including the US. We think they're trying to delay our entry by doing everything they can, *including murdering people*, to stop any research, evaluation, leasing, or development for as long as they can.

"And last, here's what I *hope*...I *hope* you're more like Gail Porter than a killer like Feng. If you want a way out, you need to tell me everything you know about Feng and this operation. If you tell the truth, you *might* get out of this without too much trouble. If you lie or don't cooperate, I'll do everything I can to fit you up for murdering Martie Remington."

Judy Benoit turned every shade of red, rose, pink, and purple known, but was now ashen and gray. She rubbed her hands on her jeans trying to dry her palms. Sweat broke out across her brow and started to drip in her eyes. Tears coursed down her cheeks. She moaned and leaned over at the waist toward me. I watched her shoulders shake and wrenching sobs began escaping her lips. After a couple minutes, the crying began to subside and she slowly raised her head. Her face was a wreck.

She took a couple of deep breaths and shuddered. "You're right on almost everything. I didn't know the truth until I was back here. You've gotta believe me. I didn't know what they were doing, and I

still don't know all of it except for one thing—*I didn't kill Martie.*
Oh, God, *I didn't kill her!*"

I let her stare into space for several seconds. "I believe you,
Judy. But, you're going to have to tell me everything. If your story
holds up, I'll do everything I can for you."

It was the lifeline she'd been looking for. She bobbed her head
several times, her face changed color to something like normal, and
she regained her breath. I said, "Let's get out of here before one of
your office mates comes back. We need to go someplace where you
can tell me your story. Where's a good place?"

She shook her head. "I definitely *don't* want to go to my apartment. We need to go where Jon can't find us. He knows about you
and that you're after him. He came to my house last night after you
went to his office. He threatened me. He said he could send the cops
evidence *I* killed Martie and unless I kept working with him he
would do it. I'm scared of him, Mr. Scott. I've never been so scared of
anything in my life."

I thought for a minute. "Let's drive, Judy. If we're on the move
and don't go anyplace he knows, we can spend as much time as we
need to sort out your story." She nodded, stood up, and grabbed her
backpack. When we got to the parking lot, I said, "We'll take my
car. Feng knows your Volvo and I don't want him to get lucky in
case he starts looking for you." She nodded again. When we got to
my rental, I had to squeeze in and back out for her to get in the passenger side.

I pulled out and went west on the first through street. I caught
the Eastshore Freeway and started north toward Vallejo. I intended
to head to Napa and the wine country where there were lots of lodges
and B&B's and I could stash Judy.

As we pulled onto the Eastshore, I spotted a black Suburban a
few cars back and it suddenly registered I'd seen it for several blocks.
Shit! I didn't say anything to Judy about the Suburban. In fact, we
hadn't said anything since we got in the car. Now, I turned to her and
said, "We'll run up toward the wine country until we find a quiet

place to stay." I thought this would give me time to determine if the Suburban was tracking us. I should have opted for one of the custom sports car rentals available in California. I could have lost the Suburban in a heartbeat. Judy stared out the side window and just nodded. She seemed to be in shock. I decided she didn't need to know about our tail until it became critical.

I got in the far right lane and slowed to the minimum of fifty-five. The Suburban stayed in the center and slowed to match me... bad sign. I accelerated to seventy, five over the limit in this stretch, and the Suburban kept pace...more bad news. Judy glanced over but didn't say anything. I drifted back to sixty-five and stayed in the center lane...no change. Near the 580 exit to Richmond and San Rafael, I got in the right exit lane, engaged the turn signal, and slowed as if to turn. The SUV followed suit three cars back. I checked the left side mirror, waited for one car to pass in the through lane, and jerked the wheel left cutting off another car and swerving to the center lane. The Suburban was trapped in the exit lane. I saw the driver hit the brakes and slide to the right, but he was in too far to get back on the Eastshore.

Judy screamed when I cut off the other car and fishtailed into the center lane. *"What's happening? What are you doing?* Oh, Jesus, *help me!"*

As calmly as I could, which probably wasn't too calm, I said, "There was somebody tailing us. I think I lost them with that move. Sorry, I probably should've told you earlier but I wasn't sure. We should be alright now."

She started to sob again. "This isn't going to turn out is it? We're going to be killed, too."

I hoped she was wrong although I couldn't promise anything yet. "I'll do the best I can to get us out of this jackpot. Here's my cell and a card with a number on the back. Dial the number and when a guy named John Nelson answers, identify yourself, tell him you're with me, and we're heading to the wine country. Tell him we'll find a place to hole up and call him to set up a meet. Can you do that,

Judy?" I took the cell out of my jacket pocket and Nelson's card out of my shirt and handed them to her.

She opened and closed her mouth like a fish out of water, finally nodded, took the phone, looked at both sides of the card, and dialed. I could hear the ring tone and it went on forever before going to message. Judy said, "It's a message box. What should I do?"

I said, "Leave a message—say 'it's Cort checking in, I've got some news, and *we'll* try again later.'" Judy did as I told her, using the emphasis on "we'll" just like I'd said it. I didn't like it that Nelson hadn't answered his cell. He'd said it was a private line and I was the only one with the number. I checked the dash clock: 1:17 p.m.

I put the hammer down and didn't worry about the highway patrol until after Vallejo and we were headed for Napa. I continued to check the rearview mirror but didn't spot any obvious tails. When we reached Napa, I decided on St. Helena and we began to talk as we cruised through the vineyards and wineries.

Judy told the story chronologically from her earliest involvement in environmental concerns. I might not have wanted to hear everything, but I didn't want to interrupt her stream of consciousness.

She confirmed her father owned a lumber company and sawmills and she'd been involved with a local group protesting the cutting of old-growth redwood stands. That had led to a lengthy estrangement from her family. That was when she'd first met Gail Porter. Porter had been tree sitting as a protest and had spent fifteen days in a tree house in a redwood. Judy was taking her food and water delivered with a pail on a rope until the timber owner hired guards who kept everybody out until Gail came down. When Benoit started at Berkeley, she'd lived with Porter for the first semester. Porter had regular meetings with protest groups from the Bay Area and several times, after meetings, her friends sat around talking about actions they'd been involved in. Stories flew about putting sugar in the fuel tanks of Cats, spiking trees by pounding big nails at the levels where loggers used chain saws, and chaining themselves to trees marked for cutting. She said Gail would laugh about the non-violent stuff

but didn't hold with doing things that might get someone hurt...
like the spiking.

Judy had followed a career in geology because she thought it
would keep her involved with the environment. She was astonished
when an offer came from the USGS for a summer job mapping in
western Colorado because she'd applied for work with the Park Service. She and Gail had discussed possibly staging a one person slow
down to monkey wrench the survey's resource evaluation program.

During her first summer, she was assigned to Martie Remington's mapping group and worked as slowly as she could. Martie pulled
her aside and said her performance was not very good and she'd have
to improve if she wanted to be considered for full-time employment.
She thought about it and decided she could only make a difference if
she was on the job so she worked harder. Her improved performance
satisfied Martie and Judy received better job performance reviews.

Gail Porter came to Colorado over the 4th of July weekend that
first year and introduced her to Jon Feng. Porter described him as a
Bay Area businessman with a great interest in the environment and
who supported several environmental groups. He seemed very committed and sincere. He said he was a protégé of Porter's and believed
in non-violent civil disobedience to achieve their goals. Judy drove
them to the Glenwood Springs area to show them what oil shale out-
crops looked like and where she was working. They'd talked about
how sad it would be to see the vistas ruined by an oil shale mining
operation. Gail Porter had flown back to California. Feng said he had
business in Denver and stayed over.

On Tuesday, after the long weekend, Judy's field vehicle had
burned. She hadn't thought much about the truck fire until she returned to Berkeley following Martie Remington's death. She had
dinner at Gail Porter's house with Jon Feng and a guy introduced
only as "Bennie", no last name. Judy described Bennie as incredibly
creepy and an outspoken member of the ECF group.

Here, I had to interrupt. "What does E-C-F stand for?"

"It means Earth Comes First. They took the first letters of each word, you know, like E-L-F stood for Earth Liberation Front."

I said, "Okay, go ahead."

Judy figured out from the dinner conversation that Bennie had met with Feng in Glenwood Springs and they'd driven to where the mapping teams were working. Bennie talked openly about putting a small, timed incendiary device in the undercarriage of one of the pickups. He laughed when Judy told him it was her truck. Porter got so mad she told Bennie to leave and expressed a great deal of remorse over the incident. She laid into Jon Feng although he defended the ECF by saying no one had been hurt and it had slowed down the project. When Judy said the project had now stopped because of Remington's death, Feng said, "Sometimes the ends justify the means." That upset Porter even more and she told Feng he was changing for the worse. He'd replied things weren't moving fast enough for him.

Feng had driven Benoit back to Berkeley and talked about things that made her wonder if he was directly involved in Martie's death. As they pulled up to her house, she'd asked him. He denied it, saying it didn't bother him because Remington's death was going to delay the evaluation. Judy said she'd almost become ill.

She didn't talk for a few minutes, just sat gazing out at the side window. I didn't want to push her and was relieved when she took a deep breath and picked up the story. "Jon started coming to my office and house several times a week. After one of his visits to the office, I noticed the GPS was missing. I searched everyplace and didn't find it until the next day, when I pulled out the desk drawer and found it right where it was supposed to be. I freaked out and accused my office mates of screwing with my stuff. They all swore they hadn't done anything."

"That's when I began putting two and two together and suspected Jon had done it. That night, he dropped by to talk about protesting oil and gas leasing of federal lands in southwestern Wyoming. When he finished, I asked about the GPS and if he knew anything about it. He stared at me a long time and finally said, 'Judy, it's time you grew up and found out things aren't always as they seem.'"

"He admitted taking the GPS and giving it to some *friends* who reprogrammed it to show I'd been with Martie Remington every step of the way to where she fell."

I glanced at her and said, "What'd you do, what'd you say?"

"I threw up right between us. I started crying and screaming at him."

"What'd Feng do?"

"He slapped me and said I'd have to do everything he said because the GPS unit would incriminate me. I told him Hank had already called and wanted it back so they could download the information."

"How'd he react?"

"He told me to stall Hank and go get the unit. I asked him why and he told me his friends would download it and run a wiping program. He said he'd keep the forged download and unless I followed orders, I'd get charged with Martie's murder."

I nodded slowly. "Well, at least you knew the truth then."

Judy dropped her face to her hands for a few moments. When she lifted it again, she said, "I think I knew it all along. I just couldn't make myself believe it."

She said it was three days later when I showed up and started asking questions. She'd panicked, called Gail, and told her everything except that Feng had the GPS unit.

***

We arrived in St. Helena and drove to the Wine Country Inn. Judy stayed in the car while I went in and asked for a room with two double beds.

After we entered the room, I said, "I'm hungry and you must be getting that way. I'll drive back to the strip mall and get a couple of Subway sandwiches. You can go through the mini-bar for something to drink. What kind of sandwich would you like?"

"Anything with turkey and lots of veggies is fine."

"Okay, I'll be right back. Don't answer the phone or the door and don't open the shades. I'll knock twice when I get back—just like in the spy movies." She smiled and I thought it was the first time I'd ever seen her smile.

I checked the lot for black Suburbans, didn't see any, and drove to the Subway for the sandwiches.

Back at the room, I knocked twice and heard the chain being undone. Judy jerked the door open. "Please hurry, you've got to see this." She'd been crying again. Her eyes were puffy and her face was splotchy.

"What's going on?" I asked.

"Just look at the TV. I think the FBI guy who gave you the card, the guy you had me call, was shot."

My stomach rolled and it felt like someone had hit me with a baseball bat. I grabbed the desk chair and sat down. Judy handed me the TV remote and I turned up the sound.

The TV was tuned to a San Francisco news station which was carrying a live helicopter camera feed of the parking garage where I'd parked earlier in the day. It was surrounded by police emergency vehicles and crime scene tape was stretched around the entire building. A serious looking woman news anchor came on. "We're live at the scene of an apparent homicide inside a parking structure across from the San Francisco Federal Building. The San Francisco police and FBI Agent-in-Charge, Mariah Martinez, have just concluded a news conference where they confirmed Special Agent John Nelson from the FBI's office in Quantico, Virginia, was shot and killed by unknown assailants. Agent Nelson had formerly been assigned to the San Francisco office and spent nearly eight years here. Agent Martinez declined to discuss Nelson's current assignment or what cases he may have been working on. She described Nelson as a career FBI agent with a distinguished service record. Deputy police chief, William Fong, said SFPD was currently interviewing several witnesses who heard gunshots or were on the streets near the parking structure exits. The chief said there are no suspects at this time. Channel 52 has talked to several bystanders who reported seeing a dark SUV leaving the building immediately after the shots were heard. None of those witnesses identified the make or model of the SUV and no license plate number was reported. Stay tuned to Channel 52 for up-to-the-minute updates on this apparently brazen shooting of an FBI agent. This is Amy Waterman reporting from the scene—back to you, Jeff."

The scene switched to the station's news set and senior news anchor. The crawler identified him as Jeff Bligh. Bligh, looking properly downcast, intoned solemnly, "Thanks for that on-the-scene report, Amy." He then looked straight into the camera and continued, "A tragic story is currently unfolding in the downtown area near the federal center. The FBI confirms the shooting death of veteran agent, John Nelson, a career FBI employee currently stationed in Quantico, Virginia, apparently in San Francisco on special assignment. Local FBI officials confirmed Nelson had formerly worked here, but are not discussing his assignment at this time. SFPD is assisting in the investigation. At this time, neither agency has identified any suspects or motive for the killing. We will, of course, keep you updated on this developing story."

I killed the sound and stared at the screen as the picture switched back to the helicopter's camera shot. I turned toward Judy who looked like I felt. "Judy, I don't know what to tell you. This is very scary and, frankly, I'm not entirely sure of our next move. Unless something changed between when I left John Nelson's office and when he was killed, I don't think the FBI actually *knows* what he was working on or why he was here. I think they thought he was taking a final swing through the places he'd been stationed." I was thinking to myself how the hell did Feng know I was meeting Nelson? Had he followed me somehow or known where I was staying? I knew I hadn't been particularly careful before picking up Judy on campus, I still couldn't figure it out. Suddenly, I had a terrible thought.

"Judy, do you have Gail Porter's telephone number with you?"

"Yes. I have it on my phone. Why?"

"I'm worried about her. It sounds like Feng was being pretty bold when he was talking to you guys about his involvement. You and Gail Porter are loose ends who are dangerous to his operation. I want you to call her. If she answers, tell her what's going on and then let me talk to her."

Judy Benoit looked even more stricken as she did what I asked. She got her phone out of her backpack, scanned the directory, and punched in Gail's number…it was on speed dial. Again, I could hear the ring tone on the other end and it was not being picked up. Finally, her voice mail answered and Judy handed me the cell. I said, "Gail, this is Cort Scott calling. I met you yesterday although I called myself Bob Colby. I'll explain that later. Right now, I'm with Judy Benoit. Gail, I think you're in great danger from Jon Feng or people who work for him. Feng is an agent of the Communist Chinese and is conducting an operation in this country having to do with oil shale. I suspect he has just killed an FBI agent I was working with. If you get this message, please pack some things and leave your house immediately. Go someplace safe, don't tell anyone where you're going, and when you get to wherever that is, call Judy's cell phone. I will be contacting the police and FBI and will try to get you some protection. Call us, Gail, as soon as you can." I closed the cell and handed it back.

Judy's hands were shaking as she took the phone. "Mr. Scott, I'm so scared! I don't know what to do. How did I ever get pulled into something like this? I mean…all I was trying to do was help with some things I believe in. Now, I'm involved in spying and, even, murder. How can this happen?" She was shivering and tears were again rolling down her face.

I took her in my arms for a several seconds, backed away, and said, "First of all, Judy, call me 'Cort.' Second, I don't have answers for your questions although I can understand how it happened. Believe me, Feng and the Chinese are experts at this sort of thing. They'll exploit any weakness to their advantage. You're not the first person to get sucked in and you won't be the last. I'm guessing that once we get out of this pickle and the truth comes out, you'll be able to continue on with your life...sadder, but definitely wiser."

She backed away and continued to hold my hands. "Oh, God, I so hope you're right, Mr. uh...I mean, Cort. I'm so sorry about everything. I don't know what I'll do if something happens to Gail. She has been a great friend and she really does care... about everything. Do you really think they'll go after her? Would they really try to kill her?"

"I don't know. It's obvious they're capable of anything."

"What are you going to do now?"

chapter

TWENTY-TWO

That was a good question and one I hadn't figured out the answer to yet. I knew I had to get someone pointed toward Feng, though. I needed to get in touch with Tom's friend in the CBI, Harry Thornton, and the quickest way would be through Tom. I told Judy, "I'm going to try and get us some help."

I opened my cell, hit Tom's number on the speed dial and was glad to hear him pickup. "Tom, it's Cort. Listen, I'm in a jackpot out here and need some help, big time! I need to talk to your pal, Harry Thornton. I've got to get some protection for Gail Porter and Judy Benoit. I'll stay with Judy until we get it, so I can't do much on my own."

Tom gave me Harry's number, told me to make the call and call him back to fill in the details. I punched in Thornton's number, waited for it to connect and hoped it wasn't going to voice mail. So far, my luck was holding; he answered "Thornton."

"Harry Thornton, this is Cort Scott. I think Tom Montgomery, in Denver, told you about me and a case I am working on."

"Yeah, sure, Scott, Tom told me about it. I put him in touch with John Nelson... *OH, SHIT!* Where are you? You're mixed up in John's shooting, aren't you?"

"I think so, but right now there're some other people who need your help before we get into that."

"Okay, give it to me fast—I'll record the call so we'll have it if necessary." I heard an electronic ping and Harry said, "Go ahead—start talking."

I gave him Gail Porter's address and telephone number and told him I thought Gail was in imminent danger and needed some police protection as soon as possible...I said I hoped it wasn't already too late. Thornton told me to hang on while he got the cops headed to her house. He was back on the line in less than a minute, asked where we were, and after I told him said he would also have a CHP car at the Wine Country Inn in about ten minutes. I was impressed; this guy had some stroke. He said, "Okay, go on... what happened to John Nelson?"

I told him about my meeting with Nelson and the rest from when I'd picked up Judy Benoit. He listened without interrupting. "John was a friend. I'm going to make sure we catch up with Feng and anybody else who's involved in this. Listen, Scott, here's what I want you to do...as soon as the CHP car gets there put Benoit in it. They'll take her back to Berkeley, she can get some stuff together, and we'll take her someplace safe until we can get a handle on Feng's bunch. Next, as soon as she leaves, get your car and drive over to the high school. It's on the west side of town about half a mile from The Inn. I'm leaving for the pad right now and getting on our chopper. We can be in St. Helena in about thirty minutes; we'll set it down on the football field and pick you up. From there, we can probably be in Frisco in an hour. We'll land on top of the federal building and walk right into the FBI office. I'll radio ahead and tell them what's happening. You got all that?"

"Yeah, I got it. I'll be at the high school."

I closed the phone and told Judy what was going on. She looked panicked. "I don't want you to leave me alone." I told her I wasn't leaving her alone; I was getting her into safe hands...hands a lot safer than mine. She finally nodded and asked, "Will you get back to me when you find out what's going on with Gail?"

"I'll try, but I can't promise. There's going to be a lot going on in the next few hours or maybe days. I'll try."

She hugged me hard and didn't want to let go. She was still hugging me when we heard a knock on the door and a voice say, "Mr. Scott? California Highway Patrol officer...are you okay?"

I disengaged from Judy Benoit, stepped to the door, looked through the peephole, and saw two uniformed CHPs outside. I opened the door and said, "Glad to see you guys...come in."

The patrolmen introduced themselves. I wasn't listening carefully enough to catch their names. One cop, a sergeant, said, "We need to hustle. The CBI guy said he wants this lady back in Berkeley in a couple of hours and in a safe place by tonight." I looked at Judy and nodded in as encouraging a manner as I could muster.

We didn't have anything to pack. I told Judy to take her sandwich and a bottle of water. She could eat it on the way. She complied and left with the two cops. I grabbed my stuff, walked to the car, and drove around to the office. I walked in and surprised the receptionist by telling her I needed to check out. She said, "Oh, my, Mr. Scott, what's wrong?"

I just said, "Oh, something has come up back in San Francisco and I need to attend to it." She asked if I'd used anything and I told her about the bottled water and the wash cloth and towels. She said she'd charge me a day's room rent with no extras and she hoped I'd be able to come back and enjoy the area again sometime. I silently hoped the same thing although, like with Judy, I couldn't promise myself anything.

chapter

TWENTY-THREE

I had the car window down and heard the whop-whop of the chopper blades. The big black and white spiraled down and made a soft landing on the practice field next to the parking lot. I grabbed my briefcase, sprinted to the plane, and climbed the stairs. A heavy-set guy strapped in one of the four passenger seats motioned me to take the seat across from his. The co-pilot pulled the stairs, locked the door and returned to the front. The vibrations increased, the chopper revved, and lifted off.

I slipped on a headset and we shook hands. "I'm Harry Thornton. Tough way to meet, Scott; I hope we get a chance to really talk after this crap is over. Tom told me a little about you...pretty interesting. Here's the latest—Alameda PD went by Gail Porter's house. Nobody answered the door so they slipped the lock and took a look around. There aren't any signs of a struggle and everything seems to be shipshape. The dishes are clean and the dishwasher was still cooling down from a run cycle. If anything has happened to her, it didn't happen at her house. Her car is gone so we're thinking she may have just gone out. The only thing strange is her cell phone is lying on the kitchen counter. It looks like she just forgot it. The last message, in fact the only message today, is from Judy Benoit's cell when you called."

I heaved a sigh of relief. "That sounds like good news. I was scared as hell you might find her with a bullet in her head."

"After what happened to John Nelson, I was thinkin' the same thing. I've been talking to the FBI and they're running around in a cluster fuck. They don't have an idea in hell about what's going on. That bitch agent-in-charge is new to the job and about as good as a fart in a whirlwind. She had no clue about what John was doing; she didn't know you'd been in their office; she says she's never heard of Feng—or anything else. When we get there, you need to tell her the whole damn story, top to bottom. Actually, it'll probably help me to hear everything again too. Once you've told them everything, we'll get an APB out on Feng. Bastard's going to have a hell of a head start and there're more places to hide around the Bay Area than a frog's got warts." Harry was colorful. "It's going to be important to keep Benoit…and you…safe until we get ahold of him. I don't know what evidence we've got at this point. It's just you and Benoit's word that he's involved at all."

That made me mad. "That's a crock. He's up to his ass in the murder in Colorado and in John Nelson's here!"

"Prove it, hotshot. What've you got for proof?"

I hated it when cops were right. "Okay, so what're we doing next?"

"Just what I said—you'll give everybody the story, including what John Nelson thought. Benoit will give a statement as soon as we can get to it; we'll kick it around and figure out something to do."

I sat back and thought about what Thornton had explained. This wasn't going to get it done. As long as Feng and his agents were running around, Porter, Benoit, and I were all in danger. I liked Harry, just as I'd liked Nelson, however, the wheels of justice were grinding way too slowly and he didn't seem to be speeding up the process. We didn't say anything else.

The view of Golden Gate Bridge was spectacular as the chopper cruised in over the North Bay. At a hundred knots, the trip had only taken forty minutes. The Transamerica Tower materialized; we slowed and began spiraling down. The helicopter air traffic was still heavy over the federal center. The CBI chopper pre-empted everybody and we quickly put down on the federal building's pad. Thornton and I descended the stairs and were met by a uniformed security guard and a guy in a suit who I assumed was a junior FBI agent. We were inside the stairwell before the suit said, "I assume you guys are Thornton and Scott...who's who?"

I had to laugh at that. Harry didn't look pleased. He jerked out his ID and badge. "I'm Thornton, *sonny*. Who the hell are you?"

That bothered the kid. He looked like he thought he ought to salute or something. "Sorry, Mr. Thornton, the boss didn't give me many details...just your names. I'm Agent Joe Riggs. We're set up in the main conference room. Agent-in-Charge Martinez said to bring you down as soon as you landed. We're anxious to hear from Mr. Scott." He nodded towards me and stuck out his hand. It might've been a bad start with Thornton, but I liked Agent Joe Riggs. "Our offices are on thirteen, the roof is seventeen. Do you wanta use the stairs or the elevator? The stairs are faster."

Harry grunted, "Stairs."

We started down as quickly as we could take the steps. At thirteen, Riggs punched a code in the security pad and we entered. It seemed a lot longer than eight hours since I'd been here. Riggs led the way to a doorway three down from the "conference room" I'd been in with John Nelson. This one was a real conference room with a glass table and ten chairs. Four people were seated in the chairs; TV monitors covered one wall and were all tuned to different news channels.

I recognized Mariah Martinez from the TV news conference, as well as Deputy Chief William Fong of SFPD. Martinez stood up, shook hands with us, and said, "It's nice to meet you both albeit under some pretty crappy circumstances." She turned to Riggs. "Agent Riggs, I'd like you to stay and listen. There's a good chance you may be accompanying Mr. Scott for a while." Riggs nodded and took a seat. "Mr. Scott, Mr. Thornton, the other people here are Deputy Chief Fong of SFPD, Special Agent Bob Walsh of this office and Agent Mark Petersen from the CIA. Agents Walsh and Petersen liaise on counterespionage activities. I understand we may be dealing with something that may fall in their bailiwick.

"Mr. Scott, obviously time is short and we need every possible detail quickly. Please tell us everything you know and include any details you believe are important." She turned to the others and said, "Hold your questions until Mr. Scott has finished." She pointed to the chairs at the head of the table and Thornton and I sat. Regardless of what Harry Thornton thought, Agent-in-Charge Martinez ran a tight ship.

I tried to be brief and since this was the third time today I'd told the story, it went quickly. Only Petersen took notes so I suspected everything was being taped. Everybody straightened when I related John Nelson's theory about what Feng and the Chinese were up to. Walsh and Petersen exchanged surprised glances. When I finished, Martinez got up, walked over to a service counter, asked if anyone could use some water or a soda. I took a bottle of water and hadn't realized how thirsty I was. I would have preferred a beer.

Martinez looked at Walsh, cleared her throat, and said, "That's quite a story, Mr. Scott. I receive a daily notice of all visiting agents and had noted John Nelson, although I didn't know what he was doing here. We have three or four visiting agents nearly every day. In general, they inform their counterpart in this office why they're here." This time she stared hard at Walsh. "Agent Walsh, did Nelson alert you of his visit or ask for any assistance?"

Walsh shook his head. "No, Mariah, he didn't. He stuck his head in my office first thing this morning to say 'hello' but we didn't talk about anything."

Martinez continued to stare at him. "Isn't that a little unusual? Did you know Agent Nelson?"

Walsh took a drink of water before replying. "I overlapped with John for three months before he went to Quantico...that was almost eight years ago. And, yes, it's probably a little unusual for any agent not to tell a local guy what he's working on."

Martinez swiveled her chair to Petersen. "Does the CIA have any information on any of the things Mr. Scott has related?"

"No, Ma'am, we don't have any active investigations into this."

Deputy Chief Fong finally spoke. "After we got his name from Harry, I ran Feng through our computers and came up with the stuff about his father getting blown up back in 1988. It was a thin case file because you guys took over the investigation and never let us follow up. It's still a cold case in South San Francisco PD's files."

Martinez nodded, "Yes, we ran the Fengs through our computers also. John Nelson worked the bombing and was also shut down on a request from the US Attorney General. There hasn't been a single thing added since he filed his report in early 1989. It *is* interesting, though, to find he'd recently accessed *all* the files—including some that should have been closed to him. We will be following up on that. Do you have any comment, Agent Petersen?"

Petersen raised his hands, shrugged, and said, "No." Mariah Martinez didn't look happy.

Harry Thornton, who'd been swiveling back and forth, couldn't stand it anymore. He erupted with, "*Goddamn it!* This isn't getting anything done. What the hell's wrong with you people? You seem to be more interested in covering your asses or pointing fingers than in running down Feng. He turned toward the deputy chief. "Fong, why the hell don't you have officers all over Feng's warehouse and his house wherever that is? With all due respect, you need shoes on the street. You need to find Gail Porter and you need to get off your ass!"

Fong stood up, clenched his fists, and said, "Harry, you're a pain in the ass. You always have been and I suspect you always will be. For your information, we've been to Feng's warehouse and searched it. There wasn't anybody there. He lives in Pacifica and we've been there too—with the same result. Look, Harry, we've reacted as fast as we can with virtually no intel—we're flying blind here. We ran Feng's name and company through motor vehicles and we've come up with five cars. They're all in the company name: a Lexus, a Mercedes, and three Suburbans. We've got APBs out on all of them and we've got people at SFO and we're trying to cover all the other airports in the area. Harry, while you were flying around, we were working...*so get off my ass!*"

Thornton looked sheepish. "Sorry, Bill, I went off half-cocked."

The feds had enjoyed the dust-up. Martinez smiled as she turned to Harry Thornton. "We had agents with the cops when they searched Feng's warehouse so we've got a little more information. You remember the shipping containers Scott described? They actually contain a very sophisticated computer center. There are some extremely high-tech machines in there along with equally high-tech communication equipment. Our IT guys are going over all of it right now." Thornton didn't say anything and I just nodded. She glared at me and said, "Mr. Scott, who knew about your meeting with John Nelson?"

I'd been waiting for that one—and dreading it. "The only people who knew were me, John Nelson, Tom Montgomery in Denver, and my girlfriend, Lindsey Collins."

All eyebrows rose as one. "Who's Lindsey Collins?" Martinez asked.

"Like I said, she's my girlfriend. She's a forensic specialist for the Arapahoe County, Colorado, sheriff's office. Look, she's a cop for

Christ sake. There's nothing to look at with Lindsey." Everyone relaxed. "I've been wracking my brain trying to figure out if I was
being tailed before I spotted the Suburban when I got Judy Benoit. I
didn't see anybody—still, it's a possibility."

Harry asked, "Where're you staying?"

"The Embassy Suites north of the airport."

"You need to go back there for anything?"

"That depends on how long I'm here. I can stay there or check
out and move. Once I'm sure Benoit and Porter are safe, I'd like to
go back to Denver."

Martinez said, "That's not going to happen until we have some
resolution here." The rest of the heads nodded like bobble-head dolls.
She scooted her chair close to the table, put her elbows on the top, and
let her gaze cover everyone. "OK, listen up. Here's the plan. Marsh,
Petersen, you guys need to delve into everything Nelson had pulled
together. For starters, consider everything Scott said as gospel and
work backwards. Download every file Nelson looked at in the last
month. We need to nail down the connections he found and figure
out how he developed his theory. Chief Fong, we'd like you to expand
your search. There are so damn many airports around here, it's going
to be hard to monitor all of them. I'm betting if Feng hasn't grabbed
Porter yet, he'll try to get the hell out of Dodge. I'd concentrate on
airports that can accommodate jets… particularly business jets. Mr.
Scott, we'll want you to move to a safe house here in the city. Riggs,
you go with Scott and collect his stuff from the Embassy Suites. Mr.
Thornton, you and I need to talk about coordinating our efforts…
and not just on this case, on everything. You can be of tremendous
service to the FBI and I think we can help you too."

Thornton smiled like the cat that ate the canary. Maybe, in the
future, he wouldn't be quite so quick to call AIC Mariah Martinez
a bitch.

Everybody stood and exited the conference room. Riggs and
I were the last to leave and cross the cube farm toward the elevator. The admin, Jen, who'd brought Nelson and me the coffee, was

pushing back from a clean desk top as we passed. She looked at me, nodded almost like a little bow, and said, "I am very sorry about Mr. Nelson, Mr. Scott. He seemed a very nice man."

She nodded again and walked with us to the elevators. In front of the building, she turned away from us and said, "Good night, gentlemen. I park a few blocks away. It's too expensive close by." Riggs and I crossed to the parking garage. The crime scene tape was gone and uniformed SFPD officers stood at each exit. They stopped each car, conducted a search of the back seats and trunks, and checked IDs. Riggs was parked on the second floor so we took the stairs. At the Golden Gate Avenue exit, the cops stopped us briefly and waved us through as soon as Riggs pulled his FBI creds and badge. He drove a Ford sedan the same uninspired color as the government-issued desks on the thirteenth floor.

***

At the Embassy Suites we parked in the back lot and went to my room. As I got out the key card, Riggs quietly said, "I'll go in first, Mr. Scott. You hang back while I check it out." I nodded, opened my jacket and took out the Beretta. Riggs' eyes opened slightly wider, he nodded, took out his own gun, and said, "Unlock it." I slid the key card, opened the door, and stepped aside.

Riggs had his Glock 9 millimeter in the approved two-handed grip as he entered. I followed him in, staying at the door as he slipped down the short hall. He stepped quickly around the corner into the room swinging the Glock from side to side. He turned back toward me and said, "You'd better come in. It looks like you've had visitors."

I holstered my gun, walked in, and surveyed the mess. The few clothes I'd hung in the closet were on the floor. My carryon bag had been cut up like the intruders had been looking for secret compartments. All the bedcovers were thrown aside and the mattress and box springs were displaced. Whoever broke in had tossed the place professionally.

My DOP kit was cut up the same way as the travel bag. They'd even taken the tops off the shave cream and deodorant cans.

"What'd you have they were looking for?" Riggs asked as he holstered his gun.

"Nothing, this is more to piss me off than find anything. Of course, they didn't know that when they started. Whoever it was made a hell of mess."

Riggs nodded as he glanced around. "Let me call this in. We'll get a team out here. Maybe we'll get lucky and get a handle on somebody. Right now, the only ones we know are the Feng brothers. We don't know anybody else."

I crammed my clothes into a laundry bag, Joe hung the Do Not Disturb sign on the door and we walked to the front desk. Joe stepped up, flashed his badge, and told the desk clerk to leave the room undisturbed. An FBI forensic team would be arriving in a few minutes and would need to be admitted. The clerk looked uneasy as he agreed.

We headed toward the back lot and the Ford. As I walked past the big sedan, I heard the crack of a pistol and a bullet whirred past my ear. Riggs yelled, *"Down!"* I hit and rolled. From under the car, I saw Riggs scrambling around to face the rear. I pulled the Beretta and jacked a round into the chamber. I could hear someone running although I couldn't tell how many. Riggs whispered, "You okay?"

I stage whispered back. "Yeah. What about you?"

"Okay," he said. "I only heard one round but there're at least two guys, maybe more. I heard 'em running."

I heard car doors slamming, a big motor starting, and suddenly a Suburban was behind us. An automatic began burping and bullets started hitting the Ford and the cars on both sides. I slid under an Explorer as a line of bullets stitched up the pavement where I'd been laying. The Suburban driver hit the gas; the big SUV peeled rubber and took off. My ears were ringing from the slugs hitting the pavement next to my head. I hadn't been hit.

"Riggs—you still all right?"

There was no answer. *"Riggs? RIGGS?"* There was only silence. I rolled out from the Explorer and ran around the Ford. Riggs was lying face down between his car and a Cadillac CTS coupe next to him. There hadn't been enough clearance for him to get under either car. There was a line of bullet holes in the middle of his back from his belt to his head which was in pieces. I didn't have to check for a pulse. I knew he was dead.

I pulled my cell and punched 9-1-1. When the emergency operator came on, I told her my name, where I was, and that I was with a dead FBI agent. She sounded shook up. She said police cars and ambulances were being dispatched. They would be there within three minutes. I told her we didn't need the ambulance. She told me to stay put and wait for the police. She didn't need to tell me that... my legs were too weak to go anyplace.

chapter

TWENTY-FOUR

I closed the cell and sat on the curb. I put my head between my knees. It didn't stop the gorge rising in my throat. I threw up between my feet and felt my brain start to spin. I could hear sirens approaching and managed to get to my feet using the front of the car as support. The black and white roared into the entrance, paused, and accelerated to where we were. It skidded to a halt behind the CTS and the cops bailed out with their service pistols drawn. The driver looked at Riggs lying between the cars and saw me standing there staring at him. The cop yelled, *"Put your hands in the air... straight up! Do it now!"* I did as he said forgetting I had the cell phone in my hand. *"Stop! Drop what you're holding!"* I started to say it was a cell, didn't bother, and let it fall. The cop didn't know…he was just playing it safe and following procedure. "Okay, step back. Step up on the curb."

"That was a cell phone. I have a pistol in a clip-on holster on my right side."

"Okay, reach across with your left hand and open your coat. Don't move too fast and keep your other hand in the air." Again, I did as I was told. The cop walked up close, told his partner to go around the car, and pull my gun. The other cop did it and everybody breathed a sigh of relief…including me.

"You the guy who called 9-1-1?"

"Yeah, my name's Cort Scott. I'm a private investigator from Denver. The dead man's FBI Agent Joe Riggs. This is connected to the murder of the FBI agent downtown this morning."

"*Oh,* man*! Two FBI guys in one day! Shit's really going to hit the fan!*"

The ambulance pulled up, the EMS guys piled out, and rushed over to Riggs. One tried to find a pulse on his neck, looked up immediately, and shook his head. I already knew that.

The cop said, "You need to come with us while we sort this out."

"I understand, but have your dispatch call CBI Agent Harry Thornton, SFPD deputy chief Fong and, most importantly, Agent-in-Charge, Mariah Martinez at the FBI. They'll speed up the process."

"Impressive. That's a lineup of heavy hitters. I'll call it in and we'll see what happens. You're in the city of South San Francisco so we'll do our own investigation. If you're ready and able, we should get going." He looked at my vomit-splattered shoes and pants and the puddle on the pavement next to the curb. "Don't worry about that—we take it as a sign of innocence. It'll be in my report."

They put me in the back of the prowl car and roared out of the hotel parking lot. We ran with flashers but no siren. It was a quick five minutes to a modern looking, one story station house.

We entered the station into a hallway with doors down each side. The cop opened a door and said, "Let's go in here to get started." The room was comfortable looking with a small couch and four tub chairs. If there'd been carpeting, it could have been a home media room or an office. Without carpeting, it was a comfortable interrogation room in a police station.

I read the cop's nametag. "Officer Donnelly, do we have time for me to hit the head? I could stand to use the facilities, wash my face, and maybe clean off my shoes."

"No problem. It's across the hall."

I stepped across the hall, used the urinal, washed my face in cold water, and tried to wipe off my shoes and pant legs. When I finished, I looked in the mirror and what I saw was not a pretty sight. I looked like I'd been drug backward through a keyhole and then slapped around. A horribly long day didn't look like it was going to end anytime soon.

Donnelly was standing in the hall. "You feel any better?"

"Not really, but thanks for the break. We'd better get on with it. There's a lot of ground to cover."

He opened the door to the interrogation room and I saw two plain-clothes cops sitting in the tub chairs. They stood and introduced themselves.

"Scott, I'm Lieutenant Mike Christopher and this is Detective Sergeant Larry Janes. We need a statement from you about what happened at the Embassy Suites. We've been able to contact everybody except Harry Thornton. Agent Martinez and Chief Fong will be arriving here, separately, within half an hour. Martinez told us that after we're finished, she'll take you into protective custody and provide you with transportation back to San Francisco."

"Thanks, Lieutenant. I'll be damn glad to see this day end." I dropped onto the couch.

"I'm sure you will. If you're ready, let's get started." Sergeant Janes set up a digital recorder. Christopher gave his name, badge number, the date, and the names of everybody else in the room. He nodded at me and said, "Go ahead, Mr. Scott. What happened at the Embassy Suites?"

I told them the story from the time Riggs and I had pulled out of the garage on Golden Gate Avenue until Officer Donnelly had arrived in the parking lot of the Embassy Suites. Christopher and Janes sat quietly for a full minute before Christopher said, "That's a tough one. Who do you think is responsible and why?"

I gave a condensed version of the whole story of Martie Remington, Judy Benoit, Porter, Feng, and John Nelson. The cops' eyes got wider and wider as I talked. When I finished, Janes said, "This is way out of our league, Mr. Scott. Frankly, we'll be glad to have the FBI take it off our hands. If everything you say is true, and we certainly don't have any reason to doubt it, they're a lot better equipped to work it than we are." The other cops nodded in agreement.

The door opened and deputy chief William Fong held it for Mariah Martinez. Fong knew the two South San Francisco detectives and met Donnelly. They all introduced themselves to Martinez who looked drained. Lines that hadn't been visible this afternoon were deeply etched on her face. Mostly, she looked very sad. Losing two agents in one day had to be tough emotionally; it was also going to be a blotch on her service record. Thornton had told me she hadn't been the boss for long and was one of only a very few women serving as Agent-in-Charge.

I didn't know what to say to her. "I'm really sorry about Joe Riggs, Mariah. He seemed like a great young man."

She looked at me as if puzzled by my using her first name. "It wasn't your fault. It wasn't anybody's fault except the bastards who did it. Losing two good men in one day is tough. This is by far the worst day of my life." Mariah Martinez cared. It was obvious. "We're going to get the bastards, you can count on that." I hoped she was right. I also knew I was going after Feng on my own—killing John Nelson and Joe Riggs as soon as I met them had made it personal.

I had to run through everything again for Martinez and Fong before everyone was satisfied. The South San Francisco cops said they

were okay with my story and had no reason to talk to me anymore...
at least for tonight. Martinez said the FBI would take over responsibility for the investigation and would cooperate fully by sharing any
information. She said she couldn't tell them where I'd be, although
she'd make me available if they needed.

Everybody shook hands, exchanged cards, and exited into the
hall. Donnelly said, "If you'll come over to the evidence room, I'll
get your gun and phone." As we stepped over to the counter, he
said, "You're lucky as hell. The crime scene team just returned; they
counted almost a hundred bullet impacts between the cars out there."
I thanked him. I felt a familiar knot in my stomach and fought it off.

I followed Martinez to her car, another big Ford sedan. This
one was black instead of gray like Riggs'. It must have been one of
the perks of being the boss. As we pulled away from the station-
house, I asked her, "Was Joe married?"

"No, he was single, thank God. In fact, he doesn't, uh...didn't
have much family at all. He had an uncle in Seattle and that's it."

"I guess that's a blessing. What about Nelson?"

"Divorced...he had two kids—boys. They're grown and gone.
According to Quantico, Nelson lived by himself, didn't go out, and
had become a hermit the last few years."

"He seemed like a good guy. Why do you think he got so
wrapped up in this case?"

"Because it's the only one he never closed. I think he wanted
to wrap it and, at the same time, shut down a Chinese espionage
operation. I can't say I blame him...it would've been a good way to
go out."

"Maybe we can close it for him."

She turned to look at me. "There isn't a 'we' in this. You're
way out of your depth, Scott. You need to leave this in our hands. I
promise we *will* get these guys. The best thing you can do is to go
back to Denver and let us do our job. I'll make you the same deal as
South San Francisco PD—we'll keep you in the loop until we have
a resolution."

I didn't say anything—just stared at Martinez' profile as she drove. Finally, she looked at me. "I know you don't think that's fair but it's the way it's got to be. You're just another thing for us to worry about if you're here."

I took back all the nice things I'd been thinking about her. Thornton was right... she *was* a bitch. "If you think I'm leaving, you're a hundred and eighty degrees out of phase. Those bastards are trying to kill *me*. They've already killed two people around me. When they started shooting, this became personal and it's going to stay personal until they're either caught or dead. I intend to be involved either way."

I saw her knuckles whiten as she gripped the wheel. "We can't guarantee your safety if you don't cooperate."

"With all due respect, that's a goddamn joke. You guys can't even protect your own people let alone me. I'll take care of myself."

"I'm going to check you into the Renoir hotel for the night. It's one of San Francisco's best boutique hotels and it also happens to be our safe house. We'll make your flight reservations to return to Denver tomorrow. We'll provide protection and transportation to the airport. If you're here, you're a distraction and an inefficient use of our manpower."

I thought about it a few seconds. "You're right, Mariah. I wasn't thinking clearly. Let's go to the hotel, book a flight for tomorrow afternoon, and you can arrange for your guys to haul me to the airport."

She relaxed, gave a sigh, and said, "Thanks. That'll make it easier on everybody."

We didn't talk for the rest of the ride to the Renoir. It was a great looking old hotel and, as she'd said, right around the corner from the federal building. She pulled under the porte-cochere and said, "I'll go in with you." Inside, she said, "Follow me" and veered off to a closed door that said Manager on the name plate. She knocked, opened the door, and walked in before there was an answer.

Inside was a small, dark-complexioned guy who looked Indian or Pakistani. His nametag read Mr. Adjani. Martinez introduced herself, showed her ID and badge, and said, "This is the gentleman we called about this afternoon. We'll need our suite this evening." I noticed she hadn't used my name. I assumed that was standard operating procedure.

Mr. Adjani spoke in a cultured British accent. "Certainly, Agent Martinez, we will take care of it, as usual. Welcome to the Renoir, sir. If you'll follow me, I'll get you to your room."

I was tired as hell and probably looked it. Martinez stuck out her hand and said, "I'm sorry for all you've gone through today. It's been rough on all of us."

I took her hand and said, "I appreciate it, my condolences to you and your officers too." We shook hands and she left.

Mr. Adjani gestured toward the door and ushered me out. He led the way around the elevator lobby and into an area behind. There was a single elevator here which Adjani opened with a key and we stepped inside. It served the tenth floor only and Adjani used his key to activate it.

We exited in a small alcove with a single security door to a hall. As we started down the hall, I noticed a fire escape stairwell located halfway down on the right. I asked Adjani if it was the only other exit. "Yes. And the stairwell is like the elevator, the doors to the other floors are locked until you reach the main floor. You don't have to be concerned about anyone accessing the tenth from one of the other floors. You're very secure here. Ah, here we are...room 'E', sir."

He opened the door with a large conventional key instead of a key card. It worked a bolt lock. Inside, down a short hall, I saw a large well-appointed living room with expensive furniture. Adjani opened the first door on the hallway. "Here's your bath. You'll find everything you need in the cabinets." I looked in and was reminded of France. The place was luxurious. At the next door, Adjani said, "And, here's your bedroom." Again, it was pure luxury with a king bed, closets, sitting chairs, and a fireplace. "Would you like us to take care of your clothes, sir?" He pointed at the laundry bag I was carrying.

"No, they're fine. I'm only staying the night anyway. I do need a small travel bag of some kind I can put them in."

Adjani opened one of the closet doors, pulled out a bag that was exactly what I needed. "It's amazing how many people come here, exactly as you have, and need a bag. The FBI provides them."

"Great...my tax dollars at work, I suppose."

Mr. Adjani smiled. "I know everyone who comes here arrives under strained circumstances, sir. I hope you'll be comfortable. Do you have any questions?"

"How do I call the elevator when I'm ready to leave?"

"Like any other elevator, there's a call button. It rings a bell in the manager's office and whoever is on duty will activate the elevator from his desk."

"Okay," I said. "Thanks."

"You're welcome." He handed me the key and left. I went into the bedroom, took my clothes out of the laundry bag, and put them in the travel case. In the bathroom, I took out a toothbrush and paste, a razor and shave cream, deodorant, and a brush. I threw them in on top of the clothes, zipped the bag, and walked out. At the door to the fire escape, I eased the door open hoping it wouldn't set off an alarm. I didn't hear anything, although that didn't mean there wasn't something in the manager's office or reception. I started down the stairs as fast as I could. By the third floor I was wishing I'd spent a little more time running the paths around my house.

At the bottom, I looked through the wire mesh window in the exit door. I couldn't see anything except an undecorated hall and some electrical control room doors. I tried the push bar again expecting to hear an alarm. I was prepared to sprint across the lobby and was surprised when nothing happened. I pushed the door open, looked around, and slipped out into the hallway. The double doors at the end of the hall opened to the lobby so I went that way. Inside the lobby, I was around a corner from the reception desk so I started toward the front entrance keeping my eyes forward and my face slightly turned from reception. I exited through the revolving doors onto the circular drive-through. I had spotted a cab stand at the corner when Martinez had pulled in. I pointed at the driver of the first cab in line. He nodded and I hopped in. He dropped the meter handle and said, "Where to?"

I asked, "Is there a rental car place anywhere close by?"

He glanced over his shoulder with a sullen look. "If you don't wanta use the concierge in the Renoir, I can take you over to Union Square. There's a Hertz office there. It'll be a whole three blocks."

I said, "That'll be fine. I'll give you a twenty for the ride."

The guy's attitude improved dramatically. "Yes *sir!*"

I glanced at the dash board clock: 11:49 p.m. I said, "How late do they stay open?"

He glanced at the clock and said, "Midnight, I think."

I said, "Let's make it, okay?" He hit the gas, slid around two corners, and ran a light but pulled up in front of a small Hertz office with four minutes to spare. I threw a $20 over the seat, jumped out and yelled, "Thanks, man."

Inside, the two counter agents were shutting down for the night. An attractive Hispanic girl smiled and said, "Just under the wire, sir. How can we help you this evening?"

"Well, I hope you'll rent me a car. You do that here, don't you?"

She smiled again. "Yes, sir, you've come to the right place. What kind of car are you looking for and how long will you need it."

"Let's say three days—if it's longer, I'll call in. Can we do that?"

"Certainly, sir. Now, what kind of car would you like?"

"Something sporty...do you have any Mustangs?"

"This *is* California, sir. We *always* have Mustangs. Are you looking for a convertible?"

"Absolutely." I thought why not? I would've liked a Mustang's horsepower this morning when I was being tailed.

We did the paperwork. I gave the Renoir as my temporary residence. She gave me the key and told me where to find the car in a garage about a half block away. I thanked her, apologized for making them late, and headed for the garage.

I took the stairs to the second floor of the garage, found the Mustang, royal blue with a camel top, threw my bag behind the seat, and drove out through an exit marked Hertz Only.

I took the Bay Bridge and hauled ass to Oakland. I didn't have a plan and needed someplace to hole up for the night to figure one out. I drove to the Bancroft. One more time, I was in luck—they had two rooms available and one was the same suite I'd had before. By the time I got to the room, it was almost 2:00 a.m. It was too late to call Lindsey…or anyone else for that matter.

I checked the mini-bar and found they'd restocked the Anchor Steam. I grabbed one, opened it, and drained half. I needed it. I carried everything into the bathroom, turned on the taps, and poured in a little bubble bath while I stripped. I finished the beer and got the other one. I shaved while watching the water level in the tub. I filled it to the drains, climbed in, and slowly settled down as deeply as I could. It was as hot as I could stand and I stayed mostly submerged for about five minutes. When I sat up and sipped the beer, I could feel some of the tension slipping away. It had been one of the worst days of my life. It didn't approach the day two years ago when my girlfriend, Gerri German, had been murdered, but it was still a damn bad one. I sipped more beer and thought about tomorrow.

chapter

TWENTY-FIVE

I'd set the alarm for 6:00 a.m. but awakened at 5:45. I used the room phone to call Lindsey's cell number. It was 7:00 a.m. in Denver. She picked up and it was good to hear her voice.

"Hey, sleuth, I was wondering if you'd call this morning. You didn't keep your promise to call last night. You have too many California girls to chase?"

"Hi, Linds...I'm sorry I didn't call—I couldn't. Things have gone to hell here."

"Are you in trouble?" I could hear the concern in her voice.

"I don't know if I'd call it trouble...deep shit comes to mind." I told her most of what'd happened without going into detail about the shooting at the Embassy Suites. There was no need to worry her any more than she already was. I did tell her I was probably a fugitive from the FBI although I'd only been in protective custody and not charged with any crimes. "They aren't going to like that I'm still here and hunting for Feng."

"Why *are* you still there? Can't they run this Feng guy down and put a stop to it?"

I'd trapped myself by not telling her everything about the shooting. "You know what, Linds? I feel like I owe it to Hank, or maybe Martie Remington. It's not as personal to the FBI as it is to Hank...and I guess to me." That probably wasn't fair. Martinez had taken the killings of her agents pretty hard.

Lindsey was quiet for a moment. "I can see that. You should stay and see it through, and you need to be careful. I know you're probably sick of hearing me say that, but I mean it. Those guys sound bad, I mean, killing the girl here and now the FBI guy..." She didn't finish the sentence as she completed the thought. The count was actually three, although she didn't know about Riggs, and I didn't know what had happened to Gail Porter either.

"Thanks for understanding, Linds. I'll try to keep in touch though I'm not going to use my cell for a while just in case the feds can trace it."

"You better call me anyway. I'm counting on it. Come home to me as soon as you can."

"That's a promise."

I hung up, poured a cup of coffee, and dialed Tom Montgomery's office.

"It's about damn time you checked in." Tom was in his normal frame of mind. Hedges had once told me Tom had a very even personality...he's pissed off all the time. "Those FBI killings are all over the police wires and you're right in the middle of John Nelson's. What the hell happened out there?"

I filled him in on everything. He listened without talking until I was finished. "So what are you going to do now? You need some help?"

"How well do you know Harry Thornton?"

"Pretty well...why?"

"I'm going to need some eyes and ears and I'm not going to get them from the FBI or the local cops. Harry seems like the kind of guy who'd like to see this thing wrapped up in a hurry and might not be too concerned about how the end game plays out."

"That's about right. You can trust Harry. He's an old-time cop, came up through the ranks by busting heads when they needed busting. He's probably got as many enemies as friends, but he's a good guy. Another thing in your favor is he'll want to burn Feng's ass. He won't want to see him go to court and end up with a sentence. If you're okay with that, Harry'll give you all the help you need."

"Good, that's what I was hoping to hear. I'm back at the Bancroft, however, if you absolutely have to get in touch with me call Harry. I don't want to use my cell. As soon as his office opens I'll call him, tell him what I'm up to, and ask for help."

"Okay, I got it. Watch your ass, will ya? You don't have me there to cover you."

chapter

TWENTY-SIX

I poured another coffee, thought better of it, and decided to try the breakfast bar instead. I pulled on some jeans and a golf shirt and took the stairs. In the breakfast room there were five people queuing up, so I grabbed a plate and got in line. It was a feast by my standards. I took a chocolate croissant, Eggs Benedict, and three slices of thick-sliced bacon, chose a two person table in the room's bay window, and set my food down while I went back for coffee. I poured an orange juice and a cup of coffee that smelled of cinnamon.

The newspaper headline read: *Two FBI Agents Slain in Separate San Francisco Shootings* and the entire front page was made up of stories about the shooting deaths of John Nelson and Joe Riggs. I read the articles as I ate, searching for my name, and was thankful not to find it. Several quotes from Mariah Martinez linked the shootings to an ongoing investigation of criminal activity taking place in the South San Francisco area involving possible links to foreign espionage activities. It was about as vague as she could make it. She attributed the FBI's involvement to a long-standing investigation by John Nelson. She said the FBI was working closely with local authorities and would vigorously pursue the perpetrators of this tragic incident.

I finished my food, poured still another cup of coffee, and took the paper back to my room. Agent Martinez was quoted as saying the original investigation had been initiated from information obtained from non-FBI sources. That was as close as she came to telling the whole story.

I finished the coffee and called Harry Thornton. "Harry? It's Cort Scott."

"I figured you'd be calling. Your good friend, Ms. Martinez, just called to tell me you left their protection and were going to be a problem."

"You might've been right about her, Harry. I think she's too damn *professional* to get anything done. I mean, two guys who were working with me yesterday got killed and she was more concerned with getting me out of town than chasing the killers."

"I told ya...so what are you going to do now?"

"I'll tell you what I'm *not* going to do and that's leave. That son-of-a-bitch Feng almost got me last night. I wanta take care of that. I owe it to the three people who've been killed to see this thing to a finish. I'm going to need your help, though, Harry."

"What can I do for you?"

"Well, first, what's the story with Judy Benoit? Is she safe and can I see her without the FBI getting in the way? Second, have you heard anything about Porter? And, third, what's the CBI doing?"

"Okay—from the top, we took Benoit back to her place; she packed up some clothes and toiletries and we've got her here in Sacramento. Incidentally, Martinez didn't like that either...said it made it *inconvenient* for them to interview her. I told her 'tough shit.' Benoit's pretty shook up but she's willing to talk about everything. She's scared as hell of Feng. I think he might have romanced her in the early going, you know—led her along with more than just a common interest in the environment. The best way for you to talk to her will be here to our office. We had to tell the feds where we have her so they're probably keeping an eye on our safe house. We can bring her into the office, though, and it'll be easy for you to slip in without anyone being the wiser.

"Next, Porter…that's a whole different story. We're wondering if Feng might have grabbed her. There's been no sign of her, nothing on her credit card, no record of airline flights…nothing. She's just vanished.

"Now, what are we doing? We're looking for Porter as hard as we can and we're looking for Feng and his gang just as hard. We're trying to stay away from the feds because they're a pain in the ass. I think our best chance of catching Feng will come from Benoit. He might have mentioned something or someplace to her that'll give us a clue. Why don't you come up and sit in when we talk to her? I think she trusts you after yesterday and might tell you something she won't to us."

"All right, I can probably be there in a couple hours. How do I get in without being spotted?"

Thornton told me to park in a public lot and board a shuttle bus like I was going to tour the capitol. At the shuttle drop-off, I'd cut through the capitol building to the CBI office located in a nondescript building on 5th Street. He said they'd bring Benoit there at 11:00 a.m. I thanked him and hung up.

I put my gun in the briefcase, used the bathroom…too much coffee…and went to the parking lot. The day was overcast and warm. I drove the quick hop over to I-80 and headed for Sacramento. Traffic was light and I made great time without speeding too much. I found the parking structure Thornton described, caught the free shuttle advertising capitol tours, and took the three block ride with twelve or fifteen tourists who must have represented every third world country on earth. They were dressed in all conceivable modes and styles of clothing. The bus smelled like a low-level United Nations meeting.

At the capitol building, the crowd charged up the steps to the guided tour entrance where there was already a line. I walked through the main entrance, down the back steps, out onto 5th, and turned toward the CBI building half a block north. Inside was another of the sophisticated security setups required in every public building. I was glad I'd left my gun locked in the trunk of the Mustang.

I signed in and wrote down Thornton's name for my appointment. The security guard glanced up as he started to enter it in his computer. He said, "Just a minute, Mr. Scott, I'll call up to Mr. Thornton's office. I think we can get you right in." He dialed, told somebody that Thornton's visitor had arrived, nodded, and hung up. He looked at me again and said, "Do you have some ID, Mr. Scott?" I took out my PI license and handed it to him. He looked at it carefully, back at me, indicated a gate at the side of his desk and said, "Step through here. Take the elevators to the third floor. They're expecting you."

The elevator opened to another reception desk. The six foot plus, shaved head, black "receptionist" looked like a 49'ers linebacker. "Mr. Scott?" I nodded and he said, "Mr. Thornton's expecting you. They're in the room all the way to the rear." He pointed at a door in the middle of the back wall. "Go ahead."

Harry opened the door, stepped out, and extended his hand. "No hard feelings about yesterday, okay? I know you were upset with some of what I said, but I could see you were getting sucked in by Martinez. I'm sorry as hell about what happened to that young agent. I'm glad you're okay. From the moment I first talked to Martinez yesterday, I got the feeling she wasn't on top of this. John Nelson was a friend and he didn't deserve to die because some commie son-of-a-bitch is spying for the fucking Chinese. Let's go in there, have a nice, long talk with Benoit, and see if we can figure out where that asshole Feng is hiding. If we can flush him out, I won't be real particular about how we bring him to justice if you catch my meaning."

"I catch your meaning, Harry, and thanks for dealing me in. I take it personally when somebody tries to stitch me up with a full auto from fifty feet. I was goddamn lucky if you want to know the truth."

Inside, Judy Benoit was sitting next to a uniformed, woman police officer. Judy looked pretty good, all things considered. Although a little pale and hollow-eyed, she'd cleaned up, done her hair, and had on nice jeans and a patterned blouse. I reached out to shake hands, but she walked into my arms and gave me a hug. "I want to thank you for getting me out of Berkeley and probably saving my life yesterday. I heard about what happened to the other agent in South San Francisco and I'm so sorry. I didn't know you'd been with him until Mr. Thornton told me. It must have been terrible."

I released her. "It was pretty bad. I was lucky. I'm glad you're safe though. We'll get a chance to go after Jon Feng and the guys who did it."

The uniform was introduced as Roberta—call me Bobbi— Walton. She was California Highway Patrol on assignment to the CBI. We sat, Harry broke out some water bottles, and we started to talk. We kept it casual as Harry led Judy through how she'd met Jon Feng, whether she'd done much in the Bay Area with him, or if she had traveled with him. He wanted to know if she knew who worked for Feng or if she'd met his brother or any friends. As she talked, it was clear she didn't know much about him or his business other than what Gail Porter had told her about his commitment to environmental issues. The more relaxed she became, the more she started remembering things, like when he told her about his father's house in Marin County and how he'd like to buy it back. Gail had told her Feng had mentioned owning a houseboat moored in Sausalito. Harry excused himself, went out, and quickly returned. I didn't think it was to use the restroom.

After an hour, Harry mentioned lunch. Judy must have been feeling better and said she was starving. Harry stepped out again and asked one of the admins to order a variety of deli sandwiches. He and Walton excused themselves to use the bathroom.

Judy and I were left alone in the conference room. I looked at her for a moment before asking, "Are you doing okay, Judy? Are you going to get through this?"

She didn't answer immediately which I took as a bad sign. Finally, she smiled slightly and said, "Yes. I'll get through it. I wouldn't have placed much of a bet on it yesterday though. You know, Mr. uh, Cort, I still haven't told you everything. I just can't seem to bring myself to tell the police."

"What do you mean?"

She hung her head and answered in very low voice. "Well, um, actually, I think Jon Feng seduced me—in more ways than one. Yes, it included sex and what I thought of as love, but now I think he seduced my beliefs and commitment too. He got me to do things I normally wouldn't have done. I'm not saying I had any direct involvement in...you know, Martie's death or anything, but I told Jon exactly where we were working. I gave him everything he needed to do what he did."

"Judy, you need to tell us everything you can about what happened to Martie. If you don't want to tell the cops about Feng seducing you, that's okay. If you need to get everything off your chest, you can tell me and it won't go any further. But, if you can think of any little thing, no matter how unimportant it may seem, about where we might find Feng, you need to tell us."

The door opened and the two cops reentered the room. Harry jerked his thumb toward the door indicating he wanted to see me outside. I squeezed Judy's hand to reassure her. She said, "Mr. Thornton, I've just thought of some other things Jon Feng said—they might help find him. Plus, I have been thinking some more about how I fit into all this...there are some other things I need to tell you." As she said it, she looked directly at me.

Harry Thornton smiled and replied, "Hold those thoughts, Ms. Benoit. Scott and I will be right back." He jerked his head toward the door again. I stood and followed him out. A few feet from the door, Thornton pointed at an agent seated in front of a computer screen across the room. "We entered Feng Li's name and came up with an address in Marin. Then we checked the real estate records—guess what?"

I took a wild shot in the dark. "Jon Feng already owns the old home place."

Harry grinned. "You're smarter than you look. He's always owned it—he got it in the estate. He was blowing a little smoke up sweet Ms. Benoit's ass. We also ran down his houseboat. It's registered to the company. We've got the slip number and location in Sausalito. Now, what's Benoit want to tell us?"

"I don't know for sure, but I think she's on our side."

"Well, that's progress...let's get back in before she gets cold feet."

We stepped into the conference room and saw Benoit and Walton talking quietly. Harry said, "Okay, Judy, what did you remember?"

Judy faced Thornton and said, "That I probably have a lot more culpability than I've told you. I don't want you to think I had any direct involvement in Martie's death because I didn't. I'm talking about my ties to Jon Feng."

She took a deep, shuddering breath, let it out, and said, "I'm sorry. I've been lying to you about some of what happened. I was deeply involved with the ELF and I participated in some of their actions. I know people got hurt although mostly there was just property damage. I'm not a member of ECF, but I know who they are and what they do. Jon Feng was a major money source for them and he got me involved in some of the things that have happened."

Harry looked up and asked, "What's the ECF?"

Judy looked surprised at his question. "I thought Cort told you. It stands for Earth Comes First. They're a small group who've been taking action against polluters and agencies, or anybody they think are destroying the environment. Most of them were in ELF but came to believe their actions weren't working fast enough to change the system."

Harry looked agitated. "You mean tree spiking and bullshit like that wasn't getting the job done as far as ECF was concerned?"

She dropped her gaze. "Yes, and a lot more too—some of it has been headline stuff…like setting fire to car dealers who sell SUVs and dynamiting power transmission lines." She looked at me again and I saw tears glistening in her eyes. "I knew the ECF was planning to slow down the USGS resource evaluation. I knew they were going to burn the truck last spring. I showed Jon Feng and Bennie where the truck was parked and I was there when Bennie rigged up the fire bomb."

She took more deep breaths and the tears began coursing down her cheeks. "I've been a member of ELF since high school. I helped them get on some timberland my Dad owned up near Yreka and I even spiked some trees with them. One of my Dad's loggers was hurt when he cut into a spike with a chain saw. That made me sick and I quit doing anything with them for a long time. I worked with Gail Porter because I still wanted to be active in environmental protest, but I didn't want to hurt anybody. When Gail first introduced me to Jon Feng, I thought he was just like Gail and me. I thought he was *really* involved and believed in nonviolence."

I interrupted. "Are you saying Gail's *not* in the ECF?"

Judy nodded. "Gail's a wonderful person—she would never hurt anybody. I think she may have been associated with the ELF early on, however she told me several times they took a wrong turn and she didn't want to be associated with them. I'm sure she knows who some of the people in the ECF are, but I can guarantee you she doesn't have anything to do with them. I *was* telling you the truth about her making Jon and Bennie leave her house when she found out they were involved in burning the truck."

I was relieved to hear it. It made me wonder about Gail though. Was she safe or had Feng grabbed her?

Judy started talking again. "When Gail and Jon Feng came to Colorado, Jon and I went out for drinks after Gail went to bed. Jon told me about ECF and that he knew I'd been involved with ELF.

He said they needed my help to slow down or stop the oil shale resource evaluation. He was soft spoken about it, however he implied if I didn't cooperate, he'd let the information get out that I'd been involved with ELF. He kept telling me they weren't going to do anything really bad—they just wanted to monkey wrench the operation. He asked lots of questions about where we were working and who was working with whom, and about our schedule. I thought he was probably going to do some more things like sabotage our field vehicles. But, I was a fool...I led Jon Feng directly to Martie."

She looked back and forth from Harry to me. "I think I fell in love with Jon and I didn't want to know what was really going on. I'm not sure I want to know now either. After Martie was killed and I heard what he and Bennie said, I started putting two and two together. There were way too many coincidences. It was after I confronted him that Jon said they could frame me for Martie's death. I was so scared I just kept lying about everything. I'm so sorry." She bowed her head and covered her face with her hands.

Harry took it all in and slowly shook his head. "You know, Ms. Benoit, I have some sympathy for you although, quite frankly, not a lot. If you knew what ELF was capable of, you should've suspected what this new ECF outfit might do. The fact Feng was willing to blackmail you into helping him should have been another big clue. I don't see how you can say you fell in love with him *after* he told you that. You're right about one thing—the fact you're a fool. Although you didn't directly murder Martie Remington, your actions led to it. I hope to hell you're finally telling us everything you know and not holding back or lying about anything." Harry wasn't cutting her any slack. I felt sorry for her although Harry was absolutely right.

I asked Judy the biggest question of all. "Why did they kill Martie Remington?"

Judy Benoit lost it. She began sobbing and gasping for breath. I slid a bottle of water in front of her. She ignored it. Finally, she inhaled deeply, picked up the water, and took a small sip. "Again," she murmured, "I think it's about *timing.* Jon kept saying if he could just delay the resource evaluation by a year or two, he'd feel like he'd done his job. He was disappointed we went right back to work after the truck burned; he said he would have to do something a little more dramatic. After you told me about Nelson's theory of Jon working for the Chinese and their needing a year's head start to begin controlling the world's oil shale, I began thinking it through. They probably figured a death would, at the very least, stall any field work until next year. It will take at least two more field seasons before the USGS can do the evaluation. When all that gets added up, it would give the Chinese the head start they want."

I asked, "Do you have any idea why Feng murdered John Nelson and the other FBI agent or why he seems to be after me?"

Benoit dropped her head and sagged before she raised her eyes and said in a barely audible voice, "I think Jon Feng has someone on the inside at the FBI. Somehow, he found out what John Nelson told you and he guessed Nelson hadn't told anyone else about his theory. He gambled you were the only ones who knew and he could stop everything by killing you both. I know I'm guessing, but it's what I think.

"When I told him about you showing up at my house, he went ballistic. He calmed down a little when I told him you were following up on Martie's death as a favor to Hank. He asked me several times if I thought you were connected to the FBI or CIA or anything else 'federal.' I told him I didn't know, but didn't think so. After that, he said maybe you'd turn out to be a good thing—you'd keep the investigation going and Hank wouldn't send out any more field teams for a while."

Harry shot me a look, slid his chair back, and said, "Ms. Benoit, is there anything else you can tell us about Jon Feng, no matter how small or unimportant you might think it is? You can see how dangerous this man is; how important it is we find him as soon as possible."

"I know he has a favorite restaurant in Berkeley and another in San Francisco; he mentioned them almost every time I saw him. The place in Berkeley is called La Note. It's a French place on Shattuck. The other one, the one in San Francisco, is The Range. I think it's in the Mission District. He used to talk about going there for business meetings."

Harry Thornton spoke in a hurry. "That's the kind of thing we need. Okay, I think that's everything we wanted to cover with you today. If you think of anything else, you can tell Walton or give me a call if you'd rather. I think it best if you stay here for a few days until we get a handle on Feng. Walton will stay with you…we'll even let her wear civvies. There's no reason to have you stand out by being seen with a cop. If you need anything, let her know. You're not under arrest, however I don't want you leaving or going anywhere. We need to process what you've told us, discuss it with the feds, and decide if you'll be charged with anything. Eventually we'll catch up with Feng and we'll protect you until we do."

The admin came back with the sandwiches; the women chose two each and left.

***

Thornton had jerked upright when Judy said she thought Feng had someone in the FBI. Now, he fixed me with a stare and said, *"Jesus Christ!* He has somebody inside in the FBI? Where?"

The same question had been bothering me. "You know, Harry, he has to be in San Francisco."

Thornton furrowed his brow. "How do you figure that?"

"Simple timing…unless it was someone who knew where Nelson parked and knew where I was staying, there's no way they could've gotten word to Feng in time for him to set up the ambushes."

Harry ran his hand through his hair, leaned forward, and the light bulb went on behind his eyes. "That would explain a lot I haven't been able to figure out, like how they ambushed Nelson in the parking garage, and how they knew where you were staying.

Hell, they searched your room *before* you and Riggs got there. And
they were set up to take you out when you went to the parking lot.

"You've got to be right. But, *who the hell is it?* There's gotta be
twenty-five agents and almost as many staff in that office. Got any
ideas on who the mole is?"

I thought for a moment and asked Harry, "Does the FBI tape
everything that goes on in the interrogation and conference rooms?"

He said, "I'd bet on it."

"If it's taped, can someone listen in directly? You know, in real
time."

"Sure. Hell, we do it here."

That got my attention. "Are you telling me this session is being taped?"

Harry shook his head. "It's at our discretion and I decided *not*
to record this one. I thought if Benoit gave us some information we
can use or if we needed her to testify later, I didn't want her testimo-
ny sullied by claims about illegal wiretaps or recordings. Of course,
the feds don't play by the same rules, although they used to. Since
nine-eleven they do whatever the hell they want and justify it on the
basis of national security."

I'd been wracking my brain from the moment Benoit raised
the issue. "I've got an idea of who it might be. Nelson called himself
a 'visiting fireman' and was bitching about a lack of support all the
way from administrative help to office space. He said the only perks
visiting agents got were the motor pool and parking in the garage
across the street. But, he *did* have an administrative assistant, an
Asian gal named 'Jen.' I don't know how their taping and monitoring
system works, but if anyone was going to listen in, I'm betting it was
her. It would have been easy to tip Feng off about what Nelson told
me...and where his car was parked.

"When you and I were there yesterday, Jen left at the same
time as Riggs and me. We spoke a few words on the street when we
left the building. It would've been a perfect way for her to finger us.
She could've already let Feng know about the Embassy Suites so his

guys could search my room before we got there. I'll bet somebody tailed us and set up the ambush when they saw where we parked."

Harry Thornton exploded. *"Goddamnit! What a fucking mess!* I don't know whether to alert Martinez or not. What if 'Jen' isn't the one? What if it's higher than that? The fed agencies don't take kindly to being accused of having leaks and double agents."

"I'll bet that's right. Any way to check her out without them knowing?"

"No, once the feds run their security checks and hire somebody, it becomes a closed file to everyone else."

"In that case, I think we need to talk to Martinez. I know you don't think much of her and I'll admit she's not my favorite either, but this is on her turf. We've got to risk it."

Harry sighed and cursed under his breath. "You're right of course. It still chaps my ass. It's always us local yokels who end up doing the shit details and having to share with the feds. Oh, well, that's just a bitter old cop bitchin' about life...I'll make the call."

He used the desk set, asked for Mariah Martinez, and waited several seconds. "Hey Agent Martinez, Harry Thornton, here—Yes, ma'am...fine, thanks for asking. And you?" He listened for a minute, looked at me, and rolled his eyes. "I can certainly understand your frustration, Mariah. Listen, I've got some information for you that could have a huge impact on this case. First, I've got a question for you...does Scott face any kind of charges from you?"

That took me by surprise. I couldn't think of anything I'd done that would warrant charges. They were probably pissed at me for running out on them, but I didn't care about that.

Thornton listened for a little while and gave me a thumb up before saying, "That's kind of what I thought. Here's the deal, Mariah, Scott is sitting across the table from me right now and—no, no, c'mon—don't get all bent out of shape. We didn't pick him up or anything. He called me this morning to inquire about Benoit. I told him we were going to talk to her this morning and he volunteered to sit in. Look, Mariah, she trusts him more than us and I figured we had a better chance of learning something if he was here. That's how we got what I'm going to tell you.

"You're not going to like this, Mariah—Scott and I think you've got a mole in your office and..." I could hear her voice as plainly as if she had been on speaker phone,

"YOU'RE FUCKING CRAZY, THORNTON!"

Harry held the receiver away from his ear and let her vent for several seconds. When the volume went down a few decibels, he quietly said, "Hang on a minute and listen, Mariah. First, when we compare everybody's stories, the only person who knew what John Nelson was working on was Tom Montgomery, the Denver PD detective. The first time Nelson's theory about the Chinese wanting to control world oil prices was mentioned occurred in your office when he told Scott. You said yourself you didn't know what he was working on and your guy, Walsh, said the same thing. Second, until I asked Scott—again, in your office—where he was staying, nobody else knew. Now, and here's the question that's going to make all the difference, do you tape the conversations in your interrogation and conference rooms? If you do, who can listen in?"

Thornton listened carefully for several minutes. Occasionally, he would nod or say, "Okay" or, "Yeah, I see." or, "I don't know." Finally, he said, "Well, that's who Scott thinks it might be. He even thinks she might have 'fingered' him and Riggs when they left your offices yesterday. They saw her outside and spoke a few words about parking spaces and stuff. It would've been plenty of time for someone to get a fix on them and follow them to the Embassy Suites. Look, Mariah, I know this is hard to hear, but I think you need to take it very seriously." He listened a little more. "Okay, I think that's wise; do me a favor—give me a call after you check it out? Now, here's some more stuff Benoit gave us and I don't have the manpower to cover everything so you can help me out." He told her about the house in Marin, the houseboat, and gave her the detail about the restaurants. He said CBI would check Marin and Sausalito and needed the FBI to stake out the restaurants. He listened a moment and said, "Yeah, you, too...okay, we'll talk later."

He closed the call, smiled, and said, "If this wasn't so damned serious, that might have been enjoyable. You had to hear her—she didn't take it very well, at least at first. Thing is, after she *listened* to what I told her, she came to the same conclusion as you—the *only* one it can be is Jen Wang. Martinez will start a complete background check.

"Oh yeah, here's a news bulletin—she's not real happy with you. She says you cost them a lot of time trying to protect you. By the way, how come you rented a car in your own name? That was one of the first places they checked because it's the closest car rental to the Renoir. She also said you're not at the Embassy Suites." He laughed as he made a pistol of his thumb and index finger and shot me.

"I don't have the luxury of a bunch of fake ID's, Harry. I had to go with what I had because I needed the wheels. Is she going to get back to you about Jen Wang?"

"She promised she would. The last thing she said was 'Thanks.' That's the first time she's ever said that to me...I guess that's progress."

Harry sat back and peered over the half glasses perched on the end of his nose. "Whadda ya think? Think Benoit gave us enough to find this bastard?"

"Hey, it's your turf, Harry. I gotta believe we've got a head start. What do you think Martinez will be up to?"

"Probably playing cover-your-ass for having two agents killed on her watch. In a way, I feel a little sorry for her...not enough to share everything, but a little sorry."

"What are we going to do now?"

"How would you feel about another chopper trip?"

"Fine by me...where?"

"Marin County. We'll go take a look at Feng's houseboat and old Feng Li's house. The feds will get on the restaurants. Who knows—maybe Mariah will get lucky instead of us. That would piss me off, but it can't be helped. I wasn't bullshitting about not having enough people to look at everything."

chapter

TWENTY-
SEVEN

We finished the sandwiches and Harry asked if I was ready to go.

I nodded and said, "I need to get my gun if we're going hunting. I left it in the trunk of my car. I didn't think it was a good idea to bring it here."

"You got that right. We'll take my rig by and get your piece. It's kinda on the way to the pad anyway. I'll have James call the chopper drivers and tell 'em we're on the way." I guessed the linebacker's name was James.

We drove to the parking garage; I retrieved my gun and we continued to the CBI's heliport. He parked the truck in a spot marked Director and pulled a Colt .38 Police Special with an ancient looking shoulder holster out of the console. I did a double take which he caught. "I've had this since I went plainclothes thirty years ago. It looks like shit but it gets the job done."

We trotted across the tarmac to the helicopter and clambered inside. The chopper shuddered as it revved up and leapt into flight. We put the headphones on and Harry said, "I'm getting too old for this shit. I feel like John Nelson—I'd like this to be the last rodeo."

I pointed at his gun and holster. "You said that setup *'gets the job done'*...have you had to use it much?"

"More than I like to remember. The seventies and early eighties were bad times out here. We had leftover revolutionaries, militias, druggies, and almost any other kind of crazy you can name. I'll be fifty-eight years old next spring and I've been a cop for going on thirty-five years. I'm not proud to say it, but I've shot seven felons in that time."

Seven seemed like a lot. "All of 'em dead?"

"No, no, *thank God*...only four of 'em. It was them or me every time though, and I'm still walking around."

"You ever get shot, Harry?"

"Twice...once in the arm and once in the foot; the arm was just a scratch. The time I got it in the foot, though—that was tough. I was laid up for several weeks. I still limp around whenever the weather turns real cold and wet. Wouldn't want to admit it's ever cold and wet in California, however the Bay Area and points north are *fucking* cold and wet. You ever get shot?"

I shook my head. "No, and, furthermore, I don't wanta be. I spent four years in the army rangers and I've had a couple of shootouts chasing bad guys since I became a PI, but that deal yesterday was as close as I've come. It scared the shit outta me."

"I hear ya. In some ways, that's a good thing. You need a healthy respect for what can happen. It keeps you sharper and you pay attention. What kind of piece do you have?" He pointed at my rolled up jacket.

I unrolled the Beretta, took it out of the holster, dropped the clip, and jacked the slide open. Harry took it and examined it carefully. As he handed it back, he said, "Nice gun—can you shoot it?" I told him again about being a ranger, some of the things I'd done, and target scores. He nodded, "Looks good on paper...makes a difference when somebody's shooting back." There wasn't much I could say to that.

As we flew, Harry explained how we'd pick up a car, drive to Sausalito, check out the houseboat, and then to the Fengs' house. "I'd love to catch the son-of-a-bitch on the houseboat. That'd be a real dead end for him, though I doubt if he's that dumb. I still can't get my arms around why he thought he had to kill John and go after you. Trying to prove a spy case is a hell of lot harder than putting someone away for murder."

I'd been wondering the same thing. The chances of keeping up the spy gig were long gone. Maybe he was trying to send a message, although I wasn't smart enough to figure it out.

We started our descent to the Marin County Sheriff's helipad. When we touched down, Harry and I piled out and met two plainclothes CBI guys who'd driven two unmarked Ford Crown Victoria Police Interceptors to meet us. Harry didn't bother with any introductions; he took the keys to one car and said, "Let's go."

Harry programmed the GPS navigation for the houseboat moorage and we sped off. It was only a fifteen minute drive and the GPS put us in the parking lot. The printout Harry had brought gave the slip number as 87B and a look at the You-Are-Here map showed two piers, A and B—87B was near the end of B pier. It looked like business was good as nearly all the slips were filled. Harry showed the rent-a-cop guard a badge and we went down an inclined ramp onto the pier and strode to the houseboat. It was closed up and no one was aboard. We tried the sliding door. It was locked. Harry said, "I *knew* we wouldn't be that lucky. Let's go check out the house."

Back at the cruiser, Harry put the house address in the GPS and we followed the voice directions. The route was north into the hills overlooking North Bay. After winding around the curvy hill-side roads for twenty minutes, we spotted a sign with the address. A driveway with a chain across the entrance disappeared up a brushy hill. We got out and examined the chain and lock. There were fresh scrapes on the chain and the eye bolt which was set in a concrete and stone gatepost. "Look at this, Harry. Somebody's had the chain off recently. See how the rust is scraped away? Let's check it out."

"I see what you mean, but I don't think we want to charge up there in broad daylight. I can't even see the house from down here, I don't know how far it is, and I'll bet you a dollar to a donut whoever's up there can see a visitor coming. It's a couple hours till dark, let's drive back to that coffee shop at the base of the hill, get some coffee, and park in the observation pullout across the road. We'll monitor the driveway until dark and come up then if we don't see anybody."

I worried about leaving the scene but didn't have a better plan. We were back in fifteen minutes, parked in the two-car pullout fifty yards from Feng's driveway, and began the stake-out. Even though it was unmarked, hardly anything says "cop" better than a gunmetal-gray Ford Crown Vic. Feng or anyone else would have to be blind not to spot us if they came by.

We sat for an hour and a half mostly talking about Harry's long and distinguished career. It got dark earlier on the east-facing hillside than on the bay stretched out below us.

Just as I thought we wouldn't have to wait much longer, a black Suburban raced up the street, pulled into the driveway, and a guy jumped out of the passenger side. He unlocked the padlock, slid the chain through the eye, and dragged it across the driveway. The driver pulled through, the guy pulled the chain back, pushed it through the eye, and padlocked it. He jumped in the truck and it roared up the driveway.

Harry said, "Well, I guess that answers some questions. You recognize anybody?"

"I couldn't see the driver but the guy who got out is *not* Feng. About the only thing we know for sure is there are at least two guys up there."

"Yeah, that's a bitch. Well, not much for it other than wait another half hour and then take a walk."

After the half hour passed, which seemed like a month, Harry said, "We might as well saddle up and go for a ride. If you've gotta piss, this is a good time to do it. You don't want a full bladder if we get in a tight spot."

He stepped out to follow his own advice. I followed suit. I slipped on my windbreaker and checked the extra clip in the pocket. Harry strapped on his old shoulder holster, attached an ammo pocket to his belt, and put on his own windbreaker. It said 'CBI' in big yellow letters across the back. He didn't want me mistaking him for a bad guy.

At the gate we listened for car sounds, didn't hear any, and stepped over the chain. We started up the driveway side by side and stayed that way until a switch back to the right. From there we could see the outline of the house against the skyline at the crest of a ridge. Harry whispered, "Let's step off into the brush on each side of the driveway. It's not much cover but it's a damn sight better than walking up the freeway. Like I said, 'I'm too damn old for this horsepucky.' I'm already winded and we've got a ways to go."

I was breathing fairly heavily too. I didn't know if it was from climbing the hill or anticipating what was ahead. "Okay, I'll cross the road and go up the other side. You can keep your head below the road-cut and shouldn't have to walk in the brush." He looked at the cut and gave me another thumbs up...he liked doing that. I stepped quickly across the drive and down the grade on the far side. Although the brush was thick next to the bank, it opened up a few feet farther in so I decided to take the easier path. We started up the hill toward the house as the last of the light faded in the west.

When I got close to the house, I saw it was built at the top of a ridge and appeared to have decks around three sides. The deck toward me would have a great view of the North Bay and Sausalito. I couldn't tell what was on the other side. The north end of the house was a four-car garage with a deck extension above it. All four doors were down and I couldn't see the Suburban. *Crap!* That meant there could be anywhere from the two guys we'd seen to a small army inside. Lights were on in the main house; unfortunately I was so far downhill all I could see were the ceilings. Fifty feet from the house, the driveway spread into a cul-de-sac and the brush and shrubs stopped. I saw Harry standing behind a big rhododendron bush looking at me. It was hard to see, but I could make him out describing a circle with his arms, pointing at himself, and pointing toward the south end of the house. He repeated the circle, pointed at me, and the north end by the garages. I gave him a thumbs up...two could play that game...and set off around the edge of the cul-de-sac.

It took forever to scrape through the shrubs and circle the house. When I made the top of the ridge, I could see the house was actually set into the ridge rather than straddling it. The west side was at ground level with an extensive patio rather than a deck. From the amount of light, the whole west wall must be picture windows and sliding glass doors. I crossed the ridge and started toward the house. I stayed outside the glow of the lights and kept bushes and trees between me and the windows. I worked my way within twenty feet of the patio and looked straight into the house. I didn't like what I saw.

A great room took up most of the north end of the house. It opened onto the patio on the west and to decks on the north and east. The room had floor-to-ceiling windows on both sides. A long table that would seat twelve or fourteen ran down the center of the room. Four guys were sitting at the table, two more in big leather chairs facing east, and two more standing at the south end of the room near a fireplace. One of the guys standing was Jon Feng. I spotted weapons everywhere: the coffee tables, the dining table, and even leaning in the corners. I saw assault rifles and full autos...the kind that killed Joe Riggs and almost got me. Feng was having an animated conversation with the other guy by the fireplace. I caught a movement out of the corner of my right eye, turned, and saw Harry Thornton slip behind an azalea bush thirty or forty feet from me. I was out of the light coming from the house. Harry was only in a shadow from the bush. I hoped nobody looked west.

Harry looked directly at me and slowly waved his hand. I acknowledged with my own wave. He made the look sign by forking his fingers and pointing at his eyes and toward the house. I looked back at the house. The occupants had moved around with two guys getting up from the table and joining Feng at the fireplace. One of them was the guy who'd been at the warehouse with Feng. His taped nose confirmed I'd caught him pretty hard. Funny what you think of at a time like this. I imagined the guy would like to kill me and wondered if he'd been the shooter at the Embassy Suites. Everyone was waving their arms and pointing without many smiles so these guys were either arguing about something or making plans. We'd watched for maybe two minutes when Harry signaled me to back off. He made the circle sign again and pointed east...the way we'd come. I waved to acknowledge and began to back up staying in the shadow.

I heard the sound of a sliding door and froze. Feng and Broken Beak came out on the patio and stood next to the low stone curb. I looked toward Harry and saw him on his knees behind the azalea. He was less than thirty feet from the two men. I was more like fifty feet and didn't want to move. I could hear their voices although I couldn't make out what they were saying.

It's hard to stand perfectly still for any length of time and I was starting to cramp up. I began imagining itches and bug bites and everything that made me want to move. I knew it was probably worse for Harry because he was so much closer. The minutes dragged until I saw a glow of headlights against the east windows and the sound of a car engine coming up the hill.

Feng and his hitter went back in the house and crossed the room to the east side. I backed away as quickly as I could, turned north, and made a wide swath around the house. I hoped Harry would do the same in the opposite direction.

It took fifteen minutes to get around the house and near the driveway where I crawled behind another bush and flattened before I turned to look back. A Mercedes sedan was pulled up facing down the driveway. Suddenly, three garage doors opened at the same time and, with the interior lights on I saw Jon Feng's Lexus and two black Suburbans in the garage bays. The whole crowd gathered around a guy in a business suit who was handing out papers. Some were carrying weapons. They talked for a few seconds and then split up with four guys getting in each Suburban. The suit continued to talk with Jon Feng for another minute, walked out, and got in the Mercedes. As he started down the driveway, the Suburbans backed out, turned, and followed. Feng walked back toward the door to the house, hit a couple of switches and two doors began closing. The door behind his Lexus stayed up. I couldn't see what he was doing but a minute or so later, I saw the lights go out upstairs and I saw him again as he got in the Lexus. He started the big sedan, pulled out of the garage, and closed the door behind him. When he reached the switchback, I stood and, taking a chance there wasn't anybody else in the house, yelled, "Harry—Where are you?"

I nearly jumped out of my skin when he answered. "Keep your voice down, dumb ass, I'm right here." He was about twenty feet from me.

"How the hell did you get there?"

"I was behind you all the way...I didn't want to go back the way I came because there's not much cover. I waited until you were in the trees and then followed you. Incidentally, for a guy who says he was a ranger, you make a lot of goddamn noise. It's no wonder you didn't know I was on your tail."

"So, what do you think's going on?"

"I don't have to think. I know—sort of anyway. These guys are splitting up and bugging out. I could hear Feng and the other guy on the patio. They were waiting for this last guy to get here with tickets and cash for everybody."

"*Jesus Christ*, Harry! We've got to get some cops to the airports."

"There's a problem. I don't know where they're going. I don't know when they're going and I don't know if they're trying to leave from SFO."

"*Shit!* What the hell do you know?"

Thornton bristled and I regretted saying it. He didn't say anything for a few seconds. "Look, Cort, I know you want to see this wrapped up and so do I. It isn't going to be easy. I heard them say the guy was bringing 'tickets', but I also heard the other guy say, 'So when does it sail?' and Feng said 'Don't worry about it, you'll have plenty of time to get there.' So, see what I mean? I don't know what they're up to."

"Okay, Harry, I'm sorry. Shouldn't we alert your guys and Martinez anyway?"

"Of course we should, and we will, but we've got to get back to the car to call it in—unless you brought your cell?"

"No, I left it in the car."

"Yeah, well, I did the same thing so let's get our ass down there and get the word out."

chapter

TWENTY-
EIGHT

We ran down the driveway and slowed as we approached the switchback. Feng's Lexus was outside the gate and he was affixing the chain. He finished the chore, got in, and sped off. We jogged down the last stretch of driveway, stepped across the chain, and sprinted to the car. We were both gasping for breath when we got in the car. Harry grabbed his cell from the console, hit a speed dial button, identified himself to the dispatcher on the other end, and issued orders to apprehend any or all of the vehicles we had seen at the house. We didn't have tag numbers for the Suburbans, but I had Jon Feng's. We assumed Jon's brother, Robert, was driving the Mercedes and its license would be in the Feng Worldwide Products records along with the Suburbans. Thornton put everything in motion.

He regained his breath and said, "I'll give Martinez a call and get her up to speed. The FBI is better equipped than us to watch the airports. We'll have to be lucky as hell to spot these assholes unless they use toll roads or go someplace where we have tag cameras. Even then, we'll be behind them at every turn. I'll try her cell—she's probably gone home for the day."

He pushed the speed dial but ended up with a voice mail recorder. He left a message recapping what we'd seen at the house. He told her what he'd set in motion and asked her to get her people on the airports. When he finished, he said, "We might as well pack it in for the night. I'll call the shack at the pad and tell 'em to get ready to head back to Sacramento."

Before he made the call, his cell chimed. He looked at the screen and said, "It's our favorite little fed..."

"Hey, Mariah, you got my message I see. Well, we got the house and the boat from Benoit when we talked to her; same time we got the restaurants I gave you. No, I decided to come over to Marin and check it out on my own. Oh, come on, Agent—John Nelson was a personal friend of mine. No, I haven't held anything back from you, c'mon, give me a break. You get anything on Jen Wang?"

Harry listened for several minutes and finally said, "I'm genuinely sorry to hear it, Mariah. I know how hard you guys work to prevent things like that from happening. I guess that's it for now, though, it'll just be another loose end till we can figure everything out."

Harry grinned at me as he said, "She accused me of sending her on a wild goose chase on those restaurant stakeouts...said we're trying to grab the glory."

"What'd she say about Wang?" I assumed it was bad from Harry's end of the conversation.

"Well, that's interesting. Wang wasn't in the office today and didn't answer her phone. They sent an agent to her apartment and nobody answered the door. True to their ways, they're sitting on their ass waiting on a warrant. They're still researching her file and digging into her background. It looks like Benoit was on to something —and you were right about Wang.

"Apparently, everything checked out back to about the tenth grade. Martinez said it gets funky before that. Supposedly, she transferred into Livermore Senior High School from Snoqualmie High in Seattle. However, when they went back further and tried to check it out, there aren't any records for her. The transfer forms look legit but there's no record of her in high school. When they figured that out, they ran her birth certificate and it's a fake. She didn't exist before she showed up in Livermore. They've already talked to some teachers and administrators at Livermore...most of 'em retired...who remember her. One thing they all seemed to agree on was she seemed *older* or more mature than the rest of the students. At the time, they chalked it up to being Asian because they're better students and more serious about school. I'm guessing she was already an adult; it's hard to tell an Asian woman's age."

Harry shifted positions behind the wheel and shrugged out of his shoulder holster. "She went to college at San Jose State and applied to the FBI while she was a senior. Before she was hired, they ran her fingerprints and there wasn't anything in the system. That's not unusual. Unless you've been arrested or applied for a license or bond, your prints won't be in the system. She's been in this office for a little over three years and, according to Martinez, has been a model employee. She's in one of those transitional positions where she does everything from filing and getting coffee to computer research. She told them she'd like to be a field agent but hasn't applied to Quantico for training. I guess the timing window is pretty tight for that and if she was serious, she needed to apply no later than this year. Martinez said all of her fitness reviews have been good although not outstanding. This is the first day she's ever missed work."

All I could do was shake my head. "How do you interpret all that, Harry?"

"I'd say she's a deep cover plant. I can't fault the feebs for missing it. Hell, we don't go back past high school either. If I were a betting man—and I am—I'd say the Chinese planted her and her records and are just now getting around to using her. If Nelson's theory's right, this idea of controlling the world oil market is probably a big enough deal for them to activate her. They needed to know what the feds were doing and I'll bet they alerted her to watch for Nelson because he was the local guy when Feng Li was rubbed out. Anything that would bring him back to San Francisco might be of interest to them."

"So, you think she was on him as soon as he signed into the office and, literally, tuned in to what he told me?"

"Yep, that's what I think."

"And, she also listened in when you and I met with them?"

"Yes, again…and now she's in the wind. She's done as much as she could here. They'll probably give her a new identity and put her someplace else."

"How'll she get past the finger print issue if she tries to go someplace else?"

"Oh, there are ways to do that. Hell, they can use plastic peels of somebody else. You know there are a billion Chinese. They'll literally transplant the peels onto her fingers; you can't see 'em with the naked eye. If they want to put her in another job or even a local cop shop someplace, they can do it. More likely, they'll put her someplace like Singapore or Vancouver…out of the US."

"Jesus, that's scary."

"If it's scary for you, how the hell do you think we feel? Remember Johnny Carson's first TV show? It was called *Who Do You Trust* and that's it in a nutshell. I don't trust anybody and this sure as hell isn't a comedy!"

***

Harry's chopper had us back in Sacramento in an hour. He drove me to the parking garage where I retrieved the Mustang and left for Berkeley. Open roads, light traffic, and exceeding the speed limit had me at the Bancroft at 10:00 p.m. I grabbed a bottle of Anchor Steam, called Lindsey, and told her the latest. She wanted to know if I was all right and when I'd be home. I didn't have an answer. I said I'd be there as soon as I could but couldn't promise anything. She wasn't happy with that. As we talked, I opened a bottle of Rodney Strong Russian River Pinot Noir and set it on the counter to breathe.

I ran a bath and decided to shave while the tub was filling. The face staring at me from the mirror looked older than the one I had seen last week. Being shot at and having people killed around you could do that. I wondered if the love of a younger woman, like Linds, would reverse the aging process. I had to hope so.

I finished shaving along with the beer, then got a wine glass and the Rodney Strong. I set them on the edge of the tub, climbed in, and sank down to my chin. I stayed that way for several minutes letting the warmth seep into my body. After a while I sat up, poured a glass of the wine, sipped it, and let out an audible sigh. That was good stuff. I was amazed to find it in the Bancroft's room stock.

It took two glasses of the pinot and a couple of warm ups to finish my bath. I ran the shower and stepped in for a cool rinse. By the time I'd toweled off and returned to the bedroom, it was almost 11:30 p.m. I put the cork in the bottle...although I considered finishing it...and crawled in. It'd been a long day and, unfortunately, tomorrow wasn't shaping up to be much shorter.

chapter

TWENTY-NINE

I was amazed when I awakened at 8:15 a.m. It was the latest I'd slept in months...maybe years. Lindsey and I had gotten up lots later—always on purpose. Just as sex is a great sleeping pill, it's also a great form of exercise...a form Lindsey particularly enjoyed on weekend mornings. Anyway, I was surprised at the hour.

I checked the Rodney Strong and it was only down the two glasses from last night. Although, I subscribe to Hedges' definition of passed out—You're not passed out if you're in your own bed—it was still good to check the wine level. I hadn't been passed out.

I slipped into the last pair of clean pants I'd brought, pulled on a golf shirt, and headed downstairs.

The little cutie, Miley, from my first stay at the Bancroft was working the breakfast room and smiled as I walked in. "Welcome back, Mr. Scott. Are you becoming a regular guest with us?"

"Well, as much as I like it here, I hope not. Are there any newspapers around?"

She glanced around the room. "That's strange. There are always papers in here. I don't know why there aren't any on the tables. I'll get one from the front desk for you."

"Thanks, Miley." She must have been all of twenty-one.

The FBI shootings were second section news and the stories repeated what Martinez had said yesterday. I pulled the business section and was greeted with a headline shouting *Oil Shale Deposits May Equal Saudi Reserves.* I began reading the article and was glad to see the Secretary of Interior lauding the efforts of the USGS in conducting a resource evaluation of the US oil shale reserves. The Secretary was quoted at great length about how important it was for Interior to get a handle on what we had and how we could develop it. He said there was more oil potential just in Colorado than in all of Saudi Arabia's proven oil fields. It sounded like good news; maybe we we're getting our act together after all. The Secretary said a lot of work remained in the evaluation, but funding was very short. Hank, who was quoted in several paragraphs, indicated the evaluation could take another three to five years. He said he was sure America was in the forefront of research and development. One quote stood out, "The US will lead the world in researching this important resource and its development will usher in a new era of American energy independence." It didn't sound like the Secretary *or* Hank had a clue about Feng's operation.

I gulped my coffee and devoured an apple fritter. I needed to let Hank know everything I'd found out. If I could get him fired up, he might push the Secretary on the resource evaluation. I also needed to check in with Harry Thornton and, as much as I dreaded it, to talk to Agent-in-Charge, Mariah Martinez. I had to find out if she was going to keep me in the loop and, although I knew she would reject it, offer my help.

I decided to start with Thornton because what he did might affect my day. "Hey, Harry, what's up? Got anything new this morning?"

Harry sounded exasperated. "Not a frazzling thing—I don't understand this at all. We should've heard something or spotted somebody by now. I can't believe all those assholes have run in a hole someplace and are waiting us out. You heard anything?"

"No, nothing on this end, either. Did you read the paper this morning, the business section?"

"Yeah, I read the article about oil shale. It doesn't sound like the Energy Department is too heated up over it...if you'll pardon the pun."

"Jesus, Harry...that's *bad*. The guy from Denver they're quoting, Hank Francis, is my friend and the guy who got me involved in this case. I need to give him a call and tell him John Nelson's theory. He might be able to push a lot harder and speed up the process. It's worth a shot, I think. I'm going to call Martinez too. I'll offer to help although what I really want is to be kept in the loop."

Thornton heaved a deep sigh. "All you're going to do is get a good ass-eating. But, what the hell do I know? Maybe she can find something for you to do."

"Thanks for the encouragement. Are *you* going to keep me hooked up? I feel like I'm flying blind out here."

"Yeah, I'll let you know if anything breaks."

"Okay, thanks. I'll talk to you later."

I disconnected from Harry and punched in Martinez' number. An admin answered, "Agent-in-Charge's office...how may I help you?"

I told her who I was and that I needed to talk to Agent Martinez. The admin told me to hold on. Martinez came on the line. "You've got some nerve, Scott! All we were trying to do was protect you. You take off like a goddamn thief. I had to spend several man-hours tracking your ass. We didn't know if you'd taken off on your own or if you'd fucked up and let Feng grab you. *Goddamn it!* The least you could've done is call me. You could've just said you didn't want to be there and we would've let you do whatever the hell you wanted!"

I let her vent and admired her range of profanities until her voice went back down the scale and it sounded like she might listen. "Okay, Mariah, I'm sorry. You're right—I should've let you know what I was doing. At the time, it felt like you were going to check me in, pick me up the next morning, and put me on a plane back to Denver. I didn't want to do that. I want to be in on the end of this deal. I want to be there when we get Feng. I want to help in any way I can. If you'll keep me up to speed, I promise I won't get in your way."

"We don't *want*, or more importantly, *need* your help, Scott. Look, I can understand how you're feeling so I'll do this much for you. If you want to stay around, maybe even work with Thornton, I'll stay in contact. If we catch anybody, I'll let you watch the interrogations. You might be able to add something to our line of questioning that'll help us. That's as far as it goes. I don't want you cowboyin' around on your own. Is that perfectly clear?"

"It's crystal clear. Now that we're straight, I can start using my cell phone again and you can reach me on it. Here's the number—"

"Oh, we've got your number, Scott—in more ways than one." On that happy note I hung up and called Hank.

I told him I'd read the oil shale article and he needed to be caught up on what I'd found out. I told him Martie's death was a murder and Judy Benoit was involved, although not intentionally. I explained Judy's background and early involvement in environmental causes and her association with ELF; about Gail Porter and how Judy's and Gail's good intentions had been hijacked by Jon Feng. Finally, I laid out John Nelson's theory. I brought it home by saying if Nelson was right, the primary goal of the Chinese was to slow down or even halt the US efforts on oil shale. Hank was a good listener and didn't interrupt or ask any questions until I'd finished.

Hank sounded stunned. "Cort, do you believe it's all true? You met with this John Nelson before he was murdered—did he seem credible to you?"

"Absolutely, this guy was as straight as they come. He didn't have an axe to grind about energy or oil shale; he just wanted to solve a twenty-year-old bombing. I probably didn't make it clear enough that Judy Benoit corroborates the story. She knew Feng was intent on slowing down the process although she believed it was because of concern for the environment. She had no clue this was a Chinese deep cover spy operation and they'd do anything, including murder, to pull it off."

"I feel sorry for Judy. Is she going to be charged with anything?"

"I don't know. There's a good chance she will. On the other hand, she's cooperating now and if Feng gets caught, she might be able to cut a deal."

"You're sure she wasn't directly involved in Martie's death?"

"For right now, I just have her word on it. But, if you'd been sitting in that interrogation room yesterday, seen her face, and heard her story, I think you'd believe her. I do."

"I'm glad of that, at least. What's the next step?"

I had to take a deep breath for what I needed to say next... this was definitely above my pay grade. "Hank, you need to go to the Director of the USGS and tell the whole story. Assuming you can convince him, the two of you need an emergency meeting with the Secretaries of Energy and Interior. You need to make a case for fast tracking your research. There's a damn good chance the Chinese already have a viable process."

"*Jesus*, why don't you just ask me to reverse climate change and reinvent the wheel while I'm at it?"

I said, "Think about it, Hank, it might already be too late. However, if you *don't* try, the Chinese win big time. The US will be a second class power within twenty years." There was a lengthy silence.

"You're right—I've got to get off my ass and change gears. What are you going to do now?"

"Well, you can take me off the clock as far as working for you. I'm going to keep after Feng, though. The son-of-a-bitch damned near canceled my ticket, so now it's personal. I want to see his ass in jail or, better yet, shot off and I wouldn't mind doing it myself."

"That doesn't sound like you. You've never been into violence."

"Things change, pards. I'm not the same guy I was two or three years ago. Having your girlfriend murdered and people trying to kill you changes your outlook."

"I'm not sure it's for the better. Of course, it didn't happen to me so I can't judge. Whatever you do, try to be careful; it sounds like a pretty bad bunch you're dealing with."

"A *bad bunch* doesn't half describe these bastards." I was looking forward to running them down, particularly Jon Feng.

chapter

THIRTY

I began listing every name I thought was associated with the case. It was time to reassess my approach; I needed a lead to help me find Jon Feng. The list got lengthy when I included Hank, his staff, all the FBI people, and even Tom Montgomery and Lindsey. I studied it and began crossing off everyone with no possible connection...like John Nelson and Joe Riggs...and Tom and Linds, still...how could I cross off names like Walsh and Petersen...or even Mariah Martinez?

It took an hour to get the list narrowed to people I couldn't rule out. The loose ends were Gail Porter, Jen Wang, and whoever "Bennie" turned out to be. I only had Judy Benoit's word that "Bennie" even existed. And why would he have been invited to Gail Porter's if she knew he was involved in the more violent actions of the ELF and ECF crowd? I knew the cops were trying to locate Porter and the FBI was after Wang. That left Bennie for me.

I needed Thornton to set up another meeting with Judy Benoit. Unless somebody found Porter, Benoit was my only connection to Bennie. I called Harry again. He wasn't in so I left a message to call me back.

Back in the Bancroft's business center, I googled ECF and got a few hits, although none of them had anything like a membership roster. Some articles mentioned people who were suspected of being involved with the ECF. Gail Porter's name kept coming up but there was no mention of Bennie or Jon Feng. I tried ELF and got several thousand hits. This was going to take some time considering my limited computer skills. One of my options was Advanced Search so I tried ELF and Bennie in the search box.

Bingo!

The first hit was a newspaper article from the *Seattle Post Intelligencer* about a violent 1999 confrontation between suspected ELF members and a logging company over timberlands adjacent to Olympic National Park. The purported leader of the protestors was listed as Bennie Weinman. The article was in-depth about the existence of a shadowy activist group called the Earth Liberation Front or ELF who organized protests by hacking into computers and sending untraceable emails and faxes. The group claimed no central organization, membership lists, officers, or anything else. The only reason Bennie Weinman was pegged as the leader was because he reportedly signed a fax that had been sent to the area newspapers, with a copy nailed to a tree where the proposed road was going to be cut into the forest.

ELF had put out homemade tack strips, poured sugar in the fuel tanks of a Cat and a grader and, "said" they'd spiked over a hundred trees in the area to be logged. The logging company confirmed the tack strips and that their equipment had been damaged. They couldn't confirm any trees had been spiked. The local cops said they didn't know who Bennie Weinman was or where he might be found. The logging company didn't think the cops were interested in finding out who was responsible. The cops said they didn't have any information.

I tried googling Bennie Weinman and Ben Weinman and, finally, just Weinman. I got lots of hits but other than a cross reference to the ELF logging company confrontation, nothing specific to Bennie Weinman popped out. This was looking like a dead end.

My cell chimed; Harry Thornton was on the other end. "You get plastered last night?"

"Morning to you, too, Harry...no, I just had enough to really get a good night's sleep. You know, if you're in your own bed, you're not passed out."

Thornton laughed. "I can use that! What can I do for you?"

"I need to talk to Judy Benoit again and I'd like to do it privately—not in the cop shop."

"What're you doing—going independent on me?"

"Nah, I just think she might talk more in a different setting. She finally started opening up a little yesterday when you and Walton were out of the room."

"We can set something up. When do you want to see her?"

"As soon as possible, I'm going to go at this from another direction. Nobody's looking for this Bennie guy Benoit talked about. You guys are looking for Porter and the feebs are looking for Jen Wang. Everybody is looking for Feng. I need to figure out if Benoit knows anything that can lead me to Bennie, whoever the hell he is. If she does, I might get a handle on Feng, too."

"That makes good sense. Walton told me this morning Benoit wants to go back to Berkeley. She's going stir-crazy sitting around in our safe house. I think we should let her do it. We've had her place under surveillance twenty-four-seven and haven't seen shit. We'd put an officer with her on a full-time basis and keep up the watch outside too. Let's do this—we'll have Walton and another CHP drive her down as soon as she can pack up. They ought to be there by 1:30 or 2:00 p.m. You plan to drop in at, say, 2:30 p.m. and we'll have her companion take a walk. You can talk to her as long as you want."

The plan and the timing sounded good. "That's great, Harry. I appreciate it; I'll keep you up to speed on what I find out."

I closed out the Google searches, went back to my room, and dressed for a run. I needed to get some exercise and hoped to clear my mind while I was at it. I wasn't looking forward to having to question Judy again.

chapter

THIRTY-ONE

I pulled up in front of Judy's place and saw a marked CHP cruiser out front. It was a good way to let Feng know—if he was watching—that Judy was being guarded. It took a moment, but I also spotted an unmarked Ford down the street near the park. That would be the backup. I rang Judy's buzzer.

An electronically distorted voice said, "Yes?" It took a moment, but I recognized the voice as Bobbi Walton, the CHP female officer who was looking after Judy.

"Cort Scott, Bobbi. I have an appointment with Judy."

"She's expecting you. Come on up." The lock buzzed and I went up to Benoit's apartment. The door opened on the chain and Bobbi Walton's face appeared; she looked at me and said, "Hang on." She took the chain off, opened the door, and announced, "We got here about half an hour ago and Judy's trying to decompress. She's lying down for a quick nap. Come in and have a seat."

A couple of minutes later, the bedroom door opened and Judy walked out. She'd lost weight in just the day since I had seen her. Her eyes were red rimmed and had noticeable bags under each one. She wasn't wearing makeup and her skin was pale. She looked like someone with a lot on their mind and who hadn't been sleeping. "Hi, Judy, it's good to see you home and I'll bet you're glad to be here."

She smiled thinly and nodded. "I *am* glad to be back. I know it's only been three days but it seems like forever."

Bobbi Walton cleared her throat. "Mr. Thornton asked me to leave you two alone for as long as you need. We've checked the house and there's no one here who doesn't belong. The only other entrance is the emergency fire door on the back side of the building and it's a bar handle, open-out style. I'll be in the cruiser out front. The other officer who rode down is taking a walk in the park and we have another car in the neighborhood."

I smiled. "Yeah, I spotted your *unmarked* Ford parked down the street."

Walton said, "I don't know if *unmarked* is appropriate...those big Fords stand out like a sore thumb."

I put the door chain in place after she stepped out. Judy sank into the love seat. She looked exhausted.

"Judy, you look like hell. Are you getting any sleep?"

"I feel like hell. I haven't slept in three nights. I haven't eaten a full meal either. I know I wasn't in custody although it felt like I was. Bobbi Walton is nice enough, but she's still a cop. She's got a job to do which is to watch me. I think she'd be a lot happier writing speeding tickets somewhere."

"Most cops would like to be doing something—almost anything really—rather than just sitting around."

"Mr. Thornton said you wanted to talk to me some more. What about?"

"I've been trying to think this through and come up with things that will give me a lead on tracking down Feng. The one thing I keep coming back to is Bennie. You said you saw him in

Colorado with Feng and again at the dinner at Gail Porter's house after you returned here."

"That's right."

"Okay, I need you to think back carefully and tell me if you can connect Bennie to anyplace or anybody we can use to track him."

"We must be on the same wave length; I've been trying to think through all of that too. I'm just not sure I know enough to help."

"Whatever you have will be a help."

She looked grateful, took a deep breath, and said, "I'm pretty sure Bennie was a member of ELF before he became radicalized and started up with the ECF." That jibed with what I'd found on the internet. "I'd never met him before Colorado although I'm pretty sure I'd heard his name. I told you I was sort of a fringe ELF member way back when. I was mostly involved in protests about logging. One of the women I met was from Seattle and I'm pretty sure she mentioned a guy named Bennie who'd organized an action in Washington state. She said he was adamant about monkey wrenching some equipment, even though the company they were protesting said they'd like to talk about the problem. She told me he said, 'Talk is cheap; they need to understand we're serious.' I hadn't put two and two together until yesterday when it all came back to me."

I still needed a tighter connection between Feng to Bennie. "When you met them in Colorado, who was making the decisions?"

She was quiet for a few seconds. "You know, that's a good question. I thought it was Bennie—he wanted to put the fire bomb on the pickup, but he kept looking at Jon Feng and sort of, you know, seeking his approval."

"Did Feng ever say anything about doing other ELF or ECF stuff with Bennie?"

"No, though I know he'd been giving money to ECF. He and Bennie talked about it when we were at Gail's—God, I wish I could remember everything from that night... we had several drinks—"

I knew how that worked so I didn't press her too hard. "Is there any chance Bennie lives in Colorado?"

Judy sat up straight and her eyes got wide. "*Oh my God*, I think he might! I remember Jon said, 'Did you get a round trip ticket this time?' He wouldn't need a round trip ticket if he lived here."

That got my attention. "That could be big, Judy. Think hard, do you have *any* clue where he might live?"

She knitted her brow in concentration. "I don't remember anything specifically— I wonder about Denver. He said he had *business* there, but I never heard him mention Denver again."

"Was there anyone else with you when you met Feng and Bennie?"

"Randy Joyce, one of the other USGS field mappers, was there earlier in the evening. He had a couple of beers and left. He said he was going to another bar."

That brought me up short. Joyce had never mentioned meeting any of these people, especially Feng. "What happened after Randy left?"

"They asked lots of questions about how long we would work in one area; where all the information went; who did the compilations and wrote the reports...stuff like that."

"What did you tell them?"

"Well, probably too much—I answered all their questions."

I was getting a bad feeling about something. "Judy, what did you tell them about where the information went and who did the reports?"

She looked at me and started to shake. Her voice broke and she stuttered out, "*Oh, God*, I told them everything went to the Federal Center in Lakewood; that Randy Joyce and Rick Russell compiled all the field studies and Hank wrote the final report. *Oh, my God*, you don't think they would go after them, do you?"

I thought about lying to her but decided not to. "Yes, I think they might. They'll do anything to keep the USGS from getting the resource evaluation done. From what John Nelson told me, they only need to delay it by a year or so. An *action* at the Fed Center would probably do that—particularly if it took out one or more of the principals."

Judy Benoit's shoulders sagged. She dropped her face in her hands and broke down in heavy, wrenching sobs.

I got her a glass of water. "I've got to make some calls, Judy. I need to talk to Hank and a friend of mine who's a Denver cop. I know it'll be tough, but you need to get some rest, maybe eat something, and then you need to think about everything you ever saw or heard from Feng. Call me with anything, can you do that?"

She nodded and with a firmer voice said, "Yes, I'll try. Please hurry—you need to warn Hank—he's a good guy. I don't know if I could take it if something happened to him—something I might have caused."

I raced downstairs and waved at Walton. She jumped out of the cruiser and asked, "What's up?"

"You need to get up there and—I don't know—*comfort* her, I guess. She remembered more stuff about Feng and this guy Bennie. I need to make some calls to Denver. She's pretty shook up right now, but she'll be okay. Try and get her to eat something and maybe get some sleep, okay?"

"Sure, I'll try...she's not been much on either of those things. You need to talk to Thornton?"

"I don't have time right now. I'll bring him up to speed as soon as I can. You guys need to keep a close eye on her. Feng is still out there and he'd like to kill her, Porter, and me...not necessarily in that order."

"Don't worry, Mr. Scott, we'll take care of her."

"Thanks, I'm depending on it."

chapter

THIRTY-TWO

I should've called from my cell but needed to sort out what to tell Hank, so I drove back to the Bancroft. I got a bottle of water, sat in the club chair, and dialed Hank. His omnipresent gatekeeper, Jamie Pearson, answered and said he was in a meeting. *"Goddamn it*, Jamie—I don't care if he's having a vasectomy—this is a fucking emergency! Get him out of the goddamn meeting—I mean it—this is life or death and I'm talking about Hank's!"

She got the message. "Yes, sir, Mr. Scott—I'll connect you immediately."

I still waited for half a minute before I heard a click and Hank came on the line. "Jesus, Cort, what the hell did you say to Jamie? She said somebody's trying to kill me and you need to talk to me."

"She might not be too far off, Hank. Look, I've just had another talk with Judy Benoit and she told me some stuff that scares the shit out of me. I think there's a good chance some people will be coming after the oil shale resource evaluation reports—or you personally. Three people who've gotten in the way are dead and these assholes won't hesitate for one second to kill more if that's what it takes to stop the report. I know you have security at the Fed Center, but these guys had someone inside the FBI office in San Francisco. If they can do that, they can get someone past the rent-a-cop at your front gate. If they get in your offices, they'll destroy everything you've got. And failing that, they'll come after you. Unfortunately, Judy gave them your name—and Rick's and Randy's as well. You need to lock down your office and take some real care on how you travel around. I'll call the FBI boss in San Francisco and see if their Denver office can give you guys some protection. I'll also call Tom Montgomery to see if there's anything he can do. Have you started trying to speed up the evaluation? Have you set up any meetings with your bosses?"

There was a long pause before I heard Hank exhale. "That's a lot of heavy duty stuff, Cort. I hope it's all BS, but I guess we can't take that chance. We've got a meeting day after tomorrow with the director—he's coming here—and we'll present an outline of what you've told me. I've briefed him and he's on board. We're meeting the Secretary of Interior in D.C. next Monday. Are you really sure we're in personal danger? That just doesn't sound possible."

"I wouldn't have told you if I didn't believe it. Feng's gang has split up and they're arranging transportation out of here. They're in the wind but haven't completed their job yet. That job is to stop your report. You need to be goddamn careful and you need to protect your family too. Is there any way you can get Sally and the boys out of town for a while?"

I could almost see a smile on Hank's face. "I guess we've been due a little luck in this mess sometime. Sally and the boys are in Europe. They left yesterday and will be gone for almost three weeks… I'm batching."

"That's super—pack up your stuff and move into a motel until we get these assholes sorted!"

"I can do that. I'll have Jamie get me a room at…"

"Don't say it! Sorry, didn't mean to yell. If I were you, I'd make my own arrangements and not tell *anybody* where you're staying. Use your cell phone for all your calls and let me know when you're settled."

"Christ, you're serious about this, aren't you?"

"Serious as a goddamn heart attack, buddy. I'll be in touch as soon as I can."

***

I dialed Tom. "It's me. Is there anything you can do, officially or not, to put a watch on Hank Francis?"

I didn't get any of the usual Tom Montgomery hard time. "Nothing official, but I know some people. Why?"

"Because Feng and company may try to sabotage his offices at the Fed Center or if they can't get that done, go after him."

"That sounds like a fed problem, but they move pretty slowly. I'll call the Jeffco sheriff and see what we can set up. What's happening on your end?"

I filled him in on the last twenty-four hours and on my talk with Judy Benoit.

"You've been busy. You have a reason to think the assholes are headed this way?"

"I don't have hard evidence. They're sure as hell scattering, plus, there's some guy named Bennie who plays a part in this and I think he lives in Colorado. His name might be Bennie Weinman, although I don't know what alias he might be using. He was definitely involved in Martie Remington's murder and burning up a USGS truck. What I *don't* know is whether he's working for the Chinese or gone off the deep end about environmental stuff. In any case, regardless of his motives, he's dangerous."

"Is he in the Denver area?"

"I don't know. He was in Denver last summer and was probably present at Remington's murder. He could be a camper or a nature freak or anything else. I doubt if he's leaving any traces wherever he is."

"That's not a whole lot to go on. I'll put it in the system and see what turns up. When're you coming back?"

"If you'd asked me this morning, I'd have said I didn't have a clue. Now, I think as soon as I can catch a flight. I keep thinking I need to be here for a chance to catch Feng; but if I'm there, I can help keep an eye on Hank."

"Okay, I'll do what I can. Check with me when you get in…it doesn't make any difference what time."

"Thanks, Tom."

United had a 4:50 p.m. flight out of SFO that would put me in Denver at 8 p.m. That was as close as I could cut it. I called Hertz in San Francisco and told them I'd be dropping their car off at SFO. That caused an argument about drop off fees, so I said, "I don't care—bill me" and hung up. Too bad the late shift agent wasn't on duty—she would've let me off the hook.

Next on the list was Mariah Martinez. "Hello, Mariah, it's Cort Scott."

"What can I do for you now?" It was the kind of greeting I'd expected.

"It's probably more about what I can do for you—I'm catching a plane to Denver this afternoon. I'm getting out of your hair."

"Well, well, well—that *is* good news, *Mr.* Scott. Not that we haven't enjoyed your company, it just seems trouble follows you around. Right now we don't need any more trouble." She didn't bother to keep the happiness out of her voice.

"Before I go, I was wondering if you had any news on any of Feng's gang…or about Gail Porter."

"No, we don't have anything new for you. We're maintaining surveillance and have activated facial recognition software at all California airports with that capability. We've also alerted all the other transportation centers. So far we haven't spotted any of the suspects. I don't know anything about Porter; Thornton hasn't called."

"Well, thanks, I guess. Since you've acknowledged I'm *involved* in this, I'd appreciate it if you'd let me know if anything breaks."

"Scott, if you're really leaving us, I'll be more than happy to *personally* inform you of any developments. Have a safe trip back." I didn't hear her laugh when she broke the connection, but she was happy I was leaving.

I had time for one last call. "Hi, Judy, it's Cort. I'm going back to Denver this afternoon. Call me if you think of anything, okay?"

"I wish you weren't leaving. I feel like, uh—I don't know—I feel safe around you."

"Thanks for that, but you'll be fine with all the cops around you. They aren't going to leave until this deal gets resolved."

"Thank you for saving my life, Cort." Her voice broke.

"I don't think I ever saved your life. I might have made it more dangerous for you by showing up here."

"There are more ways than one to save a life. I didn't know what was going to happen with Jon Feng and when he threatened to frame me for Martie's death, I was terrified. I was still scared when you showed up. I know now you've helped me—you really have saved my life."

I hung up hoping I could save everybody else's, too...including mine.

chapter

THIRTY-THREE

I threw my clothes in the Renoir travel bag, stuffed papers in my briefcase, put my gun in its travel case, and checked out. It was a quick trip to SFO. I dropped the Mustang at Hertz and caught their shuttle to the main terminal.

After checking my gun with United's security, I made it to the departure gate with forty-five minutes to spare. I used the time to buy a loaf of San Francisco sourdough bread and call Lindsey.

"Hey, it's me—the bread man."

"What's that supposed to mean? Gee, it's good to hear your voice."

"It means I'm headed home and bringing fresh bread—San Francisco sourdough to be exact. I'm wondering about the chances of being picked up by a lady cop?"

"Pretty damned good, I'd say! Do you want me to wear a uniform with a gun belt and handcuffs?"

"Well, maybe not to pick me up, although it might be fun for later."

"You got it—what time do you get in?"

"Scheduled at 7:58 p.m.—see you then?"

"Absolutely, I'll be outside door 410 at the curbside pickup."

"Perfect, see you in a little while."

My flight was announced just as I broke the connection. I was amazed at the number of Chinese on the flight. I did a double take at every man who came down the aisle. Each one looked like Jon Feng.

***

Lindsey's Edge was parked in front of the 410 exit door. She hopped out as I emerged—she wasn't wearing a uniform. "Hi, stranger, welcome home!" She hugged me and we kissed for a long time. It felt good.

Lindsey kept glancing at me and finally said, "You look beat up. It must've been a tough couple of days."

I was feeling it. "I'm not used to being shot at and having people killed next to me. I think I'm getting paranoid—every Chinese guy on the flight looked like an agent who wanted to kill me."

"That doesn't sound like you. What happens now?"

"After we have a glass of wine, I need to check in with Tom. I have to get a plan together for protecting Hank."

"I can help with the glass of wine. I opened a bottle of Chateau Ste. Michelle dry Riesling before I left. It's in the ice bucket."

"You're all right no matter what anybody else says."

***

I dialed Tom's cell. "Yeah, I'm here. You just get in?" Tom didn't make small talk.

"Just got home; I'm sipping my first glass of wine."

"Took you long enough to call. We've got some intel for you."

"Who are *we?*"

"Came from Harry Thornton...he got it from some FBI woman name of Maria Martinez, I think."

"It's Mariah—like the singer."

"Whatever...anyway, turns out the TSA cameras at DIA may have picked up Feng. He—"

"*You mean he's in Denver?*"

"It's not an absolute. They use face recognition software and got a hit on a guy getting off a plane from Oakland. Thornton said San Francisco has the technology but Oakland doesn't, so they didn't pick him up out there."

"When did they get the hit?"

"About 11:30 a.m. this morning."

"*Shit!* The FBI would've known about it before I left. Why didn't Martinez tell me when I asked?"

"Take a drink—this stuff doesn't work in real time. The computers take the live feed, digitize it, and play it back through the software program. It takes a few hours and the computers are processing hundreds of cameras, to boot. Apparently, they didn't have the ID until after you took off."

"I get it. So there was no way to put a tail on him or anything; we just know he's here, that right?"

"Yep, that's it. The local FBI guys ran the car rentals and taxis but don't have any record of him, so he was picked up or used a shuttle or a limo service. They're checking the limos now."

"I'd bet on somebody picking him up."

"So would I."

"You do anything about Hank?"

"Some—I talked to the Jeffco sheriff and they'll put a uniform on the gate at the Fed Center and an unmarked on his house."

"If he did what I told him, they can pull the unmarked. I told him to get a motel room and not tell anyone where he was staying. He's going to call me when he's situated."

"That's all I've got. Keep in touch."

I looked up Hank's cell number and was relieved when he answered. "Hey, Hank, it's Cort. I just got home and thought I'd—"

"Cort, we've got a problem."

"What kind of problem?"

"Somebody's trying to hack our computers at the Fed Center."

"How do you know that?"

"We've got some really sophisticated software monitoring our systems and it alerts us when it reads an attack. Randy told me he got an alarm; someone's trying to break in."

"Is there any way to know where it's coming from? Or, even better, who it is?"

"No, unfortunately, it's a one-way street at the moment. We just know somebody's trying to break in. So far, they haven't made it."

"I'll bet it's the MSS."

"Who's the MSS?"

"The Chinese equivalent of the CIA."

"*Oh, shit!* Are you kidding me?"

"*Oh, shit*—for sure. And I'm not kidding, these guys play for keeps. Where are you staying?"

"The Ramada Renaissance."

"Okay, I just got off the horn with Tom Montgomery. Jeffco will have a uniform on the Fed Center gate tomorrow. They've got somebody watching your house right now, but I'll get 'em to pull that one. Hank, I don't want to worry you anymore than you already are...but there's something else. Montgomery thinks Jon Feng may be in Denver. If that's true, he's going to try something. It might be your data or maybe you. Chances are he's behind this computer attack and if it doesn't work, he'll go to Plan B—and that's you."

Hank was quiet for several seconds. "I don't think anyone can break into our computers and we're transferring everything into special lock box files and wiping the mainframe. I guess we'd better make arrangements to combat Plan B."

I didn't understand the computer jargon, but I was part of Plan B. "I'll be there tomorrow morning and haul you to work myself. What room are you in?"

He told me his room number and I agreed to knock on his door at 7:15 a.m. I called Tom back and he promised to coordinate the protection detail with Jeffco. Finally, I asked for one more favor, "Can you get me a meeting with the local FBI agent-in-charge...the sooner the better?"

"Probably...I'll call you tomorrow morning with a time and place."

"Thanks, Tom, I'll talk to you tomorrow."

I hung up, sat for a minute, and walked out to the deck. Lindsey smiled and said, "You look like you could use a little R&R."

"Yeah, I'm beat, sweetheart. I don't know if I can put all of this together or not. I keep thinking about how many moving parts there are."

"Would it help to lay it out, in some kind of order, for me? I'm a good listener, you know?"

I thought about that for a few seconds and decided to do it. Everything had been happening so fast; I needed to slow it down. "You know what...that might be just the ticket. I'll get another bottle of wine. I'll talk—you listen, and then tell me what you think."

Linds fetched a carafe of ice water while I picked out a good Rioja.

chapter

THIRTY-FOUR

From start to finish, it took an hour to tell the whole story. Lindsey stood and said, "Okay, I'm going to use the bathroom and then I've got some questions."

When she returned, she reached over and took my hand. "Cort, I'm afraid for you. The most terrifying thing, to me, is the stuff John Nelson told you about the motive. Maybe not the motive per se, but more what they're willing to do to achieve the objective. I mean, how long did they have this Jen Wang in deep cover? How many more are there just like her?

"The next thing is the relationship between this Bennie guy and Jon Feng. I don't get how Bennie goes from being a tree hugger to being a murderer. That seems like a big leap and not one some greenie activist would take. There's got to be something else here we're not seeing."

I said, "Yeah, I know—it doesn't make a lot of sense."

"Do you have a physical description of Bennie?"

I had to think about that for a while. I didn't. I'd never thought to ask Judy Benoit. "That's a good question and the answer is…I don't. What time is it, anyway?"

"About 9:40 p.m. Why?"

"That's 8:40 in California. I'm going to call Judy and ask her to describe Bennie."

We went into my office and dialed her number. "Hi, Judy, it's Cort Scott. I'm sorry for calling this late. Something's come up and I need to ask you a question." Lindsey strolled into my office and sat in one of the recliners. I put the phone on speaker and leaned back in my chair.

Judy sounded tired. "No problem…it's only 8:45 here. What do you need?"

"Can you give me a physical description of Bennie? I don't think we asked you."

She didn't say anything for a while as if she was collecting her thoughts. "I'd say he's pretty average in most respects. He's probably about five feet ten with a medium build. He looks very athletic or strong and I'd guess his weight at maybe one-seventy or so. He has very black hair and kind of an olive complexion. I think his eyes are either brown or greenish. He wears his hair long and, the times I saw him, in a ponytail."

I was running through racial and ethnic profiles in my mind. So far, he could be Jewish or middle-eastern or Native American or Mexican. The name Weinman kept sticking in my brain. "Judy, do you think he's Jewish? There's some reason to believe his last name might be Weinman."

She was thinking again. "I don't know if I'd describe him as Jewish-looking—whatever that means. He has kind of a round face with more of a—oh, I don't know how to describe it, maybe, uh—I would almost say, an Oriental look especially around the eyes. *Oh my God*, do you think he could be part Chinese?"

My pulse rate increased and my brain started down a new sorting process. "You tell me, Judy, do *you* think he could be Chinese? You've seen him—I haven't."

"There's something else...his beard and moustache: they're a little thin. He doesn't wear a full beard, it's more like, you know, like he's gone a few days without shaving. It's kinda wispy or something. Isn't that an Oriental trait?"

How the hell should I know? "I guess it could be. Okay, keep thinking and call me if you come up with anything else. I'll be in touch." I disconnected the call and looked at Lindsey. "That might be the connection."

Lindsey pondered. "If Chinese espionage put Jen Wang in deep cover for what—ten or twelve years—they might have done the same with Bennie what's-his-name. It might not have been as deep if he was active in ELF or ECF, although even that could have been cover. It would have gotten him access to people who've been helping without knowing about it."

She was right. The MSS had put people in place for fifty years. John Nelson had exposed only the tip of the iceberg. Controlling world oil price was big enough for them to risk exposing the whole network. They were "all in" and this was the end game.

chapter

THIRTY-FIVE

At 7:14 a.m. I knocked on Hank's door at the Ramada. He looked at the bulletproof vest I was carrying and said, "Are you serious?"

"Absolutely, I hope it fits."

Hank laughed and patted his ample middle. "Well, if you bought it for you, it isn't going to work for me." He pulled it on and fastened the Velcro closures. It was snug. "I doubt my sports jacket is going over it—of course I don't wear one unless I'm meeting somebody."

I motioned to the door. "Let's get going. I need to be downtown by 10:00 a.m. I'm meeting with the local FBI guys."

Outside, we hurried to my truck and made the short hop down Kipling to the Federal Center. The security I'd requested was in place with two Jeffco sheriff's cars and an unmarked cruiser parked in the median between the entrance and exit lanes. I saw the normal rent-a-cop at the Dutch door check-in. Several other people, some uniformed and some not, were standing inside the gatehouse. It was crowded. The guard started to ask our business when Hank leaned over and said, "Morning, Marlon…It's me, Hank Francis. This is my new, hopefully, temporary chauffeur, Cort Scott."

The guard tipped his hat. "Good morning, Mr. Francis. Is this for you—all these cops? They said they'd be here all day—?"

I interrupted him, "Let me sign your sheet, we need to get going."

The guard looked peeved I'd cut off the questions. I didn't bother with the visitor's parking, pulled up to the entrance walk, and popped the door locks. Hank looked at me, grinned, and said, "Aren't you going to walk me to the door, honey?"

I glared at him. "Hank, take this seriously. Do everything the cops tell you and don't do anything stupid for a few days, okay?"

He stopped grinning. "All right, you've convinced me."

I waited till he was inside, pulled away, and returned to the gates. Exiting also required a stop and the guards looked carefully in the back of the Bronco. The guard asked my name and checked it off before waving me forward.

***

Rush hour traffic was over, so it was a quick trip down 6th Avenue, north on Kalamath to 14th, and downtown to my parking garage. I walked the two blocks to the Byron White federal courthouse. The FBI was on the third floor and had a security setup like a miniature of the one in San Francisco. I cleared security and went, as directed, to Room 325.

There were six men and one woman sitting around a conference table. One of the men was Tom Montgomery; the woman was Mariah Martinez. Tom looked at his watch and said, "You're late."

I shot him a glance, raised my eyebrows, and said, "How much?"

"About three minutes—where you been?"

"Delivering Hank to his office—thanks for getting the security in place."

Mariah Martinez asked, "Who is *Hank?*"

"Nice to see you too, Agent. Hank Francis is the regional director of the USGS and was Martie Remington's and Judy Benoit's boss. I think he's Feng's next target."

I glanced at the others and said, "Good morning, fellas. I'm Cort Scott, since we haven't been properly introduced."

They all stood, one stepped forward, put out his hand, and said, "Good morning, Mr. Scott. I'm Jerry Abel, Agent-in-Charge for Denver. These men are agents Jim Marshall, Monty Adams, and Hugh Sinclair." Each one shook hands. "Before you got here, Agent Martinez was filling us in on the events in San Francisco. It's a remarkable story and appears it's playing out here in Colorado. I think we have to believe John Nelson's theory was right on. We need to begin full-time protection for Mr. Francis and his staff, increase security at the USGS facility, plus coordinate our efforts with DPD and other local law enforcement to apprehend Feng and whoever's working with him."

It was the best news I'd heard since Hank had walked into my office which seemed like a very long time ago. It would mean I wasn't solely responsible for protecting Hank and every cop in the state would be on the lookout for Feng. "That's good news. I was beginning to wonder if anyone was taking me—or John Nelson—seriously."

Martinez shot me a malevolent glance. "If that's a shot at me or my office, I don't appreciate it. We take every threat seriously and this one ended up with two of my agents being killed. I've been devoting every resource I have to catching these bastards!"

I knew I hadn't phrased that right. "I'm sure of that, Mariah. I'm sorry if it came out wrong. I'm just glad everyone's on the same page now." She didn't say anything, continuing to stare at me.

Tom set his cup down and said to no one in particular, "Does anyone have a theory on why Feng is so intent on taking out Cort? I can't believe he's willing to jeopardize his mission just to get Cort."

Everyone glanced at each other before Martinez said, "If I'm to guess, and that's all it is, I'd say it's personal. Everything had been going entirely Feng's way until Scott showed up and began asking questions. Maybe this is the first time Feng's ever had anything go wrong. He knew once John Nelson told Scott his theory, his days in deep cover as a respected businessman were over. Where's he going to go? He'll have to leave the US, maybe go to China where he's never lived, or take another name and identity. Having to give up everything he's got would be a big revenge motive for wanting to get Scott."

That made sense. He would've already failed in his mission which wasn't going to make his masters happy. What was left other than revenge?

Near the end of the meeting, which took ninety minutes, Abel asked, "Mr. Scott, do you require security until we get this resolved?"

"No, security is what I do for a living. Your manpower is better used elsewhere."

"I was hoping you'd say that."

As everyone got up to leave, Martinez touched my arm. "Do you have another minute? I've just heard from Thornton—they found Gail Porter."

"*Found* her—is she alive?"

"Yes, she apparently just walked into her house, found our notes, listened to her phone messages, and called the CBI. She'd simply taken off for a few days, went up to Mendocino to meet some of her old environmentalist buddies, and relive the good old days in the protest movement."

It couldn't be that simple. "What about her cell phone—and the stuff lying around her house?"

"According to her, she tends to be a little forgetful and has never gotten into hauling a cell phone around with her. She said she just forgot to take it."

"Do you believe her? When I talked to her, she didn't seem like the forgetful or absentminded type."

"I don't know what to believe. Thornton says she was shook up when she called. She wanted to know all about Feng. Thornton went to Oakland, picked up Judy Benoit, and took her to see Porter. Porter confirmed what Benoit told you about meeting here in Colorado and about the dinner at her house after Remington's death. She said Feng *inspired* her with his support of environmental activism. However, she got a bad feeling when he introduced her to this Bennie guy. She confirmed she threw them out when they started talking about ratcheting up the violence to get results."

"I wonder why she didn't say anything to me."

"She probably thought you'd tie her to Remington. After the dinner at her house, she must have suspected they did it."

"How come she didn't hear about John Nelson and Joe Riggs?"

"What if she did? We never mentioned Feng or you or Judy Benoit in any of the news reports. You didn't use your real name when you talked to her. She wouldn't have anything to tie it to."

"I think there's more to it than that." There were too many loose ends to Gail Porter's story and something she wasn't telling us.

chapter

THIRTY-SIX

I called Sheriff Bob Colby in Glenwood Springs. "I've been following up on Martie Remington's death and have a lot of information for you."

"What kind of information? Is it good news or bad news?"

"Some of both, I'd say. Her death was definitely a murder and—"

"*Shit.* I've been afraid of that from the start. Who did it?"

"I can't say for sure. It's a pretty good bet a guy by the name of Jon Feng was behind it. If he didn't do it himself, it was probably a guy working with him by the name of Bennie."

"I've never heard of either one of 'em. Who are they and how'd they end up killing Martie Remington?"

I told Colby the whole story. It took fifteen minutes and he only interrupted a few times. When I finished, he sighed. "I can't believe a worldwide spy plot includes a murder in Garfield County—

my county. I mean, I've just listened to all this and heard what you said—it just flat doesn't seem possible. And you say this Feng is after you and nobody has much of an idea of where he is or what he's doing? This isn't a very encouraging story."

"I know, Sheriff. I wish I had a better handle on it. Thing is though, you and your office are off the hook."

"What the hell's that supposed to mean?" Colby didn't sound pleased or relieved.

"It means when we catch up with Feng, it'll end up in a federal court and not in your back yard. Remington was a federal employee working on a federal project and Feng is an agent of a foreign nation."

"I hope you're not telling me that BS to make me feel better. She got killed in my county. I investigated it and didn't come up with anything. I didn't even call it a murder. How in the hell is any of what you're telling me supposed to make me feel better?"

"I can understand how you feel. I'm staying on it because it's personal for me with Feng. I just thought you'd want to know what I found out."

"Sorry I barked at you, I *do* appreciate you giving me a call. I'll tell my deputy, Jonas Welker, what you said—he asks me about it every time I see him. Give me a call if anything new comes up, okay?"

"I'll do that, Sheriff."

"Thanks, and be careful—watch your back."

I ran everything through my mind. It came down to loose ends. How did Bennie fit and who was he? How could Gail Porter be totally oblivious to what was going on around her? Why was Feng so intent on killing me and was he in Colorado trying to finish the job?

I needed to work on the loose ends. I called Harry Thornton. "Hey, Harry—I talked to Martinez this morning and she told me about Gail Porter turning up."

Harry laughed. "Yeah, that was kinda surprising. We were glad to hear from her though. I took Benoit along when I talked to her."

"Yeah, Martinez told me. Do you believe her story about just being away and not paying attention to all the trouble in San Francisco?"

"The first time through I thought she had to be bullshitting us, but she went over it two or three times and it never changed. And she does seem about half-ass loopy—I can believe she just forgot her cell."

"She didn't seem that way at all when I talked to her. She seemed pretty much together. Here's a news flash for you if you haven't already heard—Feng is in Colorado."

"Yeah, Martinez told me. Whadda ya think he's up to?"

"I think he's trying to crack into the USGS computers or, failing that, he might be making a try for Hank Francis—anything that'll slow down the resource evaluation."

"You sure he isn't after you?"

"That might be part of it. I'd be frosting on the cake if he can stop the report."

Harry was silent for a few moments before asking, "You think he's got somebody watching you?"

"I don't know. I think the mysterious Bennie is probably in Colorado and we know Feng's got several others working with him too."

"Good point, what can we do on this end?"

"How much have you guys dug into Gail Porter's history? Do you have a chronology of her life?"

"No, we haven't gone into much depth. We haven't checked out her childhood or anything like that."

"How much problem would it be to really check her out?"

"That's hard to say. I can have the records people give it a try and see what turns up. Are you looking for anything specific?"

"I wish I knew—a connection between her and the Fengs or Bennie or any big time gaps might help. I'm spinning my wheels trying to figure lots of stuff out."

"That's a pretty broad brush request. I'll have our computer gurus get on it. I'll let you know if we find something."

I hoped he'd hurry. I needed something to move on.

chapter

THIRTY-SEVEN

I was in a holding pattern until something broke, so I resumed my research on oil shale and was quickly convinced Shell's "in situ" method was the answer. It would require huge amounts of electrical power and equally huge amounts of water; still not as much of either as the old technique of mining, crushing, heating, and refining. Western Colorado was the perfect place except for the water. Shell could get the electricity from generation plants fired by nearby natural gas fields. Eventually, hundreds or even thousands of well sites would be required but, fortunately, they would disappear as the oil was depleted. It was preferable to strip mining the entire northwest corner of the state and leaving millions of acres of slag heaps. The shale deposit was the biggest in the world. The Chinese would have to get one hell of a lot of oil on the market if they wanted to keep world oil price so low no one could afford to develop the US reserves.

Hank called to say his meeting had been set for the following week. He and the Director were meeting with the Secretaries of Interior, Energy *and* Defense. He said the National Security Advisor was going to sit in. Everything was gaining momentum and was probably out of Feng's reach. Unfortunately, I probably wasn't.

***

Harry Thornton's voice was excited. "You had a good idea and I think we found what you paleontologists call the *missing link.*"

"I'm a geologist, Harry. I look at rocks and find oil. Paleontologists look at fossils and figure out when your great grandfather started walking erect."

"Funny. Anyway, listen to this—I think Gail Porter had a kid in 1968 and, here's the blockbuster, I think Feng Li may have been the daddy. The old bastard would've been in his fifties by then and she was a teenager, but I think we found the connection."

"Holy shit—you've gotta be kidding me! What've you found?"

I could understand Harry's excitement. "It gets kinda thin in a few places, so here goes. Gail Porter was born in 1949 in San Francisco. Her parents were Jim and Maxine Porter. Jim Porter was born in China in 1918. His parents were involved in all kinds of shit, including running opium. When they came back to the US in the thirties, they were respectable business people. They ran an import/export business and—"

"Harry, I know all this stuff—cut to the chase."

"I'm getting to it! Feng Li and Jim Porter *had* to know each other. They're the same age, they were born in Chungking *and* Feng Li's father was in the opium trade. The Porters pulled up stakes not long after Chaing Kai Shek began fighting Mao and the commies in '28. For a few years Chaing's capitol was Nanking, but the Japs pushed him into Chungking. By that time, Feng Li was still just a kid, but he was in the Nationalist Army and, we're guessing, he was already spying for Mao."

"Harry, you didn't just dig all this out of the CBI files. Where are you getting this information?"

Harry snorted a laugh. "You know, you're a pretty bright guy—for a *geologist*. After we had the meeting in San Francisco, I started working with Mark Peterson. Remember him—the CIA guy? He's been giving us access to the CIA files and my guys have been doing the rest."

"What about the FBI?"

"Not much change there, they're still so fucking paranoid about turf and getting two agents shot, they won't tell me shit. Half the time Martinez won't even return my phone calls.

"Anyway, the CIA set Feng Li up in *his* import/export business in the early fifties after he got to the States. Here's where one of the threads get kinda thin...the old Porters were on the CIA's watch list because of all the left wing shit they'd been involved in before the war. Our spooks warned Feng Li to stay away from them but the dumb bastards didn't keep him under fulltime surveillance. Now, they think he must've looked up his childhood friend. What are the chances two kids from China, in the same business in San Francisco, wouldn't get in touch? I'm guessing slim and none."

I thought about it and said, "I'll bet you're right. Still, how does that put Feng Li in bed with Gail Porter?"

"We're not a hundred percent sure but here's what the CIA thinks—Feng Li was in his thirties when he got here. He apparently had a wife in China and she ended up in Taiwan when the Nationalists got kicked off the mainland. Whatever deal Feng cut with the feds didn't involve his wife...at least not at the time. She didn't get to the US until almost twenty years later, like 1969,—and get this—she was only about thirty when she got here. Either this was a different wife *or*—according to what the spooks think—she'd been one of those child brides common in China. She might have been promised to Feng when she was just a kid...maybe even a baby. They might have been *married* when she was, like, ten or twelve years old. After she got here, they had a pretty happy reunion because their kids were born in 1970, '72 and '74. Jon Feng was the one in the middle."

"Still doesn't put Feng Li with Gail Porter—"

"*Goddamn it,* I'm getting to it—and this is stuff *we* have—Gail Porter dropped out of high school after her junior year. When she dropped out, she had a straight 'A' grade average. She'd already made an application to Cal-Berkeley. When she surfaces a couple years later, she isn't in college anyplace. Instead, she's mixed up in protests and other bullshit at Berkeley. She renewed her application for Cal with a high school GED certificate and got turned down. Her GED is from a *school* down by San Jose that turns out to be a school for unwed mothers. They went out of business in the eighties. I guess girls who got knocked up by then didn't bother to go to a bad girls' school. They either got an abortion or had the kid. Anyway, the records from her school are in the state files and it took a judge's order to open them up. They show she was there for six months and gave birth to a baby boy. On the birth certificate, the line for Father is blank but the baby's name is Benjamin Li—spelled L-I—Porter."

I felt my skin crawl. Harry had connected the dots. Bennie was Gail's son and a half-brother to Jon Feng. "What happened to the baby?" I asked.

"She put him up for adoption and—here's the clincher—he was adopted by Feng Li and his wife. On the adoption papers it states they're a childless couple willing to take a mixed race child. In those days, couples like that were hard to come by so the adoption agencies didn't do a whole lot of background work."

"I'm guessing you guys did."

"Yep, the Fengs ended up with *four* kids registered in school... a girl and three boys although birth records indicate they only had three kids. The oldest boy was adopted."

"Where's this leave Gail Porter? You think she was telling the truth about Mendocino?"

Harry barked. "*Not for a goddamn minute!* I think she was lying through her friggin' teeth. What about you?"

I was standing at the window watching a fox in the brush across the street. "Doesn't look too good for her. I don't know whether she's part of the whole mess or just in way over her head. Have you talked to Benoit about this?"

"No. I don't see how she can add anything."

The fox disappeared and I returned to my desk. "You're probably right. Damn it, I like Gail Porter. I hope she's just confused about what's going on. I don't want her to be involved in Martie Remington's murder."

"I hear you, just don't get too sentimental. She obviously knows more about everything than she told you. You have any more Feng sightings? Anybody tried smoking your ass lately?"

"Nope, my luck's holding."

"Good. I'll call you if I get anything more."

"Thanks, Harry. This was an earful."

So, Gail Porter was Bennie's mother and Bennie and Jon Feng were "family." Bennie was part of the family "business" as well. I didn't know where the Fengs were but guessed Bennie was the key. I needed to find Benjamin Li Porter Feng.

chapter

THIRTY-EIGHT

No one had seen Jon Feng, or his brother, Bennie, or Jen Wang in weeks. After Harry Thornton dug up the information about Gail Porter, he put her under surveillance for two weeks hoping to catch sight of the Fengs but nobody surfaced. I finally decided to confront her with what we had. I also wanted to look Judy Benoit in the eyes when I told her everything. I'd figured out early on she was not a good liar and I would know whether she was telling the full truth this time around.

Labor Day was on September 1st so I decided to combine business with pleasure, take Lindsey, and make a four day weekend out of it at the Wine Country Inn. I wanted her along when I talked to Porter and Benoit. She knew almost as much about the case now as I did. I thought her insights might help.

I made the reservations, arranged for a Mustang convertible at SFO, called Benoit, and scheduled a meeting at her house on Friday around noon. She said she would be glad to see an end to all of this; sitting around her house, reading and thinking, was taking a toll. She sounded depressed.

I called Harry Thornton and told him what I was planning. He said his investigators called on Porter occasionally on the pretext of making sure she was all right. He said he'd tell her "someone" would be by on Friday afternoon. He couldn't guarantee she would let me in when she saw who "someone" was. I told Harry we'd drive to Sacramento on Saturday and tell him what we found out. He said I could just call—he didn't like coming in on Saturdays. When I said I wanted him to meet Lindsey, he complained but agreed.

***

We caught our early morning flight and I gave Lindsey an aerial geology lesson from Denver to around Reno. West of there, everything was foggy and Linds caught a nap. The pilot did his thing over the bay until I thought I would get my feet wet. The instant I saw land, the wheels touched and Lindsey opened her eyes. As we taxied in, she said, "Umm, is that cabernet I smell?"

I had to laugh at that. "Not quite yet, it'll have to wait until this evening. St. Helena's about as centrally located for the great cab makers as you can get. Doesn't make it any cheaper, but there are lots of places to go taste. You're going to love the Inn."

"I've been looking forward to this. It's our first trip together."

Linds corralled the bags while I signed for the car. We had to take a shuttle to the rental car lot but, for once, the bus wasn't packed. We found the Mustang...a British Racing Green beauty with a camel top. We both looked up at the sky and back at each other. I shrugged and said, "Why not?" I got behind the wheel, found the top control, and lowered it. "When in California—" I said.

We drove directly to Judy Benoit's house. I buzzed her apartment and said, "Judy? It's Cort Scott and Lindsey Collins."

She sounded startled. "I didn't expect you this soon. Come on up."

The lock buzzed, we entered, took the stairs, and strolled down the hall to Judy's apartment. I knocked and she opened the door immediately. I was stunned by how much she'd changed. Judy had been "medium" in just about every regard—height, weight, hair length and color—now, she was rail thin, her hair was cut short and colored platinum blonde. She didn't look like the same person.

I stuttered out an introduction and Lindsey and Judy shook hands. She asked us to sit and pointed at the couch. She took the recliner across the small living room, heaved a big sigh, and said, without preamble, "I'm trying to change the way I look. I've got to get on with my life and it'll be easier if I look different."

I took a moment while I appraised her. "It looks good on you—you definitely look different. At a distance, I don't think I would recognize you." I turned to Linds and pointed back at Judy with my chin, "She used to be heavier and had longer, brown hair. Losing the weight makes her look taller. You didn't have leg lengthening surgery did you?"

She smiled which was good to see. "No, although when I go outside now, I usually wear thick soled shoes or even heels. What do you think?"

"I like it. You're doing the right thing—getting on with your life. Judy, Lindsey and I are going to talk to Gail Porter when we leave here. Has Thornton told you what he found out?"

She shook her head. "About what?"

"About Gail Porter being Bennie's mother—"

I watched her carefully as I dropped the bomb. The only way I could describe her countenance was shocked. "Oh, that's not possible—his *MOTHER*! I can't believe it! How can that be right?"

I ran over what Thornton had told me. Judy listened carefully, sometimes shaking her head, and sometimes with her eyes filled with tears. When I finished, she stood, walked over to the window, and looked out toward the park. She didn't say anything for over a minute.

Lindsey and I exchanged looks and shrugs. Finally, Judy returned to the recliner. "I'm sure you're right, it's just so hard to believe. What was your clue—when I said he might have an Oriental look?"

"Thornton did all the work trying to find a connection between Gail and Jon Feng. He got access to the CIA's files and Gail's state records. He was the one who put it together and it all fell into place when you described him. Judy, think as hard as you can—does Bennie look anything at all like Jon Feng?"

Again, she was quiet for a long time and finally shook her head. "I don't think so. I didn't see any resemblance."

"Okay, here's the tough one—do you think Gail knew what was going on? Could she have been part of this from the beginning?"

This time Judy didn't take long to answer. "I don't think she's involved in Martie's death if that's what you're asking. Obviously, she knows her own son. I'd bet any amount of money she didn't know he and Jon Feng were going to murder Martie. When I think back to the dinner at her house, she was really, really mad at them for setting fire to the truck. She absolutely threw them out when they said Martie's death was actually going to be good for the cause. I don't think she could have faked that."

I nodded. "I want to believe that's the case. I'm going to hate doing it, but I'm going to lay our cards on the table with her and see how she reacts."

Judy sighed and wiped a tear from her cheek. "It's not going to be a very nice afternoon, is it?"

Lindsey and I rose and started toward the door, "No." I said.

At the car, we watched heavy clouds forming to the southwest. I wondered if they were over Gail's house. I put the top up for the trip to Alameda.

As we headed south, I asked Lindsey what she thought of Judy Benoit.

She took her time before answering. "I'd say she probably didn't have anything to do with Remington's murder. She seems like a caring person—she obviously cares about Gail Porter. I think she cares about herself, too."

"What do you mean?"

"Oh, you know—she's trying to change her life. She's willing to change how she looks and that's a hard thing for a woman. By the time you get to your mid-twenties, you have a picture of how you want to look or at least how you think others should see you. It might not be right but it's your own personal image and it's hard to change. She's changing everything which means she's committed."

***

Outside Gail Porter's house, Lindsey asked how I was going to play it. I said, "The first thing will be to get inside. If she'll let us in, I think I'll start by apologizing for deceiving her when I was here before. I'll try to explain it by saying I was investigating Remington's death and needed to talk to her. After that, we'll just play it by ear. Hopefully, we won't get tossed out on it."

I rang the bell. We could hear footsteps approaching and Gail opened the door without checking through the peep hole. I assumed she was accustomed to having the CBI investigators calling. As soon as the door opened, I saw her face fall as she recognized me.

Before she could say anything, I said, "Gail, my name is Cort Scott, not Bob Colby, and this is Sheriff's Office Investigator, Lindsey Collins." I didn't bother to say *which* sheriff's office and hoped she wouldn't pick up on it. "We're investigating Martie Remington's death and would like to talk to you."

Her face was a blank and her resentment showed in the lines around her eyes and mouth. She stared at me for several seconds before switching her gaze to Lindsey. Finally, she spoke in a firm voice. "Mr. Scott, you called on me before under false pretenses. I see no reason to allow you in this time."

"I apologize for that visit. I didn't think you'd talk to me if I told you the real reason for my call. A number of things have changed since then and I believe it would be in your best interest to talk to us. There are several things indicating you might have some involvement in Ms. Remington's death; I don't believe you are involved and this is a chance for you to set the record straight."

"What do you mean things indicate I might be involved? I didn't have anything to do with that!" Gail's voice climbed the scale and her eyes bulged.

"And I believe you. May we come in?"

She didn't say anything, unlatched her screen, opened the door, and stepped to the side. We entered and stood in the small entryway. She shut the door, sighed, and said, "Please come in—we can sit in the family room." She led the way. I could see the deck where we'd sat the first time. This was going to be more formal but at least we were in. Lindsey and I sat on a beige leather couch and Porter sat in a matching club chair on the other side of a small table. She seemed to gather her thoughts for several seconds before softly saying, "All right, Mr. uh, Scott, is it? What do you want to talk about?"

I took a deep breath and began. "When I was here before, I told you your name came up in connection with several actions taken by environmental activist groups. Some were violent and several cost some companies a bunch of money. What I *didn't* tell you was that I was investigating the death of a young woman geologist for the United States Geological Survey. She died in a fall down a talus slope, a rock slide, in western Colorado near Glenwood Springs while evaluating oil shale deposits. I don't think she fell accidentally—I think she was murdered.

"Your name came up because of ELF. I was particularly interested in your relationship with Jon Feng because he contributed to ELF and, probably, to an offshoot group called ECF...Earth Comes First. After I visited you, I called on Jon Feng and was a little more direct about his involvement in Martie Remington's death. Feng reacted violently—or at least a guy who works for him did. Later, I received information from the FBI and the CIA indicating Jon Feng is a deep cover agent of the Red Chinese government. His father,

Feng Li, was also an agent of the Chinese, except he worked both sides—the Reds *and* the Nationalists. Plus, he worked for the CIA. We believe Jon Feng was instructed to break his deep cover to prevent the completion of the USGS oil shale report. The Chinese are implementing a plan to control world oil prices by producing oil from shale. They'll manipulate the price and keep it low enough the US won't develop our reserves and will remain dependent on imports. Imports controlled by the Chinese." Gail didn't move. She just listened.

I sat forward on the couch. "The day *after* I spoke to you, I received all this information. That afternoon while interviewing Judy Benoit, we were attacked by people I believe work for Jon Feng. More importantly, the FBI agent who gave me the information was murdered in San Francisco. Still later, another FBI agent who was with me was killed." Now, Gail rocked back in the chair, pulled her legs up, and hugged them with her arms.

I decided to hit her with everything I had. "We've discovered Jon Feng accompanied you to Colorado over a year ago, and you introduced him to Judy Benoit. We also know Feng and Judy Benoit met with another man named 'Bennie.' Judy Benoit showed Bennie and Jon Feng where the USGS vehicles were parked and the three of them rigged a pickup to burn. Judy told us she participated in that *action* in her belief Jon Feng and Bennie were trying to protect the environment by forestalling a strip mining operation of the oil shale. We suspect when that step didn't sufficiently delay the evaluation, Jon Feng and Bennie raised the stakes. They killed Martie Remington believing her death would stop the project. We *don't* know whether they smashed her head in and threw her down or if they threw her down and she hit her head. Regardless of the sequence, they *murdered* her." Gail began a low keening sound. I wanted to keep the pressure on.

"After the FBI agents were killed, Judy Benoit started cooperating and, we believe, is sincere in trying to atone for her earlier actions. Judy said she had dinner, here, with you, Jon Feng, and Bennie.

She said you were dismayed by the burning of the pickup and actually threw Feng and Bennie out when they said Remington's death might be for the best. Judy's told us repeatedly she doesn't think you had any involvement with the killings."

"The trouble is, Gail—the CBI has gone through all of Feng Li's and your records in Washington D.C. and in California. We believe Bennie is Benjamin Li *Porter* Feng; *your* son with Feng Li. If that's true, it's going to make it extremely difficult for anyone to believe you're *not* involved in these murders." I went for the brass ring.

"If you want to clear your name, you're going to have to tell the whole truth and you have to do it right now. The FBI and every cop in the western US are looking for Feng and Bennie…and those cops aren't too worried about how they apprehend the suspects. If you don't understand, let me make it clear—*the cops would rather shoot them than bring them in to stand trial.* If you want your son to live, you need to tell me how to find him. Frankly, I don't care one way or another about Jon Feng. He's tried to kill me several times and I'd just as soon kill him as catch him. I am, however, willing to give Bennie the benefit of the doubt."

I stood, walked to the kitchen, opened a cupboard, and got out a glass which I filled at the tap and drained. I looked at Lindsey and pointed at the glass, she shook her head. Gail sat slumped forward with her face buried in her hands. I could see her shoulders shaking. I couldn't hear her sobs but knew they were there. I drank another glass of water. That'd been the longest speech I'd made in years. I set the glass on the counter and walked back to the family room.

Lindsey mouthed *'good job'* to me.

Gail raised her face to us and I saw the tracks of her tears to where they collected and dripped from her chin. Her eyes were red and her face was blotchy. She looked like she'd aged ten years in the last ten minutes. She tried to clear her throat, only managed to choke, and began to shake her head from side to side. I thought she was going to deny everything.

I was wrong.

"I don't want to get Bennie killed. I know he's done some bad things and I think he's involved in that girl's death but...but—he's my *son*, my only child. I don't want him to die." She looked old, helpless, and pitiful.

Lindsey spoke in a soft voice, "Gail, if you help us find him, I assure you he'll get every opportunity to come in peacefully—to surrender. If he doesn't or if he's with Jon Feng, I can't make any promises." I knew Lindsey didn't have any authority or standing. I hoped hearing it from an actual police officer might make things easier for Gail.

I tried another tack. "Tell us everything you can—we can take as long as you like. If you'd rather, we can call the other agencies and set up a meeting. That way, you'd only have to tell it once."

She hesitated a moment before saying, "No, I'd rather tell you two now. If I have to go over it again, I will. I just can't talk to a whole bunch of people right now."

She said she'd like to make some tea—it would calm her nerves—and asked if we wanted any. Although I hate tea, we both said 'yes.' When she returned with the tea, she sat back in her chair holding the mug directly under her chin as if she were inhaling the tea vapors. It took her a long time to start talking.

"You have most of the story right. Yes, Bennie is Feng Li's and my son. It's a very, very long story going back to when my father and Feng Li were childhood friends in China. After he entered the US, he sought out my father and my parents befriended him in every way. He was always at our house and quickly reestablished himself as my father's best friend. It seemed I had known him forever and, for some reason, it didn't seem wrong when we became lovers. I don't even think my father objected. Feng Li was twenty-four years older than me. He was a dashing, handsome, and mysterious man and I fell in love with him when I was just a child. I knew he had a wife in China, but I didn't think she would ever come to the States. He didn't tell me that...it was just something I thought."

Gail stood and began to pace as she talked. "I became pregnant the summer after my junior year in high school. I knew when I was three months along and I immediately talked to my parents. They were surprised although not angry. They asked me if I wanted an abortion and I told them no—I wanted to have the baby. They sent me to a school for unwed mothers. I started there in the fall and had the baby in the spring. I named him Benjamin Li Porter—just like you found out.

"We, and I mean my folks and Feng Li together, agreed I'd put him up for adoption. By that time, Feng Li's wife had arrived and they registered with the school and the state as a childless couple willing to adopt a mixed race child. It was a no-brainer when Bennie was born to give him to the Fengs." Gail stopped pacing, paused, and drank more tea.

"I was in their home most of time and helped raise Bennie for about four years while Feng Li's wife had three children. I was like a nanny to all of them. I've never told Bennie I'm his mother. He knows he's adopted, I mean, it's obvious he isn't a hundred percent Chinese. Feng Li never told him I'm his mother *or* that he was his natural father. I think Jon knows the truth, but I don't think he's told Bennie either.

"I didn't know Feng Li was a spy. I swear I didn't know that. I thought he was an importer/exporter like my dad. It was only after he was murdered that Jon told me he and Robert were working with the Chinese, the Beijing government. He also told me Bennie was working with them too. He said his sister and mother didn't know what they were doing and he wanted to keep it that way."

Although I hated to break the story thread, I had to ask Gail to hold on while I used the bathroom. When I returned, Lindsey and Gail were standing side-by-side at the sliders with their shoulders touching. I swallowed some lukewarm tea and nodded at Gail to continue. "I knew Jon and Robert were taking trips to Hong Kong and Beijing though Bennie never went with them. He'd stay with me sometimes and we would talk all night. We *never* talked about him being an agent. Jon always said Bennie wasn't really being a *spy* like you see in movies. He would just pass on information about how people felt about things like the environment and government policies. I thought he was telling me the truth and I wanted to believe him. I care deeply about the environment and Bennie and I even went to rallies together. Jon gave him money to help organize protests and actions. I knew when he branched out into ELF, but I thought it was just a natural progression—I even thought about joining him except I didn't like the way violence was increasing. We argued about that sometimes. I didn't know anything about the ECF and I wouldn't have gotten involved."

She returned to the chair, sitting on the edge. "Then, I lost contact with Bennie—something that bothered me a lot. I'd ask Jon about him, what he was doing, and where he was. Jon would just say, 'He's okay and working hard on the environment'. He never told me where. About a year ago, the two of them came by one day and we spent the whole afternoon talking about how devastating it was going to be if the government let the oil companies start mining oil shale in Colorado; about how it was going to rape the land, use up all the water, and pollute the air. They asked me if I wanted to get involved in the protests they were planning. I did. They asked if I knew anyone willing to help and I said I knew this girl who worked for the Geological Survey in Colorado. I told them we'd met at some environmental activist meetings here in the Bay Area and she'd probably help."

Now it was Lindsey's turn to use the restroom. I tried to think of something to say to Gail off the subject and drew a blank. I was glad to see Lindsey come down the hall, pat her on the shoulder, and take a seat on the couch.

Gail continued. "Jon and I flew to Colorado and I found out Bennie was living there doing what Jon called *groundwork*...learning about the workings of the geologists. I introduced him to Judy Benoit; we had dinner and talked about what she was doing. It wasn't until much later I found out they already knew about her. They were using me to make contact. I also found out Jon and Judy met with Bennie and she'd shown them around an equipment yard. I came back here and a few weeks later, all three of them showed up one night and we had an impromptu dinner. That's when I found out they'd burned a truck."

She began rocking back and forth in her chair. "Judy started talking about the girl who'd been killed and how the police didn't know whether she'd fallen or been pushed. She was very upset, almost hysterical, and started asking Jon and Bennie lots of questions, but they laughed it off. Jon actually said it might be for the best if it got the project slowed down. That was all I could take. I asked them to leave and haven't seen either one of them since."

I needed to find out something else. "Tell me about Mendocino—were you really just out of touch?"

"When I went to Mendocino, I left on the spur of the moment and left my cell phone here. I don't use it much anyway so I didn't miss it until I was already there. I never even thought about calling for messages so I didn't get Judy's call until I got back. As soon as I got her message, I called and she told me everything that had gone on. Since then, I've literally been sick to my stomach every day. I couldn't believe what I was hearing, but—God help me—I know it's true. Harry Thornton, with the CBI, came here and questioned me for hours and he keeps sending people to check up on me. That's who I thought was coming when you showed up.

"Mr. Scott, I don't want anyone else to die. I don't want Bennie or Jon or Robert to die, but I honestly don't know how I can help... or how I can stop it from happening."

Gail put her face in her hands for a moment and continued to rock. She didn't seem to be crying any longer, although she was obviously in great distress. Finally, she stopped rocking, picked up her tea and drank like a person dying of thirst.

I asked her, "Do you have any idea where Bennie is right now? He has a lot better chance if we can find him before he does something else—something that could get him killed. I won't mislead you—Bennie is going to end up doing some serious time in a federal pen, *especially* if he was directly involved in Martie Remington's death. *If* we can get him to come in or capture him *before* he does something else, he'll still be alive."

She sipped more of the cold tea, took on the thousand yard stare, and didn't say anything for a long time. Finally, she refocused her eyes, made her decision, and softly said, "He's in Colorado. He went back immediately after I asked him and Jon to leave. He lives near Rifle in a place called Battlement Mesa. It's where Exxon had an oil shale operation in the seventies—ironic, isn't it? I understand it's a retirement community with condos and apartments...even a golf course. He figured even if his real name got out it would be the last place anyone would look for him.

"Actually, it's easy for Ben to pass as Hispanic. He's living under the name Ben Castro. He's been telling people he works for one of those oil drilling rigs on what they call the daylight tour—they go to work at midnight. That way he can be home all day. I guess no one has caught on yet. I think he's been involved in some monkey wrenching around the oil and gas fields there too. When he was here, he told me he'd poured chemicals in one of the creeks and a drilling rig got shut down and the company got fined."

I wrote down where he was and his alias. "Gail, do you know where Jon Feng is?" *I knew where the son-of-a-bitch was*...in Denver. I wanted to see what she would say.

She shook her head. "I don't know. I think he might be in Colorado too. I don't know if he's with Bennie or not. I doubt it because everybody is looking for him and I don't think he'd want to lead anyone to Bennie if they happened to spot him. Bennie called the day before I went to Mendocino so I *know* he's in Colorado. He said he thought Jon was coming there soon, but that's the last I've heard." It was the right answer. I believed what she'd told me.

"Okay, Gail, I believe you. I'll give this information to the FBI and the local Colorado cops. I'll ask them to *try* and bring Bennie in alive if they possibly can. I'll contact Harry Thornton and I'm sure he'll have someone here in the next day or two and take a formal statement. This is really important: if either Jon Feng or Bennie contacts you, you need to let me or Harry Thornton know immediately. Do you understand that?"

She nodded but didn't say anything.

"I'll leave our cards. You'll have our cell numbers. If you think of anything else, anything at all, *please* call."

She'd aged even more in the couple hours we'd been there. She was just a small, wrinkled old woman; a shell of the person I'd met a few weeks ago. It was a disturbing image as we left for what was supposed to be an enjoyable Labor Day weekend in the wine country.

THIRTY-NINE

Lindsey drove so I could make calls. As we pulled away, I looked over my shoulder and saw Gail Porter standing in her doorway. I couldn't see tears from this distance, although I knew they were there.

I called Harry Thornton's cell and told him what we'd learned. He said he would personally come to talk to Gail.

Next, I called Tom's cell; when he answered, I could hear laughter and clinking glasses in the background. "What the hell are you doing calling me today? Aren't you supposed to be in California?"

"I *am* in California…I've got stuff you need to know." I told him about our talk and gave him the information about Bennie and Battlement Mesa. "I need you to get everything to the FBI and Sheriff Colby in Glenwood Springs. I didn't make any promises, but I'd appreciate it if you at least *try* to keep Bennie alive. I told Gail Porter we'd try. If you run into Jon Feng, I don't give a shit—shoot him like a mad dog if you get the chance."

"Okay, buddy, I get the message—it is what it is. I'll pass along the information, including trying to keep Bennie alive. It might be tough getting people lined out over the long weekend...I'll see what I can do. Try and show Lindsey a good time out there and I'll call if anything pops on this end."

"Thanks. I'm looking forward to drinking some great wines and showing her the countryside. I'll be in touch." I closed the call, looked at Lindsey, and said, "Tom says 'Hi.'"

"Well, 'Hi' to Tom—are we ready to *start* seeing some countryside?"

"Yep, pull over and we'll put the top down—the clouds have cleared out. I'll drive so you can see the scenery."

She took the next off-ramp, parked at a 7-11, got out an Avalanche baseball cap, and pulled her hair through the back. She leaned over, kissed me on the cheek, and said, "Okay, sleuth, show me the countryside." I tried a Paul Newman Racing Team Grand Prix look. Lindsey looked at me like I was nuts.

There were about two hours of daylight to St. Helena; I pointed out everything I knew during the drive. We arrived at the Wine Country Inn at 7:54 p.m. Linds said, "Wow! That was a spectacular drive! I need to stretch my legs and use the bathroom." She pointed to the lobby restroom and headed that way as I checked us in.

We parked in the back lot next to a vineyard stretching as far as we could see. I'd reserved a suite on the second floor of the main inn, so our room was much nicer than when Judy Benoit and I had fled here.

As I opened the door, Lindsey exclaimed, "*Oh, my God, this is beautiful!*" She dropped her bag, opened the slider, and stepped onto the balcony.

I joined her and said, "Pretty neat, huh?"

She turned, slipped into my arms, and whispered, "This is just as great as I imagined it would be. And, look, it's sunset."

The last rays disappeared into the Sonoma Valley on the other side of the low mountains. "Perfect, simply letter perfect, Linds. Hey, we have reservations at Cindy's Backstreet Kitchen at 8:30 p.m. If you want to freshen up, now's the time."

I ran my hands down her backside and pulled her close. She took my face in both hands and gave me a long, hot, lingering kiss. I murmured, "That's not going to get us to Cindy's on time."

She twisted out of the embrace, skipped into the room, and said, "You're not getting out of feeding me that easily. I'll be ready in five minutes." She pulled a makeup kit out of her travel bag and went into the bathroom.

We arrived on time for our reservation, opted for seats on the patio, ordered two glasses of Domaine Chandon Pinot Brut and prepared to dine. Lindsey looked around and said, "This is special too. Thanks for bringing me."

I touched her glass in a toast. "Yeah, it's a bit of all right, isn't it?"

I paused to savor the moment before bringing up business. "What'd you think of Gail Porter?"

"I kept thinking she'd led some kind of life! I swear she aged while we were sitting there. I don't know why, but I feel real empathy for her. She's been lied to since she was a baby and now there's probably a good chance her only child could wind up dead. And he doesn't even know she's his mother."

I sipped some of the sparkling wine. "You can see why I hope she isn't directly involved. She has enough problems without facing prison."

"Yes, I see how you'd feel that way. You know, no matter how tough a front you put up, you're basically a nice guy at heart. I love you for that." I wondered if it was the first time she'd used the 'L' word on me?

"Did you believe her?"

Lindsey nodded. "Yes, I believed her. Although it was hard for her, I think she told us the truth and, more importantly, told us everything she knew."

"Good, I'm glad. I appreciate your input."

***

When the entrees were delivered, we ate in silence for the first few minutes. Both of us attacked the food like they were going to take our plates away. After that, we slowed our pace and started *dining*. It was a memorable dinner. The finish was a sorbet for her, a crème brulee for me, and cappuccinos. By the time we'd drained the last of the coffees and I signed the check, the place was virtually deserted. I looked at the clock as we left; it was 12:15 a.m.

There were mint chocolates on each pillow and two humungous, soft, oatmeal cookies in a little basket by the coffee maker. We didn't say anything, picked up the chocolates, and walked out on the balcony. It was still warm with a gentle breeze from the south. We munched the mints and stared off into the distance.

Lindsey snuggled into the crook of my arm and put her whole body the length of mine. She whispered, "I know it's been a really, really long day but I'd like to make love."

She'd read my mind; I wanted to do the same thing. Even with the rough start at Gail's, the day had ended in spectacular fashion and it promised to be a fantastic weekend.

chapter

FORTY

Saturday was spent touring wineries, gardens, and gift shops. We were fascinated by hot air balloons drifting down the valley, so I called a number from a flyer we found and lucked into a flight at 6:00 a.m. on Labor Day.

We decided to go light for dinner with a specialty pizza at a boutique place close to the Inn. It was the perfect topper for the day and we were laughing as we cruised the Inn's parking for a space.

Lindsey commented that the Inn must be full for the weekend because the only vacant slot was two spots from the end on the far side of the lot. I had to carefully line up the Mustang for the narrow space with a Mercedes sedan on the right and a platinum colored Cadillac Escalade crowding the line on the left.

I was trying to open my door and not scratch the Escalade when a man stepped from behind the SUV with a gun pointed it at my head. "Get out, slowly. Don't do anything stupid—we've got your girlfriend." I turned and saw another guy standing next to Lindsey's door with a gun aimed at her head. A third gunman was standing behind the Mustang.

I swung slowly out of the car and stood. My guy backed off a couple of steps— he'd done this before—and didn't stay close enough for me to swat the gun or grab him. The guy beside Lindsey ordered her out of the car the same way; she complied.

From behind the car, the third guy growled, "Okay, bitch, walk out between the cars and come over here by your boyfriend." He pointed his gun at me. "You slide this way until you can open the back door on the Caddy; stand still until your girlfriend gets there." I did as he said and watched Lindsey cross behind the car and step close to me. "Both of you get in," he ordered. As I climbed in, I glanced at the third seat and saw two more passengers…guys who would be sitting behind us.

When we were in, one of the back seat guys said, "Put the seat belts on." Two of the ones from outside got in the front and the driver started the truck. The one riding shotgun turned and said, "Okay, shithead, we're going for a ride and then we're going to have a talk. Don't do anything stupid. If you do, the girl gets fucked up real bad. You understand?"

I said, "Yes, Robert, I get it."

I saw his eyes spark with surprise, although his face didn't display anything. I recognized him as the guy driving the Mercedes at Feng's Marin house and made the connection he must be Robert Feng. Lindsey turned her face towards me and raised her eyebrows. I winked at her—it was all I could think to do.

The remaining thug got in the Mercedes, started it, and backed out. As soon as he had cleared, our driver did the same and fell in behind. When we got to the highway, we turned south. Nobody spoke as we drove at the speed limit all the way to the Napa Junction and headed west on Highway 37. It dawned on me we were headed back to the Feng house above Sausalito.

I took a shot in the dark. "Are you going to open the chain gate for us, Robert? Or, do you have flunkies, here, for that kinda grunt work?"

Feng turned enough to look at me and his eyes narrowed as he stared. He didn't say anything, but he had to be wondering how I knew all this stuff about him and the house. I hoped it would give me an edge when we needed it. We drove in silence for forty-five minutes according to the digital clock in the dash.

I'd been right. We pulled up to the chained driveway. The Mercedes was in the pullover where Thornton and I had parked and the chain was down. The Cadillac pulled through and I saw the glow of the headlights as the Mercedes pulled into the driveway and stopped so the driver could lock the chain.

As we approached the garage, the driver hit the remote and the double door opened. We pulled inside, the driver and Robert Feng got out and opened the passenger doors. Feng said, "Get out and walk over to the door to the house." As the two in the back seat exited, I recognized the guy who'd been sitting behind me. It was Jon Feng's bodyguard whose nose I'd broken.

My former sparring partner leered at me as he climbed out of the SUV. "Well, well...if it isn't Mr. Montgomery—or is it Mr. Scott, today? It's wonderful to see you again." It didn't seem so wonderful the way he said it.

The Mercedes pulled in and the driver joined us. Feng unlocked the door to the house and said, "Okay, let's go. Brian you go first; then, Scott; then Kuo; then the girl." *Brian*, still sporting a couple of black eyes, flicked the lights on as he entered. The entry led up to a utility room off the kitchen. Everybody marched straight through and into the big living room I'd seen from outside during my previous visit.

Feng pointed to the curved sofa. "Scott, you and the girl sit there. He turned to the others and said, "Kuo, you and Tan go back and check out the boat; fill the fuel tanks and get ready to take off.

We'll be leaving in the morning. Brian and Michael and I can take care of these two. Take the Mercedes and lock the chain behind you."

The Mercedes driver and the other guy from the back seat went through the kitchen and down the stairs to the garage.

The odds had immediately gotten a little better with just three of them left. Of course, they had guns and we didn't—still, two against three was better than two against five. I didn't know how good Feng or Michael might be, but Brian was not the best I'd ever seen. Michael opened the refrigerator and stared at the contents. "You want a beer?"

Feng said, "No, not now...and you shouldn't be having one either."

Brian said, "Yeah, bring me one." Obviously, Jon Feng, not Robert, was the boss.

Michael chuckled, returned with the beers, handed one to Brian, and shot Robert a glance as he walked over to the deck doors. He was the only one without a gun in his hand, but I saw the bulge of a shoulder rig under his windbreaker. "I'm going to have a smoke." He opened the slider, stepped outside, and started to close it behind him.

Feng called after him, "Don't take forever."

Lindsey said, "I've got to use the toilet."

Feng looked at her with a cold, hard smile, "Tough—cross your legs."

I snarled, "Come on, Feng—you've got control of the situation. Let her go to the bathroom."

He gave me the same cold look. "I'll give the orders, asshole. Shut up."

He punched some numbers into a cell phone, waited, and said, "Hey, it's me. Yeah, we got 'em. We're at the house."

He listened for a little and said, "Yeah, I'm pretty sure everything got put on hold for the stupid-ass holiday weekend. I didn't spot anybody watching Porter or Benoit and nobody saw us snatch these two, either."

Again, he listened for a while and then yelled, "*No! Why the hell would you do that?* She can't do anything else and this gig is finished anyway. Those two bitches can't hurt us. Let's just take care of Scott and get the hell outta here."

He listened for a long time, alternating between shaking his head and nodding. Finally, he said, "Okay, okay...but you gotta do that yourself. Brian will take care of this end so don't waste any more time there. I'll see you tomorrow."

He closed the phone and looked at us. "In case you couldn't figure it out, that was Jon. He'll be here a little after midnight. Scott, you did some kind of job pissing him off. He won't even let Brian do you—he wants to do it himself."

Feng pointed his gun at Lindsey and motioned for her to get up. "You can use the toilet now. It's the second door on the left down the hall; leave the door open and come straight back. Brian, you stand halfway down the hall...and cover your ears...don't listen." Feng laughed at his own joke.

Lindsey stood, started toward the hall, and winked at me. I didn't know what she was planning, but it was going to happen quickly. I got my feet under me and perched on the edge of the couch. Feng was about five feet in front of me leaning against one of the dining room chairs.

Brian started to step aside to let her pass. As he did, Lindsey yelled as loud as she could and used a sweep kick on the outside of his left knee. He screamed as his knee caved in. Lindsey aimed another kick at his gun hand as he went down. I saw the gun fly down the hall. Feng turned his head to see what was happening and I exploded off the couch. I drove my shoulder into his gut and got one hand on his gun arm. The pistol fired and the shot went into the ceiling. We went down in a heap across the chair and Feng's head hit the floor. I managed a glance toward the hall and saw Lindsey and Brian rolling around in a tangle of arms and legs. I kneed Feng in the balls and he gasped in pain. I had his gun hand pinned, but knew I was running out of time. The third guy, Michael, would be on his way. I got my right hand on Feng's face and slammed his head against the floor. I felt him go slack, grabbed the gun out of his hand, and rolled to my left. Michael ran around the couch and I shot him in the gut. He got a surprised look on his face, dropped the gun he'd pulled, and crumpled to the floor like someone had let the air out of him.

I jumped up looking for Lindsey and Brian. He had a hand on her throat and was forcing her head back. She was clawing at his face and kicking at him. I got close and clubbed him with the pistol grip. As he toppled sideways, I hit him again. He went against the wall and slowly slid down to a sitting position.

Lindsey kicked her way out from under his legs and pushed back a couple feet. She pulled her knees to her chest and sat there breathing hard. When she looked up, she said, "You took your time in getting over here, sleuth. I was getting kinda tired."

I pulled her up, put an arm around her, and said, "You're something else. That wasn't exactly a cat fight you started. Where'd you learn that sweep kick?"

She was shaking a little and I heard her voice catch. "I guess all the martial arts training the department made us take paid off. I hoped you'd get my message when I winked. I figured it was now or never."

Feng stirred and moaned. I kept my arm around Lindsey and steered her toward him. "You figured it just right, babe. I didn't know what you were going to do; just that it was coming soon. I can't believe Feng let that guy go outside. I had just enough time to tackle Feng and get his gun."

I bent down and checked Michael. He was breathing and had a pulse, but he was losing a lot of blood.

Feng was moaning and lying on his side with his eyes closed. I kicked him in the shoulder and said, "Get up, asshole. You're not hurt." He opened his eyes, stared up at me, slowly rolled to his knees, and reached for the edge of the table to stand up. I said, "Go sit on the couch. Sit all the way back and on your hands."

Brian started to stir; I asked Lindsey to pick up the guns and bring him over to the couch. She retrieved the two guns and told Brian, "Okay, buddy, get your ass over to the couch beside your boss—you sit on your hands too." He started to stand, his knee wouldn't support him, and he had to lean against the wall.

"I can't walk." He said.

"So, hop on one foot—get the hell over there." Lindsey's voice was low and hard. He didn't hop, choosing instead to hobble without putting weight on his bad leg.

"How does it feel to have a girl kick your ass?" Lindsey taunted him. Brian grimaced as he lowered himself to the couch. Lindsey said, "What should we do about the guy you gut shot?"

"Keep a gun on the other two while I take a look at him."

I rolled him onto his back, put his hands to his side, and straightened his legs. His eyes were open, his stare was vacant. He was slipping in and out of consciousness. I checked his pulse again—it was weak but steady. I pulled up his windbreaker and shirt and looked at the bullet hole in his gut. It was an inch and a half to the right of his belly button. There was a lot of blood on the floor under him and down his side, although the bleeding had slowed.

"I think he'll make it if the bleeding stops. Watch those two, I'll try and find some bandages."

"Go ahead. They're not going anywhere. I'll put a slug in their legs if they try to move." I saw acknowledgement in their eyes—they believed her.

I found the bathroom and the medicine cabinet, grabbed a roll of gauze, some two- inch square bandages, and a bottle of disinfectant spray. I soaked a wash cloth under the faucet, grabbed a towel, and came back to the living room. I washed as much blood as I could from the wound, sprayed the area with disinfectant, wadded up a small piece of gauze, and put it in the hole. I covered it with two of the bandages, watched for a few seconds, and didn't see any blood leaking around the edges. The guy's eyes were a little clearer now; he was conscious and hurting.

"What's the verdict, Doc?" Lindsey asked.

"Like I said, I think he's going to make it. He needs a hospital pretty soon though. We need to get him taken care of and get some help before Jon Feng gets here."

I opened Robert's cell and punched in Thornton's number. When he picked up, he didn't sound happy. He didn't recognize Feng's cell number. "Harry, it's Cort Scott. I've got some heavy duty shit going down and need some help."

"What's going on? Where the hell are you calling from?" Harry sounded like he'd been asleep.

"I'm in Feng's Sausalito house and using Robert Feng's cell phone—"

"*What the fuck!* What the hell's going on?"

I quickly related the story and that Jon Feng was on his way. I told him I'd shot a guy who needed an ambulance and we had Robert Feng and Jon's bodyguard. Thornton said he'd have an ambulance on the way as soon as we got off the phone and he'd be in the helicopter headed our way in thirty minutes.

I told him about the other two who'd gone to the boat and he said he'd have them picked up. I checked the mantel clock: 10:53 p.m.

I told Lindsey what Thornton had said and added, "The timing on this is going to get dicey. Robert said Jon Feng would be here around midnight. It didn't sound to me like he's coming from Colorado, although I can't be sure. Thornton should be here long before then; the ambulance and his cops should be here quickly. This could get interesting."

***

We were drinking bottles of water when the ambulance's flashers lit up the drive. I wondered how they'd gotten through the chain gate. Lindsey opened the outside garage doors and waited while the EMTs came in with a stretcher.

When they had Michael loaded, I asked about the gate. A tall, thin black guy named Jay said, "The CBI guy told us about it, so we brought bolt cutters."

As they were loading the ambulance, two police cruisers pulled into the cul-de-sac in front of the garage and four uniforms got out. Lindsey brought the cops up the stairs and into the living room where I was sitting in a dining table chair with a gun on Feng and Brian.

The lead cop, a sergeant, looked at the scene. "You must be Scott—that right?"

"That's right. Listen, sarge, I've got a little timing problem, so you need to get these assholes out of here pronto."

The sergeant studied me carefully. "So I hear—Thornton's about fifteen minutes out from the pad so he should be here in another half hour. We've got a problem down at the harbor though. There was only one guy on the boat when Sausalito PD rushed it. That means we've got a bird in the wind."

"*Shit!* I knew this was going too well to last. Any ideas about where the other one got to?"

"Nope—no one saw him. Our best hope is that he might walk in without knowing what's going on. They moved the one they caught out of there and now we've got two cops staked out inside the boat."

"I guess we gotta take the good with the bad."

"Not much choice—how the hell did you get the drop on three guys by yourself?"

I heard Lindsey snort in disgust. I looked at the sergeant and said, "I didn't do it by myself. My girlfriend took out the big guy. I just kinda mopped up."

The sergeant did a slow appraisal of Lindsey. "How'd that go down?"

Lindsey said, "I'm a cop. I do that sort of shit all the time."

The sergeant sighed. "Let's go fellas—the bullshit's getting pretty deep in here." The cops got out cuffs and told Robert Feng and Brian to stand. When Brian tried, he couldn't put any weight on his leg. The sergeant asked, "What happened to you, asshole?"

Brian growled, "That cunt kicked my legs out from under me. I think she wrecked my knee." The sergeant stepped close and slapped him so hard he went to the floor.

"*Watch your mouth, shithead!* You're talking to a police officer." The sergeant tipped his cover to Lindsey, smiled, and said, "Good job, officer—sorry I jumped to an assumption there. We don't see many women patrol officers out here in the land of fruits and nuts."

Lindsey grinned. "It's okay, except I'm not a patrol officer, I'm a forensics type." The sergeant sighed again but didn't say anything; he turned and led the way out. Lindsey looked at me with a broad smile. "Anything you want to add?"

"Who me? Not a word!"

We watched the cops load Feng and Brian in separate cars and depart. Only seconds after they cleared, two sets of headlights swept around the curve and unmarked Crown Victorias parked in front of the house. Harry Thornton and three other non-uniforms got out and started through the garage.

We met them in the kitchen and I introduced Lindsey to Harry. He stuck out his beefy hand and said, "Well, Lindsey, that's quite a story Cort told me on the phone. It sounds like you're quite a scrapper. You did a hell of a job!"

"Thanks, Mr. Thornton, I—"

"Call me Harry."

"Sure, uh, Harry...let's not make it any bigger than it is, okay? I got lucky. We had to do something."

"Lucky or not, you did it and now we've got a chance to put an end to this bullshit—sorry, Lindsey, uh, *crap*." Harry glanced around the room and turned to me. "I got that chopper driver to kick it in the ass and made it here in record time. I assume Sergeant Bradley told you about the screw up at the harbor?"

I said, "Yeah, but the cops couldn't have known one of them was missing."

"I know. It still chaps my ass—sorry Lindsey…that one of them is loose."

"I hope he doesn't have a way to get in touch with Jon Feng to warn him off."

Thornton paced back and forth. "Whadda ya want to do now?"

I walked to the east windows. "We'll set up an ambush; you and one man stay here, have your other guys move the cars up the road and out of sight. We'll just have to hope Feng doesn't worry about the chain being down and comes directly to the house."

Harry thought for a moment, looked at Lindsey, and asked, "You staying here, Lindsey?"

"I've come this far; I'll see it through."

He nodded agreement. "Okay. It sounds all right to me. We better get moving though—it's 11:45 p.m."

We did everything we could to make the place look normal from the outside, took comfortable chairs, and waited. At 1:00 a.m., Harry stood, turned on the lights, and said, "The son-of-a-bitch got the word. He's not going to show. *Goddamn it!* Where're we going to go from here?"

I stepped across the room and stuck out my hand. "We've done everything we can for tonight, Harry. We need to catch a few hours of sleep and get back to Colorado. With the leads we've got on Bennie, I gotta believe we'll catch up with him soon and maybe we can put an end to this."

Harry returned the handshake, looked at Lindsey, and said, "Good luck, Cort. Take care of this young lady…it looks like she's a keeper."

chapter

FORTY-ONE

Harry called the local cops in and directed them to secure the Fengs' house until he could get a warrant to conduct a thorough search. We got in one of the unmarked Fords and drove to the CHP office where the helicopter was sitting on its pad. As we boarded, Harry told the pilots to take us to the Wine Country Inn.

It was 2:59 a.m. Sunday morning when we walked into our room. I called and left a message with the ballooning company that we wouldn't make the flight on Monday and we climbed into bed.

We slept until noon, made coffee in the room, and I called the airline to see about returning that evening. After listening to the spiel about change fees, I booked the seats. We packed our stuff, hit the road, and visited one last winery near the south end of the valley. We cruised into SFO with plenty of time to return the car and check in.

On the flight to Denver, Lindsey slept while I read an Ian Rankin novel featuring John Rebus as a Scottish detective. Rebus was investigating a murder and fighting his personal demons—he liked to drink. I could relate—at least to the drinking.

At 7:30 a.m. Monday morning, Labor Day, my cell rang. The caller ID said Tom Montgomery.

"Hey, Tom, what's going on?"

"Plenty ... we've got a line on Bennie and, maybe, on Jon Feng, too. Why the hell didn't you call me about all the shit that went down Saturday night? I had to get filled in by Harry Thornton."

"Sorry. Linds' and my long weekend turned out a little differently than we'd planned. What'd Harry tell you?"

"He mostly talked about Lindsey beating the shit out of one of Feng's sluggers. Incidentally, she tore up his knee pretty good—better not piss her off, bucko."

"So what do you have on Bennie and Feng?"

I heard Tom flipping papers. "After you called me, I talked to the FBI and the sheriff in Glenwood. The goddamn FBI said they wouldn't start on it until tomorrow—so much for your tax dollars at work. Sheriff Colby called and said he'd check out the apartments at Battlement Mesa. He just called back and they've got a Bennie Castro living there; he's been there a year or so. Colby and his deputy took turns staking out the place and spotted a guy leaving the apartment about 11:30 p.m. Saturday. The deputy followed him to Grand Junction. He went into a twenty-four hour coffee shop and stayed almost four hours drinking coffee and using a laptop he was carrying. He left there at 7:00 the next morning and went straight back to the apartment. Since then, he's gone into Rifle twice and he's there now."

I let that sink in. "Has Bennie had any visitors?"

"Colby didn't say, so I'm guessing he hasn't. They'll keep watching, though."

"What kind of car's he driving?"

"According to Colby, he's in a 2005 Dodge Durango."

I thought about everything for a moment. "I don't know anything else to do except wait and hope Feng shows up someplace. I don't think we should grab Bennie in case he gets together with Feng. If we snatch him up, Feng will be gone."

I should've called Tom from California; he'd made that clear. I decided I'd better call Thornton and bring him up to speed on what was happening in Colorado. I got his voice mail and asked him to call me back. I'd just poured another cup of coffee when he called. "Jesus, you don't even give a guy Labor Day off…or time to go to the crapper. What's up?"

"We've located Bennie. He's in Rifle, Colorado, not too far from where Martie Remington was killed. The local sheriff has him under surveillance. What'd the search of Feng's house turn up?"

"Not a damn thing…place was virtually sterile. There were lots of prints from the guys we grabbed plus, we're guessing, the one who didn't show up at the harbor 'cause we can't match one set. We searched the boat, though, and it was a little more interesting."

"How's that?"

"We found charts for taking a trip all the way to LA. They were planning to have five guys on board with a stop in Ventura and Newport Beach as their destination. The boat was plenty big enough to make a trip like that and the weather is good this time of year."

"What's in Newport Beach?"

"Access to a lot of airports, highways, and ships, including Chinese freighters that don't get checked out very well. The only thing that doesn't track is Feng and Bennie being in Colorado. You have any ideas?"

"I think the asshole is tying up loose ends and I'm one of them. He wants to kill me. Bennie's another loose end…I don't know if Feng's trying to get him to help or take him out, too."

"I'm betting he wants Bennie to help get you. After that, who knows—?"

"How's the guy I shot doing?"

"Sicker'n a fifty-cent chicken, but he'll make it. The slug clipped his spleen and got a piece of his intestine. It didn't go through him, so they had to dig it out. He lost a bunch of blood. You probably saved his ass when you bandaged him up. Hell, your girlfriend did more damage than you. That *Brian* guy—his name's Brian Kwok by the way—is going to need his whole damn knee repaired. She really did a number on him... better not be pissing her off, buddy."

"Funny, that's the same thing Tom told me. What's happening with the other ones you bagged?"

"They're all in slammers. Robert Feng is in San Francisco for investigation of John Nelson's murder. We've got all kinds of charges against the others; everything from weapons charges to assaults and kidnapping. I gotta go. Call me if you get anything else."

My desk phone rang and caller ID read George Albins, Lindsey's boss and my good friend. "Hey, George, what's happening with you?"

"I just had a conversation with Lindsey about your little trip to California. It sounds like more than a long weekend."

"I'll say. Lindsey saved our ass. Did she tell you she kicked the crap out of one of the bad guys?"

"She just said she got in a couple good shots on some guy. She said you ended up plugging one for real, though. That sounds kinda dicey."

"More than I liked, George. The problem may have moved here now."

"What do you mean?"

"I don't know how much Linds told you. This is a big deal and it's playing out like a damn spy novel except it's not fiction. We've got everything from a couple of FBI agents getting killed to real life Chinese spies. The leader of the whole damn thing is here in Colorado and I'm guessing he's going to make a play on me...mostly out of pure spite."

I heard George's boots hit the floor and pictured him sitting forward in his chair. "Am I involved in this?"

"Probably not, although you never know. We gotta find the guy first. We're watching his brother's place in Rifle to see if they try to hook up."

"Well, if you need some help, let me know, and try to keep Lindsey out of it, will you?"

"I'll try."

***

At 2:07 p.m., the phone rang and I picked it up without glancing at the caller ID. "Scott? Mariah Martinez in San Francisco. Do you have a minute?"

"Sure, what can I do for you? You guys decided to work today after all, huh?"

"We've located Jen Wang. She tried to get on a flight out of Seattle for Hong Kong with a fake passport in the name of Ji Liu. The new passport scanners run the pictures through the facial identity program at the same time they record the information. The computers alerted the TSA people and they grabbed her before she could board. So far, she's not saying anything and I mean that literally—she won't speak. We've got her in a federal holding facility in Seattle and will need special extradition papers to get her back to San Francisco."

"That sounds like a lot of paperwork."

"It is. We don't have any choice."

"What kind of charges are you going to make against Wang, or whatever her name is?"

"We'll sort it out when we know the whole story. For now, we'll use false applications, falsely swearing an oath, forgery and that kind of stuff. This goes back a long way. Their side got into the hospital records at least twenty years ago, found a stillborn Asian baby girl, and switched the paperwork for a live birth with the name Jen Wang. Everything after that went back to a birth certificate. All the subsequent records were faked, including her application to the FBI. Jerry Abel says you've got something going on in Colorado?"

I was surprised she'd heard already. "Yeah, the county sheriff is watching Bennie. No one has spotted Feng yet, though. I'm going stir-crazy sitting around waiting."

"I hear you. I hate waiting when I don't have any control. We're playing the same game here. If anything else breaks, I'll give you a call."

In the late afternoon, I mixed margaritas and Lindsey and I sat on the deck watching the bunnies and squirrels. We fixed a light dinner, sat and talked about nothing, hit the hot tub for a few minutes, and went to bed at ten. I had a nagging feeling that something had to happen soon.

chapter

FORTY-TWO

I was sleeping soundly when the phone rang at 1:47 a.m. I'd grown to hate digital clocks, it wasn't "around" two o'clock any-more—it was 1:47. Sheriff Bob Colby had picked an unusual time to call.

"Cort? Sorry to wake you at this hour, but I figured you'd want to know Bennie is on the move. We're pretty sure he's headed for Denver. We had a tail on him from Battlement Mesa to the Eisen-hower Tunnel. The son-of-a-bitch lost our guy in the tunnel. There were lots of cars and trucks in there and he passed two or three and kept changing lanes until our guy couldn't tell which set of tail lights to follow. We think he may have run like hell down the hill and jumped off at Silverthorne or Georgetown. It pisses me off we lost him."

"I can see how it happened, Bob. Who've you told besides me?"

"Sorry about this...you're about the last to know. I called the FBI guys and Highway Patrol first."

"That was the right thing to do. I appreciate the heads-up." I felt Linds stir as I hung up.

"Who was that?" Her voice was in still in sleep mode.

"Sheriff Colby from Glenwood; he called to let me know Bennie is headed this way."

Lindsey sat up and turned on her reading light. "Do we need to do anything?"

"You need to go back to sleep and I need to go to the bathroom. Other than that, we'll just act normal."

She turned the light back off, snuggled down in the bed, and murmured, "Okay, I know how to follow orders."

I went into the bathroom, closed the door to the bedroom, walked through to the closet, and turned on the light. I took my .38 out of the gun-safe, had a drink of water, and turned off the light before I opened the door to the bedroom. I could hear Lindsey's regular breathing as she slept. I slipped out to the front entry and checked the door locks, did the same for the garage door, and the slider to the deck. I crept downstairs and checked all the doors and windows there. I could hear the motion detector chime as I moved around downstairs and hoped it wouldn't wake Lindsey.

Back in the bedroom, I put the .38 on my table and crawled into bed. Lindsey stirred but didn't awaken. I laid there knowing I wouldn't sleep anymore tonight. After an hour, I quietly slipped out of bed, picked up my gun, and went to my office. I turned on the reading lamp over one of the recliners and got out a James Lee Burke novel I'd started. His hero, Detective Dave Robicheaux, had fallen off the wagon again and was suffering the aftereffects, including having to go to two AA meetings a day. I felt sorry for him. Hedges used to say the difference between alcoholics and drunks was, "Us drunks don't have to go to those damn meetings."

I heard Lindsey's alarm at 5:45 a.m. I'd almost finished reading about crime in New Iberia Parrish. Dave had sobered up and was on the straight and narrow…until the next time.

I headed back to the closet, waved at Lindsey in the shower, and pulled on some jeans and a tee shirt to get the newspaper. The clock over Lindsey's vanity read "about" 6:05 a.m. It had old-fashioned hands and a sweep second hand. I liked it.

***

I don't know why I went out the front door to get the paper. I *always* go through the garage. It probably threw the sniper off. The crack of the rifle and sound of the slug hitting the faux stone column on the front porch were simultaneous. Rock chips stung my face, I dove behind the column, and did a shoulder roll back through the open doorway. I dodged to the side, kicked the door shut, and heard another slug hit the frame. I stayed on my hands and knees, crawled across the entryway into my office, grabbed my gun as I went past the desk, and ducked under the window. I got as far to the side of the window as I could and carefully looked at the trees and scrub oak thickets in the hillside open space across the street. The reflective glass film on the windows would keep the shooter from seeing in, but he might make out a shadow so I didn't stand straight up. If he was far enough back in the trees or too far to the right, expecting me to come out of the garage, he might not have an angle at my office window.

Lindsey raced into the entryway and I yelled, *"Get Down! Don't get in front of the windows!"* She dropped to the floor and crawled into my office. Her hair was dripping and she was naked.

"What's going on? Was that a gunshot? Are you all right?"

"I'm okay. Somebody took a crack at me. Stay below the windows. It came from across the street, probably up in the trees. I haven't spotted anybody yet."

Lindsey crawled to the kitchen hall desk, stood, and picked up her cell. I watched her punch in a number and say, "George, this is Lindsey. I'm at Cort's place—we've got a shooter. Somebody just took a shot at Cort from out front. No, we're okay; he's trying to spot whoever it is but hasn't seen anyone yet. Yeah, okay, that'd be great. Thanks."

She dropped and crawled back to my office. "George is on his way. He's closer than the Douglas County guys; they'd have to come from Castle Rock. George said he'll radio them and the state patrol while he's on his way. He'll be here in fifteen minutes.

You spot anyone?"

"I haven't been looking. Linds, stay down, crawl back to the hallway, and then go get some clothes. My other gun, the nine millimeter, and an extra clip are in the carry bag on the dresser; get it and check out the back yard from the downstairs guest bedroom on the far end. I think the shutters are open enough for you to see out without anybody seeing in. Don't get in front of any windows because the ones on the lower level don't have reflection glass. If you stay in that corner, you can see out both sets of windows and see the backyard and the north side. Okay?"

Lindsey nodded and crawled around the corner toward the bedroom.

I hazarded another glance and saw movement in the trees up the slope. A figure, I assumed a man, dressed in forest camouflage, moved from the trunk of one tree to another. He was too far away for a pistol shot—probably a hundred yards, so it wouldn't do me any good to try from the front porch. As he moved to another tree, I saw the rifle. He was going uphill away from my house toward South Pinery Parkway. I figured he must have parked a vehicle where the brush and trees were close to the road.

Lindsey cautiously emerged from the hall in cutoff jeans and a golf shirt. She was carrying the 9 mm in her right hand.

I said, "I think he went over the hill, through the scrub oak toward South Pinery. Linds, I'd still like you to go downstairs and look out back, okay? I'm going to take the truck and try to beat him to his car. It's a long ways through the woods."

"Okay, be careful." She ran downstairs and disappeared into the lower level.

I grabbed the truck keys, ran into the garage, and blasted out into the street. As I headed east, I half expected someone to take another shot but nothing happened.

I gunned the truck up the hill heading east. As I slid around the corner onto Fox Sparrow, I spotted one of my neighbors finishing a run and he glared as I roared past. I turned left on Fox Sparrow, floored it the three blocks to South Pinery, and took another left to head west on South Pinery Parkway. As I topped the hill, I saw a white SUV disappear down Lake View headed toward The Pinery golf course. I took the turn onto Lake View on two wheels, caught a glimpse of white several blocks ahead and knew I wasn't going to catch up through the maze of streets in The Pinery. I slowed, made a U-turn, and drove back to the house. As I rounded the last corner, I saw an unmarked cruiser in my driveway and George Albins walking toward the house. He'd pulled in front of the third door where Lindsey parked her Edge; I drove straight in the other door and climbed out as George came into the garage.

"What happened? Lindsey said somebody's shooting at you." George was wearing his customary western-cut jacket, snap-fasten shirt, boots, and cowboy hat.

"Yeah, it's a tough way to start the day. I haven't even had my coffee yet." The door from the kitchen opened and Lindsey came out still carrying the 9 mm. "Hi, Boss. Out of your jurisdiction, aren't you?" She hugged him. "Sorry to call you like that, but you're the closest to us."

George touched his hat brim, "I expect that's correct, Linds. You all right?"

"I'm fine...a little shook-up maybe. I don't usually start the day with someone shooting at me." She turned toward me. "Did you see anything of them?"

"I saw one guy slipping back through the trees and figured he must've parked out on South Pinery, so I took off to try to catch a look." I pointed across the street toward the big pines in the open space. "I spotted the back end of a white SUV tearing down Lake View. I don't know if it's the shooter. Hell, he might still be standing up there in the trees someplace." With that, we stepped away from the garage door and into the house. Inside, I asked, "Do you guys want coffee? I need some pretty badly."

We all grabbed mugs, filled them, and stood around the kitchen island. I asked Lindsey, "Did you see anything out back?"

She sipped coffee, grimaced at the temperature, and replied, "No. Unless whoever that was had a driver, he must've been alone."

George sat in one of the kitchen counter stools. "I assume it was the guys who tried to get you in California."

I agreed, although I didn't know for sure. "I can't imagine anyone else."

George looked at Lindsey. "Whoever it was must have been watching you for a while. They knew where you live...of course you're in the damn phone book. They also knew enough to park on South Pinery and cut through the woods."

He was right and it was troubling. If it was Jon Feng, and I couldn't imagine anyone else who wanted me dead, he'd grabbed us in California and now had tried at my house. Somebody had good intelligence. "Yeah, it's pretty disconcerting. Somebody knows way too much about me."

We heard the doorbell ring and I walked back to the front entryway. Through the distortion of the water glass in the front door, I could make out a uniform and opened to a Douglas County sheriff.

"Mr. Scott? I'm Sergeant Miller. We got a call about shots fired here. May I come in?"

I motioned him in. "Would you like a cup of coffee? We're having some."

"No thanks. Oh, I see George Albins—the dispatcher said he'd called this in."

"Yes, George is a friend of ours. My girlfriend works for him."
We went to the kitchen, he shook hands with George, and I introduced him to Lindsey.

I told Miller what had happened. He took notes, snapped his
book shut, and said, "That's quite a story. Our office doesn't have
much to do with it other than this morning and that's not going
anywhere unless somebody walks in and confesses."

I said, "I wish some of the other jurisdictions would take that
attitude. The guy with the California Bureau is in a turf fight with
the FBI, San Francisco PD, and South San Francisco PD. In Colorado,
the FBI, Denver PD, Highway Patrol, and Garfield County Sheriff
are all in the mix. Sergeant, if we just keep you informed, will that
do the trick?"

"Absolutely, we've got plenty of Douglas County crime to fight,
anyway. Nice to meet you, Miss Collins—and George, it's always
good to see you. I'll write up an incident report and wait on you guys
to fill in the resolution sections." We retraced our steps to the front
and I showed him out.

Lindsey said, "Okay, Boss...I'll be in the office in about an
hour." She set her cup on the kitchen counter and headed for the
bedroom.

George set his cup beside Lindsey's. "I don't think there's anything more to do here. You probably ought to keep a low profile for
a while. You guys might consider staying at Lindsey's place until this
mess gets cleaned up."

I shook my head. "I'll *suggest* it to her. You know how that usually goes."

George grinned. "I do for a fact, but it's probably worth a try."

***

Lindsey was finishing her last touches when I walked in. "Hey,
Linds, how would you feel about staying at your place for a few days
until we get something figured out with Feng?"

"You mean both of us?"

"Well, no. I was thinking just you."

"I don't think anything about it because I'm not going to do it. I'm in this thing up to my neck after California. I'm not leaving you to fend for yourself now."

"I thought that's what you'd say. I told George I'd ask anyway."

"*GEORGE!* What does he have to do with anything?"

"Ah, c'mon, Linds—George loves you like a daughter. You know that. He doesn't want anything to happen to you. I didn't think it was a bad idea."

"Well, it is, and I'm not having any part of it." She wrapped her arms around my neck and pulled me close for a long time. When she released me, it was just far enough to look me in the eyes, and kiss me hard on the mouth. "I'm going to be even later to work if we keep that up. Be careful when you go out today, sleuth. I want you safe and sound when I get back tonight." I didn't have anything else to say.

***

I called Tom who answered with a brusque, "What's going on?"

"Oh, just the normal morning ambushes. Somebody took a shot at me when I went out to get the paper."

"No *shit*! That's kinda harsh. You okay?"

"Yeah, he missed. I tried to chase him but lost him in The Pinery. Albins was here along with a Douglas County sheriff. You heard anything new on Bennie?"

"Maybe...a Jeffco deputy spotted a truck like his about half an hour ago. The deputy was westbound on I-70 and saw it exit southbound onto C-470. There weren't any cops on that stretch so that's all we've got."

"If it's Bennie in the truck, it couldn't have been him shooting. He wouldn't have had time to get here."

Tom was silent for a few seconds. "It could've been Feng. We still don't have anything on him. What're you doing?"

"I'm going stir-crazy. I hate sitting around and waiting for something to happen."

"Yeah, I hear you. Do you want to come downtown and sit around my place?"

"No, if I come downtown, I'd want to have a beer. I don't need to be doing that if something breaks."

"Probably right; I'll call you as soon as I hear anything. Keep your head down."

I hung up and after making a careful observation of the backyard and open space behind my house, walked out to the deck. A young mule deer buck cruised through the scrub oak. He seemed to have someplace to go and something to do when he got there. I envied him.

chapter

FORTY-THREE

We went through five more days of nothing happening and no news until we couldn't stand to be prisoners in our own house any more. On Saturday evening we cleaned up, pulled on dress jeans, and took the Bronco into Parker. We parked behind the downtown commercial block and entered the back door of The Grape Arbor, a wine bar and tapas place.

Marv Spotswood, the owner, waved us into the smallish center dining room behind his glass walled wine case. I asked for a table away from the windows which was out of character. He nodded and found an interior table.

Just as we opened the wine list for their three-wine samplers, my cell vibrated in my jacket pocket. I checked the screen: Tom Montgomery. I looked at Lindsey. "Tom." She closed the list and laid it on the table.

"Tom—what's up?"

"Where are you?" Tom sounded out of breath.

"We just sat down in The Grape Arbor. What's going on?"

"We think we've got 'em spotted. Highway Patrol picked up on Bennie's truck on south Santa Fe Drive down by Sedalia and called it in. They already had a chopper in the area looking for some four-wheelers and were able to get on him.

"He turned west on Rampart Range Road and headed out past Indian Hills to Jarre Canyon Road, then to a ranch house up against the red rocks. The pilot said there are several other cars parked around and one of them is a white SUV."

I nodded at Lindsey as I spoke to Tom, "There's no way it's a total coincidence; it has to be Feng and the rest of his gang. I can be there in forty minutes. What's the plan?"

"I've got to call Jerry Abel at the FBI and the Douglas County sheriff, but I called you first. I wanted to give you the heads-up. Although I'm supposed to be coordinating everything for all agencies, I won't have jurisdiction at the incident scene. That's Douglas County not Denver, so it's not totally my call. I'll make the other calls and then scramble our S.W.A.T. team. Even if it's not our turf, we can roll on it. I'll probably be there in about an hour."

"Okay. I'm leaving right now. I'll see you there."

I told Lindsey, "Tom thinks they've got 'em and I think he's right. They tracked Bennie's truck to a place west of Sedalia and there's a white SUV with a bunch of other cars. It's got to be Feng. Let's go. I'll take you home, cut across Highway 86 to Castle Rock, and go north to Sedalia."

Lindsey looked at me with incredulity as she picked up her things. "If you think you're leaving me out of this, *you're fucking nuts!* I'm going! Those bastards grabbed me, too." The couple at the table next to us reeled back in their chairs as she spoke.

We ran to the Bronco, roared out of the parking lot, went west on Lincoln Avenue all the way through Highlands Ranch to Santa Fe and then south to Sedalia.

Lindsey unlocked the console and took out our arsenal: her .45 auto, my .38 and the 9 mm Beretta. She asked how I wanted them arranged. I said, "Put the nine in the hip holster and the .38 in my shoulder rig. I'll take an extra clip for the Beretta in my hip pocket. Make sure the cartridge case for the .38 is full." She made the adjustments.

In Sedalia, the usual Saturday night crowds were parked outside Bud's Bar and Gabriel's. We were doing seventy-five as soon as we crossed the tracks and made it to Jarre Canyon Road less than five minutes later.

Two hundred yards down Jarre Canyon, we pulled up to a roadblock manned by Douglas County deputies. Sergeant Miller stepped out from behind a cruiser and walked up to my window. "We heard you'd be here." He bent to look through the truck. "I didn't expect you, Ms. Collins." He didn't look pleased. "Sheriff told us to let you up to our perimeter. We've got several units about three hundred yards from the house with a couple more down on Jackson Creek Road which is the only other way out of here. The State Patrol's chopper carried four of our deputies up to a meadow behind the house. It's about half a mile back. They're going to spread out and move in to five hundred yards. I think we've got whoever's in there pretty well bottled up."

I'd listened carefully. "Do the guys inside know you're out here?"

"Probably. I can't say for sure, but they'd have to be deaf and blind not to. They can see this location by just looking up the road from the front windows. There hasn't been any movement, but we haven't tried to contact them either."

"Who lives at the ranch? Do you have phone numbers for the house?"

"No one's lived there for years. The phone company doesn't show any phone service. They've got lights, though, so the power is on. It used to be called the Allen Ranch. The Allen family used to own the whole valley all the way from Perry Park north to Roxborough Park. The fourth generation, though, was all girls—three of 'em. When they married, none of their husbands wanted to live here and ranch with the old folks.

"The old home place burned down about twenty years ago and they built the house that's there now. When the last of the old folks died, the place got split up and sold off. Some corporation bought the house and a hundred and sixty acres three years ago. The Sheriff's trying to get the county clerk to check the real estate records to see if we can come up with anything."

I thought for a moment and fixed Miller with a stare. "You guys got a plan or are you waiting on something?"

"Sheriff said to wait on the FBI although I don't know why. That's the way it's going to be. Is this all related to the story you and Albins told me at your house the other day?"

"I think so. If it's Jon Feng and his gang in there, they're responsible for killing two FBI agents and a USGS geologist. It's all part of a Red Chinese spy operation, so the FBI has first dibs on them. You guys and Denver's S.W.A.T. team will probably have to do the dirty work though."

Miller raised his eyebrows. "How does DPD figure in this?"

"Tom Montgomery from DPD is coordinating everything statewide. He said they're rolling their S.W.A.T. unit."

Miller scuffed the ground with the toe of his combat boot, looked up, and said, "We can probably use all the help we can get, but Denver cops might not be suited for this kind of cowboy country."

I stared at him. "Well, *pardner,* I don't see anybody on horseback. It looks like cars and trucks and guns to me. That's pretty much the same whether it's downtown or out here in the country."

"That's a fact. Sorry."

Lindsey listened to the exchange and leaned over to ask, "How many are in there? You guys have any idea?"

Miller bent down to look at her. "Not really. There are five vehicles parked around the yard. We're pretty sure the guy called Bennie was alone when he pulled up. Beyond that, it's anybody's guess."

Lindsey asked, "Is George Albins coming?"

"He said he is and he's bringing Arapahoe's Special Tactics unit, too. If everybody shows up, we're going to have a lot of fire power."

Lindsey said, "Good, these guys play rough."

Miller fixed his eyes on me. "So, what do you want to do?"

"Unless something changes, I think we'll wait here until everybody shows up and ride in with one of them."

He glanced up the road. "It looks like we're about ready to kick this party off— looks like two S.W.A.T trucks— probably George's and DPD's. I don't know if the FBI has any."

Lindsey snorted. "Oh, they've got 'em—I just don't know if they come out to play on Saturday nights."

We watched as the armored trucks pulled up beside my Bronco. George Albins climbed out of the passenger seat of the lead truck. He scowled as he bent down and looked across me. "Lindsey, what are you doing here? You're not checked out for an operation like this."

"I've had the same training as everybody else. I just haven't taken the deployment tests. Besides, I've got an interest in this, remember? These jerks grabbed me out in California. Hey, do you have a spare vest in the truck?"

George looked mad. "I knew you'd say something like that, *Officer* Collins. Yeah, we've got extras. We probably even have one that'll fit you."

He straightened up and glared at me. "You really know how to show a girl a good time, huh, Cort?"

Before I could answer, he stomped back to the truck, knocked on the rear door, and said a few words to someone inside. He returned with two Kevlar vests. "Here, get these on. They should fit all right. He started to hand the vests through the window, but we got out to put them on.

Tom Montgomery strolled up from the other truck in full battle gear: boots, fatigue pants, vest, and helmet. He had an army issue holster strapped to his thigh with a .45 auto in it.

I said, *"TENS' HUT!"* George grinned and snapped a salute. George was wearing Wranglers, cowboy boots, and a Stetson. He did have a vest on and his .45 was in a hip holster.

Tom snapped, "Button it up, wise ass. You're the one who started this mess and, like usual, you need the cops to bail you out." He didn't smile when he said it. The look on Miller's face was priceless.

Tom turned to George. "Don't you get tired of cleaning up after this guy, George?" He looked at George's attire. "Obviously, Arapahoe County doesn't have the same uniform requirements as Denver."

They shook hands and Albins introduced Tom to Miller. Finally, Tom grinned, "Don't worry, Sarge. Believe it or not, this knucklehead is a friend. So, what's the situation?"

Miller gave them the same report he'd given us. When he finished, he asked Tom if we were waiting on the FBI.

Tom kicked the ground hard. "About fifteen more minutes. This is your county, Sarge; your boss is going to be calling the plays. We're here to assist if you want. I imagine all the trucks are equipped pretty much the same. I did bring our sniper along, though, and he's got the new .308 military issue sniper rifle with the night 'scope." Tom glanced at the sky. "With this much light, he's probably good to damned near four hundred yards. In full daylight, he could double that."

Miller whistled. "We don't have anything like that. I'll report it to the Sheriff and he'll want to get that guy deployed. I'll talk to the Sheriff and be back before your fifteen minutes is up so we'll know how many troops we've got."

He hurried to his car and headed toward the perimeter and his boss.

Tom said, "Impressive guy; he gives a good report."

George agreed. "Yeah, he's one of the good ones. He did two turns in Iraq on Shore Patrol guarding Iraqi big shots in the Green Zone. He saw lots of fire fights and weaponry there. I tried to hire him for our department, but he grew up right over the hill from here in Deckers. He wanted to stay in Douglas County."

Tom shook his head like he was clearing his mind. "What was a Navy SP doing in Baghdad?"

"He's a Marine, Tom. He's the kind of guy we're going to want with us for what's going to go down here." Montgomery nodded.

chapter

FORTY-FOUR

Miller returned and didn't look happy. "The FBI asked us not to do anything until they're here to *take charge*. They called the Sheriff while I was standing there. He's not thrilled."

Tom and George scowled in disgust. Tom said, "*Shit!* I thought I was coordinating this shindig. How far out are they?"

"Louviers—probably ten, maybe fifteen minutes."

George asked, "How many are they bringing?"

Miller shook his head. "I don't know." He glanced at Lindsey. "They aren't bringing any heavy equipment."

Lindsey acknowledged his glance. "I told you they might not want to party on Saturday night."

There wasn't much else to say. We stood around and watched the last of the twilight fade out over the Rampart Range. After a few minutes we spotted two sets of headlights, and in another minute two gray Suburbans pulled up. The doors opened, the dome lights went on, and we saw two people in each truck. George cleared his throat and softly said, "So much for economizing on energy. Those rigs can haul up to seven people each.

As they gathered and approached, I was surprised to see Mariah Martinez leading them. Jerry Abel and Agents Jim Marshall and Monty Adams followed. They were all dressed in civvies and looked like a golf foursome. I thought Miller may have been right about city cops not fitting in out in the country.

Martinez surveyed our group, let her eyes settle on George for a moment, and then said, "Well, well, Mr. Scott—one more time, huh? Hello, Lieutenant Montgomery, good to see you again." She turned toward George and stuck out her hand. "I'm Mariah Martinez, Agent-in-Charge for San Francisco. You must be the sheriff?"

George shook his head as he took her hand. "No, Ma'am, I'm a deputy sheriff from Arapahoe County. This is Douglas County; the sheriff's down at the command post. I brought our special tactics squad to help out if we're needed."

Martinez appraised him again. It was obvious she was skeptical of the big cowboy. "Okay, thanks for bringing your team. I'll take command of your squad and—" she turned toward Tom "— yours, Lieutenant"

George interrupted. "No disrespect, Agent, but I'm not giving up operational control of our boys—especially out in the country like this."

Mariah started to puff up when Tom chimed in and said, "Well, my guys aren't *open range* like George's, but I'm not yielding command either, *Ms.* Martinez. We don't know how many people are in there, what kind of weaponry they have, or even if they're the right people."

Martinez let out a long breath, glowered at George and Tom, and turned to Abel, "Lots of cowboys in your area, Agent."

Jerry Abel suppressed a smile and said, "Mariah, welcome to colorful Colorado. Frankly, the Bureau depends on these guys and we work well with them. They know the country and, for the most part, are a hell of lot better in the field than we are. It usually comes down to us doing the investigations and relying on the local cops for the heavy lifting."

Mariah studied Abel for several seconds before saying, "I get it." She bobbed her head at George and Tom. "I'm sorry, guys. I've been after these assholes for a while now and it was my agents killed in San Francisco. I want 'em pretty bad."

Everybody relaxed. I said, "What's the plan?"

Sergeant Miller stepped up. "The Sheriff wants all of you, the officers anyway, to meet him down there." He pointed toward the command post. "He's in radio contact with the guys the chopper dropped off and we've got a map showing everybody's location."

That touched the right buttons. Lindsey and I got in Miller's cruiser, George and Tom got into one of the Suburbans with Abel and Martinez and we drove the few hundred yards to the temporary command post.

Douglas County Sheriff Hugh Wexford's dark blue and white Ford Expedition was parked behind a scrub oak thicket and the sheriff was standing next to it talking on a radio. Wexford was short and stout and dressed in the blue-gray uniform of Douglas County. He was at least eight inches shorter than George Albins. Wexford was a tough, no nonsense cop. He didn't tolerate criminals or even scofflaws. He also didn't tolerate crooked or lazy cops and had worked hard to clean up what had been a lax department. I'd met him a few times and we got along okay, although we wouldn't be mistaken for friends. He didn't like PIs. When we got out of Miller's car, Wexford stared hard at Lindsey and equally hard at Mariah Martinez. He scowled at George, "Too many women here; too many to be worrying about if this comes to a fire fight."

Mariah Martinez stepped forward and hissed through clenched teeth, "Sheriff Wexford, I'm Mariah Martinez, FBI Agent-in-Charge of the San Francisco office. We think the guys inside that house are part of a Red Chinese spy unit responsible for at least three murders, including two of my agents. I would like nothing better than to drop a goddamn bomb on that building and kill everybody in there but, like it or not, this isn't about revenge. We need to catch as many of them as possible—alive. This is about national security. I can't speak for Officer Collins, but I *can* speak for me, and I highly resent your implication we could be in the way or we can't take care of ourselves if it comes to a gun battle!

"For the time being, on the advice of Agent Abel, I'm willing to assume a support role for myself and my agents in apprehending the suspects. *But*, be forewarned, if you attempt to go cowboy on us, or if you do something that, in my opinion, jeopardizes this action, I will not hesitate to call in every federal officer in this state to take over. Furthermore, if that becomes the case, I will do everything in my power to see a federal indictment lodged against you for obstruction of justice. I will make the remainder of your term in office a living hell. Are we perfectly clear on that, Sheriff?"

Wexford never blinked. "Get your skinny ass outta here, *Agent-in-Charge of the FBI office in San Francisco!* This is Douglas County, Colorado, and *I'm* the Sheriff. You and your agents are not in proper uniform, including protective gear. More importantly, you don't have official identification as law enforcement officers.

"I'm ordering you to return to the roadblock and wait. This action will be conducted under my supervision and authorization and it's going to commence in the next few minutes. You can make all the phone calls you want…no one will be here in time to interfere. I recognize the people inside are wanted on federal charges but this, *by God*, is my jurisdiction and I will conduct this operation as I see fit.

"Now, I advise you to turn around, return to the roadblock, and stay the hell out of our way." Wexford turned on his heel and walked away.

I stared at Martinez and thought she looked mad enough to go for her gun. Her face glowed red even in the suffused light coming from the interior of the Expedition. Jerry Abel and the two agents stood stiffly behind her. Seconds ticked away until Abel stepped forward, took Martinez by the arm, and gently turned her. "Mariah, this isn't a battle you should fight right now. I understand your position, but you need to understand Wexford too. Right now, my advice is to let him do his job. We can sort out the boundaries later. This is the closest we've come to these bastards so far and the longer we wait, the better the chance they're going to slip away."

Martinez shrugged off Abel's hand, turned to Wexford, and spit out her words. "This isn't over, Sheriff." She turned back to the three agents. "C'mon, let's go up and watch this local yokel fuck this up!" She stomped to the SUV with the others in close pursuit. She jumped in the driver's seat of the lead vehicle, started it, jerked the wheel, and spun the rear tires throwing dirt and gravel around as Abel and the others scrambled to get in.

Wexford watched the taillights of the speeding FBI rig before turning back to us. "I know you Scott—and George told me who this is." He pointed at Lindsey. "I don't like having her here either, although George says she can handle herself, so I'm going to let her stay—at least at a distance. Now, let's get to it."

He indicated a map on the hood of his truck and we crowded around to take a look. Wexford pointed out our position, the ranch house, and four Xs on the hillside above the house. "That's where I've got the guys the chopper flew in. As you can see, there's way too much distance between them. They need to be closer and cut down the gaps before we start from this side."

Lindsey touched my arm as everyone nodded their agreement. I stepped back and she whispered in my ear, "I feel like one of the boys, but I'm not going to say anything. Wow, Wexford's pretty rough, isn't he?"

"Yeah, that was tough on Martinez. She brought it on herself with that stupid speech. Try and make sure you don't cross swords with him. You'll do what you need to do, I'm sure of that. And, Linds, I'm glad you're here." She squeezed my arm.

Wexford spoke into his radio and made connections with the officers on the hill. "All right guys, this is Wexford. I want you to move down toward the house and close the gaps between you. When we go toward the house, I don't want the guys inside to make a run for it and get between you. Everybody got that? Acknowledge."

The deputies answered one by one acknowledging the order. Wexford gave each one five minutes to get to their new positions. He asked George and Tom to radio their SWAT trucks and get them started toward the command post. When everybody arrived, Wexford did a head count. He had six Douglas County deputies, including Miller, plus two more at the roadblock, three on the Jackson Creek Road, and the four on the hill. Tom had five on his team including the sniper. George also had five. Including the four FBI agents, Lindsey, me, Tom, George, and the Sheriff, there were thirty-four of us.

Wexford issued his orders. "I want my guys to take the center as we walk toward the house. I want the DPD team on the left or south. The ground is a little more level on that side and there's not so much scrub oak and brush. George, you and your guys take the north end of the line. That ground is rough with lots of small gullies and there isn't much cover. Lieutenant Montgomery, I'd like to keep your rifleman right here. He'll have a full field of fire in case anyone manages to slip through. Scott, you come with me. We'll be in the center."

He turned to Lindsey. "Ms. Collins, I'd appreciate it if you'd stay here with the sniper. I have a set of night vision binoculars and you can climb on top of this truck and serve as his spotter."

Lindsey recognized the Sheriff was offering an apology as well as assigning an important task. "I can do that. I assume the radio mike will reach the roof?"

Wexford smiled for the first time. "Yes, ma'am, there's plenty of mike cord for that." I saw he appreciated her response.

He addressed the platoon he'd assembled. "OK, here's what's going to happen. It's about three hundred fifty yards to the ranch house; I'm taking a loud hailer with me and my guys have six volt portable lamps. We'll walk down to about a hundred and fifty yards out and stop. We'll use hand signals down the line for the stop. When everyone's in position, I'll hail the house, identify ourselves, and tell them to come out. I'll tell them to open the door and come out single file with their hands over their heads. Watch through the night vision scopes because we won't turn on the lights until we see they're coming out. There's no use in giving them targets if they decide to try and shoot it out.

"Now, listen up, *I don't want anyone shooting into the house on their own.* If this turns into a fire fight, they're going to be firing the first shots. *Nobody* from this side fires unless I give the order! Has everyone got that?" His gaze moved from one face to the next until he'd watched every single person nod their head 'yes' or answer affirmatively.

"That FBI agent made her point about this being bigger than just a drug bust or some damned crazy militia. These assholes are the real thing—real life spies. We need to catch them and we need to keep them alive to boot—if we can. One last thing, don't do something dumb and get yourself shot if it comes to that. If they're out in the open and are going to shoot you, shoot them first. We'll sort it out later. Okay, let's move out."

Lindsey and I remained as the men began spreading out along a line. Wexford stepped to his truck, leaned in, and extracted a pair of night vision binoculars which he handed to Lindsey. "Here you go. There are ladder steps going up the back of the truck. Try not to make to sharp a profile up there, Lindsey—I don't want to get you shot."

The sniper got on the roof with Lindsey and established his field of fire. When they were in position, Wexford signaled everybody to move out. I walked ten or twelve feet to his right. Moonrise gave us a good look at everything. There was a low hill between the command post and the house, so we didn't see it for a hundred yards or so. The cops were aligned like Wexford had indicated and we walked briskly to just below the crest of the rise. Wexford signaled a stop and he and I inched forward until we could look down on the ranch house.

We counted the five vehicles parked out front. There was light showing in two front windows and from a porch lamp. The yard was illuminated by a flood light on a pole. A large barn stood about a hundred and fifty feet northwest of the house. It had another flood light over the doors. Wexford motioned to back down below the crest.

He pushed back his baseball hat and wiped his brow. "I wish to hell we knew how many people are in there; I hate going into something blind."

I said, "Yeah, it's like going into a farm house in Kosovo. Sometimes, it was just a farm house with a family inside. Sometimes, it was a nest of Serbs."

Wexford studied me in the moonlight. "You in Kosovo?"

"Yeah, did two tours."

"What outfit?"

"Rangers."

"No shit? Tough bunch; you see much action?"

"More than I wanted. I made it through okay."

Wexford was quiet for a minute. "Well, I guess we need to get something done here. We're farther out than I wanted to be, but I'll go ahead and hail the house and see what happens. You ready?"

I nodded and said, "Ready as I'll ever be."

The Sheriff keyed his radio. "Okay, guys, everybody move up to the top of the ridge, take a position, and get ready. As soon as everyone's in position, I'm going to roust the house. Be ready…and keep your fingers off the triggers."

He gave a hand signal that each cop relayed and the whole line moved forward. We retraced our steps to the top. Wexford raised the bullhorn and his amplified voice cut through the dark. *"ATTEN-TION IN THE HOUSE; THIS IS SHERIFF WEXFORD OF DOUG-LAS COUNTY. WE HAVE THE HOUSE SURROUNDED. WALK OUT ON THE PORCH, SINGLE FILE, WITH YOUR HANDS ON TOP OF YOUR HEADS. LINE UP ACROSS THE PORCH AND DON'T MOVE."*

Halfway through his announcement, the lights went out except for the pole light and the flood on the barn. Wexford paused and continued, "*I KNOW YOU CAN HEAR ME. WE'RE GOING TO GIVE YOU TWO MINUTES TO OBEY. YOU HAVE TWO MINUTES, STARTING RIGHT NOW, TO COME OUT ONTO THE PORCH.*"

He checked his watch, scuttled over next to me, and said, "If they don't start out, we'll shoot out the pole light in the yard. That'll let them know we have sharp shooters and plan on attacking the house."

Wexford opened his radio. "Wexford, here...sniper post, acknowledge."

The shooter's voice came over the radio immediately, "Sniper post acknowledging."

The Sheriff said, "Did you follow all of that?"

"Yes, sir; it was loud and clear up here."

"Okay, mark the time; two minutes from right now, if they're not lining up on the porch, I want you to shoot out the pole light. Do you have a clear view of the house, the porch, and the yard light?"

"Affirmative, sir; I can see everything clear as day. The shot will not be a problem."

"Good—if they start out the door, *Do Not*, I repeat, *Do Not Fire*. Are we clear on that?"

"Yes sir."

Wexford checked his watch and looked at me. "Forty-five seconds to go. What's your guess?"

"They're not coming out."

Forty-five seconds took a couple of lifetimes to pass. At the end, the Sheriff sighed and said, "Well, we'll wait for the light to go out and see what happens then."

Fifteen seconds later, the pole light exploded in a shower of sparks and glass plunging the yard into darkness. A half-moon arc of light illuminated the front of the barn. The sniper's rifle was obviously silenced and fitted with a muzzle-flash suppressor. We hadn't heard or seen anything until the light exploded. We studied the house through the night vision goggles looking for any sign of movement. Nothing happened until a couple of minutes passed; then the barn light went off.

I said, "They must have a switch in the house for the barn light."

Wexford was silent for a moment. "Unless there's someone in the barn."

I hadn't thought it through. He was right.

Wexford spoke into the radio. "All right, men, it looks like we'll have to do this the hard way; start advancing on the house. Continue to advance until you're within fifty yards or I command you to stop." He hand signaled and after a few seconds the line began to advance. We moved slowly forward. Nothing came from the house; no lights were showing; no sound from inside could be heard.

At fifty yards out, I was on one side of the driveway and Wexford on the other. We were both near junipers shielding us from the house. The Sheriff signaled for everyone to stop and the line came to a halt.

He raised the bullhorn again, *"YOU IN THE HOUSE ... YOU HAVE FAILED TO COMPLY WITH MY ORDER TO COME OUT. WE ARE PREPARED TO ACTIVATE OTHER MEASURES TO RE-MOVE YOU FROM THE HOUSE IF YOU DON'T IMMEDIATELY COMPLY. YOU HAVE ONE ADDITIONAL MINUTE TO EXIT."*

When the echoes died, there was absolute silence for a few seconds until we heard a high-powered engine start. The sound came from the barn. An instant later, a black Hummer, one of the early models that looked like it had come straight from the Gulf War, burst through the barn doors and rolled up in front of the house. An automatic weapon opened up from a gun port on the side towards us. The gunner didn't know where we were so he raked the area back and forth, raising and lowering the barrel elevation.

I looked back toward Lindsey's location but couldn't see anything. A few rifles cracked along the line of cops. The rounds pinged off the Hummer. Those of us with pistols didn't bother.

Only the top of the door to the ranch house could be seen above the Hummer. We saw it open and people ran out. The cops on the left end of the line had shots, although at bad angles and the side door of the Hummer provided cover. The big vehicle lurched forward, turned toward us, and quickly picked up speed as it started up the road. Guns were being fired out both sides. The cops quit shooting as they would have been firing toward our own guys. As the rig approached me, I aimed the Beretta at the gun port just behind the cab on the driver's side and emptied the clip as the truck roared past. It wasn't more than twenty feet away. I saw sparks fly as the slugs hit the armor plate and thought a couple might have hit the mark because the gun stopped firing.

We could only watch as they roared up the road, topped the rise where we had stopped, and sped toward Lindsey and the sniper. I couldn't see anything up there and the Hummer hadn't turned on its lights. I could hear though. The engine revved as it got close to the command post. Then I saw muzzle flashes and the bark of Lindsey's .45.

Suddenly, I heard a tremendous crash followed by more roaring engines and headlights from different directions. I yelled at Wexford, "Let's get the hell up there—something big has happened!"

I ran hard up the road toward the scene at the top of the hill. I heard the sounds of footfalls behind me and saw several cops running as I glanced over my shoulder. I was glad I'd been doing my morning runs. Even with that, I was breathing hard by the time I slowed twenty-five yards from the scene of one hell of a wreck. A loud shot went off. It sounded like a .45. I saw sparks fly off the tail end of the Hummer, which was partially lit by headlights from other vehicles.

The Hummer was tipped at a high angle in the barrow ditch and sat forty-five degrees to the roadway. It had been T-boned by Denver's SWAT truck just behind the wheel well on the passenger side. It didn't look like the doors would open on the driver's side and the SWAT truck was in contact on the passenger side. The Hummer was tipped far enough that the gun ports were not in play. Both motors were running and I saw whoever was driving the SWAT truck rocking the Hummer by hitting the gas and quickly backing off. The headlights of two of the cruisers were trained on the Hummer.

I could make out Lindsey standing behind the open door of one of the cruisers. She was resting her .45 across the door and had it trained on the rear escape hatch of the Hummer. I walked toward her and she glanced at me as I entered some of the headlight glow. "Don't get in front of the lights! We're keeping the guys inside off balance and they don't have a place to shoot from, but there's no reason to take chances."

I stepped back into the shadows and approached from the side. Other cops were starting to gather and check out the scene. I said, "Christ! What the hell did you guys do? It looks like a ski season, eastbound pileup at the Eisenhower Tunnel!"

Lindsey chuckled. "Well, you and Sheriff Hard-Ass didn't seem to be having much luck stopping those guys, so we did it."

Wexford arrived and surveyed the scene. He still had the bullhorn in his hand and was breathing like a steam engine. He approached and said, "What's the situation, Lindsey?"

She straightened to an *At Attention* stance and told him, "We were watching through the night vision glasses when they broke out of the barn and pulled up in front of house. The sniper, his name is Jack Redmond incidentally, had a decent look at the house over the top of their rig. We're pretty sure he winged one of the guys coming out of the house, but they got him inside the Hummer.

"Anyway, we had to think fast so we decided to stop them by using the SWAT vehicle. Jack pulled it up behind Arapahoe County's rig so they couldn't see it as they came up the road. I got behind your Expedition and when they got close enough, I emptied my .45 at the driver's windshield. I didn't figure anything would penetrate. I was just trying to make one hell of a noise and maybe distract him a little. As soon as I fired, he slowed down; Jack timed it and T-boned him broadside with the SWAT truck. It pushed the Hummer into the ditch and on its side a little. Jack's bumping them every few seconds so they can't stand or get oriented. I ran back here and turned on the headlights so we can see if they try to get out. They're all still inside. I changed ammo clips and when I saw the door start to open, I fired one round at it and they turtled up."

The rest of the cops had arrived, including the four deputies who'd been dropped off by the chopper on the hill behind the house. They'd made good time getting here after covering another three or four hundred yards. After he let them catch their breath, Wexford asked, "Is everybody here? Everybody accounted for?" He did a quick head count and came up with the right number. "Are there any injuries?"

A young-looking DPD officer stepped forward and said, "I think a shot grazed my ankle when the truck first came out of the barn." He walked in front of the lights and we saw a rip in the top of his boot. Tom bent down and looked at it carefully.

"You're lucky, Bobby. That's a bullet hole for sure. It doesn't even look like it broke the skin. Do you feel anything?"

The young cop said, "Well, I felt kind of a thump and it went a little numb. It doesn't hurt or anything."

Tom looked around "Anybody else?"

Two deputies had sprained ankles and that was it. Wexford heaved a sigh of relief. "That's the best news I've had all day. Let's get these assholes sorted. I can hardly wait to go up the hill and deliver my *report* to Agent Martinez." It was the first time I'd seen him grin.

chapter

FORTY-FIVE

Suddenly, everyone heard the sound of motorcycles coming from the direction of the house. A few seconds later, we saw two lights going up the hill behind the barn. Wexford yelled, *"SHIT! Somebody stayed in the goddamned barn. GODDAMN IT!"* We'll never catch up with them from here." He turned and spotted Miller. "Miller, is there a trail back there? Where does it come out?"

Miller said, "Yes, sir—there's a trail. It kinda winds around before it comes out on the Rampart Range Road maybe two or three miles south. We *might* have a chance of intercepting whoever it is at the road."

Wexford yelled, "Get moving!"

Miller sprinted toward his cruiser and I followed. We piled in and tore out towards the roadblock. Miller grabbed his radio and told the officers at the roadblock to open the barricade; he'd be there in less than a minute. The heavy Crown Victoria bottomed on the rutted road and was nearly airborne when we topped the low hill before fishtailing onto the pavement.

The cops barely had time to move the barricade as we flew through the opening and headed toward the highway. I could see the FBI vehicles parked to the side. Miller didn't use the flashers or siren. There was no reason to let the bike riders know we were coming. We made the turn onto Rampart Range Road on two wheels, accelerated to the first set of curves starting up the mountain, and had to slow. Miller cursed under his breath. "I need my goddamn road bike. I could take these corners twice as fast." I tightened my seatbelt and held on.

"Think we can beat 'em to where the trail comes out?" I asked.

"We should...it's shorter the way they're going, but they have to stay on the trail. We'll be moving a lot faster."

"Do you know exactly where the trail intercepts the highway?"

"Yeah, I've used that trail several times. There's a pullout on the west side of the highway where people park their cars and bike trailers. I'm betting they have a car parked there. They wouldn't be dumb enough to try and outrun us on trail bikes.

***

Five minutes later, Miller said, "Okay, we're almost there...I'm going to kill the lights. They can't hear us over the noise from their bikes." He shut off the headlights. I could see surprisingly well in the moonlight.

We rounded a sharp corner and spotted a white SUV parked in the pullout. Miller stopped behind a large granite boulder on the east side of the road. "That's gotta be their rig. We beat 'em here. The way the trail comes up at an angle, they can't see the car here. We need to surprise 'em so let's split up. You go down this side to the trail head and hide in the scrub oak. I'll go on the other side next to their car and slip over the edge. When they get here, let 'em cross the road to their car. As soon as one of them goes to the driver's side, I'll jump him while you get the drop on the other one."

We stepped out of the cruiser and immediately heard the growl of trail bikes. Miller said, "Let's go!"

We deployed as quickly as possible. I crouched in the oak brush and watched Miller approach the SUV, glance inside, and slip over the edge of the road. I was only five feet off the trail at the base of a steep road shoulder. I figured the bikers would have to get off and walk the bikes up the shoulder if they wanted to get them to the SUV. They'd have to do it single file and they'd be separated when the first one topped the road and started across. I'd make my move on the second guy then and hope Miller could time his attack to take advantage of the commotion.

The bikes were close now and I saw flashes of the headlights through the brush as they steered up the switchbacks. Fifty feet short of my location they stopped, shut off the bikes, and began walking. Damn it! They were leaving the bikes. We should have anticipated that. At twenty-five feet, I could see them quite clearly in the moonlight and saw the machine pistols slung over their shoulders. Both were walking with their hands on the pistol-grip stocks. The tall one in front was Jon Feng. I assumed the other one was Bennie.

They stopped right beside me on the trail. I held my breath. Jon Feng turned to Bennie, "I think we got here first. Dumb bastards could've probably beaten us here if they'd have come up the highway. We still need to be careful when we get to the road. I'll climb the shoulder first, take a look, and run across to the truck. I'll yell when I'm across. You okay?"

Bennie was breathing heavily. "Yeah, I just can't catch my breath. Too many fucking cigarettes, I guess. Go ahead—they'll be coming as soon as they figure it out."

Feng started up the road cut, slipped on the gravel of the steep slope, and slid back a couple feet. "Shit! This ain't easy." He took a slower approach and made it up the bank. Bennie bent over, put his hands on his knees, coughed, and exhaled loudly.

I stepped out of the brush next to Bennie and clocked him in the right temple with my gun. He went down in a heap. As I started to turn, Jon Feng launched himself from the top of the road cut and tackled me onto the trail. I fell heavily on my left shoulder, felt a snap and a lot of pain. I dropped my gun when I hit the ground.

I managed to roll out from under Feng and regained my feet. He got up at the same time and tried a leg kick that barely missed as I hopped backward. The momentum carried him off balance and directly into my roundhouse right. It was a good punch and hit him high on the forehead. He went to his hands and knees but scrambled back up and fumbled for the machine pistol still slung on his shoulder. I couldn't see my gun so threw myself into the brush doing a tuck and roll. My shoulder felt like someone was jabbing a knife in it. I knew Feng would open up on full auto as soon as he found the trigger, so I stayed on the ground behind a skinny scrub oak. I could hear him on the trail and thought this was going to be a crappy way to die.

The blast of a large bore pistol came from the road. I heard Feng scream and the sound of his body hitting the ground. Miller yelled, *"Scott, you all right?* Stay put. He's down but probably still alive."

I followed orders but yelled back, "I'm all right. Keep your gun on him. He's got a machine pistol."

I heard Miller scrambling down the embankment and then slow footfalls on the trail. I raised my head enough to see Miller's outline go past me. A few seconds that seemed an eternity passed before Miller said, "Come on out. He's alive, but he isn't going to be doing any shooting."

I got to my knees using my right arm—the left one hurt like hell—and then to my feet. I stepped out of the brush and looked at the two figures bathed in the moonlight.

Feng was lying on his right side across the trail with his head and shoulders lower than his legs. His left arm was along his side with the hand behind his back at the waist. Miller was standing behind and above Feng with his gun pointed at him. I took the few strides to stand beside Miller. "Where's he hit? You looked at him yet?"

Miller didn't change his gaze, "He took it in the upper right side of his chest. It went all the way through. Look at the back of his coat."

I stepped closer and saw the gaping exit wound and shredded fabric just to the right of center in Feng's back. Even from this distance, I could hear the distinct sound of a sucking chest wound and then he moaned. It wasn't the sound of someone who was going to recover. I stepped closer and saw his gun trapped under his body. I walked around Feng and tried to pull the gun out but it was still on the sling under him. He couldn't use it anyway. I looked at Miller. "Thanks. He'd have chopped me up. There wasn't any place to go."

Miller nodded. "I saw him get to the road cut, but then he whirled around and dove over the side. I knew the plan had changed, so I sprinted across and saw you knock him down and dive into the brush. I couldn't figure out what the hell he was doing until he came up with the gun. I shot him just as he was raising his arm."

Feng moaned again and I squatted beside him. "Hurts doesn't it, you son-of-a-bitch! Now you know how Nelson and the FBI kid musta felt!"

His eyes flickered and opened. He started to open his mouth but blood began flowing down his chin and cheek and he closed it. He tried to cough and blood spray flew out of the hole in his chest. He closed his eyes, shuddered once, and died. I couldn't help thinking it was ironic. Here he was dead at the bottom of a steep little mini-talus slope...just like Martie Remington.

We both turned as Bennie stirred and started to sit up. Miller yelled at him to stay put, took a few steps up hill, and grabbed the gun off his shoulder. Suddenly, police flashers were everywhere and several cars pulled up. We heard car doors slam and loud voices.

Miller yelled, "Hey! We're down here over the bank! It's Miller and Scott—we've got one bad guy dead and another one who needs some help—and some cuffs."

Several heads, outlined against the moon, appeared at the top of the road cut. Wexford's voice bellowed down. "You guys all right? What's happening down there?"

I answered, "Yeah, we're okay, Sheriff. John Feng just cashed in his chips. Bennie's a little groggy, but he'll get over it. We could use a couple of guys to help get him out of here."

Wexford said, "Hang on. We'll be right there." He started down the bank while he was still talking, lost his footing, landed on his backside, and slid to the bottom. Two deputies were more careful and arrived in time to help him up. The deputies stopped beside Bennie, jerked him to his feet, and cuffed his wrists behind his back.

Wexford walked to where we were, looked carefully at Feng, and at us. "What happened?"

I told him what had gone down and that Miller had saved my ass when he shot Feng.

Wexford nodded. "Sounds like a righteous shoot...good work, Miller; you too, Scott. I didn't know if you guys would be able to beat those bastards to the trailhead. We kinda got hung up digging the rest of 'em outta their Hummer."

We heard another person slide down the cut and then a laugh as Lindsey hopped up and strode to us. She grinned and said, "I hadn't even gotten my pants dirty until now." She looked at me, stepped in close and put her arms around me. It hurt to raise my left arm to her shoulder, but I did it. "I'm glad to see you in one piece, sleuth."

chapter

FORTY-SIX

Everyone made their way up the bank, although Lindsey had to help me, and we emerged onto the road where it looked like a police officers' convention. Several Douglas County patrol cars, the two FBI SUVs, and the SWAT trucks were parked at every conceivable angle. Most had headlights and flashers on. As we got to the center of the road, Mariah Martinez jumped out of her truck and approached. "What the hell happened?"

I was already tired of repeating the story, but told her everything from the time Miller and I had arrived at the trailhead. The other cops, plus Tom and George, all crowded in close to listen.

Martinez was silent for a few moments and then said, "Okay, it sounds like we're done here—at least for tonight." She turned from side to side until she spotted Wexford. "Sheriff, I was out of line earlier this evening—although I began to wonder when all hell broke loose and you started chasing these guys. Anyway, I just want to say that everyone did a good job. If you'd be so kind as to lock Bennie up in your jail until I can get the federal paperwork to you, I'd appreciate it. I'll call you tomorrow." She shifted her gaze to me. "Well, Scott, I guess you got your wish—you got Bennie alive and Feng dead—nice how that worked out. Can you come by our office for a meeting tomorrow? Say, 1:00 p.m.?"

I said, "Sure, I'll be there."

Wexford began issuing orders for processing the men who'd been in the Hummer, transporting and jailing Bennie, and getting some officers back on patrol. As they began to disburse, he turned to me, offered his hand, and said, "I meant what I said down there. You did a good job...and Lindsey did a *damn* good job with that Hummer. I'm glad she came along. I'll withhold judgment on Agent-in-Charge Mariah Martinez."

***

Lindsey and I rode back to the Jarre Canyon Road checkpoint with Miller. On the way, as I complained about my arm and shoulder, she offered to drive home and I accepted.

On the way home, she told me that after Miller and I had sped away hoping to intercept the Fengs, Wexford had supervised the unloading of the Hummer. He'd made the occupants come out one at a time through the rear door which was at such an angle it was like a hatch. Six men had evacuated after throwing out their weapons. One was shot through the shoulder...Jack Redmond had been right. The last man was wounded in the right arm; he'd been the gunner at the port when I'd unloaded my pistol.

***

I awakened at 9:37 a.m. to an empty bed and an aching shoulder. As I grimaced and sat up, I heard kitchen noises, footsteps, and

Lindsey appeared at the bedroom door with a tray. "Hey, sleuth—you back from the dead?"

"Probably not my favorite analogy of all time but, yeah, I'm back. God, my arm hurts! What've you brought me? Coffee, I hope."

"That's right, plus orange juice, water, and some extra-strength Tylenol. I figured you'd be hurting when you woke up. You'd better see a doctor today."

I tried to raise my arm, but could only get it to shoulder height and that hurt like hell. "Bastard did a job on me, didn't he?"

"That's an understatement. Of course, it's not as bad as what happened to him. Miller's shot really blew him up."

"I can't say I'm sorry, Linds. If Miller was a half-second slower, Feng would have killed me first." I shook out three pills and washed them down with a gulp of water. The coffee smelled good.

"What do you think will happen now?" She brought her coffee and sat beside me on the bed.

"Probably nothing for a long time…it's going to take the feds and the locals forever to sort out the charges. Linds, I need you to do something—I'm not sure I'm up to it right now. We need to let Gail Porter know Bennie's alive."

"I'll call her soon as we're done talking."

chapter

FORTY-SEVEN

Three months passed; my separated shoulder was mostly healed. I was studying oil shale trying to figure out a way to get involved and make some money when the phone interrupted my research. I glanced at caller ID and saw Judd Lampley's name. Judd was the US Attorney for Colorado and I'd had several conversations with him following the apprehension of Bennie Porter Feng and the rest of the oil shale spies. "Mr. Scott?"

"Yes, what can I do for you, Judd?"

"I thought I'd give you a heads-up on what's coming down today in the Feng spy cases."

"You bet. I'd appreciate it. You guys finally get everything together?"

"We've got a deal and it's all going to hit the fan late this afternoon."

"What do you mean by *hit the fan*, Judd?"

"Well, you're not going to like this. There've been all kinds of negotiations almost from the time we brought back the indictments."

"What kind of *negotiations*?"

"Well, it turns out the Chinese have a Viet Nam-era CIA operative in jail over there. We've been trying to get him back for forty years. Now, the Fengs have given us some trade goods and we're going to make a deal."

"I'll guarantee you I don't like the sound of this. Who's getting traded and who's going to take the heat?"

"We're giving the Chinese Robert Feng, Jen Wang, and the rest of their cell for our guy. We're charging Bennie with being an unregistered foreign agent, committing domestic terrorism, and conspiracy to commit murder. And, here's where you're going to really be pissed, we're going to charge Judy Benoit with the same stuff."

"Shit! What about Gail Porter?"

"That's part of the deal with Bennie. After she told him she was his mother, he changed his attitude about a lot of things. He's agreed to plead guilty to everything if we keep Gail out of it."

"What kind of time is he looking at?"

"Twenty-eight years in a federal pen. He'll do the first ten in Leavenworth and the rest in California...close to Gail."

"Are you going to do a deal with Benoit?"

"Probably."

"What's that mean...she's a victim in this deal."

"That's questionable...she knew what was going on."

"C'mon, Judd—yeah, maybe the monkey wrenching, but not the murders!"

"That's where Bennie comes in again. He's agreed to say Benoit didn't know about their plans, and we're going to reduce our charges to failing to register as a foreign agent and drop everything else. She's going to have to do a year in a federal pen...probably minimum security in Pennsylvania...and she won't be able to get a job requiring a security clearance of any kind."

I thought about it for a few moments. "I guess that's probably as good a deal as she could hope for. The part that sucks is letting Robert Feng walk away. There's no question he pulled the triggers on John Nelson and Joe Riggs. What do Mariah Martinez and Harry Thornton say about this?"

"That's a tough one. Martinez fought it like hell. I'm pretty sure Washington put the pressure on her to go along. She doesn't like it but, frankly, her job is at stake. If she wants to have a career in the FBI, she's going to have to swallow hard and shut up.

"Thornton's a different story. He's been making threats to go public about us letting a murderer walk."

I tried to keep my voice flat. "Sounds to me like he's on to something. How is it *punishment* for Feng to walk away from a sure death penalty conviction?"

"Between you and me—and this is what I told Thornton—he probably won't escape a death sentence."

"How do you figure?"

"Look, Robert Feng has never lived in China; he isn't even a Chinese citizen. He's going there in disgrace—their mission failed after all, and the MSS doesn't look kindly on failure. From what we know about them, he'll be lucky to last two years. They'll put a bullet in his head at their first opportunity."

I exhaled. "I can only hope. You know the son-of-a-bitch was trying to kill *me* when he got Joe Riggs and he's the one who grabbed Lindsey and me. Have you *thoroughly* explained all of this to Thornton?"

"Yeah, I just got off the phone with him. I'll admit, he still doesn't like it much, although he's willing to go along. Anyway, he's going to put in his papers on July 1st—he's retiring."

I sighed into the phone. "You were dead right about me not wanting to hear about a deal, but thanks for telling me before I read about it in the papers."

"You probably won't see much, if anything. We'll keep it pretty quiet."

***

It was time to complete the circle and let Hank know what had happened. "Hank? It's Cort. I've got some news about Judy Benoit."

"Oh, yeah—what's up?"

"There's good news and bad news depending on how you look at it. The good news is that this thing is coming to an end. The feds have been making deals. As part of the bad news, Judy will have to do some time, but probably no more than a year. The rest of it is she won't be able to work for you...or anyplace else requiring a security clearance. The *big* thing, however, is she won't be charged with murder."

"*Oh, man,* that's going to be rough on her as far as a career goes. But, at least, she won't be branded as a murderer or a spy—her life isn't over."

"It's about the best she could expect. I'm sorry I couldn't do much for her."

"You kept her from getting killed and convinced her to tell the truth. That had to help in the long run. What about the rest of them?"

"The feds are letting Gail Porter off the hook. Eventually, they'll put Bennie in a California pen where she can visit. It damn neared killed him when she told him she was his mother—it changed his whole attitude and he started cooperating. He told the feds he and Jon Feng had trailed Martie and Judy all over their mapping area on the day Martie was killed. They tried to grab her up there on top of the ridge, but she got away from them and started running down the slope. They were chasing her when she fell and hit her head. Jon Feng caught up with her and hit her with the rock that killed her. The odd thing was, according to Bennie, she never screamed or anything. Judy wasn't lying when she said she didn't hear anything.

"Bennie is going to be an old, old man when gets out of prison—but alive. That's better than Jon Feng and, according to the feds, his brother Robert. They're trading Robert for some old spook of ours and shipping his ass to China. Apparently, since he screwed up their mission to slow down your evaluation, he's as good as dead. The

Red Chinese spy outfit doesn't reward failure. The rest of their gang will also get sent to China. I don't care what the hell happens to any of them—they tried to kill Lindsey and me."

Hank was silent for several moments. "You're a good guy, Cort. Thanks for everything."

***

I was preparing a celebration feast when Lindsey wandered into the kitchen and hopped on a counter stool. She rotated and I stepped close. She put her arms around my neck, pulled me to her, and we kissed. It was one of those long, lingering kinds of kisses that made me warm all over.

"I'm glad everything's over, Cort. I realized something while you were in California and I was here by myself. I love you. I don't want anything bad to ever happen to you or to us. I want us to be together forever."

My heart skipped a beat, but reality set in...it was time to turn the steaks. When I returned, I'd managed to stall long enough to organize my thoughts. I poured two glasses of the Pinot Noir that had been breathing for half an hour, touched her glass with mine, and said, "I love you back, Linds. Here's to forever."

ACKNOWLEDGEMENTS

I couldn't have written this novel, or more importantly, my first book, *The Murder Prospect,* without the help of several people. First of all, my wife Jan's unwavering support makes everything possible. She's also a wonderful proofreader, critic, and editor. Thanks, "Special."

My first editor, Eugene, Oregon, based author, LJ Sellers, gave my writing form, structure, flow, and direction. Some editorial suggestions hurt, although in the end they proved to be, not only necessary, but indispensable. Check out LJ's books on her website. I found LJ through Nashville based, bestselling crime fiction writer, JT Ellison, who just keeps getting better and better while encouraging the efforts of new authors.

Ms. Tina Foster of Foster Literary Agency read my edited manuscripts several times, offered innumerable suggestions, corrections, and editorial comments. Her suggestions led me to createspace.com. How do I thank her for that?

Very special thanks are due Bob Lent, Linnea Peterson, Bob Ragsdale, Mary Caughey, and Fred and Mary Anne Beesley for reading one version or another of *The Murder Prospect* or *The Talus Slope.* Their comments and suggestions added greatly to both books.

Thanks, also, to Bob Grabowski and Ann Padilla for all the encouragement and support.

Lastly, kudos to the incredible project staff at createspace.com ...They get it done!

Made in the USA
Charleston, SC
10 October 2015